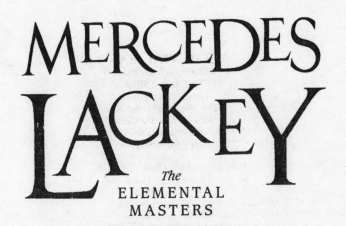

MERCEDES LACKEY

The
ELEMENTAL MASTERS

JOLENE

TITAN BOOKS

Jolene
Paperback edition ISBN: 9781789093759
Ebook edition ISBN: 9781789093766

Published by Titan Books
A division of Titan Publishing Group Ltd
144 Southwark Street, London SE1 0UP
www.titanbooks.com

First Titan edition: December 2020
2 4 6 8 10 9 7 5 3 1

A CIP catalogue record for this title is available from the British Library.

Printed and bound by CPI Group Ltd, Croydon CR0 4YY.

To the Memory of Ruth Bader Ginsburg

AUTHOR'S NOTE

This book is set in Tennessee, in around 1890. As such it contains characters whose attitudes, language, and behavior reflect harmful ideologies that were prevalent in that place and time, including racism, anti-Native sentiment, and other forms of bigotry. Readers who are sensitive to depictions of these things are encouraged to read with caution.

1

The sun shone thinly through the ever-present smoke and dust above the coal-mining town of Soddy; it should have been warm, but Anna May huddled in Ma's darned and discarded shawl as her hands busily shelled peas. She was almost always cold, except when other people were fanning themselves, opening their collars and complaining about the heat. From where Anna May sat on her Pa's porch, if you raised your eyes above the roofs of the clapboard houses across the dirt street, and squinted just a little, the haze that never left the air of Soddy looked pretty instead of dirty, and the hills and the tops of the trees outside of town were like something in a dream.

She didn't dare daydream, because Ma would be after them peas before too long. She druther look at the trees just past the roofs of town, concentrate on shelling, and try not to listen to Ma and Pa inside, argumentin'.

Ma had set her to shelling the peas she'd picked out of the garden, and told her to go out on the porch to do it. She knew what that meant. It meant Ma was going to have something to say to Pa as soon as he got back from the coal mine, and she didn't want Anna to hear what it was.

That was what she always did whenever she wanted to give Pa a piece of her mind. The two-room house was too small for anyone to keep anything private. The bedroom in the back barely had room enough for Ma and Pa's bed, the washstand, and the clothes chest, and when Anna's narrow trundle under the big iron bedstead was pulled out for sleeping, there was hardly room for a mouse to pass. And the main room was just as cramped, what with the deal table, the three stools, the iron sink, the cupboard for the food, two mismatched chairs at the hearthside, and the cast-iron cookstove. She supposed the cookstove was a blessing, though it took up so much room and needed such careful tending. All the Company-built cabins had cast-iron stoves; people didn't burn wood 'round here, they burned waste coal, and the Company reckoned that what with coal soot building up in the chimbleys faster than wood did, there was a bigger fire risk with an open hearth than with a coal stove. After all, the Company didn't want its investments burning down.

There wasn't much at all pleasing to look at here in Soddy itself. This dirt street they were on was all Company houses, clapboard two-room Company-built cabins all alike, all originally whitewashed, all of them gray and dingy with the soot that came out of the coke ovens. That soot was everywhere, and it was worse in winter, when everyone stoked their little coal fires (in freehold cabins) or coal stoves (in the Company houses) all day long and most of the night. Soot and coal smuts were just a part of life in Soddy. You couldn't never get anything clean, or at least, it didn't stay clean for long, no matter how hard you tried. Wash left hanging out was gray by the time it was dry, even if you bleached it until your hands burned, iffen you could afford the bleach. Even if you could afford to whitewash your house every spring, by early summer it was gray again. Folks coughed and sneezed a lot, but the Company said all that coughing was prosperity.

She tried not to breathe too deeply, because that always set off her coughing bad, but there weren't nothing good here in town to smell anyway. Nobody that had a garden wasted space and compost on flowers. And some people, naming no names, didn't keep their privies as clean as Ma did.

She dreamed most nights of running out of town, down to the Lake, all the way to Soddy Crick, or just out to them trees, where things was green and there must be the wonderful scents of green grass and flowers, and she could walk in the grass or paddle in the Lake's edge. She'd never in her life done that, even though them woods was only a few streets away. When she was little and couldn't help around the house and garden, Ma had tied her to the table to keep her from toddling off or touching the hot stove. Maybe Ma had done that because she'd tried to run off to the woods even back then, when she couldn't get down the porch steps without crawlin' down 'em; she obviously couldn't remember. But as soon as she was old enough to hold a rag, Ma had put her to work, like every other kid in Soddy was, as soon as they was old enough. It was only once there were more kids in your family than there were chores that anyone got to play, and Anna was the only child in her family.

Not that there were store-bought toys to play with, but you could make toys easy enough, like corn dollies and corn horses out of shucks, and if you had a knife you could carve out whistles and all manner of clever things, and if you were careful they could last for months or even a year. And there were games you could play without much but a stick or a piece of rope, or a pocketful of conkers. Boys could always fish, and that wasn't considered playing, that was putting food on the table, even when it was sham-fishing with nothing on the end of your line, not even a hook. As a young'un, she'd often looked up wistfully from scrubbing the porch or weeding the garden to see other kids playing tag or skipping rope, or trudging toward the Lake or the Crick with poles over their shoulders, wishing she could be one of them. Especially if she'd been a boy. If she'd been a boy, there wouldn't be no house-chores to speak of, maybe weeding or hauling waste-coal, whitewashing the fence, but no cleaning and cooking. She'd have been one of them boys with a pole and a pail of worms, off for a day of freedom.

But Anna was the only one in her family to take on chores, and she was proper obedient. She'd always tried to do what she was told. So even as a little bitty mite, she'd done chores from the moment she woke up until after supper, when Ma would teach her letters and numbers until bed. There was a school, but Ma said she couldn't be spared, and nobody in Soddy that mattered cared if someone's Ma and Pa kept them out of school, 'cause so many households needed their kids to work. So even before she'd gotten so puny, she'd never got to run off to the woods and the water like some of the others did whenever they got a spare minute. Because Anna never had no spare minutes, Ma saw to that. Not even on Sunday. Sunday was for Service in the morning, then Sunday school, then Sunday dinner and wash-up, then Bible reading, then Service before supper, then supper, then prayer after supper until bed. Well, for her and Ma. Pa used to vanish after the morning service; now he just went to lay down and Ma couldn't budge him except to eat—unless he felt good enough to go throw a line into Soddy Crick himself. Ma said that was sinful; Pa said that Jesus produced loaves and fishes on a Sunday, so there was no reason why *he* couldn't produce some fish.

And now, of course, even if she didn't have chores from morning till night, she'd never get as far as the woods, much less the Lake or the Crick, as tuckered out as she got, so quick.

So she just tried to imagine what the woods might be like, and did her best not to think about the fact that she was surrounded by Company houses full of tired, shabby people like her, in this tired old coal town, where the Company owned everything but your soul and every house on every street was the same till you got to the part of town where the few good houses were, for the bosses and suchlike, or the part where the freehold shanties were.

The only difference from house to house was what kind of chair, if any, you had on the front porch, and how many people got crammed into the two rooms. And if you were really pressed for space and could find or buy some boards, you could cram all the kids into a loft you could build across the rafters. Anna knew that compared to most here, their living arrangements were spacious, with her sharing the bedroom only with Ma and Pa. There could be six or eight kids rammed into some of these places, the loft packed edge to edge with corn-shuck mattresses, with a granny or granpappy or two bedding down in the living area thrown in for good measure.

Her hands were busy shucking peas, while she tried to keep her mind on anything other than the urgent voices in the house behind her. Because they were talking about her. She dreaded the times when the talk came down to being about her. Because no matter how it started, it always, always came down to the fact of her poor health, her small size, her weakness, her coughing, and how Something Needed To Be Done.

Ain't my fault I'm sickly. Not like I did this t' m'self.

She actually could remember a time when she'd been healthy, able to take on any chore Ma set her, and always obedient like the Bible said to be. Plain cooking, cleaning, sewing, working in that sad excuse for a garden behind the house where the plants were always covered in soot—though at least the soot kept the bugs off. And the garden did produce enough to make sure that in summer they were never hungry.

It was when she turned womanly that she started sickening. Tired all the time, short of breath, coughing, little appetite and always nauseous. Just this spring, after the potions Aunt Jinny sent stopped doin' much good, Ma insisted she be looked at, and they found the twenty-five cents to take her to the Company doctor. But that didn't help. The Company doctor couldn't find nothing wrong with her, ruling out consumption immediately. Just as well. The likes of them couldn't afford sanitariums in Colorado or hot springs in Arkansas. Ma had thinned up her lips and looked angry as they left the doctor's office; she'd plainly expected more for their two bits, which could have bought a lot of beans. Pa said, "She'll grow out of it," and that was an end to it as far as Pa was concerned.

Except she didn't grow out of it, and that wasn't an end to it. She didn't get much worse, but she didn't get better, neither, and now she was puny and thin, looking closer to twelve than sixteen, and there wasn't much she could do for long without running out of breath, unless it involved sitting. So she could plant and weed but not hoe and water; sew and mend, but not clean or do the laundry. Do things like shucking peas, but not cook, unless it was stirring something while sitting down. All the "easy" chores, things Ma could do in a minute, and even then Anna took so long over them that sometimes Ma chased her off to do something else and finished the job herself.

"...if I'd had my way I'd've sent her to Jinny two years ago. That there *doctor's* about as much use as a hound-dog that won't hunt. He kills more people than he saves. A pure waste of two bits."

Her throat closed up, and her chest got tight, and her cheeks burned with embarrassment. That was her mother, who'd raised her voice just enough that now Anna could hear her clearly. Ma did that, making it sound like something *she'd* pressed for was somehow someone else's fault if it didn't go well. So Pa could take it as *he'd* been the one to urge the doctor, or even that Anna herself had begged for it, and he'd probably misremember it as the second, and she would be the one that wasted a whole two bits.

And the "her" that was to be sent away, of course, was Anna. The "Jinny" was her aunt Jinny, someone Anna had never seen, but who was nevertheless a constant presence in this household. It was Jinny who sent regular basketfuls of "potions" that Ma sold or traded to folks in Soddy and even Daisy, who mostly couldn't afford the Company doctor. It was Jinny who sent other potions that Ma gave to Pa and Anna, and something Ma called her "tea" that she didn't share with anyone, but Anna suspected was a potion too. Jinny lived east, near to Ducktown, all alone, in a cabin that had belonged to her granny. And that was all Anna knew about her. Except that Pa never liked hearing about the woman, though he never complained about the extra pennies the potions brought in.

Pa coughed. She hated that cough. It wasn't like her cough. It sounded like there was something deeply wrong with him—and she knew he didn't seem as strong as he'd been only a couple of years ago. But Ma insisted he'd be all right, they just needed to find the right potion from Jinny...

But so far no potion he'd been made to drink had done him much good for long. And lots of other coal miners in Soddy got that cough too. And they, too, would get weaker and weaker, and then they wouldn't be able to work, and then—well, usually as soon as the weather turned, they'd get the Winter Fever and it would carry them off. She was pretty sure Ma knew that too. And from Ma's tone of voice, Anna reckoned she'd decided she wasn't going to have two people she had to nursemaid on her hands.

And of course, there was another factor in her wanting to send Anna to that *particular* place. *Other folks don't have Aunt Jinny.* She knew that was what Ma was thinking. That Jinny would have a better chance at making Anna better if the old lady got her hands directly on Anna. And even if Jinny *couldn't* make her well, at least Anna would be out of the way and Ma could concentrate on saving Pa from the Miner's Cough. And she knew Ma would fight anything, be it beast, man, or sickness, that got between her and her Lew.

"Girl belongs with her kin," Pa said, after he finished coughing. "Not gallivantin' around the hollers with a wild woman. She kin stay right here."

"You allus say that," Ma said crossly. "I dunno why you allus say that. There ain't no good reason to keep her here. It ain't as if you give the girl two hoots and a holler."

Tears stung Anna's eyes at that awful truth. Because it *was* true. Pa didn't give a pin about her, because she weren't the son he wanted. Maybe if she'd been strong, tall, and beautiful, like Sally Macray, with boys after her and willin' to do just about any favor to her Pa if he'd give 'em leave to court her, he'd have given her some heed—but small, weak, and plain meant she was barely earning her keep in the household, she had no prospects of getting married and being off Pa's hands, and she knew it. And so did Ma.

"Girl belongs with her kin, givin' her ma help, like God intended," Lew repeated, once the coughing fit had subsided. "And not with the likes of Jinny. Not with some crowin' hen what lives all by her lonesome with no man jack to see she cleaves to Godly ways."

Ma snorted in that way that meant *yore a fine one to talk, Llewellyn Jones, with yore whisky and yore chaw, and the way y'all used ter stay up nights with yore friends, a-drinkin' and a-yarnin' afore y'all took sick. Thet's prolly why, even with me a-prayin' on my knees every Sunday, Jesus don't heal y'all.* But she didn't say nothin'; that wasn't her way. She'd just wait for you to get all uncomfortable and change the subject back to what *she* wanted to talk about.

But then Pa went too far. "And who knows what she's up to with them potions. She's probably a witch!"

"Wall, yore quick enough to drink them potions, an' even quicker to take the money what comes from 'em!" Ma retorted. "An' I know what I know, and I know thet Anna ain't never gonna come 'round right here, but Jinny can *make* her right once she gets the gal under her roof. And Jinny herself invited her!" she added in triumph, and there was a crackle of paper—presumably Ma flourishing Aunt Jinny's latest letter, which had come with the last batch of potions. Ma wrote to Jinny every time she returned the basket with orders for more potions, and Aunt Jinny allus wrote back when she sent the potions. They used soot-ink and brown paper the fatback came wrapped in, one writing on one side, the other returning on the blank side, grease-stains and all. "It's right here! She says she wants Anna to come now, right now, while it's summer and easy travel! *And* she got it all arranged in advance. It ain't gonna cost us nothin'—Jinny's a-takin' care of all of that. So Anna's goin' to her, and *there's* an end to it! And one less mouth to feed won't come amiss, neither."

Well Ma almost never went agin Pa's wishes, but he knew better than to keep palaverin' when she did. So he shut his mouth, and there was the clatter of cookery for a moment or two, twice as loud as normal 'cause Ma was still mad. And then Ma made as much of a stompin' noise as she ever did, which weren't much, and stomped out to the porch where Anna sat on the stoop.

"Y'all done with them peas?" she asked.

Anna held back her tears with an effort. "Yes, Ma," Anna replied, and held the two bowls up to her, the one with the shelled peas and the other with the pods. You didn't throw away nothin' in the Jones house. Ma would make a soup out of the pods and that'd be what she and Ma ate for lunch, with cornbread, while Pa took a hunk of cornbread and some cold bacon and pickled slaw in his lunch bucket. Pa needed the extra food, and every scrap of meat they got went to him; every miner needed as much food and water as could be packed into their lunch buckets to keep up their strength. So Pa got a big breakfast, as big as Ma could manage, and a big lunch, and the lion's share of what she made for supper. And Anna and Ma got the ends of everything, like thin soup made from pea-pods, and plain grits with just salt, and poke salad and potlikker from the greens. Pea-pod soup and a little bit of cornbread wouldn't satisfy most folks, but Anna never had much appetite anyway, and the taste was all right. Better'n cabbage soup, which was all she got come winter.

"Come inside and read yore Bible until supper," Ma ordered, which probably meant she was to show Pa she was a Godly girl, and Aunt Jinny wasn't gonna corrupt her no matter how much of a Jezebel Aunt Jinny was. Although Anna couldn't imagine how anyone who lived alone in the woods could be a Jezebel in the

16

first place. Nor how, if she lived all by herself and was doing all the things you needed to do to keep body and soul together *and* making all them potions, she could ever find the *time* to be a Jezebel. Anna had a hazy idea of what it took to be the kind of woman that one could call a Jezebel, and it required an awful lot of time to make yourself pretty. It probably needed servants too, because you couldn't stay lookin' pretty if you was out weedin' the garden or choppin' wood.

Ma stared at her hard, which made her scramble to her feet, flushing painfully, aware that she had been wool-gathering again. She trotted into the house, obediently got the Bible she'd been given at Sunday School as a prize for memorizing the longest passage, and sat down with it on a little stool near the window, opening it at random, which you were supposed to do if you needed guidance. Which right now, she surely did. Because it seemed like Ma had arranged it, and Pa wasn't going to fight it anymore, and she was being sent off to Aunt Jinny. She wasn't sure if she wanted that or not.

But the first thing her eyes lit on when she let the pages fall open was a page of "begats," which was no help at all.

Supper, which was cornbread, peas and carrots from the garden biled up together, and cabbage from the garden fried with a little fatback grease to give it more flavor, and a mess of poke salad, was extremely uncomfortable. Finally, Pa cleared his throat, and she alerted to him like a coon dog catching a scent. "Your Aunt Jinny done said y'all's to come to her," he said shortly. "Yore Ma thinks she can set y'all up. Y'all can come home when you're stronger."

And that was that. He went back to his food. Anna looked to Ma. Ma looked faintly triumphant. "We'll pack up yore things ternight and y'all'll leave in the mornin'," she said. "The feller what brought the potions today will take y'all part-way, and another feller will get y'all the rest of the way. Jinny got it all arranged."

Anna just sat there, stunned. She hadn't even got her mind wrapped around the idea that she was being sent away—and now Ma said it would be *tomorrow*?

"Finish yore supper," Ma said, sharply, as she continued to sit

17

there with her fork in her numb hand. Mechanically, she obeyed, mashing peas and soft carrots with her fork and somehow getting them into her mouth. She chewed and swallowed, but it tasted like ashes.

She didn't remember getting up to clear the plates like she always did, but somehow found herself drying while Ma washed, and Pa sat next to the cold fireplace in the one good chair. Ma was telling her how this was a grand thing, how Jinny would make her well again, and repeating herself a *lot*, and Anna May just let it all wash over her like rain she couldn't get out of. Eventually Ma gave up, and sent her off to bed.

Like the other houses, this was a two-room "shotgun" house: bedroom in the back, kitchen and living area in the front. Anna plodded numbly into the bedroom, pulled off her dress and folded it neatly, leaving it on a stool. Then she washed up at the basin, pulled the narrow little trundle out from under Pa and Ma's cast-iron bed, and crawled into it in her chemise and knickers. She was old enough for a corset … but like so many things, they couldn't afford one. Ma still used the corset she'd got married in.

Ma was still talking, but now that Anna wasn't there, she was saying different things. "Jinny was right. Anna bein' so puny wouldn't hev happened if we'd'a lived anywheres else."

Pa snorted. "So I shoulda been a farmer like yore Pa? I ain't got any idea of what end of a plow to hold. I'm a miner like my Pa was, and his Pa was in Wales, an' that's what I know. Where else is a miner supposed to work but a mine? Mining's a good, honest living, and it'd been no better at the Burra Burra mine. No better pay, an' ye cain't even grow a blade'a grass there, let alone a garden."

"It woulda been closer to Jinny. Close 'nuff we coulda lived with her. We wouldn't owe nothin' to the Company," Ma countered. "We coulda saved the rent money we's spendin' now. 'Tween me an' Jinny, we'd hev a garden wuth hevin'."

"Fancy me and Jinny livin' under the same roof! And her always lookin' crosswise at me, like I cain't provide for my own damn family!" Now Anna knew that her father was angry, because he never swore unless he was really angry. "Y'all didn't have no complaints when I brung you here!"

"That was afore—"

18

"And this is *now*. I'm givin' in 'bout Anna, even though I think it's a load of heathen trash, like Jinny's witchy potions, because it's plain the girl ain't no help to y'all no more, but I'll be damned if I sit here with you naggin' at me and let y'all tell me what a man should do to provi—" And that was when Pa broke into a fit of coughing, and Ma rushed to get him a drink of one of those potions and said soothing words, and apologized, and begged him to forgive her.

Anna would have loved to have heard Pa say "Anna's staying," rather than "It's plain the girl ain't no help no more." But … that hadn't happened. And wouldn't happen. Pa had made up his mind, and when he did that, there was no changing it. And it appeared that her fate had been sealed. Her chest felt so tight now she could scarcely breathe, and her eyes burned.

She knelt and said her evening prayers, quick as quick, then pulled the quilt over her head as she had as a child to block out the rest of the world and pretend she was somewhere else, like King Solomon's Palace, or with the Pharaoh's daughter, because it would have been lovely to take care of little Baby Moses. Not that she had many ideas what those places looked like, but that was part of the fun of trying to imagine it. There had been a picture in her Bible of Pharaoh's daughter finding Moses in the bulrushes, in which the Pharaoh's daughter was wearing what looked like nothing more than a bit of cloth wrapped around her and tied at the waist, with a strange round collar-like necklace and a kind of scarf over her head, draped in stiff folds, but that didn't give her any ideas about how the Pharaoh lived. As for King Solomon, there had been two pictures. All the one picture showed was a couple of big pillars and a throne with Solomon on it, draped in what looked like a lot of shawls, on top of what looked like a sort of loose bag-garment. And the other showed Solomon and a different Pharaoh's daughter in the same get-ups, promenading in front of a bunch of girls playin' harps and tambourines and dancin', and all of them done up in the same sort of outfits.

The clothes seemed odd. But the pictures of Jesus and the Disciples and Mary all showed the same baggy things, and the Pastor called those things "robes," and the Bible talked about "robes," so that was probably what they all wore when they weren't wading into the Nile after babies.

There was nothing to hint in the pictures about what the Palaces looked like. But there would be lots of gold, surely. And flowers, masses and masses of huge flowers. And the robes would probably be soft, like the best cloth at the Company store, and in beautiful colors, and with all kinds of fancy trim on them. There would be soft pillows everywhere, all made of velvet, and beds and chairs like clouds. And clear, clean skies without a hint of soot. And lots and lots of sweets to eat. Sweets were the one thing that she could work up a shade of appetite for.

She fell into the old daydream, of being the Queen of Sheba visiting Solomon, a queen in her own right and equal to Israel's king. She'd be wrapped in a white robe with the middle pulled in tight with a wide gold belt to show how small her waist was, and there'd be gold trim on all the hems, and she'd have little gold slippers. And a big necklace of gold and pearls around her neck and gold bracelets on her arms. She imagined herself into that outfit, looking as tall and pretty as Sally, with her hair covered by one of the draped headdresses Pharaoh's daughter had on in the picture. She imagined herself going through a big crowd of people, with those girls playing harps and tambourines and dancing in front of and behind her, walking on a carpet of flowers they threw down in front of her. With a whole town full of servants coming behind the dancing girls, and Solomon on his throne like in the picture, staring at her with all his eyes, because she was so beautiful. She imagined him coming down and handing her up the stairs his own self, and putting her in his golden throne with the velvet cushion on it, and little servant boys offering her trays of sweets.

The sweets were where her imagination really had to stretch, because the only time she ever saw anything sweet to eat was at the Methodist Independence Day Picnic and the Christmas Party for the miners' children. So, gingerbread, probably. Peppermints and jaw-breakers and butterscotch to suck. Pie. Pretty squares of white-flour bread spread with honey and jam, bowls of strawberries and cherries and peaches—she'd never seen a fig or a pomegranate, but she guessed they were some kind of berry and apple, so she imagined a big, juicy raspberry the size of her thumb and an apple the color of gold. And nuts dipped in honey and rolled in sugar. She'd seen other sweets in the Company store, in the jars of candy behind the counter, so she imagined all of them too, though she didn't know what they tasted like. And she imagined Solomon at her feet, looking up at her the way Ma looked at Pa.

And it worked to make her unhappiness go away, because just as she was imagining herself biting into a peach so sweet it made her tongue curl up with delight, she fell asleep.

She woke with Ma shaking her shoulder. It was just come sun-up. Thin light came in through the tiny window over Ma and Pa's bed. She could tell by the silence in the house that Pa was already gone to the mine. And that hurt, hurt more than she expected, that he didn't even wake her to say goodbye. Her chest went tight again.

"Jeb'll be here in a right minute," Ma was saying. "I got yore things all bundled up in my old shawl. Get dressed and get some breakfast into yore belly or it'll be a long pull till lunch."

She scrambled out of bed into morning air so cold and damp it made her shake, made a quick wash at the basin full of even colder water, and pulled on her dress and apron as Ma stood there impatiently tapping her foot. Ma didn't even let her do her own hair; as soon as she took it out of its braids, Ma snatched the brush out of her hand and brushed it so roughly it brought tears to her eyes, then braided it in the two braids she hated, because it made her look like a child. As soon as she was decent, Ma all but shoved her into the kitchen, and plunked her down at the table, where there was a bowl of grits and a hunk of cornbread waiting for her, with some potlikker from the greens on the back of the stove to sop up with the cornbread. Ma didn't even go back to the bedroom to pour out the wash-water or to make up the trundle; she just stood there, as if to make sure Anna ate quickly. It was much more than she usually ate, but with Ma staring daggers at her, she obediently took up her spoon and did her best. The grits had some bacon fat in them from cooking Pa's lunch, which was a surprise. Usually all she ever got in her grits was salt. Maybe Ma was feeling a mite sorry for sending her off like this.

Or maybe not, given how Ma was staring at her.

When she'd gotten down as much as she could, Ma snatched the uneaten cornbread from the table, put it in a square of clean rag with another couple of pieces of cornbread, and tied it all up. And just at that moment, out there on the quiet street, she heard hoofbeats and the creak of a wooden wagon.

"There, that'll be Jeb Sawyer," Ma said. "Come on! No keepin' him waitin'!" She picked up a bundle from the floor and shoved it into Anna's right hand, and stuck the packet of cornbread into her left, and chivvied her out the door.

There was just a sliver of sun above the horizon, the damp air made her shiver, and in someone's backyard a rooster crowed. There was a buckboard wagon with a black mule in the traces right outside the front door, with a weather-beaten man just getting down off the seat, a man with grizzled hair under a battered straw hat, wearing red longjohns with the sleeves rolled up, under a pair of faded jeans overalls. The man looked surprised to see that she was ready to go, but didn't say anything other than "Mornin', Missus Jones."

"Mornin', Jebediah," Ma replied. "I wasn't gonna make y'all wait around, I know y'all got a long way to go, and this's a kindness."

"I'm a-bein' paid for my pains, Missus Jones," the man reminded her mildly, and turned to Anna. He had kindly-looking brown eyes, and his face crinkled up when he smiled encouragingly at her. He took her bundles from her and stowed them under the wagon seat, then handed her up, climbing in and taking his seat beside her. He picked up the mule's reins, but waited for Ma to say something to Anna.

"Y'all obey yore Aunt Jinny and read yore Bible," was all Ma said.

"Yes, Ma," Anna said, ducking her head.

"Don't be no trouble. Aunt Jinny'll have y'all right fixed up, but y'all gotta do ev'rthin' she says, and do it exactly as she says, an' no argumentin' about it." Ma looked as stern at her as the Pastor when he was preachin' hellfire.

"Yes, Ma," Anna repeated, shrinking in on herself, and feeling as low as a snake's belly.

"And don't you pay no heed to what yore Pa said about her. Jinny's a Godly woman, for all she's a strange one with strange ways. Never no finagling with Jinny. But she does things as she likes and she don't cotton to no man comin' into her life and a-bossin' her around, and she and yore Pa got sideways of each other from the minute they met. She's done forgave him, but he ain't never gonna forgive no woman for bein' uppity to 'im." Ma softened just a little bit at that. "So you mind yore manners and don't pick up Jinny's ways."

"No, Ma," Anna agreed.

Ma turned her attention to the driver. "Thenkee again, Jeb. Safe journeys."

Jeb took that as the signal to leave. He slapped the reins against the mule's back. "Walk on, Daisy," was all he said, and with a little lurch, the mule put the wagon in motion.

Anna looked back to wave goodbye, but all she saw was Ma's back as she went back into the house. She swallowed down tears, and turned her attention to the road in front of her. Bad as she felt, she wasn't going to cry in front of a stranger.

Anna had never ridden on a wagon before, and the sensation of sitting on something that was moving was extremely unsettling, and very quickly drove out every other feeling but borderline fear. She clutched both hands on the worn board seat and gritted her teeth. It seemed very high up here, and as the wagon lurched in the ruts of the dirt road, more than a little precarious and not a little scary.

But by the time they reached the edge of Soddy, where the Company houses ended, and the much more ramshackle shacks of those who had cobbled together their own "houses" out of boards and tarpaper began, the road smoothed out some, and she started to relax. The mule didn't seem inclined to go any faster than a walk, Jeb didn't seem inclined to urge her to, and Anna loosened her white-knuckle grip on the seat as her fear ebbed.

The transition from "Soddy" to "farms outside of Soddy" was abrupt. The shacks ended, the farm fields began, and already there were men and women out in the fields, either doing something with a mule dragging some sort of implement between the rows of growing plants while a man steered the thing, or with a man dragging the implement himself and a boy or a woman guiding it. Plow? Harrow? Hoe? She didn't know. She didn't know nothin' about farming.

That must be cruel hard, she thought with astonishment, looking at the men dragging a plow their own selves. No wonder Pa was contemptuous of farming. At least he wasn't being treated like a mere beast. Was he? She realized at that moment she didn't know much about mining either. For all she knew, his foreman could be driving him as harder or harder than that man pulling that plow. Pa might be contemptuous of farming, but was mining really better?

But if you farm, at least you ain't gonna starve ... and you ain't allus owing the Company more money than you got.

Jeb turned the mule onto a new road, going south and east, and soon they were driving along parallel to the Lake. For all that she had lived all her life within shouting distance of the Lake, this was the first time she had ever set eyes on it, and she tried not to gape at the expanse of water. Until now, the most water she had ever seen at one time was when Ma had the extra wood to heat water for everyone to have a bath in the old tin hip-bath—which normally lived next to the rain barrel, with both set to catch extra water so Ma didn't have to go to the pump as often. Ma kept pieces of old rag stitched together over the tops of both to keep out the critters, the bugs, the leaves, and the soot. There was a pump shared by all the nearby houses where they otherwise had to get their water, which was why it was much more convenient to have the rain-water handy.

Wonder where Aunt Jinny gets her water? Does she have a crick nearby? Walking all the way to a crick in the winter to get pails of water would be a powerful lot of work. And cold. And she didn't have shoon, so she'd have to wrap her feet in rags and straw and hope they didn't freeze going to and fro. She hoped Aunt Jinny wasn't going to expect her to do it. She wasn't sure she could haul a half-full pail, much less two full ones.

Little wisps of fog floated over the surface of the Lake. It wasn't *exactly* a Lake, it was more like a very, very wide part of Soddy Crick, because barges came up the Crick all the time, passing through the Crick and on, to take up the coal and coke from the mine at Soddy and the bigger one at Daisy, south of Soddy, and haul it down elsewhere to sell. The view was unexpectedly beautiful, with the sun just coming up and glinting off the ripples, and a passel of ducks floating on the current, and she found her heart going still for a moment at the sight. And suddenly, instead of smelling soot and smoke and someone's dirty privy, she smelled—

Green. There was no other way to describe the scent, except as green. And clean water, and a hint of something sweet. Flowers? And she heard birds *singing*, which she could never do in town. The air felt clean on her face, and despite the morning being cold, the sun felt warmer than it ever did on her own porch.

She straightened up a little, and took in lungfuls of the lovely clean air, and somehow, didn't cough.

And a little spark of hope sprang to life inside her.

Mebbe this ain't gonna be bad.

2

The route they followed took several turnings, away from the Lake, across smaller cricks that she didn't know the names for, but generally going more south than east, and through farm country. By this time, she'd managed to lose her sadness in something like excitement at all the things that were new to her. She'd never seen so much food growing before, and in her mind, she started to question Pa's contempt for farmers even more. Of the people who were out there, there weren't more than a couple out of dozens that were pulling a plow themselves. So mebbe the ones that were doing that were just *bad* farmers. It appeared to her that if you were farming, even if the harvest was poor, well, you didn't *owe* nothin', you just didn't *get* much.

As for mining ... well. Things had been better before Pa started coughing, but they had never been precisely *good* in her memory. The miners got paid by the weight of coal they brought out, and paid in Company scrip, which could only be used at the Company store— and how overpriced things were at the store was made evident by the difference between what Ma paid at the general store with the cash money she got from potions, and what she paid at the Company store in scrip. But the Company store did one thing the general store didn't—it let you take things on account.

Which is why pert near ev'body allus runs a debt at the Company store ...

She shook away these uncomfortable thoughts, and admired

the green fields spread out around her, taking long breaths of air that somehow got deeper into her lungs than ever before. She hadn't coughed once since they left Soddy! Most of the stuff out there in those farm fields she recognized; she knew corn and beans even at a distance, and squash was obvious from the rounds hanging on the vines. But other things were a mystery.

But all that corn! Even flint-corn was tasty when it was just milky, soft, and done as a roasted ear, and she longed to jump off the box and pick a couple of ears to have at lunch. But—that would be stealing, and that was breaking a Commandment. She couldn't be tempted to do that, though the boys in Soddy boasted all the time out of the hearing of adults about how they'd sneak out after dark when they was supposed to be in bed and raid cornfields at night, and have themselves illicit corn feasts. A few ears of corn wasn't worth the amount of praying for forgiveness you'd have to do, after a theft like that. At least, not as far as she was concerned.

They kept going mostly south and a bit east while the sun kept climbing up into the sky, and Anna watched everything going on around her with complete fascination. These were all things she had *heard* about, but never seen. The only cows and goats she had ever seen were in pictures; the only geese and ducks were the ones she spotted flying overhead when she was weeding.

Some few people in Soddy kept chickens, so of course she'd seen those, but her family had never been able to afford to do so.

So many animals out here! And wild ones! Rabbits froze beside the road as they passed, and squirrels ran across it, and she'd never seen either alive, only skinned and gutted and ready for the pot when Ma could trade potions for them. The same with 'possums; she was not prepared for how ugly and odd they were, and she only knew what they were by the bare tail. They were good in stew; some people said they were greasy, but in winter she positively craved the taste of fat.

As for the farms themselves, the more she saw, the more she envied the children out there in the fields, helping their Mas and Pas. Ma scrutinized every weed that got pulled up, on the chance it might be added to the poke salad she kept stewing on the back of the stove, the food of last resort when even the Company store wouldn't give you a speck of flour on credit. And when Ma was watching, Heaven forbid you sneak so much as a single pea for yourself. As she squinted to see what was going on at them farmhouses, there was at least one girl younger than her, shelling peas on the porch as they passed, and Anna could tell that for every pea that made it into the pan, at least two were going into the little girl's mouth. The freedom to eat as many peas as you wanted ... she'd never had that. Every bit of food had to be accounted for and shared, with the lion's share always going to Pa.

Every time they crossed a crick, there was at least one boy fishing it, or hunting for crawdads. Every farm, if it didn't have a cow, at least had a goat, which meant milk and butter and maybe cheese. And *all* of them had chickens, which meant eggs, and when a hen got too old to lay—stewed chicken! She hadn't had an egg in—forever. And she'd never tasted chicken. Well, maybe having to pull a plow your own self instead of having a mule or ox to do it was cruel hard ... but wasn't it made up for in all the good things you got to eat?

They passed a tangle of wild blackberry bushes standing between the road and a field of tall, leafy plants she didn't recognize; she spotted the red and purple berries growing there, and it was all she could do not to beg Jeb to stop—

But then, he did. "I fancy a bite a' fruit with lunch," he said conversationally, as he got down off the bench and tied the mule's reins to a young tree. "How 'bout y'all?"

"Yessir!" she said eagerly. "Please, sir!" And he laughed, and pulled an empty basket out from beneath the seat before helping her down.

"Lessee if we kin fill this quick," he told her, and set to picking.

A few berries went into her mouth (to make up for the pain of being stuck by thorns), but most went into the basket. And most of the fruit was fully ripe, so it wasn't too terribly long before the basket was, in fact, full.

It occurred to her that Jeb was treating her like a little girl, and not the woman-grown she was by her years. But right now—she didn't care. Not if being treated like a little chile was going to get her *this* kind of treat.

"Mistuh Jebediah?" she asked, because she was dying to know.

Was it some kind of green to eat? The leaves were enormous. She could scarcely imagine how someone would cook it—would they eat it raw? "What's the stuff a-growin' in the field on t'other side of the blackberries?"

He laughed and laughed. "That there's 'baccy, young'un! Ain't you never seen it afore?"

"Not a-growin'," she admitted. The whole way, she'd seen field after field of the stuff, and wondered what it was. She knew enough about farming to know that this, and not corn, was a farmer's cash crop. He grew corn for his family and his animals, but he grew 'baccy for money.

"Wall, there 'tis," he said, and looked at the basket, which was almost overflowing. "Huh. Missy, most young'uns I know'd et more than they picked, but since y'all didn't, I reckon we got us 'nuff fer dinner an' supper too. We'll stop at next crick we cross."

He helped Anna back up on the seat, and picked up the reins. Daisy, who had been contentedly munching the weeds growing at the foot of the blackberry bushes around her bit, obediently picked up her head. "Walk on, Daisy," Jeb ordered, and off they went again.

But before too long, they came to another small field of corn, with a farmer working in it, and he stopped her with a "whoa-up." "Howdy, neighbor!" he hailed the stranger. "I got me a hankerin' fer roastin' ears. Y'all got any t'trade?"

The farmer straightened up from his hoeing and moved over to the road, as Anna sat quietly. "Reckon I do. What's t'trade?"

Jeb leaned over between his own legs and extracted a bit of metal from beneath the wagon seat, and held it out. "Knife blank. Been worked to a finish, jest needs a handle an' sharpenin', an I reckon y'all for the kinda man what knows his way 'round a good knife."

The farmer took it from Jeb and examined it critically. "Reckon it's wuth 'bout two ears," he said, starting the bargaining, which carried on in a spirited manner until Jeb was the possessor of a full dozen young ears of corn and some termaters for good measure, and the farmer appeared right satisfied with his potential knife.

"Now, that there's supper and breakfus' sorted," Jeb said as he got Daisy moving again. He looked over at Anna and his old blue eyes twinkled. "Saw y'all a-hankerin' over thet corn, an' I'm partial to a roastin' ear m'self."

"Thenkee, sir," she said quietly, her hands clasped on the edge of the seat. "Where'd y'all get thet there knife?"

"Make 'em m'self from scrap iron," Jeb replied. "I ain't no smith, but m'Pa taught me how, so's I'd allus hev' somethin' t'trade fer. When winter sets in an' there ain't so much cartin' t'be done, I takes my liddle scraps of iron an' I makes blanks. Man allus has t'hev two strings t'his bow, my Pa useta say, and I gets a better bargain tradin' than payin' fer most liddle things."

For the first time in a very long time, Anna was actually feeling *hungry* by the time they crossed another crick, and Jeb declared it was dinnertime. He slipped the mule's bit this time so she could eat proper, tied her up near enough to the crick so she could drink, and they set up upstream, under the trees, amongst the moss and roots. It was cool and breezy, the moss was soft to sit on, and the crick sounded cheerful. Jeb brought down a tin cup to share, the basket of blackberries, and her little packet of cornbread and a bigger packet folded in a square of cheesecloth. When she opened her packet, he stared at it a minute and frowned, then patted her shoulder. "Y'all put thet away fer now," he said, and opened his own packet. "I got too much t'et by m'self, reckon y'all kin he'p." And he handed her a fat half-moon of piecrust stuffed with something.

Piecrust! They almost *never* had pie. You needed flour *and* lard or suet for it; flour was better saved for bread, and lard hard to come by.

She wrapped her cornbread back up, and held the piecrust-thing he had given her in her lap, staring at it. "What is it?" she asked.

"Fancy a good Taffy gal not knowin' a pasty when she sees one!" he scoffed. "Must be 'cause yore Ma niver learnt t'do 'em fer yore Pa. That there's a pasty. Miners et 'em. Pie crust nice as nice, stuffed with whatever y'all got at hand. Missus Davies, what I stay with in Soddy overnight, makes 'em fer m'trip home. Now—" He ducked his head and clasped his hands and she did the same. "For what we're about to et, thenkee, Jesus," he said, then watched her until she took a tentative bite of the thing before he tucked into his own. She nearly dropped it in surprise to taste the meat in among the carrots, turnips, and potatoes, little shreds of meat and enough gravy to hold it all together too. "Now, that crimpy crust 'round the edge, y'ain't supposed to et that. Y'all throw it down the mine fer the tommyknockers, so they don't steal yore lunchpail or let the mine roof fall on ya. Now, we ain't gonna give our'n t' the tommyknockers, but we're a-gonna save it anyway, 'cause I got a notion." He nodded wisely, and said nothing more; after thanking him profusely—and marveling at the idea of being able to th*row good food away*—Anna was too busy enjoying every bite to talk. And she was stuffed so full that she couldn't have eaten that outer crimped crust anyway, so she handed it over to him and he folded it with a little bit of his in the cheesecloth. Then, for no reason that she could determine, he stopped and cut a couple of willow rods and threw them in the back of the otherwise empty wagon.

It wasn't until they were back on the road that it occurred to her belatedly that he had just probably fed her his supper, and he'd given her that pasty out of pure kindness of heart when he saw how poorly provisioned she was. But she couldn't un-eat it, so all she could do was be thankful for it, determined to add him to her evening prayers. At least they had roasting ears, her cornbread, and berries, so he wouldn't go to sleep hungry.

Finally they moved onto a road running down the middle of a broad spit of tree-covered land with a couple of small houses on it that ended at the Lake. And here the Lake was even broader than it was back at Soddy. Late afternoon sun made everything a mellow gold, the rippling surface of the Lake looked molten, and that green-water smell was back again.

Dead ahead of them was a dock, and tied up to it was a contraption so perilous-looking that Anna felt a wash of terror at the thought that this thing and it alone was going to take them across the lake to the other side.

It was a cobbled-together raft-like contrivance roughly big enough to hold a couple of wagons, with nothing more than a couple of ropes serving as railings. It looked as if it was floating barely above the water. There was a sort of shack at one side of it in the middle, and on the opposite side, what looked like a water wheel.

"That there's the Igou Ferry," said Jeb. "Thet'll get us t'other side, an' if the current ain't bad, we kin get fur enough along the road on t'other side that there's a farmer I know'll let us use his haybarn fer the night."

Anna wasn't given a chance to comment or object. As she clung to the wagon seat, the mule pulled the wagon aboard the rickety thing, not stopping until her hooves were nearly in the water at the front. Jeb climbed down, took eight wedges of wood from under the seat, and wedged two under each wheel to keep the wagon from rolling either forward or back, then came around to her side and held out his hand to her. "Gotta come down, Annie," he coaxed. "Y'all bein' up there so high, least little move y'all make'll start the whole thing a-rockin', an' y'all don' want that."

No, she most assuredly did not! Moving as carefully as if she and the wagon were made of glass, she eased herself down to the wood of the raft with his help. And since the dubious shelter of the cabin seemed to be the least fragile spot on the entire ferry, she plastered her back to it.

Smoke came from a tin chimney on the roof, puffs of steam from the window in the rear of the shed, and she felt and heard a steady thumping and chuffing on the other side of that wall. A man with a cloth "bucket" hat on his head, in overalls streaked with black grease and a faded flannel shirt, came out of the shed to greet Jeb. They clearly knew each other very well, and exchanged some jokes she simply didn't get. "An' who's this?" the man asked after a bit of joshing, turning to her.

"Anna Jones, outa Soddy. I'm a-takin' 'er to 'er Aunt Jinny Alscot up Ducktown way. Anna, this's Cap'n Clem. He's in charge of this here ferry."

"*That* Jinny?" The man's eyes widened. "Tarnation! Wall, then, no charge fer extree passenger. I'd'a not be on the water without Jinny Alscot's potions." He held out a greasy paw to Anna, who shook it with no hesitation, since he seemed to know and be respectful of Aunt Jinny.

"Permission t'throw a line off th' stern, cap'n?" Jeb asked with a grin. Clem grinned back.

"Yore th' on'y man I know what asks permission, or calls me cap'n," the cap'n replied. "Permission granted. Jest don' foul the rudder."

Jeb took something out from under the bench seat on the wagon, and the two willow rods from the back. The "something" proved to be a cigar box with a couple lengths of string wrapped up neat, and other oddments. Meanwhile Clem bustled about, pulling off ropes from logs holding the front and rear of the ferry to the dock, then vanished into the cabin. The smoke turned from white to black, the chuffing sound increased, the wheel on the side of the raft started to thrash the water, and the whole thing started to move.

Anna glued herself even tighter to the cabin. Jeb held out his hand. "Come along, missy," he coaxed. "Y'all ain't gonna fall off. And even if y'all did, water's still as a glass here. Y'all could swim back to the ferry easy as pie."

"But I cain't swim!" she wailed.

"Then I won't let y'all fall in," he said reasonably. "Lookit Daisy! She's so easy she's a-fallin' asleep!"

She turned her head nervously to see that he was right; the mule was standing hipshot with all her weight on her left leg, her head hanging comfortably, her eyes closed.

Still so terrified her knees shook, she took Jeb's hand and let him lead her to the rear of the contraption. There he rolled up his pants legs, sat down on the edge of the raft, and went to work with his string, a willow rod, and a cork, the pasty edge, and a fishing hook—and now she knew what he was doing. In a moment he had a fishing rod all set up, with a cork for a bobber and a blob of dough made from crushed crust and crick water on the hook. He handed her the rod.

Gingerly she sat down beside him, with her legs crossed under her skirt.

"Jest drop th' hook inter th' water and let out the string while y'all hold the rod," said Jeb patiently. "When y'all feel a fish pull on't, lemme know an' I'll take it from there."

He did the same for his own rod, and after a while, under the warm sun and the mesmerizing, slowly changing view of the shore passing beside them, she finally relaxed. So that when she suddenly *did* feel a strong tug on the rod, she yelped.

Quick as quick, Jeb handed her his rod and took hers, and patiently, with much waiting, reeled in the string hand over hand. Finally he brought up a struggling catfish, which he hit on the head with the haft of his knife, before carefully taking the hook out of its mouth and stringing a piece of string between its gills. Then he tied the piece of string to the raft and dropped the fish over the side.

"What—" she asked.

"I knocked it out, an' the water flowin' through'll keep it alive till we git t'other side. That way it'll be fresher when we et it, than it'd be if I gutted it now." He re-baited the hook and let it back into the water, then grinned at her. "I was a-hopin' y'all'd hev beginner's luck."

Slowly Jeb persuaded Anna to pull up her skirt a little and let her feet dangle in the water. She was still unreasonably afraid, right up until the point where she actually did it, that the water, or something in it, was somehow going to grab her feet and pull her in. After nothing of the sort happened, she relaxed, as the ferry chuffed its slow way upstream north and east to the landing point.

"Why don't the ferry go straight across?" she asked Jeb when she had caught her third fish and he his second.

"Two reasons. On account'o this's still Soddy Crick, the water's a-flowin' south, an' if y'all tried t'go straight across y'all'd end up south of where y'all wanted to land. T'other reason is on account'o the carts are mostly goin' east empty an' west full, like mine. So Clem gets the he'p o' the Crick when his load is heavier a-goin' west by letting the Crick do most'o th' work for 'im, an' saves on the coal by goin' downstream. Comin' this way, we're lighter, an' it don' take as much coal t'head upstream."

It was nearly suppertime by Anna's reckoning when the ferry chuffed and wallowed its way into the dock on the other side. He overshot the dock, which alarmed Anna all over again, until she understood he was letting the stream help him turn the unwieldy craft so that Daisy and the front of the cart would be getting straight off rather than having to be backed off. Clem left Jeb to do the tying up; he was fussing with his little steam engine and just gave them a dismissive wave from the shed. Anna got off ahead of the cart; the poles, fishing tackle, and fish, still somewhat alive and now wrapped in wet cheesecloth, went into the back of it, and Jeb led Daisy out onto the dock. By this time Anna knew how to get up onto the seat herself; she pulled herself up next to Jeb and off they went.

Jeb frowned at the sun, though, which made her worry. "Reckon it's jest as well we got corn'n fish," he said. "Gonna be too late to stir up m'farmer, so best we set up camp fer the night. This here—" he waved at an inlet just to their right "—is Blue Springs Slough. There's a nice liddle crick runs inter it, Blue Springs Crick; we kin use the crick fer water, an' there's plenty'o green stuff fer Daisy. We'll be all right."

There were a few houses in the distance to the north, but Jeb evidently didn't know the people who lived there, or at least didn't know them well enough to ask for shelter, she guessed. She supposed she should have felt alarmed at the prospect of spending the night without even canvas over her head, but she was getting too tired and hungry to think about anything other than food and a place to lay her head.

The spot Jeb picked was very like the place he'd chosen for lunch: in the woods, near the crick he'd talked about. But it differed from that one in that they were actually in a little meadow among the trees, where a bigger tree had fallen and taken several more with it, leaving a place that others had clearly used in the past to camp, because there was a circle of bare earth with the dead cinders of a fire in it.

"Y'all go pick me up as much dead wood as y'all kin carry an' bring it here t' the fire-circle," Jeb instructed. "Do thet 'bout four times. Then iffen y'all wanta sleep soft, break off stuff t'pile up an' y'all kin either sleep in th' wagon or under it. Whichever y'all pick, I'll take t'other."

"Wagon bed, please, Mistuh Jeb," she said, thinking about all the creepy-crawlies on the ground. Then she trudged off in the direction of the top of the felled tree. She didn't have a lot of hope of finding much deadfall there, if this was commonly used as a place to camp, but to her surprise, there was quite a bit, and all of it of a size she could handle.

She brought in her first lot and returned—

And that was when things took a turn for the odd. Because she was *certain* she had picked that particular spot bare—but there was wood there. All of it a convenient size, both for the fire, and for her to carry.

She stared at the spot for a moment, then shook her head. *Must be gettin' so weary I'm all a muddle*, she thought, and stooped to start gathering again, bundling it all in her apron for ease in carrying.

Sure this time she had picked the spot bare, she left the load beside Jeb, and went back to explore further—

And there was more wood. Right in the same place she had picked over.

A chill ran up her backbone. Wood just didn't walk itself over to that spot. Something or someone had to have carried it there.

Was Jeb trying to play a trick on her?

She looked back over her shoulder. No, she could see him at the edge of the trees.

Was someone out there in the woods, watching her? Right now?

She almost ran away, back to the safety of Jeb and the wagon. But she had been told to gather wood—so she fumbled it up as fast as she could, and scuttled back to Jeb and the security of the campsite. To her immense relief, he told her, "Thet'll be enough an' t'spare, missy. Now, take this here spade t'the crick an' scrub it down with a rock an' sand till all y'all kin see is bare metal."

Well the crick was well within both line of sight and earshot; she could be back to Jeb in a lick if someone was out there. She told herself sternly that nothing bad had happened; in fact, whoever had been piling up that wood for her had been doing her a favor. Maybe it was a trapper or hunter who didn't like to bother other people, or thought he might frighten her with his wild appearance. She knelt beside the crick, found a good piece of sandstone to scrub with, and scoured away.

When she brought back the immaculate spade, the sunset had turned the tops of the trees above them to flame, and in the deepening shadow beneath the trees and in the little meadow, the campfire Jeb had lit looked very welcoming. He took the shovel from her and directed her to ferns to break off and grasses to tear up until she had a decent pile in the wagon bed.

At that point she was so tuckered out that she dropped down next to the fire and stared at it for a long time before she realized that, besides the ears of corn roasting in their shucks at the edge of it, Jeb had the blade of the shovel over the coals and was frying the fish in it.

She blinked in surprise at how clever that was. *She* never would have thought of doing that!

The basket with the remains of the blackberries and the termaters was between them, and as Jeb tended the fish, he ate 'maters absently. She reached in and got one herself, and bit into it. It was wonderful. Much better than the peaches of her imagination.

Jeb had split one of the larger chunks of wood in half, and presently he scraped some of the fish off onto the raw, fresh wood of each half. He'd left the skin on, so while the skin stuck to the shovel, the meat didn't. He turned the shovel on its side in the middle of the fire to burn the skin off, then reached into the chest pocket of his overalls and pulled out a twist of paper, sprinkling some of the salt that was in there onto each pile of fish and bones. Once again, he clasped his hands and said a brief "grace." "Don't et them bones," he warned her as he handed her the chunk of wood. "Go slow and be careful."

She was no stranger to catfish. Before Pa had got Miner's Cough, if he had time and strength, he'd take a try at catching a fish or two himself. 'Twasn't as easy as catching 'em from the ferry—lots of competition, for one thing. But it was always worth trying. Fishing was free, so were worms, and you could get a decent meal without debt to the Company store.

The fish was hot, so she had to be careful not to burn her fingers; she knew to go slow and mindful and eat nibbles, not bites. She even knew to suck the bones bare and put them in a pile at her feet. When the roasted ears came out of the fire, all they needed was a squoze of 'mater juice to hold the salt, and they was heaven.

For the second time that day she stuffed herself, finishing up with 'maters and berries, and there was still some of everything but the fish left over for breakfast. The cornbread, which she split with Jeb, filled in all the rest of the corners.

Jeb rummaged under the seat, which seemed to be a mysterious place that held practically anything, and came up with a folded bit of old canvas she could put between her and the pile of vegetation. When she lay down, it was no worse than her corn-shuck mattress at home, though it seemed strange to be sleeping in her dress.

She said her prayers lying down and silently, because she didn't want to disturb Jeb, and she made sure to include Jeb and Cap'n Clem in her "God blesses" because both of them had been so good to her on this trip, Clem not charging a fare for her and all, though *what* she would have paid for a fare with, she had no idea. She heard Jeb grunt and snort for a while as he got himself comfortable, and then there was silence filled only by crickets and...

...and strange sounds.

She hadn't noticed them so much when she and Jeb were eating, but the night was full of sound. Some, she did know: the peeps of little frogs and toads, the louder croaks of big ones, and the booming of bullfrogs. And crickets. But there were other noises out there she'd never heard before, and some of them were hair-raising enough to wake her right out of drowsiness. Hisses and screeches, and a weird *huh-huh-huh-huhHOO-ah* that put the hair on her head straight up.

Bears? Panthers?

Wisht Jeb wasn't asleep...

But she heard him snoring away, and she heard Daisy shifting her weight and making smacking noises, and it finally occurred to her that if the mule wasn't alarmed, there probably wasn't anything out there to be alarmed *by*.

And she started to relax. As she started to relax, she started to get sleepy again. And just as she was about to fall asleep, she noticed how there were stars peeping through all of the branches overhead.

Wait ...

There was a dense canopy of leaves over them, enough to block out all the sun by daylight. So how could there be stars shining through the leaves now?

And ... those stars were in *pairs*!

Pairs of eyes!

Dozens and dozens of them, and what she had taken for twinkling was the eyes blinking now and again.

She absolutely froze.

What ... are ... those?

She stared at the eyes. The eyes stared back, blinking every now and again.

She could not have told how long she lay there, staring at all those eyes, but at some point exhaustion overcame her.

The next thing she knew, she was curled up, having somehow wrapped the old canvas around herself, and had awoken to the smell of the campfire, the sound of Jeb moving about, and birdsong.

She unwound herself from the canvas and got out of the wagonbed. Daisy had eaten everything around her and strained at her rope, so she dragged all the bedding out of the wagon and dropped it in front of the mule, who seemed pleased enough to see it.

"Iffen y'all're gonna wash up, it's private up that-a-way," Jeb said, nodding toward where the crick cut through the trees. She hesitated a moment, remembering the incident with the wood last night, then took the canvas to dry off with and her bundle from home with her. *Iffen I see anythin', I can scream*, she decided.

She got a good scrub without taking more off than her dress. Her comb was in the bundle, so she was able to tidy her hair and rebraid it. Not as good as Ma could, but good enough. She was old enough to put her hair up, of course, but they couldn't afford hairpins, and Pa hadn't been able to find any bits of wire to fashion into pins for her the way he had for Ma, so she kept her hair in braids like a child. She'd tried to make pins with bits of this and that, mostly garden stuff, but they always broke or were too slippery to work.

There was no hint of anything out in the woods but the things that ought to be there, but she hurried over her wash and got back to Jeb quickly. Grace said, breakfast over, fish bones and corn shucks buried (Daisy ate the cobs with gusto), fire put out with water and the dead coals buried, they were on their way again.

3

This was not farmland. This was real forest. Once they got out of sight of the couple of cabins near the shoreline—and she guessed the people living there were probably more fishers than farmers—there was nothing on either side of the road but trees. She kept taking deep breaths of the air, because after Soddy, it was absolutely intoxicating. She realized with a sense of wonder and surprise that she had literally never felt as good as this in her entire life.

Maybe she was getting better? Maybe she could stay until fall with Aunt Jinny, then go home? If she felt like this, she could do *anything* Ma asked her to do—all the garden work, *and* go out a-foraging, *and* help with the housework! Why, feeling this good, she might could get a little extra money by working in the kitchen of one of the mine owners or foremen! Last night's alarm seemed ridiculous now. The firewood? She'd likely misremembered, and each time had just gone farther than she'd thought. The eyes? Tree frogs, more than like. And mice, there were mice everywhere, the Good Lord knew. She'd just never seen eyes shine in the dark like that, but they were probably reflecting the campfire. And of course it seemed as if there were more of them than there actually were, because she was so scared.

And this place was just beautiful. Pa had said Aunt Jinny lived all alone out in the woods, so maybe her place was just as beautiful. If that was true, well…

She found herself looking forward to getting there.

"Mistuh Jeb?" she said, as a thought occurred to her. "What d'y'all *take* t'Soddy iffen y'all go there all the time?"

"Stuff what the rich folks order from Sears Roebuck," he replied promptly. "And stuff fer the gen'ral store. Sometimes stuff fer the Company store. Mail. All manner'o this an' that, 'cause there ain't no railhead. It's 'nuff thet I gits trips ever' three days or so. An' iffen I ain't haulin' t' Soddy, I'm doin' bits'a haulin' 'round Cleveland, where I live. Thet's where we're a-goin'."

"I thunk Aunt Jinny lived in Ducktown—" she said dubiously.

"She do, but I'm on'y takin' y'all as far as Cleveland. They's wagoners yore aunt knows good thet haul copper ingots from the Burra Burra mine in Ducktown to Cleveland regular, an' one of 'em's gonna take y'all to Miz Jinny."

Another stranger! She grew a little anxious at that, but reminded herself that her aunt had a fearsome reputation, and was apparently a very good judge of character. Jeb had been wonderfully kind.

"Happens I know th' feller m'self," Jeb continued, as if sensing her apprehension. "He's a good, Godly man, is Caleb Strong. Won't carry a whip, much less use one on 'is mules. They say y'all could ask him to carry a leddy stark naked with a pot of gold from Ducktown t'Cleveland an' when he got t'Cleveland, wouldn't be a coin missin' or a flyspeck on th' gal. An' I b'lieve 'em."

Well, if Jeb vouched for the man, that made her feel much easier.

The thick woods hid all sorts of things ... and before long, she began to wonder if she hadn't been too quick in dismissing the incident with the firewood and all the shining eyes in the darkness.

Because she started getting glimpses of things out of the of her eye that were definitely *not* songbirds and rabbits. She thought she saw *faces* peering at her from the trees above, or the bushes and weeds below. But she couldn't be sure, because when she turned her head to look, whatever she had thought she had seen wasn't there anymore; it had whisked away out of sight, leaving behind only a little bit of movement in the leaves or grass to show where it had been. If it had been there at all.

But Jeb didn't seem to notice anything, and he was quick enough to point out a doe with a fawn at the edge of a meadow, a gray fox whisking out of sight, and a badger peering at them suspiciously from under a bush.

But mebbe he's seein' 'em too, but he don't want ter scare me. He knew she was a town girl, after all.

And last night, absolutely nothing had happened to her, despite all those eyes staring at her.

Pastor allus says iffen y'all is Godly, ain't nothin' kin happen to you from hants an' spirits an' suchlike. And Aunt Jinny lived in woods like these, and she never came to no harm.

"Mistuh Jeb? Where y'all live in Cleveland? What kinda town is it? Is it like Soddy?" she asked, as she thought she spied something not unlike a doll made out of sticks with an acorn cap on its head, whisking under the bushes.

He guffawed. "Bless yore heart, no! It's away bigger! Even Daisy's bigger nor Soddy!" He proceeded to regale her with a description of something she could scarcely wrap her mind around—a town where the main streets were all paved, and there were so many buildings that were two and even three stories tall that there were "too many to count." What he described sounded like a traveler's tale. Houses with water that came from pipes inside, not pumped, hauled up from a well, or carried from a crick—and lit at night by gas that was brighter than dozens of candles. Privies *inside* the houses, with all the waste being magically carried away somewhere. Not just one store, or two, but *dozens*, an "opera house" and a "trolly" (whatever those were). And factories! She suspected Ma would have been a lot happier if Pa had gotten a job in one instead of in the mine. And a railway station! And he said there were almost two thousand people living there! The very idea made her head spin.

"But I ain't livin' *in* Cleveland," he added, with a laugh. "An' the fancified stuff's fer the well-off. So don't 'spect no inside privies, nor gas-lights, and jest a pump at the kitchen sink."

Quite frankly, a pump of your very own at the sink sounded like unimaginable luxury to her.

"It useta be a farmhouse, but the city growed up to it an' the fields got sold off, so it's got the barn fer Daisy, an' we got a garden an' a pig an' some chickens, but not much else," he continued. Which sounded like heaven to her.

The woods abruptly changed to farms again, and she stopped seeing things out of the corner of her eye. And oddly, rather than feeling comforted, she felt a little disappointed. The things weren't offering her any harm, and she really wished she had been able to get real glimpses of them so she could have made up her mind if there actually were things there, or it was just her overactive imagination.

Not so much in the way of hills on this side of Soddy Crick, so it was easy to see Cleveland long before they got near it. She gaped at the spires of what must be churches by the crosses on top, the tall chimneys and buildings that were, as he had promised, two and even three stories tall!

But the nearer they got, the more she began to feel that all-too-familiar weakness. It wasn't nearly as bad as it had been back home, but—did this mean that her sudden improvement had only been temporary? If she couldn't get well, completely well, Ma would never let her come home to be a burden again. The thought cast a bit of a gray pall over the otherwise beautiful, sun-filled morning.

But her growing weakness didn't seem to have the old symptom of nausea attached, at least.

They didn't actually go into the part of town where the streets had been paved with bricks, although in the distance she could see the place where dirt gave way to brick, and marveled all over again. If you never left that part of town, think how easy it would be to keep the hem of your dress clean! No dragging it in the dirt and mud, no laborious scrubbing away at it with a brush and bucket of water before you went to bed!

Jeb's house was at least three rooms bigger than Pa's, maybe more. And the barn was near as nice as the house, all neatened and painted up with red lead paint. He didn't even have to guide Daisy; she knew her way and knew a rest in a stall with hay and water was waiting for her. She picked up her pace right smart, her ears up, her head bobbing. Jeb's kids must have been watching for him, because the wagon got swarmed by them before Daisy even came to a halt. Jeb laughed, and shouted out orders. Somehow the mule got led into the barn, unharnessed, and put in her stall before either of them were ready to climb out of the wagon.

Jeb lifted her down, got her bundle from the back, and handed

43

it to her. By this time the swarm of kids resolved itself into a mere three: a boy her age or a little older, a girl about ten, and a boy about six. The boys didn't interest her much, but the little girl's neat white pinafore over a gingham dress that clearly was *not* sewn from flour sacks inspired her with a surge of envy. Ma had never had a dress that wasn't made from flour sacks, at least not in Anna's memory. And Anna had never had a dress that hadn't been cut down from one of Ma's that couldn't be patched together no more.

"This's Anna," Jeb said to his kids, with a stern look. "She's Miz Jinny's kin. Anna, this's Hal, Sue, an' Bobby."

"The witch?" the older boy blurted, his eyes gone big and round. "She's kin t'the witch of Lonesome Holler?"

"We don' call her a witch, boy," Jeb corrected. "She's a Root Woman. An iffen it weren't fer her potions, you'd likely be under sod right now." He glared at the boy, who dropped his eyes to his bare toes and scuffed them in the straw on the barn floor.

"Is she a-stayin'?" asked the girl, eyeing Anna with interest.

"On'y overnight. Then she goes to Miz Jinny, her aunt. She's stayin' in the barn, an' *you* are a-gonna go to bed at bedtime and no sneakin' out an' larkin' about in the hay." The oldest boy came in for a glare that made him *and* Anna blush, likely because they both knew that "larkin' about" did not mean games and giggles as the younger children thought. *I'd never!* Anna thought indignantly—but then, from the fact that Jeb had glared at his son and his son only, there might be a bit of history there she was better off not knowing.

"Now come on in, Anna, and we'll all have lunch," Jeb continued, in a much less stern tone. "Y'all can meet my wife, an' give her a hand with the washin'-up."

Well it was clear she was not going to be set in the corner as a guest. Not that she had expected to do anything but earn her keep. At least she was still feeling good enough she *could*.

She was more than a bit apprehensive about Missus Sawyer, having spent the night unchaperoned in the presence of her husband and all, but she need not have been. Missus Sawyer, a round dumpling of a woman with a merry face and brown braids wound around and around her head, was waiting at the back door. "You mus' be Anna!" she said, with welcome and enthusiasm. "I

hope my Jeb didn' wear yore ear out with his jawin'!" Before
Anna could answer, she had taken Anna's shoulders in her hands
and held her out at arm's length, examining her closely. "Lawsy,
you're hardly bigger nor a ladybug! Y'all better come on in an' set
right down t' some vittles afore the wind blows y'all away! Come
wash up, an' we'll et." And she didn't give Anna any choice about
it; she hustled Anna into the house with a shooing motion, as if
she were chasing hens, crowded her in with the rest to wash her
hands and face at the pump, and pulled out a ladder-back chair
for her at the gingham oilcloth–covered table.

The kitchen was a bit warm, given that the iron stove was right
there, but Anna didn't mind. Compared to the kitchen part of
the Jones house it was downright opulent. A nice bucket of coal
and stack of firewood beside the stove, a sink *with a pump* under
the window, a counter purpose-built next to it for working on,
three pantry cupboards and a dresser with china displayed on it, a
rag rug under the round table and six matching chairs, and food
stored literally everywhere, including sausages and hams hanging
from the rafters.

"We et th' big meals at breakfus' an' dinner," Missus Sawyer
said, as the rest took their places around the table. "Supper's
naught but some soup an' bread. So mind y'all et hearty now."

Anna was doing her very best not to look shocked at the sheer
amount of food on the table, but it was very difficult not to gape.
Hot biscuits with butter and jelly in little bowls. A bowl of pickles.
A dutch oven full of stew, and not just the thin, soup-like stuff her
Ma made, but with a thick, brown gravy. Fried squash—a heaping
platter of it. Roasting ears. And pie! A glorious pie with dark juice
bubbled up through the slits in the crust!

She wondered how much she would be allowed to take. Better
be cautious. Just a little of each …

But Missus Sawyer forestalled her by taking her plate, heaping
it with stew and squash, adding a roasting ear, and topping it with
two biscuits before setting it back down in front of her. "Now
y'all et all that," she cautioned. "There's no wastin' in this house."

She waited, of course, until the whole family clasped hands
and bowed heads; she did the same, and Missus Sawyer said a
much, much longer prayer than her husband did, slipping in a few

admonitions to her offspring along the way and adding gratitude that her husband was home safe, and a little coda at the end well-wishing Anna on her journey that made Anna blush. *Then* they could eat.

The stew was rabbit—she would have recognized the bones, but Hal piped up when his father asked what was in the stew. "I got me two rabbits in the garden, Pa!" he said proudly. "Jest like y'all showed me t'do."

"Wall! Thet's fine!" Jeb said with enthusiasm. "That'll larn 'em! Et our garden, get et yore own self!" He laughed heartily over that, and Hal beamed proudly.

It occurred to Anna halfway through this meal that she had eaten more food in the last two days than she normally did in a week—and better food than she had seen since the children's Christmas Party at the Methodist Chapel. The jelly, deep red and shining in its bowl, was *exceedingly* tempting, but she wanted to have some of that pie—so she ate carefully, using the tender, flaky biscuits to sop up the gravy from the stew so Missus Sawyer wouldn't think she was wasting anything. Biscuits didn't happen very often in the Jones house, because they required lard and baking powder as well as flour and salt, and bread only required the starter, flour, and salt.

"Ev'body got room for pie?" Missus Sawyer asked rhetorically, when the plates were all clean (and Hal and Jeb had had second helpings of everything). Without waiting for an answer, she cut the pie and began serving pieces around the table.

By this point, Anna was nearly in a trance of pleasure. The food had gone a long way toward mitigating the slightly sick feeling she'd had when they neared Cleveland. But oh! That pie! It was blackberry, and while the fresh blackberries she and Jeb had picked and shared had been delicious, the pie was just so much more!

"Lemme he'p y'all with the dishes," she said as soon as she had finished, licking the last of the sweet berry-juice she had scraped up off her plate from her fork. If she'd been alone, she would have licked that plate clean—but, no. Manners.

"Lawsy, no, I got a better chore for y'all," Missus Sawyer corrected. "Them blackberries ain't a-goin' ter last ferever. I want all four of y'all t'fill me them baskets by th' door." She pointed with her chin at a pile of empty baskets. "The more blackberries I gets, the more jelly I kin put up."

She hadn't even gotten all of the words out of her mouth before her own children were scrambling for the baskets and out the door. Anna got the last basket, the largest of all, and went hurtling after them, afraid they had forgotten that she was a stranger to these parts and didn't know where the blackberries were.

She was right; she had to run to catch up with them, and that persistent weakness did not make it easy. She was panting and had a stitch in her side by the time she did.

But it was worth it; they led her down little lanes between fields of tobacco until they came to a stretch that was entirely hedged in blackberry bushes. There were several other children out here already, but the fruit was so thick that it hadn't been picked over. Anna gratefully settled herself down in the weeds and set to picking in earnest.

When she glanced over at the other children, it appeared that for most of them, far more fruit was going into mouths than into baskets. How the Sawyers could manage that, after that enormous dinner, she had no idea. It was very like a magic trick.

As for her—this was easy work, sitting in the shade of the hedge and moving over little by little as she cleared each section of hedge of its ripe berries. Eventually Hal sauntered over to her, swinging his half-empty basket, and looked down at her full one, an expression of admiration on his face. "Say, Anna Jones," he declared. "Y'all are the best picker I done ever seed! I'll jest take thet basket fer y'all, 'cause I knowed it's gosh-darned heavy, an' leave this 'un—"

"Y'all kin leave yore basket, Hal Sawyer," she retorted. "But y'all're leavin' mine too! I didn' pick them berries so's y'all could et half!"

He flushed, caught.

"Y'all go he'p Sue," she continued. "Mebbe 'tween y'all, thet basket'll git fillt."

Shamefaced, he went away with his proverbial tail between his legs to help his little sister—and cram berries into his mouth.

By the time she had filled his basket as well as her own, the sun was westering and the Sawyers were ready to trudge back. That basket she had filled was mortal heavy—and bigger than Hal's—so she let him take it for her on the solemn pledge that he wouldn't eat any berries out of it on the way home. It was probably an easy promise for him to make, seeing how many he'd already eaten.

Missus Sawyer greeted them and their bounty with pleasure and enthusiasm, stowed the baskets under the sink, and directed them to wash their hands again. Then it was grace around the table, and cold bread, butter and jelly, and the remains of the stew, thinned down, bones strained out, to make a fine soup. *Nothing* like the thin cabbage-and-onion soups Ma made, that gave you wind without satisfying your hunger.

But then, it was very clear that though Jeb Sawyer and his family were quite modest about it, they were a lot richer than the Jones family was, and Missus Sawyer had pretty well cottoned to that fact. Anna tried to be cheerful about that, but it seemed to her that Missus Sawyer regarded her with pity. And pity is not a comfortable thing to endure when it's directed at you. After dinner, she helped with the dishes, then joined the others on the front porch where Missus Sawyer read to them—not from the Bible, as Anna would have expected, but from a book of very strange stories indeed. *German Popular Tales and Household Stories*, it said on the worn cover of the book. Hal obviously considered himself too old for this stuff, and made a great show of carving something with a penknife he was clearly very proud of, but Anna could tell he was listening anyway. The stories were fascinating— and horrifying. Girls drowned by their jealous sisters, their bodies dismembered and turned into harps—a brother and sister from a family as poor as her own, sent off into the wilderness by their mother for spilling the milk that was to be their supper and taken prisoner by a child-eating witch—a naughty little girl who stumbled upon a house owned by three bears—though the fact that the bears had a house and furnishings did make it clear that this tale, at least, was completely made up.

The others were obviously familiar with these tales and the youngest two clamored for this or that favorite. Anna was torn between enchantment at the ones that were obviously imaginary and terror at the ones that actually could have happened. And she wasn't entirely certain she was going to sleep without nightmares tonight.

As the sun touched the western horizon, the sound of crickets filled the air, and lightning bugs began to appear in the bushes, Missus Sawyer closed the book with a decided *snap*. "Time fer bed," she said. "Thet means all y'all. Yore Pa has ta be up in mornin' early t' look fer work, an' we decided y'all's old enough to he'p him now, Hal, so bed fer *y'all*."

"Yes'm," said Hal, looking a little rebellious and a lot excited. His siblings just looked raw with envy. Anna wondered why, if they had decided—obviously not *today*—that he was old enough to join his father at work, he hadn't been along on her trip. And then she remembered that interchange between Hal and his father about how she was to sleep in the barn, and it came clear. Jeb had been taking no chances on Hal's good behavior, alone with a strange girl and plenty of chances to take her off to the side to try for some kissing. There had certainly been some moments over the supper table and out berrying when he'd attempted to make cow-eyes at her, too, so that had very probably been a wise decision on their part. Hal clearly considered himself quite the ladies' man.

"Wait here, Anna," ordered Missus Sawyer, and shooed her offspring inside. She came back out with Anna's little bundle, some folded fabric of some kind, and something small held in her hand. "Foller me," the woman ordered, as the sun sank below the horizon and the sky turned red. Anna obeyed, following her into the barn itself. Missus Sawyer motioned to her to go up a ladder, and followed; Anna found herself in a hayloft about half filled with hay.

The big window that allowed you to bring hay in from wagons outside was wide open, allowing the sunset light to stream in. Missus Sawyer shook out one of the pieces of fabric she had carried up, and laid it down over the hay. "Thet there canvas'll keep y'all from getting hay in y'all's dress," she said, and shook out the second piece of fabric. "An' this's an old shawl I ain't used fer years. It'll serve fer a cover." Then she handed Anna what was in her hand—a biscuit wrapped in a bit of brown paper. "An' this's iffen y'all gits hungry, but mind t' et it, or the mice'll get it." She smiled at Anna, again with that uncomfortable tinge of pity.

"Sleep tight, missy. I'll come git y'all in the mornin'—or if y'all wake up afore us, jest come wait in the kitchen."

Then she climbed down the ladder, leaving Anna alone in the hayloft. Anna took her bundle, got out her comb, sat down on the canvas, which was old, soft, and pliable, and unbraided her hair to comb it out. She found an embarrassing number of tiny bits of blackberry bush in it. Probably too small to notice, or at least she hoped so—but maybe that was why Missus Sawyer had looked at her with pity, thinking her some slovenly sort who didn't know any better.

By the time she was finished rebraiding her hair, the sunset had become twilight, and she decided she probably did have room for that biscuit after all. She unwrapped it carefully, bit into it, and discovered it had been halved and filled with strawberry preserves.

She ate every crumb and licked her fingers absolutely clean, then wrapped herself in the borrowed shawl and lay down, watching the hay-window. The hay was surprisingly soft to lie in, yielding and firm at the same time. And it smelled really good. She felt all of herself relaxing into the embrace of the hay, warm without being too warm. It was good to lie down after such a long day. She remembered just in time to say her prayers, adding Missus Sawyer to the list, but couldn't manage to get to her knees to do so when she was so comfortable. More than in her bed at home, with the hard straw mattress.

And once again, things took a turn for the odd.

Something climbed in through the window. It was about the size of a raccoon—but it wasn't a coon. It *looked* like a human being— only not a baby, but a miniature man, lean, muscular. She froze and held her breath, but all he did was perch on the ledge and look out over the yard. It was hard to tell in the light, but she *thought* that instead of a cloth shirt and trousers, he was wearing a leather shirt and leggings. His hair was definitely in two braids, like hers. Slowly it began to dawn on her. This was a miniature Indian!

At that point, she became convinced that she had somehow fallen asleep without realizing it. There was no reason why there should be an Indian lounging about in the window of the Sawyers' hayloft—much less one the size of a doll. So she was surely dreaming. She tried opening her eyes, but they seemed to be open already, which could happen in dreams. So she tried closing them. That worked. At least she wasn't seeing the tiny Indian anymore.

Given the blood-curdling tales Missus Sawyer had been reading, she was actually relieved that all she was dreaming about was a tiny Indian.

And the next thing she knew, the Sawyers' rooster was crowing, practically in her ear, and she woke up with a start. The rooster, naughty thing, stood in the window where she'd seen the tiny Indian, looked her brazenly in the eye, and crowed at her again before flapping down into the yard to join his hens.

When she had combed and braided her hair again, and folded up the canvas and the shawl to carry with her down the ladder, she took a look herself out of the window to see if there were any signs of life at the house. Missus Sawyer, scattering grain for the hens in the thin morning light, must have caught movement in the window out of the corner of her eye, because she looked up and waved.

Anna waved back.

"Toss me them things so's y'all don't hev t' carry 'em down," Missus Sawyer said, in tones that suggested this was probably a good idea. Anna tossed down the folded canvas, then the shawl, then her own bundle, and went back down the ladder.

"Go wash up at th' pump," Missus Sawyer told her when she emerged from the barn. Since this was not framed as a suggestion, Anna obeyed her. Jeb's wife seemed to set a high store by cleanliness, and Anna was not about to disobey her.

The table was already set, and almost as soon as she had finished washing up, Jeb came in, followed by Hal, followed by the two younger children. They all took their turns at the pump, while Anna took the seat she had been given last night and waited for Missus Sawyer to come in from her chores. The kitchen was already full of wonderful scents.

Missus Sawyer had not been exaggerating when she had said that breakfast was one of the two big meals of the day. There were biscuits again, and tomato gravy to dip them in. Everyone got an egg from the batch Missus Sawyer had brought in from the henhouse. There was fried bread and jelly, and pickled okra, and if you wanted it, the leftovers of last night's soup. And cornmeal mush and blackberries to stir into it.

And somehow, even after all of the food she had eaten yesterday, she was starving, as if her body was trying to make up for all the years of cabbage soup and plain grits.

Just as she finished helping to clear the dishes, there was a jingle of harness, the sound of many hooves, and the rolling of wheels out at the front of the house. She and Jeb and his wife went to the front to see what the noise was. There, atop a very tall wagon pulled by six mules, was someone she was certain was Caleb Strong, the man who was to take her to Aunt Jinny.

"Hello th' house!" the man called out, then spotted them coming around the side. "Hope I ain't afore time."

"Jest in time, Caleb," Jeb said heartily, and reached up to shake Caleb's hand. Anna, meanwhile, could only gape at his rig-out.

It was a truly enormous wagon, with a deep, deep bed, tall wheels, and *six* mules to pull it! What must he be hauling to need that many mules?

Caleb himself was slightly older than Jeb, with a smooth-shaven, open face, much tanned by sun and wind, and weather-bleached yellow hair. He was wearing something very similar to Jeb: flannel shirt with the sleeves rolled up to the elbow, and denim overalls, with stout boots. He peered down at Anna from the vast height of the box and smiled. "This'd be Miz Jinny's gal?" He handed Jeb down a woven willow basket without waiting for an answer. "This'd be her pay for bringin' her t'Cleveland, then."

"Obliged," Jeb said, taking it, as Missus Sawyer took Anna's elbow.

"Let's go git y'all's things," the older woman said, and Anna followed her back to the kitchen.

"Here's your bundle," Missus Sawyer said, and put her old folded shawl on top of it. "An' take thet shawl. I ain't usin' it, an' y'all will want it if th' weather turns." She picked up an identical basket to the one that Jeb had taken from Caleb from under the sink, without waiting for Anna to stammer her thanks. "Time's a-wastin'!" she said cheerfully. "Le's go!"

They returned to find Jeb and Caleb still chatting amicably, coming up alongside the wagon as Jeb was saying, "...thenkee kindly fer that, Caleb."

"T'weren't nothing." The man grinned. "But y'all owe me a drink next time."

"Here's the gal," Missus Sawyer said, "an' here's her bundle, an' here's dinner fer th' two of y'all," she added, handing up the basket.

"Dinner? Reckon Jeb don't owe me no drink arter all," Caleb replied, smiling broadly as he hefted the basket. "All right there, missy. One foot there, that's right. Reach up y'all's hand—and *up* y'all come!" He took her by the hand and hauled her up as if she weighed nothing at all.

Once on the high wagon seat beside him, she looked down at Jeb and his wife. "I cain't thenkee enough," she began awkwardly. "Y'all be so good t'me—"

Jeb waved her words aside. "Jest doin' as the Good Lord says," he replied modestly.

Including feeding and clothing the poor, she thought but didn't say aloud. Because they *had* done that, and even though charity galled, that wasn't their fault.

"I'll make sure t' let Aunt Jinny know how good y'all been," she replied after a bit of awkward silence.

"Best be on our way," Caleb interjected, diplomatically. "I'll be a-seein' y'all in a couple days, let y'all know this liddle gal's got t' Miz Jinny safe. H*up*!" That last was to the mules, as he slapped the long reins on their six backs, and the mules stepped out. The wagon lurched forward, then began rolling smoothly, and soon the Sawyers' house was out of sight.

Caleb's mules were either of a brisker disposition than Jeb's Daisy, or they found the unladen wagon no more burden than a feather, or both. Or perhaps they knew they were going home, which put a spring in their step.

Or maybe it was just the overnight rest, because surely Caleb had not driven all night long to get to Cleveland.

As these thoughts went through her mind, Caleb broke—well, it wasn't silence, since it was full of the jingle of harness and the sound of twenty-four clopping hooves—

"Y'all know Miz Jinny good?" he asked, conversationally.

She shook her head. "Ain't never seed her," she confessed.

"Hrm." Caleb considered this. "Wall—she takes some gettin' used ter. Don' let what she looks like put y'all off her. Ain't a smarter, better Root Woman in—wall, betwixt here an' Memphis, an' tha's a fact! If she minds t'teach y'all, y'all ain't niver gonna lack for work."

Aunt Jinny—teach me? The thought had never occurred to her, and it startled her. She'd thought—well, she'd thought that her aunt was going to try to cure her up, that was for sure. And she'd thought maybe Jinny was on the lookout for a kind of servant she wouldn't have to pay.

But—*teach her?*

She wasn't sure how she felt about that. The idea both excited her—because Caleb was right, Jinny's potions were highly sought after, and she'd always have the means to make ready money— and nauseated her, because of what else Caleb had said. *She takes some gettin' used ter. And don't be put off by what she looks like.*

Just what kind of a woman *was* her aunt, anyway?

Images out of those stories Missus Sawyer had read to them last night rose unbidden into her mind. A twisted crone, nose so long it touched her chin, clad in tattered black robes and spiderwebs. With black cats and toads at her feet, and a cackling laugh. Gray hair like dead straw sticking out from under a pointed black hat. A house made of gingerbread was absurd—but a little stone hovel, barely big enough for a fireplace and a bed, certainly was *not*. And where would *she* sleep? In a shed? In a haystack?

All manner of strange possibilities ran through her mind, and none of them made her feel in the least little bit hopeful.

4

Jeb's Daisy had ambled. Caleb's team was not minded to amble. They moved about as fast as a strong boy could run, full-out, which did not make for a comfortable ride until they got well clear of Cleveland and onto a road that was not so rutted. The discomfort of being atop the swaying wagon overcame the weakness she'd been feeling since yesterday noon, and it wasn't until things smoothed out a bit that she noticed that weakness was gone.

By that time she and Caleb were chattering away like old friends. Or rather, he was making slow, steady conversation, and she was listening. She learned that he and his son had a cartage business hauling copper ingots from the Burra Burra mine to Cleveland and the railhead, although he could haul ore from the mines or timber from the river to the smelters as well, which was why his wagon was so deep. That right at this very moment his son would be setting out from Ducktown with a heavy load of metal.

That he had six children, and they did *not* live in Ducktown, or even the Ducktown Basin. "I wouldn' let my wust enemy raise a fambly there," he said, matter-of-factly.

"Why?" she asked, because it was an obvious question.

He scratched his head. "They melt th' ore inside them smelters, and they feed them smelters with timber, 'cause there ain't no railhead t'bring in coal. They done cut down ever' tree in th' Basin, an' there's somethin' 'bout the smoke that pizens th' air, so the rain's— bad. I cain't 'splain it no better. But ain't nothin' grows in Ducktown an' around it. Ain't nothing but bare ground. Now, Lonesome Holler, where Miz Jinny lives, is fur 'nuff away, with 'nuff mountain 'tween her an' Ducktown that they ain't a-comin fer her trees when they kin cut 'em north and float 'em downriver easy. But you wouldn' b'lieve what Ducktown looks like. It ain't natural. And I ain't a-goin' t'let my fambly live thar. We live 'bout a mile from Lonesome Holler, an' thet's all the closer I aim's t'get."

But why do y'all work fer 'em, iffen y'all feel thet way? she thought. She didn't say it, though. That was not the sort of question you asked someone. Ma would'a slapped her face for being pert if she spoke like that in Ma's hearing.

And … his description seemed entirely unreal. How was it possible for there to be nothing but bare ground where nothing would grow? Here, in the middle of thick forests and green fields? Even back in Soddy, things grew. They didn't grow real well, 'cause of all the soot, but they grew. Surely he was exaggerating.

But she didn't even think of challenging him. He was a man growed, and she was just a girl.

Caleb waxed eloquent about his family and their—well, it wasn't a farm, no more than what Jeb Sawyer had was a farm. But it did sound like a little spot of paradise. There was an extensive garden, and they had several pigs, a lot of chickens, and a cow, but it wasn't a farm they relied on to supply their prosperity. The bulk of the family fortune was tied up in cartage: the two big wagons for hauling copper, ore, or timber and the twelve mules, plus two spares, for pulling them. Caleb knew every one of his mules by sight, personality, and name, and described each of his team and its temperament in great detail, while she listened attentively. It was clear he thought of them as family, too.

When they stopped for dinner, it was deep within heavily wooded hills, covered with trees right up to the roadway. But they didn't have the road to themselves, not by any stretch of the imagination. All the way, they'd met with other dray wagons, coming the opposite direction, heading to Cleveland. And when they stopped, it was at an enormous clearing and pond, with three other carts already there, and it was clear this was a usual stop for all the carters. There was not just the clearing itself, there were water-troughs hewn from the trunks of trees for the mules, and buckets to fill those troughs from the nearby pond. Caleb made the point of unhitching his three pairs, taking each pair to the trough and watering them and hitching them back up again, before helping Anna down off the seat and taking Missus Sawyer's cheesecloth-covered basket out of the bed.

The basket was full of sandwiches. Bread and butter and thin-sliced country ham, bread and strawberry jam, bread and butter and sliced cucumbers. Missus Sawyer's bread was much better than Anna's Ma's was. The butter was a positive revelation. The ham was sliced so thin it was practically transparent, but its flavor was powerful enough to make you feel like you'd eaten a thick slice. But after eating one and seeing Caleb wolf down two, while ignoring the cucumber ones, Anna left him the ham out of pure politeness and ate jam and cucumber. She'd never had cucumber sandwiches before; her Ma only made sour pickles with cucumbers.

He didn't dally over the food, though, and didn't join the other muleteers in jawing. She quickly realized he wanted to be back on the road as fast as possible, and practically swallowed her last half-jam-sandwich whole so they could.

Only when they were on the way again did he look at her sheepishly out of the corner of his eye and say, "I'm plumb sorry I rushed y'all. But I don' trust them other rascals 'round a young leddy. Not—" he added hastily, "—thet they would'a hurt y'all. But they talk ugly. Things y'all ain't niver oughter hear."

She wasn't sure how to respond to that, but he didn't seem to expect a response. She supposed he meant there would be a lot of swearing, and taking the Lord's name in vain. Pastor had a lot to say about that in his sermons, but that didn't seem to stop any of the miners from using whatever language they pleased any other day of the week.

Ever since they'd gotten into the deep woods, she'd been almost-seeing things again, but Caleb Strong did not seem to see a thing, even when he was looking in the same direction she was, so finally she came to the conclusion that she wasn't seeing *things*, at all. She was seeing things she didn't recognize, that was all. She didn't actually know what a lot of birds and animals other children had told her about looked like, and there were sure to be many more in the woods that *they* didn't know. And her mind was seeing bits of things and her imagination did the rest. *I can 'magine a lot*, she acknowledged, a little ruefully. After all, she could conjure up the entire Court of Solomon when she was minded to! When absolutely nothing came of all these vague glimpses, she started to relax and ignore them. They weren't hurting her, after all.

Caleb continued to regale her with proud stories about his wife and children, and it was clear he was a very fond husband and father. If she was to believe him, no one made better jelly, pie, and pickles than his wife did. No one fried a better hoe-cake. His boy was the best muleteer on the Ducktown-to-Cleveland road, bar himself— and actually, she believed this one, if only because he surely had trained his boy to take as good a care for the mules as he did. His eldest daughter—who was Anna's age—was as pretty as a flower and could sing like a bird, and picked up songs on a single hearing. The rest of his children were similarly talented.

Wisht Ma and Pa'd talk 'bout me thet way.

When praise of his family ran out, he told her odd stories about his mules, and how he chose them, and all about what excellent creatures they were. According to him—and she had no reason to doubt him—a mule was superior to a horse in every way except speed. "An' iffen y'all kin give a mule a good reason he can unnerstan' why he should run, he'll outrun a hoss ever' time!" He grinned, but with a hint of chagrin. "Trouble is, I ain't niver been able t' figger out how to give one a good reason he can unnerstan'!"

She learned more about mules in the time it took them to get from that lunch stop to Lonesome Holler than she had ever known in her life.

She knew she was about to meet her aunt at last when Caleb turned off the main road onto a little bare track he probably could not have managed if the cart had been fully loaded. As it was, it took some very careful work by the mules to make the turn. The track took them between two hills, but there was more than enough space between them for a good farm, as she quickly learned when they passed by just such an establishment. A lively crick ran through the holler, deep enough to turn a small water wheel—and this farm had just such an object, attached to what must be small millhouse. It also had a good, big garden, a lot of corn, two mules, a pigsty, a big henhouse, and four cows, two of them with calves. There was a huge house, not built of clapboard, but of logs, and a big barn to match. Why, there must have been at least four rooms in the house, plus a big loft, or even a full second story! It even had two chimneys, which meant two fireplaces!

For a moment she thought wildly that this must be Aunt Jinny's place, and wondered how her Pa could ever have thought that Jinny was some sort of crazy woman out in the wilderness. But then she saw a man coming out of the barn, and a woman with a younger one—probably her daughter—coming out of the house with a basket of laundry to hang, and she realized her mistake. No, this was a proper farm that belonged to a family. But that meant neighbors for Aunt Jinny. So she wouldn't be out here *all* alone with her aunt.

The mules had to pick their way slowly and carefully once they got past that farm. Roots had grown across the track, and the cart swayed from side to side as it rolled slowly over them. She held on to the seat with both hands, and the empty dinner basket bounced around in the cart bed with a rattling noise. The huge trees met overhead, closing them in a tunnel of dim, green gloom.

They must have gone on for at least another hour when she saw light ahead; there was a clearing up there. Was that Aunt Jinny's place, finally?

It was not; it was merely a clearing, though one big enough that the mules could turn the wagon around. And standing at the other side of that clearing was—a figure.

At first, Anna thought it was a man. It wore denim overalls, a red flannel shirt, and a straw hat. But then Caleb hailed it as he *whoa*'d the mules.

"Howdy, Miz Jinny! I got the liddle gel, safe an' sound!" He beamed at the figure, who came forward and tipped up its head, showing, by its beardlessness at least, that it was a woman.

"Howdy, Caleb Strong. Niver doubted y'all would." Aunt Jinny smiled slightly at him. "Le's get her down so y'all kin git home in time fer supper."

The mules stood, steady as statues, as Caleb hopped off the seat, came around to Anna's side, and helped her down by the simple expedient of putting both hands around her waist and lifting her down. Anna stood there awkwardly while he got her bundle and managed to get hold of the basket as well, handing them both to Jinny.

Jinny reached down and picked up a similar basket that had been hidden in the weeds at her feet. "Here y'all be, Caleb. Much obliged. An' give my thenkee to Jebediah Sawyer when y'all see 'im."

"It's me that's obliged, Miz Jinny," Caleb replied with deep respect. "My Mary sets a powerful store by y'all's potions." He stowed the basket under the wagon seat and fastened it there securely with a bit of twine he took from his pocket. "Now I'll get my team turned about and be on my way."

"Safe journeys," Aunt Jinny said. She took the basket with Anna's bundle in one hand and Anna's elbow in the other, and steered her up the path, deeper into the holler, before Caleb had even gotten to the front of his team to lead them back around to the track.

This was not a track; it was a path. Ferns encroached on either side, and foliage met just above their heads. There was barely enough room for the two of them to walk side by side, but the moss-covered path felt quite cool, soft, and utterly wonderful on Anna's bare feet.

Aunt Jinny let go of her elbow once they'd gone a few feet. It wasn't as if she was going to have to guide Anna anywhere, when the path was clear. And it wasn't as if Anna was going to run back to Caleb Strong to beg him to take her home—although given how odd and stern Aunt Jinny looked, that idea had certainly passed through her mind.

They walked on for almost an hour. The path went up a slight incline, and there was bright light at the end of it, so presumably there was a house up there and Aunt Jinny didn't actually live in the woods, or a cave, or a hollow tree.

They emerged from the forest into a clearing under bright sunlight. If there had ever been any trees here, the least vestige of them had been cleared away a long time ago. The path went to a split-rail fence with a stile they used to get over it, then passed between two farmed sections: one all corn, the other a mixed garden of vegetables and herbs. Or—wait, no, that wasn't *just* corn in the first field; each hill supporting a corn stalk also had a winter squash vine trailing out of it, and a pinto bean bush.

Bean pods studded the bushes, and the squash plants each had hard little green shapes on them. Chickens, brown, white, and speckled, scratched at the earth and hunted vigorously for bugs in both fields, watched over by a sharp-eyed red rooster. The sheer amount of food growing here, presumably all for just one person, left Anna feeling stunned.

Ma was right. We all coulda lived here, an' Aunt Jinny wouldn't hev noticed.

At the end of the path was a log cabin. There was a stone well with a little roof over it to the left of the cabin, a sturdy henhouse built of smaller logs to the right of that, and a stone pigsty beside that. At this end of the garden plot were four beehives. Aunt Jinny might not be as prosperous as Jebediah Sawyer or Caleb Strong, but she clearly was several pegs above the Joneses.

Anna stood mesmerized by all this bounty, as her aunt went on ahead, then paused to look back at her. "Foller me, girl," she said. "Don' stand there with yore mouth open. Happen my bees might take it fer a new hive."

She snapped her mouth shut and followed her aunt, who stopped right by the well, turned, then seized Anna's chin in a hard, strong hand, turning her head this way and that to look her over critically without saying a word. "How long since y'all had a bath?" Aunt Jinny demanded, scowling. "A proper bath. All over."

Torn between acute embarrassment and indignation, Anna stammered, "Soon's it got warm in April, an' agin in May…"

"Lawsy." Aunt Jinny shook her head. "Take off yore close. All on 'em." And when Anna hesitated, flushing to the roots of her hair, embarrassment now total, Jinny snapped, "*Now, goldangit!* There ain't nobuddy t'see but me'n God, an' nuther one of us cares whut y'all look like nekkid!"

Hands shaking, she pulled off her dress, then her petticoat, her thin, sad little excuse for a chemise, and her drawers. Aunt Jinny snatched them up, but held them in a way that made it look like she thought they were filthy, and went into the cabin with them and the basket with Anna's bundle in it. When she came out again, she had a big piece of flour sack, a smaller rag, a wide-toothed comb, and a rough chunk of yeller soap. "Here," she said, thrusting the soap, rag, comb, and sacking at Anna. "Scrub. All over. Hard. Wash yore hair. Keep pullin buckets'a water outa the well t'do it with." Then she stomped back into the cabin, leaving Anna standing there, stark naked, with a rag in one hand and the piece of soap in the other. It was handmade soap, and she'd seen pieces like it before; it came in the baskets of potions her Ma got from Aunt Jinny to sell. And it smelled wonderful, like all the flowers in the world.

Well ... there didn't seem any good reason, or any reason, really, to disobey. A bath wouldn't hurt her, to be sure, and it wasn't as if this were the dead of winter. So Anna pulled up her first bucket of water and began to wash.

The water was quite cold, but the sun, in the windless little clearing, was hot. And it wasn't too long before Anna forgot her embarrassment and began enjoying how a really good, thorough bath was making her feel, a much more thorough bath than she could ever have gotten in the old tin tub. She hadn't really thought about it, but the ugly on the rag didn't lie; she had soot and grime almost everywhere, especially her hair. As she washed and poured water from the bucket over herself, the water all ran down the slight incline into the garden, where it quickly soaked into the earth.

When the water finally ran clean from her hair, she dried herself on the sacking and began to comb her hair out. That was when Aunt Jinny emerged and handed her a shapeless white garment.

Shapeless—but not ugly. There were pretty little ruffles all around the hem, at the ends of the sleeves, and around the drawstring neck. When she slipped it on, it was softer than anything she had ever worn, and although there was a darned spot where it had been ripped a little, it was almost as good as new. There were ribbons at the wrists to draw the sleeves closed, and another ribbon threaded around the neck, so you could gather it tighter, or let it looser.

"Tha's a nightgown, an' it belonged t'y'all's Granny, my Ma," said Aunt Jinny. "Reckon I got some more pieces of her close, an' y'all are about her size. Yore stuff ain't fit t'wear till it's been give a good wash."

Anna opened her mouth to object, then closed it again. The dirt on the rag and in the water didn't lie. Her clothing was probably just as filthy as she'd been.

"*Now* y'all're fit t'come in," Jinny continued, and turned and went back into the cabin. Anna followed, still combing the knots out of her wet hair. Without any drawers or petticoat on, being in the loose nightgown, which came down to just above her ankles, felt like being naked. It was disconcerting, but also cool and comfortable at the same time.

It was a one-room cabin, although the room was surprisingly large, with a pair of lofts. And the very first thing that caught Anna's attention was the fireplace—because it didn't look like any fireplace she had ever seen in her entire life.

It absolutely dominated the room and took up most of the back wall. It was made of stone that had been plastered over and whitewashed, so it *really* stood out in the dimly lit room. It stuck out into the room at least six feet. It was at least five feet tall! There was a hearth with a fire in it—but it was set deep into the fireplace, at about waist-high, and not directly under the chimney, a big alcove with a hearth large enough for three pots, and the fireplace deeper in that.

It occurred to her using this kind of fireplace—if you could even call it a fireplace—would be as easy as cooking on the Jones's coal stove, if not easier. No getting down on your hands and knees, no real bending over.

There was another deep place to the right and directly under the chimney that looked as if it could be a hearth—or maybe it was an oven—and several more niches along the side to the left. Did the whole big construction keep things constantly warm? There was a ladder going up to the flat top, which must have been about five feet off the ground and big as Ma and Pa's bed. And there was, in fact, bedding up there. As if—well, if someone slept up there in the winter, it would keep them mighty warm and comfortable.

There were two pots and a fry-pan at the hearth, and more in the niches.

It was such an extraordinary contraption that it took Anna a while to look away from it and survey the rest of the room.

Unlike the Jones's clapboard house, where you could see light coming in through tiny spaces between the boards, the logs were chinked so tightly and expertly there was no chance of a draft once you closed the doors and the solid shutters over the windows. There were two windows in the wall behind her, with the front door between them, two windows in the wall to her right, and two and a door in the wall to her left. There were two lofts with ladders going up, one above the front door, the other above the fireplace, and she thought she saw a hint of a window up in the wall of the loft above the fireplace. Running under the one window to the right of the door was a counter with a sink in it, and beneath the counter, shelves laden with pots and jars and a few full or mostly full sacks. Above the counter, more shelves, one with a few books on it. At the end of the counter against the right wall was a huge cupboard. In front of the fireplace was a small table and a pair of stools atop a rag rug. The rest of the cabin held another huge cupboard, shelves loaded with bags, baskets, pots, jars, and rough boxes, another two chairs made of small, peeled logs, and a bed made of the same peeled logs. And that made Anna stare as well; she had never seen furniture made of logs before. Especially a bed. The well-off had fancy brass beds with wool mattresses. The not-so-well-off had iron beds with straw mattresses. Those just getting by had box beds made of whatever planks they could find and a corn-shuck mattress. The Joneses had an iron bed and a straw mattress with a trundle under it that her Pa had made with another straw mattress. The really poor slept on whatever they could find, piled up on the floor, sometimes contained within the confines of a rough plank bed. She didn't know what to make of a log bed.

And there was food and bunches of drying plants *everywhere*: not only (presumably) in those bags and boxes and pots and jars, but hanging from peeled saplings tied up to the rafters. Sausages and hams, smoked meat she couldn't identify, smoked fish. Onions in bunches. Potatoes in nets.

Before she could get over the shock of seeing such bounty, her aunt went over to the hearth and started frying something. There was the mouth-watering scent of bacon in the air. And when she turned back from the hearth, she had two plates in her hand, which she set on the little table. A moment later two bowls joined the plates. All four dishes were made of wood. So were the two cups she filled with liquid from a metal pitcher she took from one of the niches in the fireplace. "Set," Aunt Jinny ordered.

Anna sat herself down, and took the spoon Aunt Jinny handed to her. She couldn't identify what it was made of, until it dawned on her that it was cow horn.

She waited for her aunt to say grace, but Jinny just sat down and dug straight into her food. After a moment, so did Anna.

The plate held a thick, fried-cornmeal hoecake. The bowl held soup virtually identical to the one Missus Sawyer had served her last night, except that there was less pepper and more things she couldn't identify in it. The liquid was an herb tea of some sort, and there was honey to spoon into it to sweeten it. There was blackberry jam as well, and a horn knife she and Jinny shared to spread it on the hoecake. She ate carefully, so as not to get a crumb or a drop on the white gown she wore, and she felt—well, she felt a little like Pharoah's daughter in her white shift with naught underneath, feasting on fine vittles. Jinny didn't say much, except to ask when her plates were empty if she wanted more of anything. She hesitated, and Jinny sighed with exasperation. "This ain't Lew Jones's house," she said crossly, and waved her hand at all the food. "I could feed three more of y'all and niver notice the lack. Are y'all hungry, or not?"

Anna allowed as how she was hungry, and got another helping of soup. There didn't appear to be any more hoecake batter, but Jinny went to the nearest cupboard and opened it, and came back with a square of cornbread for her to crumble into the soup.

When the meal was over, Jinny showed Anna that the privy was, as she had hoped, in a little shed attached to that side door, was made of logs, and smelled not at all, except of dried peppermint and spearmint, from the bunches tied to nails along the inside. So—in bad weather you didn't even have to go through the rain or snow to go to the privy!

Her aunt got warm water from another big metal pitcher in the niches along the fireplace, and wordlessly washed the dishes while Anna dried and stacked them on the counter.

"Now, lessee what we kin do about close," Jinny said when the chore was done. She went over to the tall log bed and pulled a wooden chest out from under it.

The first things to come out were a couple of sets of drawers, a petticoat, and a couple chemises. Jinny held them up and examined them critically, then turned to Anna.

"C'n y'all mend?" she demanded.

"Yes'm," she said obediently.

"Take thet there stool an' go outside fer the last light," Jinny ordered. Once Anna had set herself down beside the front door, Jinny put the underthings in Anna's hand along with a woven willow workbasket full of spools of thread, a needle-flannel, a pincushion, and a pair of scissors and let her go to work.

The one thing that Anna prided herself on was her needlework— not fancy-work, because for one thing she never had time to learn it, and for another, she had nothing to spare to make it with, unless she unraveled rags for colored threads. No, it was her plain-sewing and mending she was proud of. She was better at it than Ma.

She found white darning cotton and a proper-sized needle and went to work, and before long all the tears and small holes had been neatly dealt with. She held up one of the chemises to admire it, and noticed the little touches of white-on-white embroidery around the square yoke. Just then her aunt came out with more fabric in her hand, and paused to look over Anna's work with a critical eye.

"Ain't bad," she said. "Stand up."

Anna stood up, and Jinny held a plain brown canvas skirt up against her. The waist was going to fit, but it was only going to come to above her ankles, like the nightgown. "Thet'll do," Jinny declared. "Ma were a little shorter than you be. Won't drag in th' dust'n' mud. Got shirts t'go with't, an' termorrer we kin cut up a petticoat fer more drawers'n suchlike." She cast a glance at the sky; Anna had just managed to catch the very last of the light to do her mending by, and now the sun was below the level of the trees. The flaming red color painted across the western horizon proclaimed tomorrow would be a fine and sunny day. "Thet lot ye done will do fer termorrer. Iffen y'all ain't tired, y'all should be. Bedtime fer y'all."

She led Anna inside—but not, as Anna had feared, to the bed in the corner, nor the bedding on top of the fireplace. Instead she motioned to Anna to go up to the loft above the fireplace. Wearing this "nightgown" was extraordinarily freeing. Since it ended just above the ankle, there was nothing she had to do in the way of gathering skirts out of the way except to climb the ladder.

There *was* a small window cut into the wall beside the chimney, which let in just enough of the twilight that she could see there was an enormous box on the floor shoved up against the chimney, made up with sheets and a pillow, with quilts over one end. The box was filled with something puffy. *Probably a sheet over hay, and not a proper mattress.* Still, the hay in the Sawyers' barn had been more comfortable than her proper straw mattress at home, and had smelled better too. She made her way to the box, all bent over beneath the peak of the roof, and lowered herself down—

—only to have the surprise of lowering herself down into a cloud.

... a *featherbed*?

She'd *heard* of featherbeds, of course, as in, any time someone wanted to describe something particularly comfortable, they'd say "soft as a featherbed," but she'd never actually lain in one.

It was warm, probably from being in contact with the chimney all day, and just as soft as a cloud looked, and she had never been so comfortable in her entire life. Once the sun had gone down, it had started to get cool; the warmth of the bed was more than welcome, and between it, and her full stomach, it was all she could do to force herself to her knees to say her prayers. Once she had done so, she just fell over on her side into the softness, grabbed an edge of the sheet and a quilt, and pulled them over herself.

But somehow, she didn't manage to get to sleep. Not immediately, anyway.

The night sounds here were very different from those in the Sawyers' barn, much more like the deep woods where she and Jeb had camped. And there were all manner of novel sensations keeping her awake. Her comfortably full stomach, for one. The unaccustomed luxury of this featherbed. The equally unaccustomed sensation of being totally, completely clean. The strangeness of being in this loose, soft "nightgown"—it was like being naked in the bed.

Downstairs she heard Aunt Jinny moving about—and there was one dim light down there, besides whatever was coming from the strange fireplace. That fireplace! She had never even heard of anything like that before. Who had built it here? It must have taken forever! But it certainly looked like the work was worth it.

Had that been another featherbed on top of it? Imagine *that* on a cold night!

Aunt Jinny certainly hadn't been anything like she'd expected. Did Ma know she dressed like a man? If she had known, would she still have sent Anna here? Was dressing like a man what had Pa set against her? She couldn't make up her mind if Aunt Jinny wanted her here or not. Yet Ma had said her sister had all but *demanded* she come here. Was that something Ma had just made up in her own mind? Or was Aunt Jinny just ... kind of crotchety and peculiar, but really did want her here? She certainly had shown no hesitation in doubling Anna's wardrobe, and out of her own Ma's old clothing, to boot!

She turned over onto her back and looked up into the roof ... and there were dozens of eyes up there, looking down at her. Just like in the forest.

But this time, she was not lying in an open wagonbed, vulnerable and half-listening for bears. This time she was inside, in her aunt's cabin, a cabin so stoutly built, with every single possible crack and chink stuffed, that the light down below her didn't even waver from drafts. Whatever was in here with her was harmless, because if it weren't she had no doubt Aunt Jinny would have Done Something about it—whatever "it" was—a long time ago.

Probably mice. She could tell from how the meat had been hung from those willow rods, with wooden cones on the metal hooks to prevent anything from climbing down to get to the food, that Aunt Jinny had secured every bit of the smoked stuff from the mice. And everything else was put away in stout, lidded boxes, or jars, or bottles. So they couldn't steal food, and there was nothing in the bed to attract them.

Maybe they were in here to be safe from owls.

She stared at the glowing eyes, defiantly. They stared back.

But eventually, they must have gotten bored when she didn't do anything. Pair by pair, they blinked out, until there was nothing up there. And Aunt Jinny put out the light and grumbled her way to bed.

And Anna fell gratefully asleep.

5

She woke to her aunt banging on the loft floor with a stick from below. "Time's a-wastin', girl!" her aunt proclaimed, as Anna struggled up out of a dream in which she was Pharoah's daughter, lying back on a silk divan like she'd seen once in a Sears Roebuck catalog they'd gotten for the privy, being fed bits of bread and jam by mice wearing nightgowns. "Things t' git done!"

She fought her way out of the featherbed, her nightgown up around her armpits, got everything tugged down into place, and climbed down the ladder to find her aunt working at the hearth, and the table all laid. Outside there was *barely* enough pre-dawn light to see by, so Aunt Jinny had lit three wax candles to work by. She got to the bottom of the ladder and her aunt jerked her head at the sink. "Wash up. Do a good job of it. Y'all's new close is on th' bed."

Wax candles! Most people she knew had tallow-dips at most, maybe an oil lamp, though oil was expensive. But then, most people she knew didn't have beehives.

She obeyed her aunt, and made her way over to the bed, where the "new" clothing waited. The outfit certainly wasn't going to turn any heads, but she was grateful to be able to put something clean over her clean body. Unsure of what to do with the nightgown, she folded it up and draped it over one of the ladder rungs, then went to take her seat at the table.

"Here," said Aunt Jinny, and plonked down a bowl of

cornmeal mush in front of her. The mush was followed by a fried egg, bacon, and fried bread, all washed down with that herb tea. Jinny watched her eat with a sharp eye—but not the way Ma did, making sure she didn't get more than her fair share. No, this was more like Jinny wanted to make sure she ate every scrap, and if she was still hungry, asked for more.

"Dishes, then chores," Jinny said when she was finished. "Y'all pay heed. I ain't a-gonna show y'all twice, an' this'll be what y'all do ever' mornin' afore breakfast when I'm a-cookin'."

"Yes'm," she replied, resisting the urge to bob a curtsy.

The first chore was to let the chickens out of the roost and feed them. "Y'all ain't niver had chickens?" Aunt Jinny exclaimed, when Anna showed confusion about how to handle them. Anna shook her head and her aunt pursed up her lips in a way that made Anna wonder what she had done wrong. "Wall ... look, jest scatter 'em some grain, like this—" she broadcast a few handfuls. "That'll get 'em started, an' once they get t'eatin', they'll go down inter the garden on their own. They'll spend th' day chasin' bugs'n ettin' weeds."

"Ain't y'all afeerd they'll wander off or get et?" Anna asked.

Aunt Jinny just shrugged. "I got my ways," was all she said, and led the way to the rock-walled pigsty. There was a sow with six half-grown piglets in it.

The sty had to be mucked out, and clean straw spread in it. Anna was grateful that it was her aunt who did the shoveling out; all she had to do was take another shovel and spread the muck over the compost heap. But of course—tomorrow it would be her turn. She'd have to figure out a way to keep her skirt and petticoat out of the muck.

Then the pig got a pail full of the scraps from last night's dinner—scraps that, in the Jones household, would have been made into soup or stirred into the pot of poke salad.

The third chore was one that Anna at least knew how to do well: sweep out the cabin. She took the twig broom and applied it to the cabin floor with a will, while her aunt got some warm water from the stove-niche and a washboard and began scrubbing vigorously. A moment later she realized that it was *her* clothing that her aunt was scrubbing. By the time she had finished sweeping the floor, then mopping it with a damp rag-mop, her aunt had scrubbed every stitch she owned, and rinsed them, and the clothing was wrung out and ready to be hung outside, along with another couple of garments.

"Thet's the last time I do thet fer y'all," her aunt said, as they pegged the garments to a line strung from the top of the well to the cabin. "I 'spect y'all t' scrub underthin's so's y'all allus got one clean pair on an' one t'wear in case somethin' gets y'all wet or dirty, an' one ready t'wash or on th' line. Iffen y'all's skirt'n petticoat gets mucky, wash 'em, otherwise wash 'em oncet ev' two weeks an' sponge th' hem ev' night. Wash shirt once a week, unless it gets mucky. Wash apron iffen it gits dirty."

That was ... well it was a lot more washing than was done in the Jones house. But in the Jones house there was little fuel to spare to heat water, hauling water took a lot more time, and there wasn't much money to spare for soap. Not to mention that Anna and her mother didn't have but two sets of clothing apiece. Now, thanks to her aunt and her late grandmother, her wardrobe was, by comparison to what it had been, enormous.

The next chore was weeding, one she knew well. Except instead of saving every bit of green scrap to put in the pot of poke salad, her aunt had her just leave the weeds in the dirt for the chickens to eat. Which obviously, given the abundance of food here, made more sense than deciding whether or not it was edible by humans. And it was an absolute pleasure to weed here, where every plant, every row, promised plenty of meals to come. And, just to make everything perfect, the air sparkled; every lungful brought pleasure instead of coughing. Even the dirt here smelled better than at home.

She hummed under her breath as she worked, quite thoroughly happy, despite Aunt Jinny's frowns and odd manners, for the first time in a long time.

"The dove, she is a pretty bird, she sings as she flies. She brings us glad tidings and she tells us no lies ..."

"Anna! Dinner!" came the hail from cabin, and she came to herself with a start, realizing she was halfway down the low slope, having weeded half the garden-plot. She picked herself up, shook the dirt out of her skirt, and hurried to the cabin.

It became evident that, like the Sawyers, Aunt Jinny's two biggest meals were breakfast and dinner. It wasn't as big a spread as the Sawyers had, but it was plenty. Poke salad and cornbread, thick bean soup with either ham or bacon in it (she couldn't tell which), pickles, more of that herb tea, blackberry jam. "You best get used t' bean soup," Aunt Jinny cautioned, as she ladled out a big bowlful for Anna. "I keep a pot a-goin' most o' th' time."

Anna was too busy trying to eat the delicious stuff and not burn her mouth to reply.

Then it was time to take the clothing down off the line. Aunt Jinny eyed it critically, then sat her down with the workbasket to mend and patch using the contents of a scrap basket. Then she handed Anna a pile of pieces of slightly yellowed, soft fabric. "Y'all kin sew as well as mend, I hope?" she asked, and without waiting for a reply, continued, "I cut up a petticoat inter two sets of drawers an' two chemises. Set to 't."

Anna began to stammer her thanks, but Aunt Jinny just cut her off with a gesture. "'Twas close jest sittin' in a chest doin' nobody no good. Might's well be useful. When y'all finish thet, we'll see what else kin be turned t'use."

And with that, she turned her back on Anna and began working at her sink, doing something with the dried plants and herbs that were everywhere. Presently, Anna figured out that she was making some of her famous potions, and reckoned the best thing *she* could do right now was prove she could do as she was told.

She was a very good seamstress—that being one of the few things she *could* do without getting tired. Good enough that she sometimes got work from one or another of the miners' wives sewing for them, their husbands, or their children. And it was a pleasure to have absolutely everything she needed, right there at hand, without having to make do. There was even a reel of narrow cotton tape for drawstrings at the waist and knees of the drawers and the neck of the chemise. How—and why—did Aunt Jinny have all this if all she wore were men's shirts and dungarees?

She'd finished a pair of drawers and a chemise and was well on her way to finishing the second pair of drawers when her aunt finished her work at the sink, and interrupted her. "Stand up," she demanded, a thick wooden pencil in one hand, and a piece of leather and a piece of that cotton tape in the other. Anna obeyed. Her aunt directed her to stand on the leather with her skirt hiked up to her knee. Aunt Jinny drew around her feet, then took the cotton tape and measured around her ankle, and then around her knee, marking each length with a knot, then told her to go back to her work. "What's thet fer, please?" Anna asked as she sat down.

"Y'all didn' brung any shoon," her aunt said with that familiar frown.

"Don't need shoon in summer," Anna demurred. Because although she was enjoying herself on the one hand … and certainly reveling in the food! … she didn't really want to think to winter. Winter … she should be home, shouldn't she? She never left the house in winter, so all she needed was something to wrap around her feet to keep them warm. She was feeling so healthy now! A couple of months of "fattening up" and she'd be able to be a real help to her Ma. Why, she might be able to get a job, and that would help even more!

"Y'all're gonna need 'em come winter," came the discouraging reply. Her heart sank just a little. Surely her Ma would want her back before winter came! And Aunt Jinny was hard enough now. What would she be like when they were both cooped up together in the small space of the cabin?

Supper was the very last of last night's bean soup, and Jinny set Anna to scrubbing the pot it had cooked in with sand as the next-to-last chore before bedtime. The last chore was to bring wood in from the woodpile, while her aunt set a pot of cornmeal and water onto the hearth to cook into mush overnight, and a pot of beans to soak. But Jinny didn't seem in any hurry to send her to bed tonight; instead, she poured them both mugs of that herb tea, and indicated that Anna was to sit down in the deepening twilight, while she lit a couple of candles. The scent of honey filled the room; pleasant, and so unlike the stink of the cheap tallow-dips they had used at home.

"I'm a-goin' ter arst y'all some thin's," Aunt Jinny said. "An' y'all answer me straight." The way she said it made it an order, and Anna cringed a little.

And what followed was an acutely uncomfortable dissection of the Jones's daily life, down to exactly who got to eat what. It made Anna blush furiously to reveal their poverty, but the more she told, the more stony-faced Aunt Jinny became, until at last she finished her questions and sat, brooding, staring at the mug of cooling tea she held in both hands.

But what she said, when she finally broke the silence, shocked Anna into near paralysis.

"If I'da knowed y'all was that bad off," she said, bitterly, "I swan, I'da kidnapped y'all once y'all was weaned. Yore Ma made 'er bed with Lew Jones an' she kin lay innit. But there ain't no call ter starve a helpless child that ain't even wanted."

What does she mean, I "ain't even wanted"? How kin she know thet?

Then she looked up at Anna. "I swore I weren't gonna interfere, not after Lew Jones treated me th' way he did, but y'all deserve t'hear th' truth. Y'all's Ma didn' want ye."

Before Anna even had a chance to take that in, her aunt continued talking. "My Ma died when I'se 'bout ten. Arter th' War, my Pa'n me 'n m' brothers an' yore Ma all lived in Shady Holler, near t'Soddy, afore most of the minin' an' coke-makin' started. Afore th' War, my Granny and Granpappy on my Ma's side had this here cabin, an' afore we moved ter Shady Holler, we had the farm y'all passed at the mouth of the Holler, but thet's another story. Y'all's Ma's Ma was a widder-woman. Pretty liddle thang, *delicate* liddle thang. My Pa promised her dead man t'look arter her, an' by his way of thinkin', that meant marryin' her." Aunt Jinny shrugged. "I didn' care, I was s'posed t'go to my Granny t'learn t'be a Root Woman like 'er. An' I did. Then yer Ma's Ma had Maybelle an' up an' died, an' my Pa spoilt that liddle girl rotten. I seed it when I come home now an' agin. I was there when thet Lew Jones an' a buncha Taffies like 'im came breezin' inter Soddy, all set t'make a for-tune. He had eyes on plenty'o gals, but Maybelle put eyes on 'im an'—" Jinny put down her cup and threw up her hands. "Weren't no reasonin' with 'er," she said in disgust. "She were gonna hev Lew, an' thet was thet. I reckon Lew thunk Pa was better off'n 'e was. Pa 'ad a war-pension; thet died wi' 'im. Lew didn' know thet, or I reckon 'e'd not hev married yore Ma, and thet's the plain truth. An' I reckon when there's hard words between 'em, he don't stint t'tell her so. So yore Ma was an' is pure desperate t'keep 'im. So when she knowed she was gonna hev a chile, she thunk it was a boy an' was desperate t'be rid of 't, on account of she reckoned it likely Lew would dote on 'is son an' fergit 'bout 'er. An' I reckon she was right," Jinny added. "She wrote t'me, fust time since Pa died, she did, tol' me she was gonna hev a baby, an' begged me fer a potion t'be rid of it. *I* reckoned she'd made 'er bed, an' tol' 'er 'twas too late, anythin' I give 'er 'ould kill 'er too. But then she had y'all, an' ev'thin' was fine, cause Lew 'ad no use fer a girl-chile, an' she reckoned she could make you inter a help right quick. But she kept a-writin' me, wantin' potions so she wouldn't hev no more chillen, an' then potions she could sell on. I didn' want 'er throwin' herself down stairs or somethin' else jest as stupid, so I give her the potions she wanted fer herself. An' I figgered pickin's was getting thin in the Jones house when she wanted ter sell my potions. Which I seed a-comin', on account of thet Lew Jones was so big about bein' th' on'y man in the Soddy Mine thet knowed how t'use a steam drill, an' them things ain't called 'widder-makers' fer nothin'. I knowed 'e was gonna start a-sickenin' an' money was gonna get scarce, cause a miner's paid by what 'e digs, an' purdy soon 'e'd be too puny to run thet drill for long, an' he'd be diggin' with a pick like ev'body else. But—I'm a Christian woman. So I sent them potions, on account of she's still my sister, an' on account of there weren't no call t'make y'all suffer because yore Pa is a damn fool. An' when she started beggin' fer potions fer Lew, I sent them too. Then she started tellin' me how y'all was sickening, an' I *knowed* what caused it, an' I started a-tellin' 'er t' send y'all t'me."

"An' she finally said aye," Anna whispered. This—was all too much to take in at once. She knew, of course, that her father didn't have much use for her, except that she was *his*, and therefore no one else's to take. But she had thought her mother cared for her. At least a little bit. But now to discover she hadn't been wanted *at all* … it was a terrible blow.

"Why's my Pa so mad at y'all, Aunt Jinny?" she asked, finally, as her aunt picked her mug back up and finished her now-cold tea.

Her aunt chuckled. "'Cause when 'e come rooster-struttin' around

Maybelle, I tol' 'im to 'is face what I thunk of him. *Pride goeth afore a fall, Lew Jones*, I tol' him. *Y'all think yore better'n a farmer, cause y'all kin run a steam drill. Thet there steam drill's a-gonna be the death of y'all. An' y'all're gonna leave a widder what owes ev'thin' she's got, which ain't a-gonna be much, t' the Company store*. I tol' 'im that straight. An' thet's what's a-gonna happen."

In that moment, Anna might have hated her aunt—except that Jinny didn't sound triumphant. She sounded weary, resigned, even sad. Like one of the prophets in the Bible who tried to tell people that something terrible was going to happen, and they ignored him, and it happened, and people suffered because they wouldn't listen to him. And he didn't exult in their suffering, he grieved because he couldn't convince them and save them.

"I might'a been a bit hard on 'im," Jinny added after a very long silence. "The Good Lord knows he's a-payin' th' price fer bein' a damn-fool now. Them mines eat men an' spit 'em out t'die afore their time."

Anna bit her lip. She wanted to ask, "Is my Pa really going to die?" But she knew the answer. Her aunt was right. Everyone knew that when a miner started to get *that* kind of cough, he was going to die. The owners claimed that breathing coal dust was good for you, that it protected you against things like wasting fever and winter fever, but Anna didn't believe them, and it was clear her aunt didn't either.

"Won't yore potions do him no good?" she asked timidly.

"They'll do some," Jinny admitted. "Dunno how much. Yore Ma thinks I kin work some kinda miracle. Ain't nobody does miracles but God Almighty." She reached out awkwardly and patted Anna's hand. "I knowed that were hard t'hear. But I allus think it's better t'know th' truth. In the long run, lies'll hurt y'all more than truth. Now y'all prolly oughta go up t'bed."

Obediently, Anna undressed at the foot of the ladder to her loft, left her skirt, petticoat, and shirt folded over the side, and put the drawers and chemise in a basket by the sink to be washed tomorrow. As she climbed the ladder to the loft, in a moment of distraction from her woes, she realized that today, on the line beside her own clothing, there'd been a peculiar garment that was a sort of chemise and drawers in one. So that must be what Aunt

Jinny wore under her flannel shirt and dungarees.

She said her prayers, especially for Pa, and was sure she never would get to sleep. But she was wrong. After all that work, she fell asleep almost immediately, scarcely noticing the tiny glowing eyes lined up along the rafters, shining in the darkness after Jinny put the candles out. And somehow, her rest was troubled not at all by the revelations of the evening.

I should be feelin' bad, she thought, as she donned her clothing for the day. But ... she wasn't. It was more like she had always known these things about her Ma and Pa, but just hadn't wanted to think about them. And now that her nose had been shoved into the truth—what she felt was more a hollow feeling of loneliness and emptiness than anything else. Sad, but not ready to burst into tears. At least, not yet.

Turning the chickens loose and feeding them helped. They were so sweet with their happy little clucks, and the rooster was so funny, strutting around like he was the owner of all he could see. Aunt Jinny told her to sweep the cabin rather than muck out the pigs. "Not sure y'all's fit to muck out the sty, not till y'all is stronger. I'll muck, y'all build th' compost, an' we'll do't arter breakfus'," was what she said as Anna went out the door. So she came back to the cabin after setting the chickens loose and swept with a will until her aunt called her to eat.

Breakfast helped some more, with bounty she was rapidly becoming accustomed to. This morning there was fried mush, eggs, and sausage, and something brown and clear that Aunt Jinny poured generously over the mush. She noticed Anna was staring at the stuff askance. "'Tis maple syrup, chile," her aunt told her. "I makes it m'self in spring. Try it. Figgered today y'all should hev some sweet t' meller out the bitter words y'all got last night."

One taste, and Anna was in heaven. It wasn't like honey; it wasn't like molasses. It was something all to itself and she couldn't get enough of it. Aunt Jinny watched her eat with amusement.

Did Aunt Jinny even understand remotely how much food had come to mean for Anna? The lack of it was literally sickness and pain, and abundance like this felt like coming home to Heaven.

"If I'da knowed how bad thangs were for y'all," Jinny said, in soft tones she had never heard out of her aunt before this, "I'da niver left y'all there thet long. I swear. An' iffen I still couldn'ta got y'all away from that Lew Jones, I'da done more. Sent Maybelle parcels. Food, more thangs she coulda sold. Lookit this!" She waved her hand at the ceiling, and its festoons of smoked meats and fish. "Th' Holcrofts 'n me already put up parcels fer poor widders in Ducktown. Some o' thet could go t' yore Ma. Weren't hardly no more work t'raise one more pig a year and smoke it up. I'da done it. I would. It hurts m'cold old heart t'think how starved y'all was."

Anna paused, and looked into her aunt's eyes, and believed her. She nodded slowly. "Ma don' like bein' beholden," was all she said. "Reckon she figgered makin' them potions weren't nothin' but pickin' a few weeds and packin' 'em up and it weren't no time or trouble t'y'all—and it weren't like y'all sold them potions over to Soddy yore own self. So thet weren't makin' her beholden to y'all." She scratched her head. "It don't make no sense, when I say it out loud, but could be thet's how she's a-thinkin'. An' Pa—well, y'all knowed Pa. He'd as likely send it back, or throw it out th' door, as take it."

Her aunt muttered something about "damn fools" under her breath.

Just then, a movement out of the corner of her eye caught Anna's attention, and she turned to see what it was. But there was nothing there. She frowned, remembering the eyes in the rafters. "Aunt Jinny, y'all need a cat."

Her aunt raised an eyebrow, and then guffawed. "What in tarnation do I need a cat fer?" she retorted.

"Y'all got mice, an' a powerful lotta them," she replied, glad to get the subject off her parents. "I seed 'em the fust night I was here, an' last night too. All lined up on th' rafters an' a-lookin' down at me with liddle shiny eyes."

Her aunt's eyebrow stayed where it was. "Didja now? What makes y'all so sure 'twas mice?"

"Dunno what else it could be," she replied, then bit her lip, because she had come perilously close to contradicting her elder. She put her face down and assiduously finished her mush.

"Wall, there ain't no mice in *my* house," Aunt Jinny stated.

"But there's plenty'o small critters what come in an' out an' don't do no harm." And she left it at that.

Together they mucked out and fed the pigs. Jinny showed her how to collect the eggs from the nestboxes in the henhouse—and showed her the two hens currently sitting on eggs she was going to allow to hatch. They scrubbed their underwear and hung it to dry, emptied the soapy water into the garden ("Chases slugs," said Jinny), and she set Anna to weeding. This time she weeded down the side of the garden that had the rows of corn, squash, and beans. She would have thought that the three plants would choke each other out—but they seemed to be thriving together.

After another amazing dinner, Jinny called her over to the counter. "Y'all wanter be a Root Woman?" she asked abruptly.

Anna was so taken aback for a moment she could scarcely breathe. Did she? Of *course* she did! Why, as a Root Woman she would *never* lack for a way to keep herself fed! "Yes, please, ma'am!" she managed to get out, and Aunt Jinny looked pleased. She reached up to a shelf over the counter and took down a little, leather-bound book, one among a handful of books up there. "This here's my receipts," she said. "My Granny niver wrote nothin' down, on account'o she wanted me t'larn things by mem'ry, but I copied ever'thang she taught me right here." She tapped the cover of the book. "An' y'all are a-gonna copy my book. Copy a receipt, then we make it t'gether. Then y'all make it on yore lonesome, while I watch."

She sat Anna down at the table with four pieces of good, thick paper folded in half and stitched together at the crease, a little jar of ink, and a goose-quill pen—and her own all-important book. "Copy down th' fust receipt," she ordered. "Don' use more paper than I used in my book."

For a moment Anna felt paralyzed. There could be no making mistakes with this good paper and ink. Every letter would have to be perfect. *I kin do this*, she told herself over and over, but it was a long, long time before she got the courage to dip the quill in the ink, carefully drain off the excess, and write the first letter. With her tongue sticking out of the corner of her mouth and her brows furrowed with concentration, she dipped and wrote, dipped and wrote, until she had filled the entire page. She had no idea what the words were that she had just written, because she had been so concerned about copying them correctly, but she looked up from her task with triumph when she had finished.

"Done!" she exclaimed, and her aunt left her work at the sink to come look it over.

"Done, an' done well," Aunt Jinny agreed. "Now, what's it *say*?"

"*One part chamomile*," she read, stumbling over the name of the herb. "*One part lavender. One part purple coneflower. One part lemon balm. Steep a tablespoon in bilin' water fer as long as it takes t' say Psalm 100, strain, an' drink. Good for gen'ral ills, coughs, an' bad sleep.*"

"Thet's the tea we been drinkin'," her aunt told her. "Gen'rally good for whatever liddle troubles y'all got, an' tastes good too. Now le's go make it up."

Her aunt made her look at the samples of fresh herb, gathered from the garden that morning, then the dry, then crumble the dry in her fingers and taste and smell it, until they were both sure she would know what they were in any form. Then she made up the batches of tea, first with her aunt, then alone.

She looked up from the last task to find Aunt Jinny smiling with approval. It was the first smile she had seen on her aunt's face since she had arrived here, and she found herself blushing with pride.

"Y'all got th' touch," Aunt Jinny said. "Le's put these up."

Together they portioned out generous amounts to be enclosed in the packets Anna had seen the potions packaged in before—round, unstructured pouches made of woven grass. When the pouch was packed full, all the loose grass stems at the top were gathered into a bunch, and tied up, and Aunt Jinny finished by tying a tiny spig of chamomile and lavender to each packet to identify it. "I weaves these in winter," she said, pulling one off the stack to her left and filling it with the tea. "When I runs out, I gotta use scrap cloth, an' people don' seem ter like that as much. With y'all here, I likely won't run out anymore."

Anna had never woven anything in her life, much less a grass basket, but she was willing to try. These things were pretty, and she had used them when very little (during the few moments of the day when she was allowed to play instead of work) as dresses for her corn dollies.

When they had packaged up all the loose tea, they checked to make sure the ink had thoroughly dried in Anna's "receipt book" before putting it, the bottle of ink, and the cleaned quill up on the same shelf as Aunt Jinny's book. "Y'all's gonna do one a day," Aunt Jinny said with warm approval. "Mostly. There's a-gonna be days when we ain't got time, 'specially in fall, and there's gonna be days when y'all ain't gonna do it right. And there's gonna be days when I take y'all out in them woods t'gather. But soon or late, y'all's gonna hev yore very own receipt book. An' y'all will be a Root Woman." She gave Anna a sideways look. "Whatcha think of thet?"

"Niver heerd of no Root Woman goin' hungry," Anna said, finally. "But ... Aunt Jinny, y'all said yore potions cain't cure ever'thang."

Her aunt nodded. "No more can they. Y'all does yore best, an' leave th' rest t' God Almighty. Jest like a doctor, on'y I reckon a good Root Woman gits more people cured than a doctor." She laughed humorlessly. "Leastwise, we don't kill as many."

"Ma wanted me took to a doctor an' got mad when he couldn' find nothin'," she ventured.

"Wall, a doctor ain't a-gonna find what was wrong with *y'all*," her aunt said enigmatically. Then she changed the subject. "I'm partial t'somethin' sweet with supper ternight. Le's check them strawbs."

Well the mention of anything sweet was going to get Anna's attention, and checking the strawberries yielded four big handfuls. "Who's the neighbors, Aunt Jinny?" she asked, as they brought their harvest, cupped in their aprons, up to the cabin.

"Got two. Got th' ones as y'all passed comin' inter th' holler and ones deeper inter th' holler. The farm b'longs t' th' Holcrofts, an' like I said, they bought it from my Pa. They's got six chillun, oldest boy's Joshua, oldest girl Sue's 'bout y'all's age. Deep inter the holler's Old Raven and Young Raven, an' I *think* Young Raven's wife—I ain't niver seen 'er, on account of they make thesselves pretty scarce most of the time, but he's spoke of her a time or twain. An' some more people I gen'rally don' see. They's Cherokee."

At Anna's start, her aunt nodded. "I know. They was supposed t'be Removed. But my Granpappy didn' cotton to thet notion, so when Jackson's sojers came 'round, he made like he was too stupid t'unnerstand what them sojers wanted. The sojers knocked 'round the woods fer awhile, got thesselves chased off by bears, an' decided there weren't no Cherokee in Lonesome Holler at all. Then my Granpappy, he went inter town an' put the claim on all the holler land soon's claimin' was open. Nobody wanted ter mess wi' him t'make a counter-claim, an' ever since we all jest pretend there ain't no Cherokee back thar." She shook her head. "Sometimes I wunner iffen folks read th' same Bible as I do; rippin' famblies off th' land an' even farms they've had since Methusalem was a pup, an' all so a buncha greedy layabouts what happens t'be white kin claim it."

Anna looked at her aunt in shock at such an astonishing statement. Her aunt looked back at her sideways. "Who d'ye think taught my Granny most of what she knowed 'bout bein' a Root Woman?" Aunt Jinny demanded. "She knowed the plants she brung with 'er t' Lonesome Holler, but she didn't know the ones that was already here. 'Twas Old Raven's granpappy and granny taught 'er, when he saw—" And then, unaccountably, she stopped. "Wall, niver mind. The Ravens be wuth twenty of the no-good layabout white trash that would'a took what they'd made, iffen they'd had thesselves a farm." She snorted. "Asides, my Granpappy didn' want none of thet kind around. They don't put no work in on th' land, they's allus borrowin' an' niver payin' back, an' when it all falls t'pieces they turns up on yore doorstep with six hungry chillun, a-whinin' an' a-cryin' thet they got nothin' t'eat an' no wood t'burn an' fer the love of God let 'em in."

Well this was the first time Anna had heard *anyone* say anything good about an Indian; she didn't know quite what to think. Except that ... Aunt Jinny had the respect of everyone who knew her. And Aunt Jinny was rich by Anna's standards. And Aunt Jinny was *smart* by anyone's standards. So ... maybe everyone else was ... wrong?

As she and her aunt washed up before supper, and she changed into her nightgown, she decided to ask more about Aunt Jinny's Granny, who seemed to have been a formidable person.

"Granny? Oh she knowed more'n anyone hereabouts had any notion," Aunt Jinny said with a smirk, as she dished up bean soup and cornbread, with sliced strawberries drizzled with honey on the side. "She come over from England. Devon. But afore thet, she met Granpappy, and he's the one what built this here cabin all hisself, with his bare hands an' the sack of tools he brung with him. An' when my Pa's Pa turned up an' homesteaded the front of the Holler, he he'ped raise thet house an' barn too, cause he could see my Ma was gettin' sweet on my Pa. Built that there stove," she added, nodding at the peculiar fireplace.

"Stove?" Anna exclaimed. "It don't look like no stove!"

"But thet's what 'e called it. He was from a place I bet y'all niver heerd of. Roosha! He was Rooski!" She chuckled at Anna's bewilderment. "'Tis as fur from England as England is from here. Halfway 'round the world! They gots them kinda stoves all over where he come from, on account of the winter's so bitter hard. 'E useter tell me our winter was like spring t'him. 'E made friends with Old Raven's Granpappy Eagle Sight fust, then brought Eagle Sight t'meet Granny. Sometimes 'e useter talk t'me in thet Rooski palaver an' I couldn' make heads nor tails of it. But 'e made this 'ere cabin so it were good for a Rooski winter, an' I reckon thet's one reason why Granny lived as long as she did. Nary a chink t'let in the winter wind. An' y'all kin sleep up there on t'stove if yore bones ache."

"Why'd 'e come t' 'Merica?" she asked.

"Same as 'bout anybody else. It were purdy bad where 'e was." She shrugged. "He didn' talk 'bout it much, so I reckon it were plenty bad. He purely loved these hills. An' he was blood brothers with Eagle Sight. It were Eagle Sight an' his wife what taught him how t'plant the Three Sisters t'gether, an' as I said, taught Granny the Root Woman ways."

"Three Sisters?" Anna asked, now thoroughly bewildered.

"Corn, beans, an' squash," Aunt Jinny told her. "Maybe a liddle manure or fish head in each hill fer good measure. The three of 'em are like sisters, they he'p each other grow. Corn give beans a place t'climb, beans feed corn 'n' squash, squash leaves cover th'ground so no weeds grow, an' the prickles on the squash leaves is nasty t'bugs."

"I ain't niver heerd that," Anna marveled, knowing it *had* to be true, because hadn't she seen the results with her own eyes?

"Tha's on account of fools don't listen t' them as knows, 'cause they's too busy a-babblin' 'bout how smart they be," Jinny said, with a touch of acid. "But wise men keeps their mouths shut, and gets wiser."

And that certainly gave her something to think about, as she climbed the ladder to the loft and her warm feather bed. Roosha! What must *that* be like, if Tennessee winters were like spring to Aunt Jinny's Granpappy?

When she slept, she dreamed of dreaming, drowsing in a warm featherbed on top of the stove, while snow piled up to the roof, and the fire sang to itself on the hearth.

6

The next day was Sunday by Anna's reckoning, but Aunt Jinny showed no signs of it being any different than any other day. So finally, as they were finishing breakfast, Anna spoke up timidly. "Aunt Jinny? Ain't we a-gonna put on our good thangs an' go t'church?"

Her aunt didn't even pause in gathering up the dishes and taking them to the sink. "Nearest church is Ducktown. Even *if* I'd let y'all go there, which I ain't gonna, we ain't got no wagon nor mule. So we'd hev t' hev started out at dawn, we'd just get there 'bout time for afternoon service, an' it'd be past dark when we got home. Who'd feed an' muck out th' pigs? Who'd see the chickens was put up? Leave 'em out arter dark an' there won't be no chickens left."

"But ..." she was bewildered. "If we ain't a-goin' t'church—"

"Y'all kin sit an' read yore Bible arter supper, while th' light lasts," Jinny replied, in tones that brooked no argument. "We got work t'do, Sunday or no Sunday. Ain't no day of rest fer a farmer till winter."

After that, Anna didn't dare say anything. She just washed her clothing as always (including, at Jinny's prompting, the nightgown), and weeded as always, and there was no real change.

Though Jinny proclaimed that this was the day for the weekly full bath. "I allus takes mine on Sunday, so y'all might as well too." They both took their baths at the well, Anna doing her best to avert her eyes from her aunt's nakedness.

Then it was a full day of chores, and writing down a new receipt—this one for "coughs and croup" that featured comfrey and "Indian tobacco," which, her aunt explained, was not tobacco at all, but a kind of bellflower. They sat down to supper. There had been a second nightgown on the line next to Anna's, and that was what Jinny was sporting at supper. Well, now she knew what her aunt wore to sleep.

Then they both took stools out to sit on the front porch in the last of the light. Anna read her Bible. But Jinny didn't have a Bible, or, indeed, any book. Instead, she stared fixedly at what looked like a black glass or ceramic plate that she had taken down from the shelf where she kept her receipt book.

Anna could not understand what she was doing ... but ... maybe it was a way of praying? Certainly Jinny wasn't doing anything else but staring into the shining surface.

When it got too dim to see the letters clearly, Anna shut her Bible and went back into the cabin. She felt a little guilty, because she actually hadn't been reading anything improving, like out of the New Testament. Instead, she'd been reading some of her favorite parts about King Solomon and the Queen of Sheba. No morals, nothing "sacred" about it, just beautiful words. And ... secretly she had kind of been wishing for one of those books like Missus Sawyer had. Those stories had been scary—but they'd been exciting and fascinating too. And she wished she could read more of them.

Her aunt followed and put that black plate back on the shelf. "I'm hankerin' fer tea," she said aloud. "Iffen y'all ain't sleepy, jest put by yore book an' set a spell. Happen y'all might hev some more questions by now."

Well, actually ... she did. She put her Bible up on the same shelf as the receipt books and accepted a sweetened mug of tea from her aunt. "All this," she said, waving her hand at the cured meat overhead, and vaguely out at the garden. "Is thet all y'all need fer a year?"

"Prolly more'n a year, but I allus put by plenty in case somethin' happens," her aunt replied. "Hailstorm, wet spring, early frost— iffen what I put by is older'n a couple years, I takes it down t'Matt

Holcroft ev' six months, an' he an' Maddie take their extrees, an' makes up boxes fer widders in Ducktown. I got money put by, too, from sellin' potions, but I try not t'spend it iffen I kin he'p it. I got trade-deals a-goin' with Matt an' Old Raven. Matt's got a water mill; he grinds my corn. Thet was part'a the bargain Granpappy made with his Pa for helpin' build it. I tans my own leather, makes my own shoon. With y'all here, I reckon I'm a-gonna hev t'buy some cloth, on account of yore gonna fatten up iffen I hev anythin' t'say 'bout it, an' Ma's close ain't gonna fit y'all fer long; other than thet, I jest buys a liddle flour now'n agin, salt, bakin' soda." She thought a moment. "Vinegar. Some other trifles. Pots an' jars fer preservin'. Could make m'own, an' I useter, but I cain't make glass. When I gets a hankerin' fer butter or cheese, I go trade with Matt. Don't go t'town much; iffen y'all think Soddy's done been pizened, y'all's got no ideer what Ducktown's like."

Looking around at the shelves filled with the fruits (and vegetables) of her aunt's labor, Anna could well believe that Jinny had enough for "a bad year." Shelves as high as she could comfortably reach, all loaded down with supplies and bunches of dried herbs above that. Ranged, now that she came to think about it, by type, according to some system only Jinny knew.

Other people would have had pictures on the walls, even if they were nothing more than pictures cut out of an old newspaper or a magazine nobody wanted anymore, and framed by hand with scrap wood. Not Aunt Jinny. Every exposed inch of wall was covered in food, tools and cookware, herbs, and a couple of shelves of odds and ends that were supremely practical, like her receipt book, ink, and quill pens.

"Got a storage shed an' a root cellar behind th' cabin too," Jinny continued. "You ain't niver had call to go there yet. I'll shew y'all termorrow." She sat in thought for a moment. "I'fact, I'm a-thinkin' it's time y'all met Matt an' Maddie Holcroft. We'll go visit 'em termorrow."

And with that astonishing statement she shooed Anna up to bed.

The next day, Jinny was as good as her word. She showed Anna the storage shed, as stoutly built as the cabin and definitely bear-proof, full of pottery jars and wooden casks—mostly corn and dried beans, her aunt said—plus an emergency supply of seed in case the first planting was completely ruined. And she showed her the root cellar—dug under the cabin and entered by a trap door in the floor, barren of everything but a couple sacks of white and sweet potatoes, and some other odds and ends of last fall's root vegetables, waiting for the fall harvest.

"Didja ever hev a hankerin' fer a cow?" Anna asked, as they closed up the cabin, and set off down the trail to the Holcroft's farm.

"Too much trouble," her aunt replied. "Iffen y'all want milk, gotta keep 'er in calf. Cain't rely on a tether t'keep 'er where y'all want 'er, an' cain't tether a calf. They'd be in the garden ever' time my back was turned. More work than it's wuth for one person, even two. A fambly now, thet's different. There's 'nuff call fer milk t'hev a herd an' clear an' fence off a pasture."

The walk down the long, gradual slope was lovely—even if Anna did keep catching those odd glimpses of things that weren't quite there out of the corners of her eyes. "Aunt Jinny?" she said finally, with great hesitation. "Is these woods got hants in 'em?"

She was afraid Aunt Jinny would laugh at her. But instead, her aunt just pursed her lips a little. "Not *hants*, 'xactly. But they say there's things what ain't what y'all'd call proper critters. The Ravens got lotsa stories 'bout 'em."

Once again, her aunt gave her an odd, sideways look when she thought Anna wouldn't notice.

There's somethin' there that she ain't tellin' me about, Anna decided. *I wish't I knowed what 'twas.*

But her aunt immediately changed the subject by turning the walk into a lesson on various plants along the way, and what they were good for. And she kept quizzing Anna on what she'd been told, so Anna didn't have any time to think about her aunt's enigmatic statements.

Brilliant light at the end of the tunnel of trees told her they were about to meet the actual road, and come to the Holcrofts' farm. By that time she was as eager to end the lesson as she was to meet the neighbors.

When they emerged into sunlight, the farm lay spread out in front of them on the left side of the road. And now that she had a better look at it, it was clear that the log farmhouse was not one, but two full stories, and the second probably held as many as six rooms. Certainly four, which were probably bedrooms for the children. The whole was quite a bit larger than her aunt's farm, but then, there were six children here besides the couple themselves. *I reckon that not only means more mouths t'feed, but more hands t'he'p.* A figure she supposed was Matt Holcroft worked in the distance behind a team of two mules. She wasn't sure what he was doing—wasn't plowing supposed to be over by now? But then again, everything she knew about farming she'd learned most of in the last couple of days.

I didn' know plants fed each other. Didn' know I was s'posed to feed them. *No wonder our garden didn' grow thet good.*

A dog started barking just as they approached the house, and a woman came out of it, hands shading her eyes to see what all the ruckus was about. She obviously recognized Aunt Jinny, because she took her hand away from her eyes to wave enthusiastically.

"Jinny!" the woman called in a throaty voice—the kind that carries far when someone is calling errant children in to supper. "Come up t' the house! Been too long!"

Aunt Jinny just waved in return, and lengthened her steps a little; Anna had to trot to keep up, and despite the fact that she was feeling better than she had in a long, long time, she started feeling breathless.

Mrs. Holcroft was a tall woman, with yellow hair with just a couple of gray streaks in it done up at the nape of her neck in a knot. She wore a nice sprig-cotton dress in blue and white with a worn white bib apron over it. That dress fabric never came from flour sacks. Anna was very glad she was dressed decently in that nice canvas skirt with a proper shirtwaist and petticoat; if she'd come to visit turned out in the shabby flour-sack gown she'd arrived in, she'd have been mortified.

Not that Mrs. Holcroft seemed to take note even of Aunt Jinny's outrageous men's bib overalls. Unlike Mrs. Sawyer, Mrs. Holcroft didn't seem to care what Jinny and Anna wore.

But Anna would still have been mortified.

Now that they were out of the trees, the sun beat down on them in a way she couldn't remember ever happening in Soddy. Maybe it was because of all the smoke and soot in the air in Soddy, that thinned out the sunlight. She was hot and uncomfortable when they reached the welcome shelter of the cabin's cooler kitchen.

The first thing she noticed was that there was no fire in the hearth nor in the stove, and she wondered why. How could you get any cooking done if you had to keep building the fire over and over? The second thing she noticed was that the enormous kitchen was a room all to itself; this huge cabin wasn't just one big room downstairs, it was partitioned up. The upstairs must be, too. But the Holcrofts weren't so high-falutin' as to have a parlor, or that's where she and Aunt Jinny would have been invited, so the rest of the house probably was made of a workroom and several bedrooms.

There were many cupboards and pantries here, a circle of ladderback chairs at the hearth, and a proper spindle-leg table and set of ladderback chairs around it. The table had a red-and-white checkered oilcloth tablecloth on it.

"Set a spell, I got some'a yore tea right here," the woman said, nodding at the table and chairs as she picked up a pitcher and began pouring cups of tea—proper pottery cups, not the wooden ones Aunt Jinny used. Without being asked, she dripped some honey into all three. "So, this must be yore sister's gal?"

"This's Anna May," Aunt Jinny confirmed, as they took their places at the table. "Anna, this's Maddie Holcroft."

"Please ter meetcher, Missus Holcroft," Anna said shyly, ducking her head a little.

"Reckon I should make 'er known t'yer," Jinny continued. "Seein' as she's stayin'."

"Wall, good. I worry 'bout y'all up there all alone," Mrs. Holcroft said. "I ain't a-gonna worry iffen y'all got a young gal stayin'." Aunt Jinny snorted.

"There ain't nothin' t'worry 'bout, Maddie," Jinny retorted. "I'm meaner'n a rattlesnake and sneakier than a panther. Ain't no man nor beast a-gonna meddle with me."

"It ain't man nor beast I'm a-worried 'bout, Jinny. It's slips of th' axe, a branch a-rollin' out from under y'all, and y'all fallin' an' crackin yore fool haid, or fallin' on th' ice." Maddie chuckled. "Though hard as thet haid of yores is, prolly no harm 'ud come to y'all."

"Takes one ter know one, Maddie," Jinny snickered, and then the two of them were off, chattering away, with Maddie offering gossip about people Anna had never heard of, and Jinny asking about the six Holcroft children. Early on in the gossip session, Maddie offered around a plate of pale yellow sugar cookies. Jinny took one absently. There was nothing absent-minded about the way Anna helped herself, but she did manage to restrain herself to taking only two.

Four of the six Holcroft children were scattered about the farm. One was milking, one was fishing, one was gathering vegetables, and one was chopping wood. The eldest girl was in the "kitchen-shed." And that explained the cold stove. In summer, people who were well enough off to afford it moved their cooking to a shed attached to, but separate from, the house. Everything that needed heat from a stove or a hearth—baking, stewing, or frying—was done there instead of in the house. Anna had only *heard* about people well off enough to do this; she'd never actually known anyone who did, herself.

"An' Josh has another job fer ol' Cavenel," Mrs. Holcroft concluded.

"Who died?" Jinny asked with a sort of morbid interest, although Anna could not connect "having a job" with someone dying.

"It's fer Hopper, what runs the Company store. Their baby took sick an' died last week." She shook her head. "Poor liddle thang, it weren't even four months old. Missus Hopper took it hard, an' so did he."

"Said it afore, an' I'll say it agin. Thet there mine pizens ev'thin' around it," Aunt Jinny growled. "Half the babies in Ducktown niver see their fust birthdays. It oughter be shet down."

"An' y'all won't hear nothin' contrary from me." Mrs. Holcroft nodded. "But it's more work fer Josh, an' he's makin' a good job of't. Hopper, he wanted a big ol' weepin' angel, 'bout yay high." She measured roughly five feet tall with her hand. "Josh tol' him, sure, he could hev it, but it'd take six months or more. An' the boy talked Hopper inter a liddle sleepin' baby instead. A lot less money, but—I dunno how we'd'a got somethin' thet big back inter town w'out it fallin' over an' breakin'. Nor how we'd'a got the stone here in the fust place. He coulda carved it in Ducktown, but I don' like th' notion of him spending hours travelin' there an' back ever' day, an' I like th' notion of him boardin' with

Cavenel even less. Statue's gonna be a purdy thang."

"Wall, I'd admire t' see it," Aunt Jinny said.

"Then y'all will." Mrs. Holcroft got up from the table. "He's jest in th' barn."

Their hostess led the way to the barn, which, unlike the house, was a standard, plank-built affair; a steady but irregular *chink, chink* sound emerged from it. From the tiny amount of information she'd heard, Anna could not imagine what it was that Josh Holcroft was supposed to be *doing* that involved a dead baby, but she certainly was interested to find out.

"Joshua!" his mother called as they entered the straw-scented semidarkness of the barn. "Miz Jinny Alscot's here t'see yore work, an' her niece Anna Jones is with her."

"I'm in m'workshed, Ma!" came a light tenor voice. "Come on back!"

At the rear of the barn was an attached shed. Full sunlight poured in through a window that had no glass, but a tight wooden shutter that was currently standing open. It had a clever little wood stove made out of metal odds and ends. The stove was cold right now, since it was warm enough in the sun to be slightly uncomfortable, but Anna thought it likely the makeshift stove would keep the small space cozy in winter. There was a wooden bench filling up most of the shop, and on the bench was a piece of white stone about the size of a yaller hound all curled up. But it wasn't in the shape of a dog; it was in the shape of a baby, curled in sleep, one pudgy fist against its cheek. There was a suggestion of a pair of small wings in the rough rock where its shoulders were. Anna gasped to see it; it was *astonishingly* lifelike, even in this rough form.

"Wotcher think, Ma?" asked the young man standing next to it. He was not handsome; his features were far too irregular for that. With a prominent nose, chin, and brows, he looked more unfinished than his creation. His unruly mop of straw-colored hair hadn't seen a comb for most of the day and had stone dust and a couple of chips in it. But his bright blue eyes were intelligent and thoughtful, and did a lot to reassure Anna that he wasn't as rough and ready as he appeared.

He had big hands, one of which held a mallet, the other, a

chisel. He had stone dust all over his overalls, and stout boots on his feet, to protect them from bits of stone, no doubt.

"My!" his mother exclaimed. "I thank it's *fine*! What would y'all say, Jinny?"

Aunt Jinny examined the work with a critical eye. "I say iffen y'all showed it t' Missus Hopper right this minute, she'd bawl her eyes out. And when y'all give it t'her finished, she might wanter hev it in her parlor t' bawl over regular."

Josh tossed his head so that his hair flopped out of his eyes, and grinned. "Wall, then, thet'll jest mean ol' man Hopper'll hev t'pay me t'make another, won't it?"

His mother looked affronted, but Aunt Jinny laughed and patted him on the shoulder. "Tha's a smart young feller thinkin'," she said. "This's m'sister's girl, Anna Jones. Anna, this here is Joshua Holcroft, an' the best carver I ever seed, bar my Granpappy."

Joshua blushed, and so did Anna. They shook hands awkwardly. His hand was so big it completely enveloped hers, but he held her hand so gently, it was as if he were holding a new-hatched chick. "Please ter meetcha," he said, then finally looked her straight in the eyes, and smiled.

She blushed even harder. That smile had completely transformed his face, by some magic she didn't understand. He still wasn't *handsome*, but now he was—attractive. Very attractive. She suddenly found herself thinking about going for a long walk with him in the moonlight, or sitting on the porch and talking for hours. She shook herself out of such daydreams with difficulty. "I dunno wotcher doin'," she confessed. "But thet there's a purdy liddle baby angel."

"Joshua carves all the headstones fer Mister Cavenel, th' undertaker," his mother replied before he could answer. "Mos' people jest want a stone, with names an' dates, an' maybe somethin' t' 'member the dead by, like y'all hev prolly seen in graveyards. An' thet pays good. But sometimes he gets somethin' special. Like this, which's fer the Hoppers' dead baby."

"An' when I ain't a-carvin' fer graves, I carves liddle bits of this an' thet," Josh put in, looking modest. "Gewgaws an' the like. Knife handles. Them panels on the sides of pocketknives. Rifle stocks. Men'll pay good money fer carved bone 'n horn 'n 'specially mother of pearl. Wood, not so much, but if they wants somethin' fancy in wood, they'll still pay. Sometimes purdy liddle things fer the ladies, but thet don't pay as good as rifle stocks an' knife handles. Fellers like t'show thet off."

His mother shook her head. "An' men say women is vain!"

"Aw, Ma!" Joshua complained, but at the same time he made a sidewise glance at Anna, and she blushed all over again. She had no idea why she was having this reaction to Joshua. None of the boys in Soddy had ever made her feel this way.

But then again, none of the boys in Soddy had ever taken a first glance at her, much less a second and third the way Joshua was doing. Their eyes had always slid right over her, as if she weren't even there. Josh was certainly not doing that. He kept looking at her as if he found her as interesting as she found him.

"Back to thet work, Josh," his mother said. "Gotta make th' best of th' light."

"Yes, Ma," he said obediently, and went back to tapping lightly at the stone with his hammer and chisel, considering each blow before he took it.

Mrs. Holcroft led them back to her kitchen, with a glance into the kitchen shed where her daughter, who looked like a younger version of her mother down to the dress in the same sprigged cotton, presided over another stove, this a proper cast-iron one, made for cooking. *An' Pa thinks farmin' ain't wuth doin'!* she thought to herself, admiring the display of such signs of success. Not one, but two proper stoves, and plenty of fuel to keep them going! Not to mention the wealth standing in the fields as a sign of admirable prosperity.

There was more tea to be poured out, and more gossip shared; Anna kept her mouth shut and her head down over her tea. But then a question was addressed to her.

"And how's yore Ma, Anna?" Mrs. Holcroft asked.

It was a commonplace question, but Anna was not given a chance to answer.

"Maybelle's 'xactly where I said she'd be, which's hand-t'-mouth," Aunt Jinny replied grimly. "Look at this chile! Skin an' bones an' a hank of hair! Thet no-good Llewellyn Jones cain't even keep his own fambly fed!"

Anna wanted to sink into the chair and vanish.

"Niver shoulda married th' boy," Mrs. Holcroft agreed. "I dunno why a woman with a lick'a sense'd marry a miner, an' a coal miner at thet!"

"Maybelle's jest like her own Ma. Not a lick'a sense atwixt 'em." Aunt Jinny shook her head. "On'y smart thang that woman ever did was marry my Pa. Wall, at least she made 'im happy, so there's thet in her favor."

"Wall, her Ma was a sad case, an' I feel a *liddle* sorry fer her," Mrs. Holcroft said charitably. "Weren't her fault th' boy she married turned out to be a gol-durned traitor."

Hurriedly, Anna counted backward in her head, and realized that Mrs. Holcroft must've been referring to the War. "Y'all mean—" she blurted, about to say—*he was a durned Yankee?*

But Mrs. Holcroft interrupted her, and said the most surprising thing, with great venom. "He was a gol-durned Reb is what he was." So it was a good thing she hadn't had the chance to say that last piece.

Her face must have been a picture, because Mrs. Holcroft laughed, and actually slapped the table, she was so amused. "Lawsy me, chile, didn' y'all know this part'a Tennessee went with the *Nawth*?"

Dumbly she shook her head.

"I was gonna tell 'er all 'bout it later, Maddie," Aunt Jinny said, with faint disapproval.

"Wall she might as well hear it now," retorted Maddie Holcroft. "Ain't no sense in lettin' her go down to Ducktown an' git herself in hot water on account'a ignorance."

"She ain't a-goin' to Ducktown if I have any say," Jinny muttered, and might have said more aloud, but it was becoming evident to Anna that Maddie Holcroft at her kitchen table was a force to be reckoned with where gossip was concerned. Like a summer thunderstorm, all you could do was ride the torrent out.

"Yore Granny on your Ma's side was quite the beauty, so they say," continued Mrs. Holcroft with the relish that would have been due gossip of last week, not decades old. But maybe she just liked having a brand-new audience. "An' 'bout as much sense as a baby rabbit. She cotched hersel' Parnel Parry, a *right* good-lookin' feller with about as much sense, who was your Granpappy's best frien'. Wall, up an' starts th' War, and Parnel gets his fool head stuffed full'a romantical fol-de-rol by an idiot cousin, an' *off* he goes t'be a occifer with the Rebs iffen y'all please, an' not even yore Granpappy can put any sense inter his haid. Weren't nobody'd even say g'bye t'him but yore Granpappy an' his wife. He left in the dead of night, like a thief. So th' last thing he does afore he leaves, is get your Granpappy t'promise t'take care of th' gel iffen anythin' happens t'him. Then yore Granpappy goes t'fight fer th' Union."

"An' we was livin' *here*, not up the Holler. This useta be my Pa's farm, an Granny on my Ma's side, the Root Woman, was still alive, an' lived where I live now. My Ma was daid then, but my Granny an' Granpappy on my Pa's side lived wi' me an' my brothers, so me an' th' farm was tended to without Pa," put in Aunt Jinny. "My other Granpappy was gone by then, but Granny was close enough t'this farm t' git he'p if she needed it."

"She means where her an' her brothers an' her Pa all lived, her Pa's farm, thet was *this very farm*," said Mrs. Holcroft, helping Anna get all the relatives sorted out again. "So, yore Granpappy Alscot come back, an Parnel didn', an' since your Granpappy's notion of 'takin' care of a pretty widder woman' was a-marryin' her, thet's what he done."

"It weren't as if she was gonna get a widder's pension from th' Rebs," said Aunt Jinny. "Not like Pa got from th' Union Army."

"But *ev'body* in Ducktown know'd she was married t' a Reb, an' plenty of tongues was a-waggin' 'bout how *she* Jezebeled Parnel, then did the same t' yore Granpappy, an' thet she was a schemin' hussy, an' what with one thing an' another, she couldn' even buy a reel of cotton in th' store wi'out people gossipin' 'bout it. Thet's why I feel sorry for 'er."

"I reckon I did feel sorry for 'er then," Aunt Jinny admitted. "Mind, she could'a stiffened 'er spine an' shame the divil, but she niver did hev much spine t'begin with, an' Pa jest cosseted 'er. She wouldn' leave the house, an' *setch* a lotta weepin' in corners!"

"So yore Granpappy figgered make a fresh start over t' Soddy way, sold th' farm t' Matt's Pa, an' we got it from him as a weddin' present. So thet's how we're here."

"An' yore Granny an' yore Ma an' Granpappy an' me moved. He was 'bout tired of farmin', so's he used th' cash from th' farm t'rent a house offen a feller, an used the pension money fer spendin'. Arter about six months, I come back here, stayed with my Granny, an' learnt t' be a Root Woman. I will admit the three of them, Pa an' yore Granny till she died and Maybelle, did live high on the hog then," Aunt Jinny mused. "Which's why I reckon that layabout Lew Jones thought he was a-marryin' money. But it all went bust when Pa died. There was the bit left over in the bank from a-sellin' th' farm, but the pension died with Pa. Pore Pa prolly thought Maybelle was doin' all right by marryin' Lew. He prolly b'lieved all them stories about how Lew was a-gonna be a foreman soon. So he didn' worry none that he wasn't gonna leave 'er much." Aunt Jinny sighed. "An' thet's how y'all ended up in Soddy, when all yore kin come from here."

Anna had finally gotten all the Mas and Pas and Grannys and Granpappys sorted out in her head, and just had one question. "But—how'd y'all keep th' Yanks *an'* th' Rebs from takin' yore stock an' crops an' all?" she asked—because tragic tales of farms being stripped bare by invading soldiers of both sides were prevalent enough even she had heard plenty of them.

Aunt Jinny and Mrs. Holcroft exchanged a *look*. Aunt Jinny set her chin stubbornly and Mrs. Holcroft looked full of mischief. "Don't go—" Aunt Jinny began.

But Mrs. Holcroft bent over the table and whispered, "It were the *spirit bears*!"

Aunt Jinny groaned.

"Spirit—bears?" Anna replied, in utter bewilderment now, which was more than enough to encourage Maddie Holcroft to unleash the tale.

"I heerd it from them as saw it for thesselves, so don' y'all conter-dick me, Virginia Alscot," Maddie Holcroft said firmly. Then she turned back to Anna. "Y'all knowed how long the road is t'git here t' the Holler, 'cause y'all done been on it t'git here. Wall! Along comes a raidin' party on th' road. An' afore they gets fur, they's attacked by a giant black bear what kin run as fast as a horse! What's more, bullets don' even tech it! An' when they try t'keep a-comin', wall, there comes *another*! Them two bears is racin' in an' outa their lines, a-slashin' up their hosses, an' a-crackin' haids right *off* their bodies. So they go back they gets more men—on account'a they's sojers an' they's stupid—an' try again. An' the same thing happens. Then they try a third time, an' they's a *third* bear, as big as th' other two put t'gether! By the time them bears git done, they's mebbe one or two men left t'tell th' tale. An' the sojers cain't take it out on anyone livin' 'round 'bout here, nor blame 'em either, 'cause ev'one knows ain't no way nobody c'd train a bear t' do all thet, much less train three bears. Ain't no side ever tried more'n three times t'get here."

"It were jest a bear with her cubs, Maddie Holcroft," Aunt Jinny said crossly. "It weren't nothin' unnatural. Get a-twixt a mammy bear an' her cubs an' y'all might as well call th' undertaker."

"I heerd these weren't no cubs."

"An' I *knowed* these was a buncha city boys an' plantation sons what niver seed a bear in their lives," Jinny retorted.

"An' the bullets thet bounced right off?"

"They was turrible bad shots. Ain't nothin' magic 'bout thet." Mrs. Holcroft was obviously taking a great deal of pleasure out of teasing Aunt Jinny with this story and making her cross. Perhaps Aunt Jinny was one of those people who did not like magic, because it was the Devil's work.

Perhaps the reason Mrs. Holcroft enjoyed telling this story was as simple as the fact that it wasn't easy to get under her aunt's skin, and this story for some unknown reason did exactly that.

But there was only one really important part about the story as far as Anna was concerned, and it had nothing to do with spirits or magic.

"Is there still bears?" Anna asked, in a small, frightened voice.

"Not 'round this farm nor my place, chile," Aunt Jinny said, patting her hand. "Old Raven an' Young Raven see t'thet, don't y'all worry none. Bear thet gets close, ends up in they pots an' on they smokin' racks. An' asides, I ain't no city-born fool. Go out in the woods wi' me an' yore safe as safe."

"Are you *sure*?" she asked.

"I'm certain-sure." Jinny glanced out the door. "An' I'm certain-sure thet we need t' be gettin' back, or there won't be no hot supper, an' I don't reckon t' et cold cornbread an' drippin'."

"I'd ast all y'all t' stay fer supper, 'cause Matt'd admire t' see y'all an' meet Anna, but I know better," laughed Mrs. Holcroft. "But yore allus welcome. Both on y'all, t'gether or alone."

"Thenkee kindly fer th' tea, an' I do admire thet liddle angel o' Josh's, an' I'm right glad I got a chance t'see it afore it ends up in a parlor I ain't niver gettin' invited to," Aunt Jinny said with a smirk, standing up.

Maddie Holcroft snorted. "Not us neither," she pointed out, but her face showed her pride in her son's talent. "But at least we gets t'see it fust."

The walk back was more tiring, since it was up the gradual slope. "Aunt Jinny?" Anna ventured. "Do the Holcrofts go t'church on Sunday?" Because the fact that she had not gone was wearing on her mind, and the arched vault of the branches overhead put her powerfully in mind of a church roof. It felt wrong not to go to church, no matter what Aunt Jinny said. So maybe she could walk down here and go with the Holcrofts.

Plus ... well, if she could go with them, it would be a weekly chance to see Josh.

"B'lieve they do," Jinny admitted. "They do got mules an' a wagon."

"C'd I go with 'em?" she asked.

Jinny stopped right in the path and turned to look at her. "Is this 'bout church-goin'?" she demanded. "Or is this 'bout a-seein' Josh Holcroft?"

"I don' feel right, not goin' t' church," she temporized, but she was afraid that her blush gave her away.

Aunt Jinny shook her head. "I unnerstan'. I do. But I'm a-gonna tell y'all no. Thet wagon is full 'nuff, wi'out y'all, but thet ain't the main reason. Y'all ain't strong 'nough yet t'bear Ducktown. 'Member thet y'all felt sick in Soddy? An' when y'all got near t' Cleveland y'all started feelin' a liddle sick agin?"

Reluctantly, she nodded.

"Wall, Ducktown's a hunnert times worse nor Soddy," her aunt told her sternly. "I keep a-tellin' y'all thet, but y'all don't seem t' get it in yore haid. *Nothin' grows there*. Not a garden, not a tree, not hardly a weed. Some people, they don't feel th' pizen. Some, they do. Some, like thet pore liddle dead baby, *it kills them daid*.

I ain't a-makin' thet up jest fer foolin' y'all. Y'all wanta find out that pizen is gonna do thet t'y'all?"

Numbly she shook her head.

"Wall then. There's yore answer." She set off back up the hill, and Anna perforce followed her.

But she suddenly realized as the end of the trail came into view that the visit to the Holcrofts had brought up as many questions about her aunt as it had answered.

7

Today Anna was dealing with a particularly complicated receipt. Aunt Jinny had written in smaller letters than usual to fit everything on the page of the book, and there were a lot of ingredients. This wasn't a receipt to be making any mistakes on, either; it was specifically for "Winter Fever," a dangerous illness that could carry off even a strong man in his prime. Anna concentrated on getting every letter and number of it exactly right, focusing so fiercely that when a shadow fell over her, her immediate reaction was annoyance that her light had been blocked as she looked up.

And then she froze. Because standing in the doorway, blocking off the sun, was an Indian.

She knew that it had to be an Indian; the man had long, flowing black hair with a single feather tied into it, and a fancy leather vest with beadwork on it, though he also wore a perfectly normal collarless linen shirt with gaiters on each arm and perfectly normal dungarees, the trouser-type rather than the ones with a bib like Aunt Jinny wore. A shriek of shock died in her throat, as her mouth dried instantly, and all she could think about was stories of scalpings and massacres.

"Virginia, am I disturbin' y'all?" said the man, politely.

Aunt Jinny looked up from her potion-making. "Not a-tall, Old Raven. I been expectin' y'all fer a couple days. This here's m'niece, Anna. Come on in."

The man came further into the cabin, making no noise at all. So *this* must be one of the Cherokee that her aunt had mentioned as living in the holler. As Anna's heart slowly stopped racing, she looked up at his grave face. He appeared to be older than Aunt Jinny by the gray threading his black hair, but she couldn't tell how much older.

And a second man, who could have been the twin of the first at a much younger age, came in behind him. He was holding two dead rabbits by their hind legs. "We got rabbits t'trade fer honey, Miz Jinny," the younger man said.

"Two rabbits? Seems fair," Jinny agreed. "I figgered y'all was about due t' trade fer some, tha's why I been expectin' y'all. Anna, this here is Old Raven an' Young Raven. I told y'all 'bout 'em. They lives futher up th' Holler."

Anna told herself not to be a goose. Aunt Jinny wouldn't leave her cabin door open all the time if there was the slightest chance of danger. And now she was embarrassed for thinking what she had about them. They were both striking men, with their strong features and long black hair. But what was most astonishing about them was their economical way of moving. They didn't fidget, or shift their weight from foot to foot. They remained absolutely still until the moment they moved, and when they moved, they did so silently and precisely. Young Raven was dressed like his father, with the addition of a bone choker at his throat, and his shirt was a deeper shade of brown. Both of them wore their shirts over their dungarees instead of tucked in, and had leather belts around their waists that supported a variety of pouches and sheathed knives. Both of them carried rifles slung over their shoulders.

Young Raven took the rabbits to Aunt Jinny, who laid a flour-sack towel over what she was doing to prevent anything from being disturbed. But Old Raven examined Anna closely, uncomfortably closely actually, as if he was looking for something. Aunt Jinny put the rabbits up for the moment, reached to the shelf that held some of her sweets and jams, and passed the younger Cherokee a sealed pot of honey, then exchanged a look with the older man.

And there was a bit of unspoken communication in that moment that Anna would not have seen if she had not been paying attention. Old Raven slightly raised his right eyebrow. Aunt Jinny cocked her head in Anna's direction and gave a slight shrug. Old Raven pursed his lips a little, then nodded so very little it might not have happened at all. And Aunt Jinny smiled, ever so faintly.

And then it was over, making Anna wonder what on earth they had just said to each other. It was about her, she thought—but what did it mean?

But there was no time to think about it. Aunt Jinny invited the men to sit down at the table and poured them some of her tea, and offered cornbread, both of which were accepted. While they sipped and nibbled in silence that was very much a contrast to Mrs. Holcroft's chatter, her aunt deftly skinned and quartered the rabbits, and added them to the soup pot. "'Scuse me while I go stretch these here hides," she said then, and before Anna could say anything, she was out the door.

Anna looked down at her hands, awkwardly, and then to look as if she was doing something, capped the ink, cleaned the quill, and blew on her page to dry it.

"Anythin' y'all'd like t'know 'bout Lonesome Holler, liddle Anna?" asked Old Raven, ever so politely. "Me'n my kin been here since the days afore the white men came. There ain't nothin' 'bout this holler we don't know."

She looked up and something sprang into her head. "I heerd," she began, hesitantly. "I heerd that durin' th' War, there was *bears* here, what couldn't be shot, keepin' the sojers away." She looked up shyly. "Was there really? Whassa *spirit bear*?"

Old Raven smiled very faintly. "Th' Ole Men tol' this t'me when I was a boy, so it must be true," he said. "A time ago, there was a clan called Ani'-Tsa'guhi an' there was a boy in that clan who'd wander away for days inter the mountains. An' he never et in his house, jest slept. An' his parents begun to notice his hair was a-growin' out all over his body. So they arst him what was a-goin' on, an' he finally tol' 'em he was a-eatin' jest fine in the mountains, an' th' food was better there than with th' clan. An' he tol' 'em, 'Iffen y'all fast fer seven days an' a-go with me, all y'all will allus hev enough t'eat an' y'all will niver hev t' work fer it.' So the whole clan had a palaver with th' headman, an' they decided t' do thet. An' they fasted, an' off they went, an' they started t'look like th' boy. With hair all over. 'Nother clan heerd of this, an' they sent messengers t'talk to 'em, but th' Ani-Tsa'guhi wouldn' come back. 'Y'all call us yanu from now on,' they said, an' then they said somethin' else, on account'a they figgered they owed somethin' t' th' rest of th' nation. 'An' because we're one nation, iffen y'all gets hungry, here are the songs t'call us by. Call us an' we'll come an' give y'all our very own flesh. Don' worry 'bout killin' us, y'all cain't, an' we'll live ferever.' So they taught th' messengers the songs, an' went on, but when th' messengers looked back, all they saw was a big drove of bears a-goin' inter th' woods. Th' Ole Men tol' me this when I was a boy, so it must be true."

Well, that didn't really answer her question, but she felt it was rude to persist any further. Unless—

Unless Old Raven meant that there *were* such things as spirit bears, and that they were the unkillable bears that had driven off the Yank and Reb soldiers to protect the Holler, and that they had once been humans and Cherokee.

"Bears ain't a-gonna bother th' Root Woman an' her kin, Anna," said Young Raven. "Not niver, not nohow."

Well that answered a different question, though how Young Raven could be so certain of that, she was entirely unsure.

Her aunt was back before the silence became awkward, and the two men stood up to go. "Thenkee, Virginia," said Old Raven. "It'll rain soon. We'll come by the day arter with mushrooms."

"I'd admire thet, thenkee," her aunt replied. "I'm still a-showin' Anna here what she needs t'larn, an' she ain't ready yet t' traipse 'round the woods too far from my house."

Old Raven smiled faintly, made a sketchy little salute with his hand, and then the two of them were gone, as silently as they had arrived.

Aunt Jinny looked down at the half-finished receipt. "Uncap thet ink an' get back t'writin', Anna," she said. "Y'all ain't done an' y'all still need t'learn how t'put the potion t'gether."

That night after supper, Aunt Jinny asked her if Old Raven had said anything to her. She bit her lip, because she didn't want to irritate her aunt, but Jinny *had* asked her, and she knew she had to tell the truth. "I arst him 'bout the *spirit bears* what Mrs. Holcroft tol' me 'bout," she said, carefully.

"An' what'd he say?" she replied.

"He tol' me a story 'bout a Cherokee clan what turned inter bears an' live ferever," she answered. "But thet didn' answer m'question a-tall."

"Didn' it?" her aunt countered. "Wall, when y'all arst Old Raven a question y'all don't allus get a straight-out answer. Most times, y'all get a answer what leads t' th' answer, iffen y'all think 'bout it enough." She got up and headed for the front porch. "I'm a-gonna set a spell outside. Issa nice night, an' them fireflies is purdy t'watch."

Before Anna could say anything, Aunt Jinny went out to sit in her chair in the dark on the porch, leaving the only light in the cabin that which was coming from the banked coals on the hearth. Anna didn't particularly want to go out on the porch; it was chillier than was comfortable for her in her nightgown, and she didn't want to climb up into the loft to get Mrs. Sawyer's gifted shawl only to climb back down again just to sit on the porch. The fireflies and stars might be pretty, but she got bored with them a lot quicker than Aunt Jinny did. So she moved her stool closer to the stove and tried to puzzle out what Old Raven had been trying to tell her.

Was it that there really *were* bears that couldn't be killed? Was it that he and his son knew how to control bears in general, somehow? *Was it both?* There was magic in the Bible, after all; Pharaoh had had magicians that had fought a magic battle with Moses. They'd turned their staffs to snakes and everything. The Preacher back in Soddy hadn't talked much about magic, except around Halloween, when he'd do at least one sermon on the evil that came of "playing" with it, on account of it was pretty much guaranteed that there'd be parties that night of girls that were courtin'-high trying to cast spells to figure out who they'd marry. Mostly he was too busy with the sins of drink, lust, and disobedience to fret much about witchcraft. Back home, none of those serious sins had worried Anna; she didn't drink, she never hardly even thought about disobeying, and as for lust, well—she was never around boys much, and when she was, they paid no never-mind to her.

And now her wandering mind took that, and ran off with it, and the pressing issue of magic gradually took a back seat to the issue of young men. Or rather, a particular young man. *But what about Josh Holcroft?* came the persistant thought. *He sure weren't ignorin' y'all, Anna Jones!*

She found herself blushing and getting a little warm and uncomfortable, but somehow in a good way. And why bother thinking about witchcraft when there was a young man who had finally *smiled* at her?

The more she thought about meeting him again, the more distracted she got. This was such an entirely new situation for her, the sheer novelty of it alone could have occupied her for hours.

And she might indeed have sat there, drowsily thinking about Josh, wondering if there was a way she could get Aunt Jinny to send her down to the Holcrofts for something so she could find out if this was just her overactive imagination or he really did...

Except right about then was when she looked up for a moment saw ... it.

It crept out from underneath the stove—even though there was no "underneath" there. It was small, about waist-high to her; in fact, it looked very like a wizened little old man, with long hair and thick beard as gray as fog. Except it had cat-ears, and blazing eyes. It didn't seem to be aware that she was there.

This changed as she gasped. It reacted to the sound by disappearing instantly back under the stove, leaving her to wonder if she had even seen it at all. Had she fallen asleep and actually been dreaming? She got up and felt the place where it had been, but couldn't tell any difference in temperature between one piece of floor and the next.

And how could it have gotten *under* the stove? The thing was a gigantic piece of solid stonework!

Finally she stood up, hugging herself and shaking a little. There were only three possibilities here. She could be going mad. She might have been dreaming. Or the creature had actually been there.

She closed her eyes and told herself to be sensible. She wasn't going mad; at least, she didn't think so. And that creature could not possibly have been there. That left the middle. And if she'd fallen asleep without even realizing it, next to the stove—

—then she definitely should be falling asleep in bed instead.

She went around to the ladder and climbed it, trying not to

hurry, hoping that the feeling of being watched was all in her imagination. And when she got into bed, she pulled the quilt over her head. Tonight was not the night she wanted to see eyes staring down at her from the rafters.

She woke up, not thinking about Josh or the strange vision of last night, but of the two Cherokees who had visited them yesterday. Almost everything about them had been—unexpected. And when she sat down at the little table, her aunt had that look in her eye at breakfast that warned Anna that Aunt Jinny was about to say something Anna would probably find uncomfortable. So to forestall her, Anna asked the first thing that came into her head.

"Aunt Jinny, why do them Ravens talk jest like us?" Because it had seemed odd, hearing familiar accents and words coming from them. She wasn't sure now what she had expected before they spoke, but it hadn't been that.

"Because they *is* us, fool girl," Jinny said a little crossly. "Up till Jackass Jackson got it inter his fool haid t' Remove them Cherokee, most of 'em had farms like ourn, an' shops an' trades too, an' went t' school alongside our young'uns, and ever'thang y'all kin think of. Iffen y'all walked inter a Cherokee cabin wi' yore eyes closed an' opened 'em when nobody was around, y'all couldn't'a told the difference." She scowled. "Thet no-good trash Jackson reckoned he'd buy hisself some votes, I guess, by Removin' 'em and givin' their property t' no-accounts."

"It seems kinda strange they's on'y th' two or three of 'em," she said, thinking out loud.

"Wall, I dunno ac'chully how many Cherokee is back there in the holler," her aunt admitted. "I know I tol' y'all it was on'y two or three, but I ain't sure. On'y one who knew for sure was my Granpappy. I niver see nobody but the Ravens, so there could be a whole tribe livin' quiet-like back thar. Come t'think 'bout it, there prolly is, or at least, a couple famblies. Holler's big enough fer all of us. Ain't no biznez of mine. Figger they's at least one tribe Jackass Jackson didn' cheat outa their land."

It was very clear that, even though the Removal had been decades ago and Aunt Jinny could not possibly have firsthand knowledge of it, she had inherited a fearsome grudge against President Andrew Jackson along with her farm.

But ... it kinder sounds like it's justified.

"Me an' Matt Holcroft oughta figger out how t'transfer th' deed t'them one-a these days," she finished. "But they ain't no rush. Matt's deedin' his farm t' Josh or Jacob, an' my place'll be a-goin' t' y'all, an' neither one of y'all's gonna mess with th' Ravens."

That astonishing statement surprised Anna so much that you could have knocked her over with a feather, and she tried to think of something else to ask about, now that she had—she hoped—gotten her aunt onto something other than whatever thing Jinny had wanted to bring up. *Why give this place t'me, when she said she has brothers an' sisters?* she thought. And she was about to ask how many relatives she actually had, when Jinny shot her a sharp glance.

"And y'all ain't gonna distract me none, missy," she said. "They's somethin' I aim t'show y'all terday. 'Tis 'bout time y'all knowed about y'all's *real* inheritance."

Jinny made some odd gestures in the air. Odder still—a little scary in fact—her fingers left glowing golden trails in the air!

The sight held Anna paralyzed for a moment, and she could not believe her eyes. But what happened next made her yelp and jump on top of her stool, like a silly goose seeing a mouse.

A dozen strange little creatures came running in the front door. *Not animals*, but not anything she had ever seen before either. Some of them looked like the dolls she'd made out of twigs and leaves. Some looked like rough clay figurines. There was even one that looked *exactly* like the tiny Indian man she had thought she'd imagined in the loft of the Sawyers' barn!

But then her aunt called out, "Domovoy, come forth!" and that hairy old man she had been *sure* was a waking dream crawled out from under the stove.

The things surrounded her, and she didn't know whether to shriek or faint.

"Wall," her aunt said. "It's purt plain y'all kin see 'em."

That elicited an understandably hysterical response from her. "*A'course I kin see 'em! Make 'em go away!*"

"Don't be sech a baby," Aunt Jinny replied with faint scorn.

"They ain't a-gonna hurt y'all. I'fact, they's gonna he'p y'all. Stop dancin' on thet stool like a tavern Jezebel wi' five whiskies in 'er."

It wasn't so much Aunt Jinny's matter-of-fact tone as her allusion to a "tavern Jezebel" that got Anna to slowly, and carefully, and with many a doubtful look, lower herself to the floor and take her seat on her stool again. Although she certainly kept her feet well tucked under her skirt and away from the … things … which now clustered around her, staring up at her face.

"These," Aunt Jinny said, "is *Elementals*. Earth Elementals, ac'chully."

"Whassa Elemental?" she asked, not sure she wanted to know the answer.

Aunt Jinny put on the face that told Anna she was about to get a lesson. "There's a thang I call Glory. Some folks call it witchery, I don't hold with that. An' I niver liked th' word *magic*, on account'a *magic* sounds like it ain't no work, an' it's plenty'a work. The Glory's jest a nachural thang. Some got it, some don't, like yaller hair. Issa tool, like a knife. Y'all c'n cut up dinner wi' a knife, or murder a man. Thet don't mean th' knife is bad or good, an' that don't mean the Glory is bad or good, it jest is. They's five kinds-a things what people with Glory can call on. They's called Elements. Earth, Air, Fire, Water, an' Spirit. Each one's got critters. Th' critters kin do stuff fer th' folks what has the right Glory. I got Earth Glory, an' so do y'all. Old Raven's got Spirit Glory. Young Raven's got Fire Glory. Ghosts an' other spirits is what Old Raven kin see an' get t' do stuff fer 'im, but someone wi' Spirit Glory kin see what kinda Glory other people hev, iffen they got it." Jinny smiled with satisfaction at Anna. "An' y'all got it. Like I said, y'all's got Earth Glory. An' *thet's* why y'all got sick back in Soddy. What happens t' th' earth, *y'all* feel, an' I feel, 'cause we're linked by the Glory t'the earth. We get sick, cause th' earth's so pizened there, an' y'all are gonna *get* sick anywhere's th' earth's pizened. Most towns won't hurt y'all much, but y'all ain't a-gonna feel comfortable. Towns like Soddy, wi' all thet pizen from coal an' soot—they'll make y'all dog-sick. Towns like Ducktown, where ain't nothing kin grow? Till I shows y'all how ter pertect yoreself, they'll kill y'all *daid*."

The thing that Jinny had called a "Domovoy" nodded its gray

head ponderously in agreement. "*Daid*," it echoed.

The little creatures clustered about her, all but the tiny Indian. He hopped up on the table and helped himself to cornbread.

It was that—and the glance full of mischief that the tiny man gave her as he stuffed a crumb in his mouth—that finally made her relax a little.

But only a little. "How'd I git this Glory thang?" she asked, a little desperately. "What iffen I don' want it?"

"I dunno where y'all got it. I got it from my Granny an' Granpappy on my Ma's side," Jinny replied. "Yore Ma ain't got it, no more did her Ma. My Pa didn' hev it hisself. My Pa knowed 'bout it, 'cause my Ma had a liddle bit an' Granny and Granpappy had a *lot*. Some people got a liddle, some got it middlin', some got it a lot. I got it middlin'. Ole Raven, he thinks y'all got a lot."

"But what iffen I don' *want* it?" she repeated, her voice getting a little shrill.

"Reckon Raven kin block it up," Jinny admitted reluctantly. "But it'd be a damnfool thang t'do. Y'all wanted t' be a Root Woman on account of y'all *know* y'all ain't niver gonna lack fer a way t' et, right? Wall, this works *with* bein' a Root Woman. Makes all yore potions work better." Anna must have looked as though she was unconvinced, because Jinny scowled. "Hell an' damnation, girl! The fact thet I got Glory's th' reason yore Pa ain't sicker than he is!"

She quailed a little, and felt herself trembling. "But … this's *witchery*, right? Y'all said some folks call it witchery! An' don't the Bible say 'Do not suffer a witch to live'?"

"The Bible *also* says some damn fool thangs like y'all cain't et cheese an' meat t'gether, nor hev linsey-woolsey skirts, nor et crawdads an' ham an' bacon!" Jinny retorted. "It *also* says damn fool thangs like that God kin send bears t' et up liddle kids what makes fun uv a prophet's bald haid! Th' Ole Testyment's *fulla* damn fool thangs, an' tha's a fact!"

She wanted to object … but she knew good and well that the Bible *did* say those things. And … bacon. And ham. Why shouldn't you eat pork? Pigs were easy and cheap to raise—and wild pig was available to anyone who was a decent shot, no matter how poor. She began to waver. Maybe Aunt Jinny was right …

The little critters began to get bored, and fidgeted. Her aunt made a shooing motion and they all ran off. All except the Domovoy. It turned its heavy, bearded head to look at her solemnly.

"*You must be to listening to devushka Virginia,*" it said, in a strangely accented, gravelly voice that seemed to come from inside her head, not through her ears. "*I will go now.*" And just like that, it slipped under the stove, as if it were no thicker than a piece of paper.

She stared. "What ... *is* thet?" she managed.

"Issa Domovoy. Came with Granpappy from Roosha." She got up and went to that shelf where the receipt books were kept. This time she took down a second book, and brought it over to Anna, putting it into her hands. "Here. He wrote some down 'bout all of it. I ain't read all of it. Mostly just bits, but what I read had plenty'a common sense in it. Mebbe it'll help y'all decide y'all don't want t' throw away th' gift God gave y'all." One corner of her mouth quirked. "Y'all said how much y'all liked them stories Missus Sawyer read. Wall, that there book's fulla stories like them. And they's real."

As if this sort of thing happened all the time to her, Aunt Jinny calmly began eating her breakfast. Anna put the book carefully to one side, and ate hers as well, though she was far from calm.

Witchcraft! Her father had accused Aunt Jinny of that, and it turned out he was right!

"Does my Ma know—" she began.

"Thet I got the Glory?" Jinny sniffed. "Why d'ye think she knowed what was wrong with y'all an' thet I could fix it? Why d'ye think she arst me fer potions fer Lew? It weren't no secret, even iffen she couldn' see th' Elementals herself if they was a-standin' on her nose."

So Ma knowed. An' Ma said Aunt Jinny is God-fearin'. Ma ain't niver lied. She might not have told all of the truth—but if Anna and her Pa had known the truth, would she have been willing to go, and him willing to let her? Probably not.

Aunt Jinny clearly knew her Bible too. All those things she had cited ... Anna had read them for herself.

"Time's a-wastin, girl," Aunt Jinny said, interrupting her musings. "Eggs ter collect. Pigs t'feed. Garden t'tend. An' I aim t'teach y'all 'bout where t'find some of the makin's fer potions i' th' woods terday. We ain't a-goin' fer, but we don' need to."

Reluctantly, Anna finished her breakfast, helped with the dishes, and put the book with her Bible, though she did wonder if it was going to burst into flames when it touched the Holy Book. But when it didn't, she wondered, with everything there was to do—would she ever have time to actually read it?

Anna and her aunt returned to the house with baskets overflowing with the makings of several different potions. Jinny's tutelage had been very simple: show Anna the plant she wanted *once*. Wait while Anna examined it carefully. Then Anna herself had to seek out more, until they had enough for a bunch to hang up and dry. Then start over with a new one.

This was probably the least chore-like chore that Anna had done since she had gotten here. This was more like wandering in the woods and picking flowers, except the "flowers" generally weren't pretty, and you had to hunt for them. But other than that—the woods were cool and fragrant, and if she ignored the little eyes peeping at her from odd places—

She told herself desperately they were just wild things, mice, chipmunks, that sort of thing. She didn't believe what she told herself, however, and just as she started feeling relaxed, she'd see one of *them* again, and get unnerved all over again.

She and Jinny came back to the cabin, hung the herbs to dry, washed up, and sat down to supper. Aunt Jinny had warned her that "she'd better get used to bean soup," but the truth was, she never really got tired of it. And she doubted she'd get "used" to it, either.

Even after almost two weeks of eating well, it still seemed like something of a miracle to have three solid, satisfying meals every day—and to end the day with a soup that was substantial enough to be called a "stew" put the cap on days that were mostly good, and often excellent. Besides, her aunt would "tinker" with the soup a little each morning, so that by evening, the taste was always a bit different from the day before.

"I reckon y'all should start on thet book ternight," her aunt said, as they did the dishes. "I'll be a-workin' with the potions t' strengthen 'em up with the Glory." She glanced over at Anna, amused. "Thet's one good thang 'bout finally tellin' y'all. I ain't gotter wait till y'all goes up t'bed no more."

So *that* was what Aunt Jinny had been doing late at night! Another mystery solved …

"Y'all wanter read on th' porch or inside?" she continued.

"Wall …" she hesitated. "I *wanter* read in bed."

"I ain't a-gonna let y'all take a candle up there, fall asleep, an' burn th' house down," her aunt replied, but with a slight smile that took the sting out of the words. "I'll let y'all use th' stove so's I c'n keep one eye on y'all an' th' candle iffen y'all nods off. Climb up."

Astonished that her aunt was permitting her to do this, she took the book and climbed up the ladder to the top of the stove. As she had thought, there was a featherbed up there, covered with a beautifully quilted coverlet. It was warm and exceptionally cozy. But dark.

That is, it *was* dark, until her aunt handed her up a lit candle in a holder with a reflector in the back of it, and showed her where to put it. There was a place made right into the stove, a kind of shelf at the head of the bed before the stonework rose to form the chimney proper, that ensured that even if the candle burned down and guttered into the holder there was no chance of catching anything on fire.

Anna curled up and opened the book.

The first thing she noticed was that Aunt Jinny had almost certainly learned her penmanship from her Granpappy. The words looked almost identical to the ones in the receipt book.

But the moment she started to read, she was transported elsewhere in a way that nothing in the Bible save a very few books, like Esther, and Solomon, had ever done.

By grace of my beloved wife Sally and the Elemental Creatures we share, I, Pavel Ivanov, am writing here for the amusement and education of those of my blood who will follow me.

It was only when the candle guttered out and she suddenly couldn't see to read that she emerged from her self-imposed trance. By this time she knew what a Domovoy was, that her great-great-

grandfather had been driven from his home when the boyar—or
"great lord"—who owned the land his village was on decided to
have a hunting preserve and forest there instead. She knew that
while technically a "serf" ("one very short step from a slave"),
Pavel had been a very learned man because of his magic. That a
priest in his village, also with magic, had taught him the use of
his powers, and his letters, both from the exceedingly young age
of six or so. That when the boyar had driven the villagers from
their homes and set fire to them to force them to leave, he had
gone to the new location and just kept going westward, making
use of his abilities to keep from being pursued. And finding allies
and helpers along the way. It was very like a series of short fairy
tales, except all of the incidents he described ended well instead of
tragically. The candle went out at the point when, in the book, he
had reached Hungary.

She looked up from the book to find that her aunt had finished
her work and was looking up at her with an amused expression.
"The Glory ain't so bad now, is it?" Jinny asked with faint irony.
"Iss like anythin' else. Y'all kin use a axe t'chop wood, or t' take
a feller's haid off. Same with th' Glory."

"How'd he get the Domovoy t' come with him?" she asked,
as she handed the book down to her aunt and climbed down the
ladder to the floor. "I mean, I *guess* this here Domovoy's the same
one he had in Roosha?"

"House got burned up," Jinny said shortly. "The rich man
what wanted the village burned the whole place down. Weren't
no house fer the Domovoy t'stay in. So it follered him. On'y he
didn't know thet till he built this here house. An' iffen y'all don't
go t'sleep yore gonna be dreadful sorry come mornin'."

"Yes'm," she replied obediently, took the book from her aunt
and put it with her Bible, and climbed the ladder into her loft.

But the mere act of placing the book *with* her Bible awoke all
those doubts again, and a few more. Despite what she had learned
about how her mother felt about her, *she* still loved her Ma, and after
reading about Pavel's longing for the home that was lost to him, *she*
was homesick again. Aunt Jinny had let slip that it was possible to
learn how to protect yourself from the poisons in Ducktown and
Soddy—so what if she could get Aunt Jinny to teach her that, right

away? Wouldn't that mean that she could go home after all? And as strong as she was now, she could help with everything, including adding to the family larder by foraging and fishing.

And when Ma sees how much he'p I kin be ... I bet Pa'll figger I'm a he'p too! Why, I'd be jest as good as a boy, almost!

But then, the inescapable truth—to do that, she'd have to learn how to use the Glory. Which was witchcraft.

But Aunt Jinny wasn't the only person in this cabin that knew her Bible ...

And Aunt Jinny was right. There wasn't a single thing in the whole durned New Testament about witchcraft. Not even Apostle Paul, who had *plenty* to say on other subjects, like it being "better to marry than to burn" and about women keeping their mouths shut tight and obeying their men, didn't have a thing to say about witchcraft.

Even Revelations didn't have anything to say about witchcraft, and it was chock *full* of lakes of fire and demons and the Whore of Babylon.

And even in the Old Testament, right there next to the business about not allowing a witch to live, there was King Saul, going to visit the Witch of Endor—who *he* had obviously allowed to live!—in order to consult with the spirit of the Prophet Samuel! And the Prophet Samuel turned right up without anything bad to say about the Witch herself, and gave King Saul the advice he need for fighting the Philistines. So at least *that* book of the Bible seemed to imply that it was perfectly all right to consult witches as long as they were doing the right thing, and not going around flinging curses about.

On top of all of that ... there were some of the things that Pavel had described himself doing that she would very much like to be able to do. How could it be a bad thing to be able to do what Aunt Jinny did, and make potions *better* so they could make people well? How could it be a bad thing, to be able to talk with all of those little critters, and bargain with them to help you? How could it be bad to get them to make it so your crops didn't fail, and your animals all prospered, as long as you shared with them as needed it and weren't selfish about it? Hadn't Aunt Jinny *said* she made up bundles of food and distributed them to widows in

Ducktown? If that wasn't doing *exactly* the kind of good Jesus said to do, then what was?

Finally she got back out of bed and onto her knees again. The cabin was completely dark now, except for the very faint, red glow of the coals in the stove, banked until tomorrow.

Please, Lord Jesus, she prayed, squeezing her eyes tight shut and clenching her hands together so hard they hurt. *Please. I don' know what ter do. I need Y'all t'show me what ter do! Please, please give me a sign. Show me iffen this Glory, this witchery Aunt Jinny wants for t'teach me, is good in Yore Sight or evil. Please, Lord Jesus, show me th'way! Amen.*

And it felt, as she whispered the word *amen*, that a great weight had been lifted from her shoulders. *Really* tired now, she climbed back into the featherbed and sank down into its softness.

And she opened her eyes again, without ever being aware that she had fallen asleep, to find that it was morning.

And a little critter seemingly made of oak leaves, twigs, and earth, with an acorn for a head, was staring at her from its perch on her pillow, not three inches from her nose.

Before she could move, or even take a startled breath, it *giggled*, and vanished with a tiny *pop*.

She stared at the pillow for a very long time.

Wall … I reckon thet's a sign …

8

Jinny had made hoecakes and bacon for breakfast, and Anna had noticed a pattern about breakfast. Whenever Jinny felt pleased, she made hoecakes, and cut into the bacon. When Jinny was preoccupied or annoyed, it was mush, or fried mush. So—she must be feeling pleased about the way the conversation had gone last night.

She's a-gonna be happier'n a dead hog in the sunshine in a moment. "I reckon y'all better teach me how t'use the Glory, Aunt Jinny," she said, trying to sound like something other than "resigned." Truth be told, it wasn't too hard, not with hoecakes and bacon in front of her.

Aunt Jinny just smiled—the self-satisfied smile of someone who is refraining from saying "I told you so"—and drizzled maple syrup over Anna's hoecake. "Good, we kin start ternight," was all she said out loud. "Plenty to do till sundown."

Oh, good. Anna was a little relieved that they weren't going to jump straight into this. She was entirely sure that she wasn't ready for getting all wound up in witchery, no matter that Jesus had granted her a sign, and she'd much rather put it off entirely for a while until she got used to the idea. She finished her breakfast, helped Jinny with the dishes, then went to collect the eggs while Jinny mucked out the pigs.

From there, Jinny sent her down into the bottom of the vegetable garden, near where the lane ended and the fence around the huge garden plot began, to weed. Knowing what was coming next when a human went into the garden—tasty weeds uprooted for them with no effort, and bugs picked off the plants and tossed within easy reach—the chickens followed her down.

The garden was surrounded by a rail fence, which looked deceptively crude and weak, but was strong enough to climb and jump on. There wasn't a gate in it—there was a stile that you used to climb over it. Knowing what she knew now, Anna suspected that this fence was witched in some way to keep critters out of the garden, because Aunt Jinny never seemed to have any trouble with anything but a few persistent bugs and the usual weeds, even though there were plenty of succulent vegetables to tempt deer, rabbits, possums, and raccoons. And the chickens never strayed outside that fence, either, and they certainly could have gotten over it with no effort at all. More witchery?

Prolly. But that just underscored the fact that so far, nothing she had seen or inferred about this witchery was *bad*.

Kinda looks like thet sign was th' right one, she thought, reluctantly.

Down on her knees in the soft, fragrant earth, she soon got into the rhythm of things, and the gentle chickens scratched along beside her, making soothing, crooning noises and happily gobbling up whatever she tossed in their direction. It occurred to her in that moment that, here with Aunt Jinny, life was truly excellent. The chores she had been set, although they were not exactly *fun*, certainly had more about them that was pleasant than they had at home. She wasn't breathing in smoke, she felt wonderful, and she was surrounded by growing things that were thriving instead of struggling to live. The chickens in particular were amusing; particularly desirable bugs elicited a competition that sometimes ended in the winner being pursued the length of a row of vegetables, at least until she swallowed her prize. It was peaceful down here, and if she could just shake the feeling of being homesick, it would be a little slice of Heaven.

But even with feeling homesick at this moment, the world around her was drowsy and quietly beautiful.

Then, between one moment and the next, everything changed.

The chickens suddenly alerted, heads all going up and swiveling toward the lane. And then, abruptly, they left. Not running, but not dawdling either, they moved quickly and with unnerving quiet in a tight group up to the cabin, as if they wanted to escape something that was coming.

Everything suddenly got brighter, and oddly, a little colder, a chill as if a goose had walked over her grave. And Anna felt a prickling between her shoulder blades, as if someone was watching her.

Something inside her told her to be very careful about what she did next.

There could be a bear behind her in the lane—but the Ravens had promised that there would be no bears near the cabin. There could be a wolf or even a panther, but neither of those would have brought cold and brightness with them, would they?

They might if they's witchy-critters.

But it probably wasn't some*thing*. It was probably some*one*. If there was someone there in the lane ... it would be extremely rude to ignore them and keep weeding. But if that someone was witchy—which she suddenly suspected was the case, given how oddly the chickens had acted—she needed to *think*, and not act carelessly or impulsively.

And there was the chance that the person wasn't merely witchy. It could be a devil. Aunt Jinny wasn't devilish, but devils were attracted to witchery, and devils were always ready for a chance to trick you into a "bargain" that was no bargain at all, and wouldn't a devil do his best to catch a budding witch? Seventeen Halloweens-worth of stories about devils and hants that she had absorbed sitting in the shadows at firesides and on porches warned her that if that was the case, she needed to be twice as careful as she would be with a witchy-human, and never show a lick of fear.

And even if it wasn't a devil, the way the chickens had acted and the prickling between her shoulder blades warned her this was someone who could probably do her a lot of harm if disrespected.

So she stood up, still with her back to the lane, brushed her skirt and apron off carefully, dusted her hands, so that she'd show proper politeness by making sure she was clean and tidy, and *then* turned.

To see what was literally the most beautiful woman she had ever seen in her life standing a little distance away in the lane, with her head cocked slightly to one side. She had the face of an angel, the body of a heathen goddess, and her garments were— unbelievable.

She wore a gown of vivid green that was like nothing Anna had ever seen before. It had no real waist, and nothing like a full skirt; instead it fell down from the shoulders in a widening column, with full sleeves gathered into cuffs, and a neckline gathered with a gold ribbon. In fact, if it hadn't been that it was so glorious, it would have reminded Anna of her own nightdress. The cuffs were of gold embroidery, there were more bands of gold embroidery on the sleeves, and gold trim that matched the cuffs at the hem, and it was made of no fabric that Anna had ever seen before, but it looked soft and lustrous, sleek and shiny, with a metallic sheen to it. Over it she wore something *like* an apron, that wasn't an apron, of a slightly darker green; it appeared to be a front and back piece sewn together under the sleeves. The shoulder straps were of bands of the same gold embroidery. There was a panel of that embroidery across the top of the garment, and a thicker band of it running down the middle of the front from the top piece to the hem— which also had a band of gold embroidery around the bottom, just like the dress worn beneath it. This appeared to be made of a thicker fabric, not quite as shiny, but just as soft and lustrous.

But most astonishing of all was what the woman wore on her head. It was a kind of pointed half-moon of gold-embroidered fabric that was fastened to a kind of cap of gold beads that hung over the woman's forehead, with fringes of gold beads on either side of the woman's head. This astonishing piece of headgear was held on with a huge swath of ribbon tied in an extravagent bow around the hair at the nape of the woman's neck.

And her hair! It was—crimson. There was no other name for a color that intensely red. It was decidedly *not* ginger, nor strawberry blond. It was red as holly berries, or completely ripe strawberries, glossy and thick as the mane of a prize horse, cascading in a shining waterfall all the way down to her feet.

The woman's features were so perfect it seemed as if they could not be real, like the face of an angel. Her complexion was exactly like cream, with a hint of pink on her cheeks. And the crown jewel in a face that literally left Anna feeling stunned was the pair of eyes an impossible green with hints of blue in it, eyes that looked at her with an expression she simply could not read. The cool, dispassionate gaze, the expressionless face—there was something so uncanny about both that it made Anna shiver.

Then the woman's eyes widened as if in surprise; something like a heat-shimmer passed over her—

And then she was wearing a perfectly ordinary—and yet, extraordinary—dress. Perfectly ordinary, in that it was no different than any dress and apron you'd see on anyone who was moderately prosperous from Soddy—anyone who was just ordinary folks, that is, and not someone like a mine owner's wife, who'd wear gowns not made for heavy work. Just a print dress with full sleeves and a full skirt with a round collar, and an apron tied over it. Extraordinary in that Anna had never, ever seen a print like this, *anywhere*. It wasn't a flour-sack print, nor a store-bought muslin, nor a simple, plain color. It was as green as the last dress, but subtly patterned in curling, irregularly waving lines of lighter and darker green, and the apron was a light green that matched the lighter stripes, instead of the usual white or cream. Her hair—still that brilliant red, but this time in a tidy braid wrapped primly around her head then coiled into a knot at the nape of her neck, put up like a grown woman's should be, had a huge green ribbon bow above the coiled knot.

Anna found it very difficult to breathe. Because the woman was still so beautiful that she didn't seem to belong on this earth.

And Anna felt herself to be as plain as a mud brick, and as clumsy as a newborn foal in this woman's presence.

Footsteps behind her told her that her aunt had seen the newcomer and was approaching. And she had never felt so grateful for the presence of another person in her life.

"Howdy, Jolene," her aunt said dryly, as if the woman's appearance was nothing out of the ordinary.

"Hello, Virginia," came the reply, in a low, dulcet voice, made for breaking hearts. The woman smiled. "So this is your new apprentice." It wasn't a question. As if this Jolene knew exactly what Anna had said to her aunt over breakfast.

"My niece," Jinny corrected, with a certain hardness in her voice that surprised Anna. "Y'all ain't t' interfere with her, no way, nohow. I got my limits, an' messin' with my kin is one 'f 'em."

"I wouldn't dream of interfering," Jolene replied, in tones that suggested the opposite, and smiled again, this time finally wearing an expression—an expression of mischief. Not malicious mischief, or at least, not intentionally malicious—but the sort of mischief gotten into by someone who is generally careless of the repercussions her mischief causes. Especially when those repercussions happen to someone else, and not her.

Who is this woman? Anna wondered with bewilderment. *Or maybe ... it ain't a who. It's a what.* Because she didn't seem human, somehow. And now Jolene was bending the full force of her concentration on Anna, head tilted to the side in a way that reminded Anna of an emotionless insect. *Or maybe I'm the bug to her.* Anna wasn't sure what had prompted that thought—but the instant it sprang into her mind, she was convinced it was true.

Whatever she was—it was witchy. Anna *knew* in her bones that what she was looking at right now was absolutely nothing like the "real" Jolene. Nor was the "Jolene" she'd seen in that gold and green gown a few moments ago. The real Jolene might not be something a human could easily look at—as the Bible said about angels, where their mere appearance made people fall on the ground, unable to look on them.

"Wall. We both know th' truth o' thet," Jinny replied, with no inflection whatsoever. "What brung y'all t' Lonesome Holler so early this here mornin'?"

"A stirring in the earth," Jolene replied. "A hint of news. I came looking for it, and here it is! You've finally taken an apprentice!"

"She's my kin," Jinny repeated. "Seems fittin' I teach 'er what I knows."

Anna kept her mouth shut. Jinny was very much on the defensive. It was clear that she wished Jolene would go away, but didn't dare do or say anything that might offend her. There was more than respect; there was fear.

"And have you introduced her to the Ravens?" Jolene persisted.

"The Ravens innerduced thesselves to 'er." Jinny was giving absolutely no information away. She could have said something about how the elder of the two seemed to approve of Anna, but she didn't.

"And so now you are all good neighbors together." Jolene clapped her hands together, briefly applauding this bit of information. "Good. Peace in the Holler is something to strive for, and pleases me."

Jinny looked as if she was going to say something, but held whatever it was back. "Just so," she said finally.

"But I should give your apprentice a little welcome gift, something to mark her entry into the world of magic," Jolene continued, eyes sparkling now with that spirit of mischief. "What do I have—" She plunged her hand into her apron pocket as Jinny stepped forward to put herself between Anna and Jolene. "Ah, here, just the thing!" She held out her hand, palm open. On it were resting a dozen wire hairpins.

They were probably brass, but they shone like gold in the sunlight, each one the sort of U-shaped pin with crimped arms that Anna's Ma used, but each one finished with a blue-and-gold bead at the head of the U, so that the bead would nestle in the wearer's hair when the pin was in place.

"Go ahead, Virginia, you can take them and look them over, and see I mean no harm." There was that hint of malicious delight in making Aunt Jinny uncomfortable.

Aunt Jinny held out her hand over the fence, and Jolene tipped the pins into it. Jinny examined the pins minutely for a very long time before sighing, as if she was oddly disappointed in not finding poison or an evil spell on them. Jolene took them back and beckoned to Anna. "Come here, apprentice," she ordered imperiously. "I shall give my gift properly."

Anna glanced at her aunt. Jinny nodded reluctantly. Anna approached the fence.

Jolene seized her braids, brought them up to the top of her head, pinned them in place, crossed them over each other, and pinned them in place again, then turned Anna around by the shoulder so that Anna's back was to her. There was some deft and surprisingly gentle pinning going on at the back of her head, then Jolene turned her back around and looked her over critically. "Much better," the woman declared. "Now you look like the woman you are, not the child you were."

"Thenkee, Miz Jolene," Anna said awkwardly. Then added,

"Them pins is somethin' I been hankerin' arter fer a while."

Jolene smiled, as if she was very much aware of that.

"She do look all growed up," Aunt Jinny admitted reluctantly.

"Good. Let this remind you to treat her as an adult, not a child," Jolene stated.

"What's them beads, iffen y'all please, Miz Jolene?" Anna asked, touching the pretty things in her hair and blushing a little with pride. "They's purtier than flowers." Oh, how long she had wanted to be able to put up her hair! It had been so mortifying to have it down in a little girl's braids! To have the pins alone, made out of any old wire, would have been a great gift, but to be given such pretty ones! No matter what Aunt Jinny thought, Jolene had already given her something precious.

"Lapis lazuli," Jolene replied. "It isn't a *precious* gem, but it is a gemstone. It suits your hair better than my malachite." She patted her own hair, and now Anna noticed that bright green beads studded her braids as well, beads with the same pattern of dark and light wavy lines as the print of her dress. "Useful too; thanks to the beads, you shan't have to hunt in your hair for the pins when you take it down for the night."

"Yes'm," Anna agreed. "Thenkee ever so kindly, Miz Jolene," she added earnestly.

Jolene looked pleased, and waved the thanks off. "Just a *neighborly* gift of welcome. I look forward to our next meeting. Good day, apprentice. Good day, Virginia."

And with that, she turned, and although she didn't seem to hurry at all, nevertheless she walked with great speed and unnatural grace down the lane, and either due to the color of her gown or some other, uncanny reason, she was soon lost to sight in the shadows.

Aunt Jinny let out a huge sigh, as if she had been holding in her breath. "Thet coulda gone wuss," she said aloud. "Much wuss."

"Is ..." Suddenly Anna didn't want to say Jolene's name out loud, as if by doing so she might be summoned. "Is she a witch? Has she got the Glory?"

"She ain't a witch," her aunt replied. "But she got the Glory, and *powerful*, and you be keerful, *real* keerful, 'round her. She ain't a proper woman." And she held up her hand to stop any more questions. "I'll 'splain later, when y'all know more. Right now, I reckon I need a big cuppa tea, right quick."

Anna kept touching her hair with delight as they made their way back to the cabin; once they got there, Aunt Jinny poured them both cups of tea, and for the longest time just sat there with her cup in her hand, not drinking at all. Anna kept quiet, leaving her aunt with her own thoughts.

Finally she drank the entire cup in one long gulp and set it down. "Fer some reason, Jolene thinks kindly of y'all, girl," her aunt said, looking at her penetratingly. "She respects me, but she thinks kindly of y'all. Maybe on account of yore young. Don't 'spect that t'last. She's got her own ways an' her own notions, an' *do not ever get 'twixt her and somethin' she wants*. The 'kindly' face'll turn stormy in a heartbeat, an' I mean the kinder storm what flattens crops an' kills what's in its path."

Thet—seems kinda harsh, Anna thought, but she hoped she wasn't letting her face betray her skepticism.

"Y'all don't b'lieve me," Jinny observed. "I'm a-tellin' y'all, Jolene ain't a proper woman, she don't think like us, an' she's dangerous. Stay outen her path, things'll probably be all right. Get in her path, an' she'll trample y'all like a runaway hoss without thinkin' 'bout it twice."

Well, that seemed a lot more likely. Anna had seen plenty of ruthless women in Soddy, women who were *quite* willing to knock down and walk over anything and anyone to get what they wanted.

This was just someone—or some*thing*—with a different kind of power than social power to get what she wanted.

Cain't think how I could get a-twixt her and what she wants.

"And don't go next or nigh her," Jinny continued. "Not iffen y'all kin he'p it. And make it *Yes'm* and *No ma'am*, and real polite. Don't git her mad."

"Yes'm," Anna agreed. Then ventured, "But she was awful nice t'me. She not only give me them hair-pins, she put up my hair fer me."

"… an' it looks plumb fine, too," Aunt Jinny admitted. "I cain't account fer that. It don't make no sense, 'cause—" She paused, searching for words. "Y'all iver see big hoss, a herd mare what knows she's in charge?"

"No ma'am." Anna shook her head. "Leastwise, not iffen she weren't bein' rid or drove."

Aunt Jinny searched her memory again. "What 'bout a big cat?" she offered. "Big ole tomcat what runs th' neighborhood, an' ever'thang gits outer his way, even dawgs. An' iffen he gits inter yore house and goes marchin' 'long a shelf, ever'thang on that there shelf goes right t'the floor on account of he shoulders it right outa his way? Jolene's like thet. She jest shoulders ever'thang outa her way, an' ever'thang with any sense high-tails it afore she kin git there."

Anna just nodded, because it was obvious Aunt Jinny was going to hammer on about this until Anna agreed with her. And probably past that, until she was certain-sure Anna agreed with her and would do as she said.

Aunt Jinny sighed, and seemed convinced. "All right. Time's a-wastin'. Let's git some dinner, an' do th' laundry, an' we'll do 'nother receipt."

"Aunt Jinny, when y'all a-gonna teach me how t' put th' Glory in them receipts?" she ventured.

Her aunt barked a laugh. "Y'all're gitten th' cart afore the horse, girl," she said. "Fust, y'all gotter be able t' *see* th' Glory. An' we're gonna see 'bout thet ternight."

She found it hard to concentrate on anything other than that—up until the moment when they finished the laundry and she went to copy down another receipt in her receipt book. Then, there was no choice but to concentrate. The scorn her aunt would—rightly!—heap on her for making a mistake did not bear thinking about.

So she copied it down, letter by careful letter, and then made it up, pinch by palmful by handful, and got her aunt's curt nod of approval. And then it was time to herd the chickens into their house, close them in for the night, wash up at the well, change into her clean nightdress, and have supper. Aunt Jinny seemed to have recovered her aplomb, because she was back to her usual laconic self.

It was only when the dishes were clean and dry and put away, water was set in jugs to warm in the stove niches for tomorrow, the coals were banked, and the sun setting that Jinny turned to the subject that had been burning in Anna's mind since Jinny had proclaimed she was going to learn to "see" the Glory.

Jinny led the way out to the porch and ordered her to "set." Jinny moved the other chair to a position closer to Anna than Anna remembered her ever being before.

"This's a tricksy thang," Jinny warned her. "It ain't gradual. It takes a kinder peculiar twist in yore haid t'make it work, an' y'all might not do it th' fust, or second, or even twentieth time."

"Yes'm," Anna said, since a reply seemed to be required of her.

"Look out there over yonder, at th' fence," Aunt Jinny directed. "I gotta lotta Glory down thar, concentrated inter somethin' high-falutin' folks call a *shield*, what keeps critters I don' want comin' past th' fence. Thet includes th' bad Elementals."

There're bad Elementals?

Jinny glanced down for a moment. So did Anna. And she discovered in that moment that they had an audience, a little circle of watching twig-critters, and rock-critters, and mushroom critters. And peeking over the edge of the porch were shyer things that looked human—at least, the tops of their heads did—although it was hard to tell in the growing gloom.

"What's bad that *can* get in?" she wanted to know. She wasn't going to ask about Jolene directly, obviously …

"Anythin' what's got enough Glory of its own," her aunt told her, and reminded her with a *look* that she'd said Jolene was almighty powerful.

"So how'm I s'posed to see this shield thing?" she asked. "Or the Glory?"

For once, her aunt seemed uncertain. "I dunno," she said, finally, after a long and uncomfortable pause. "My Granny said it was diff'rent fer ev'body. I allus saw it, from th' time I was a liddle thang. Like I allus saw th' Elemental critters. But bein' in Soddy, y'all'd niver hev seed the critters, and there weren't nothing givin' off 'nuff Glory fer y'all t'see thet, either."

Anna looked down at the ring of critters around her chair—or rather, she looked down into the darkness where they were, because by this point the sun had completely set, and down here in the holler, things got dark quick.

She kind of squinched her eyes up to try to make them out, and that was when she realized she *could* still see them. There was a faint glow around them. Was that the Glory?

Just as she noticed that, the glow seemed to get stronger and stronger, until it was no problem at all to make out the little critters, each of them surrounded by a sort of halo of dark golden light, like the kind of light that lies gently over the land just before sunset on an autumn afternoon.

She carefully raised her eyes, still keeping that glow in her mind, until she had the fence in her field of vision.

And there it was. That same golden glow at the edges of the garden.

"It ain't a wall!" she exclaimed with surprise. "It's—kinda a bowl, clapped down over th' garden, iffen th' bowl were sorta squared off!"

"Wall, knock me over with a feather!" her aunt exclaimed in an astonished voice. "I sure didn' thank y'all'd see it thet quick!"

"Why ain't it a round bowl, Aunt Jinny?" she asked, because she could *see* how the Glory swirled and ebbed and flowed, and how it knotted up at those corners. And she understood, somehow, that if the shield-thing had been based on a circle rather than the rectangle of the fence, none of that would be happening.

"On account'a I cast it on th'fence, t'give it somethin' t' anchor on, like Granny taught me," her aunt replied. "I know, I know. Thangs don't flow smooth 'round corners. But Granny said 'twas stronger iffen it got a anchor."

Now Anna turned her attention to the garden, and to her astonishment, she saw that every plant had a very, very faint glow in that same golden color. "The plants!" she gasped. "Th' corn's a-glowin'!"

"Great hop-toads!" her aunt exclaimed. "Old Raven *was* right! You got it *strong*, girl! I cain't see thet! Thet there's what ev'thing what's alive has of th' Glory, just on account'a it's alive. Not one of our kind in a hunnert'd see thet!" Then she paused and added, "Don't get all hoity-toity over thet. Jest 'cause y'all kin *see* somethin' it don' mean y'all know what t'do with it!"

"Yes'm," Anna said, still looking around her in utter entrancement at how *pretty* everything was with that glow about it. "Iss like a receipt. I kin write her down, but thet don' mean I know how t' make her up, I don' know what the plants in the receipt look like a-growin', an' I sure as shootin' don' know how t'put the Glory in 'em t' make 'em better."

"My land," Jinny replied, sounding relieved. "My flibbertigibbet sister done give birth t' a gel with sense in her haid. Lawd hev mercy, it's a miracle."

She sounded sincere. Anna smiled a little.

Then she started to notice pain. It started out as a sort of dull throb, and the feeling that her eyes were dry and tired. Then it grew until the pain was definite, sharp, and located right behind her eyes. "Aunt Jinny!" she exclaimed. "Is this s'posed t' hurt?!"

"Let it go!" her aunt ordered sharply, and somehow, she did; the world plunged back into ordinary darkness, lit only by fireflies and the rising moon, and the pain dulled immediately to nothing more than sore-ish eyes and a light, dull headache.

"Usin' the Sight is like usin' a muscle y'all ain't niver used afore," her aunt explained, as Anna rubbed her watering eyes. "It hurts at fust. Th' more y'all use it, th' less it'll hurt, an' the longer y'all will be able t'use it."

"Like runnin'?" she asked. "When yore legs git all sore, but they gets better, an' the more y'all run, th' better y'all run?"

"'Zactly like runnin'," Jinny replied, and tapped her on the shoulder. "Come inter th' house. We'll hev some tea. Thet'll he'p."

Anna was not at all loath to do that, because the headache reminded her sharply of the headaches she had back in Soddy that never seemed to end. When both of them were sitting at the table, a lit candle between them and cups of warm, honey-sweetened tea in their hands, Jinny beamed at her with approval. "Y'all done good, Anna," she said. "Y'all done real good. I dunno where y'all got the Glory from, but y'all got it strong. But more'n thet, y'all got good sense. Thet's a good combination."

Anna sipped her tea, noticing a slightly more astringent aftertaste than usual. "Y'all put more willerbark innit," she said aloud.

Her aunt smiled even wider. "An' here, when I fust tol' yore Ma t'send y'all t'me, I figgered y'all was gonna be a burden an' I was gonna hev t'lead y'all around like a liddle chile," she said. "Y'all ain't been here but a fortnight, an' y'all kin see the Glory an' th' Elementals, y'all kin foller a receipt an' knows what th' makin's look like a-growin', an' y'all kin tell when I added somethin' t' y'all's tea. I swan, I am 'bout to bust with how proud y'all are a-makin' me!"

Well … this was unexpected, but very welcome. Anna smiled, and felt far better than just the tea could have made her. "I got th' *best* teacher!" she burst out. "An' not nobody could'a arst fer a better aunt!"

And at that moment, every bit of her homesickness faded away.

Her aunt flushed, apparent even in the candlelight, but looked pleased. "Pshaw," she said. "Teacher gotter hev a good pupil too."

Anna knew by this point that this was as demonstrative as her aunt was going to get, so she just smiled and nodded, and sipped her tea until it was gone. "I'll wash up," she said, standing up and taking her aunt's cup from her. "Y'all got potions t' put th' Glory inter ternight?"

Her aunt yawned and covered it with the back of her hand. "Not ternight. I do a passel of 'em t'gether an' I ain't got 'nuff t'trouble with yet. I'm a-thinkin' bed would be good fer both of us. Don' ferget t' take yore hair down an' put them pins somewhere's safe till mornin'." She paused as if to say something, but didn't. Instead she made a shooing motion with her hands.

Anna pulled the pins out of her hair, counting them carefully to make sure she got them all out—though the beads made that a lot easier. There was an empty pottery jam pot that she had washed out earlier sitting on the counter next to the sink. "Aunt Jinny, kin I hev this jam pot fer my pins?" she called, as her aunt sat down on the edge of her bed.

"Take't," her aunt said. "Iffen I need more, I kin trade fer 'em or make 'em. I'll show y'all later. They's good clay at the stream, an' th' Domovoy'll he'p."

Assured by this, she fetched the pot, put the pins in it, and put both safely with her great-granpappy's book and her Bible. *Could* she claim Pavel as her great-granpappy even though he wasn't strictly her blood? But they shared the same power. It felt right that she should.

Then she blew out the candle, felt her way up the ladder to her bed, and although the bed was *extremely* tempting, took the time to say her prayers.

But tonight, they ended a little differently.

Thenkee, Lord Jesus, fer givin' me thet sign. This feels right an' good.

Then she paused a moment, and added—
An' please let me not get acrost of Jolene.

Then, prompted by an impulse she couldn't resist, she added one more thing. *Iffen she'll let me—I'd like t'be her friend. Amen.*

9

The cabin shook with a mighty thunderclap that sent Anna catapulting out of her dream with a shriek. It was still dark out, but a flash of lightning followed by an immediate crash of thunder lit up the loft. Rain made its own muted roar on the roof.

"Aunt Jinny?" she called in alarm, not knowing whether or not the next lightning bolt was going to hit the cabin and set it afire.

"Jest a thunderstorm." The sound of the door being opened, followed by a cold gust of wind, sent her scrambling on her hands and knees across the loft to close the window. It was wet, but not *too* wet, and fortunately she hadn't left anything under it. "I gotta lightnin' rod *an'* I put th' Glory on th' house so it ain't gonna get hit, there ain't hail, an' the rain ain't so bad it's gonna flatten the crops none. Ac'chully, it'll do 'em some good, it's been a mite dry."

The door closed again. Anna peeked over the edge of the loft and saw her aunt poking up the fire. "This's jest a good, soakin' rain—" She was interrupted by another peel of thunder that shook the house. "'Cept fer th' noise. Reckon it'll rain most've th' day. Good day fer bakin'. When it gits light, y'all run t' the chicken house an' feed 'em there, an' give 'em a pan o' water. They ain't a-gonna come out in weather like this."

"We ain't a-gonna need t'muck out th' pigs, at least," Anna observed from above.

"They's a-gonna stay in their house too, I reckon. Mebbe come out fer a bath. Pigs like a bath. Go back ter bed; ain't no

132

use gettin' up till they's light 'nuff t'see by."

Another lightning strike, but this time it was far enough away that Anna was able to count to "seven-Mississippi" before the thunder came. Then it was just the rain on the roof, which was always soporific, and she drifted right off, only to be awakened again by her aunt tapping on the ladder with a broomstick.

She opened her eyes on thin, gray light; it was enough to see by but just barely.

On the other hand, the enticing aromas of fresh cornbread and bacon came from below, which was more than enough for her to climb out of bed and down the ladder.

"Breakfus' fust," Aunt Jinny told her. "Then git yerself dressed, give them chickens feed and water, come back ter the porch, an' I'll hev a pail of slops fer the pigs." She set to her breakfast, but her aunt didn't seem in any great hurry for her to go, so she took her time over it.

When she went to get dressed, however, her aunt frowned for a moment, then got some twine. She passed the twine under Anna's skirt and up through the waistband on the right side, hiked the skirt up with the twine, and tied it off, then did the same on the left side. "Now y'all got yer hands free," she pointed out, as Anna blushed at her exposed legs. "An' yore skirt ain't gonna draggle in th' mud. Consarned stupid thangs, skirts," she added, crossly. "It's why I got m'self rid of 'em as soon as I could. Won't even wear one t'town."

"But don't people *talk*?" Anna asked, taking the square of oilcloth with a hole in the middle that her aunt unfolded and handed to her, and pulling it over her head.

"An' gi' me one good reason why I should care?" Aunt Jinny countered. "What're they gonna do? Ruint my marriage prospects?" She laughed sardonically. "I be old 'nuff thet I c'n do what I wants, an' nobody burns ol' wimmin as witches no more. Asides, they need me more'n I'll ever need *them*. They knows it. Now skedaddle."

Anna skedaddled, scuttling off to the chicken coop where some very hungry chickens assessed the weather and grumpily settled down to eat and then go back to their nests. The pigs, however, were perfectly happy in the rain. *She* was perfectly happy to get back inside, and then, at Jinny's suggestion, change out of her damp clothing back into her dry nightdress.

"I'm a-gonna bake, an' I don' want y'all underfoot," Jinny told her. "Y'all been pretty good 'bout chores, an' I reckon y'all deserve a restday. So jest broom up th' floor, then climb up on th' stove with yore Great-Granpappy's book an' have a read till dinner."

The rain had brought a definite chill with it, Anna's feet were still cold from paddling through the puddles, and that sounded like a prescription for a perfect morning to her. She swept the floor—possibly with more haste than accuracy, though her aunt didn't complain— got her book, and climbed up onto the warm stove. The featherbed was heaven, even if she did have to prop herself into a somewhat awkward position to read in the thin light coming from the windows. Her great-grandfather's handwriting was so neat and precise she didn't have to squint; it was as good as book-printing.

She had left him at the border with Hungary. This was all new to him. Now he was about to enter a land where the language was entirely different from his own, and he was exceedingly cautious about approaching this place.

I crossed in the wilderness, away from roads, villages, and potential border guards. I made my camp for the night, and took such a thin meal as I could manage from nuts, mushrooms, and plants that I knew were nourishing. But my provisions were scanty, and winter fast approached. I knew I would need to attempt to contact another Elemental Master and beg help of him, soon. So that night, before sleep, I invoked the curious Elementals of this place and begged them to teach me the local languages as I slept.

She had to read that twice before she was sure she had read it correctly. *What? Them critters can give y'all a different language?*

She looked up from the book to ask her aunt; Jinny was hard at work on a pie crust, from the smell of things there was cornbread in the oven already, and she was *surrounded* by the little critters seemingly made of sticks and stones, leaves and flowers, no two of them alike, all of them watching her as if she was providing them with the best entertainment they had ever seen.

And movement to her side caught her attention.

One of them was sitting on the edge of the featherbed, watching *her* intently.

This was a little thing that looked like a crude doll fashioned of mud, with two shiny, dark brown pebbles for eyes. It stared up at her fearlessly. She looked back down at it, not entirely sure what to make of this.

Finally, she called down to her aunt. "Aunt Jinny? This here book says Great-Granpappy got the critters t'larn him languages."

"Iffen he says so, then thet's what they c'n do," her aunt replied, not looking up from the careful lattice-work she was weaving on top of what looked like a rhubarb pie.

Pie! Her mouth watered, and for a moment she was distracted. Then she recalled herself. "Wall, how does I do thet?"

"Arst 'em," came the short answer. She waited a moment, but when nothing more was forthcoming, she turned to the mud-man. "C'n y'all larn me Cherokee?" she asked, hopefully.

The mud-man put his head to one side, and mimed sleeping.

"I gots t'be asleep?" She wasn't entirely certain she wanted any of these critters near her while she was sleeping and unable to keep a wary eye on them. On the other hand—knowing Cherokee could be really useful.

The creature nodded. She sighed, but made up her mind. "Wall, *will* y'all larn me Cherokee?"

She had expected some sort of bargaining session to ensue. She wasn't sure what she had that she could bargain with, but she certainly did not expect to get her wish for free.

But the little man just bobbed his head *yes*, without any more prompting on her part. She waited, but the subject seemed to be closed. She went back to the book.

Her aunt startled her by reaching up to where she was curled up and slapping her knee. "Y'all c'n come outa thet book now," she said, amused. "Dinnertime. Pie fer arter."

Well, she didn't have to be invited twice! She closed the book, marking her place with the strip of embroidered ribbon she had found in it. She wished she had more of it, to decorate the bottom of a skirt and the cuffs of a waist—though then she'd have been afraid to wear either for fear of spoiling them. She climbed down and put the book up on the shelf before setting the table for dinner.

Still, her mind was back in that book even as she ate. Great-Granpappy Pavel had been seriously alarmed when the only "Earth

Master" he could find was what he called a "boyar," a title he had mentioned before, and obviously was someone very important and very rich—the same kind of person who had burned down his village and destroyed the crops to make a hunting preserve out of the area. He had been even more alarmed to awaken the next day—the Hungarian language fortunately well implanted in his mind—to find himself surrounded by the boyar's men. He had been certain he was about to be ushered into a prison.

But instead, he was escorted to a house of the sort that surely only a President could live in! Rooms and rooms and rooms, furnishings that, despite Pavel's careful descriptions, she could not quite wrap her mind around. And to his shock—but eventual delight—he found himself welcomed as a guest and an equal. His shabby clothing was all replaced "in the Hungarian style," whatever that meant, he was feasted and given his own room as big as this cabin with a soft, soft bed in it of the like she had never heard. She had just begun the next part, where he'd recovered from the journey so far and his host was asking him what his intentions were, when Aunt Jinny interrupted her for dinner.

"I reckon today we'll get inter th' last'a the close in thet chest, hev a look in 'nother place I might'a stashed a thing or two, then reckon what I'm a-gonna need fer when y'all get a liddle more meat on your bones," Jinny said, dishing out a slice of pie with scarlet juice running out of it. "Then next time Matt goes inter Ducktown, I c'n go with 'im an' git what we'll need."

Anna wanted to just inhale that pie at the first bite, but she went slowly, carefully savoring every bite—because it was obvious at this point that Aunt Jinny didn't use a lot of wheat flour, preferring to make baked goods with the corn meal she herself could raise. So when she *did* make something with wheat flour, it was a special occasion.

"C'n I go with?" she asked timidly, expecting the usual answer. But this time, Aunt Jinny paused.

"We'll see," she said, surprising the heck out of Anna. "Y'all took t' usin' th' Glory faster nor I'd'a thunk. An' y'all hev it powerful strong. So … mebbe. Iffen y'all hev larned how t' pertec' yoreself. We'll be a-crossin' thet thar bridge when we gits to't."

Well that actually drove all thoughts of the book out of her head for a moment. She might *finally* get to see Ducktown, and see for herself if it really was the hellscape her aunt described. *And* she'd get to go to at least one store! *And* they'd be getting cloth—or at least flour or chicken feed in matching flour or feed sacks—to make her something new!

"Y'all's gonna need a wool skirt fer winter," her aunt continued. "They don' put up flour an' feed in wool. Wool coat, too. An' wool stockin's. Ain't a-gonna hev y'all freeze, an' a shawl ain't gonna be enuff."

That—sounded alarming, to someone who was used to not having so much as a rag to spare. "Won't thet be dreadful dear?" she asked timidly.

"Y'all's a-gonna be wearin' thet there skirt fer a long time," her aunt pointed out. "Twenny years, iffen y'all takes good care, don' let th' moths git to't, an' don't tear it up."

But her eyes filled with tears when she realized how much this was going to cost Aunt Jinny. "But—all I done since I come here is et up y'all's food an' use up yore Ma's close—" she choked. "I don' know how ter—"

"Oh, hush," Jinny cut her off brusquely. "Yer my kin. An' what else'm I a-gonna spend money on? Y'all pulls yore own weight now, an' I'm a-spectin' y'all ter take care'a me when I'm old an' jest sit 'round an' complain!"

"I'll do thet!" she pledged. "I promise!"

"I'll hold y'all t'thet," Jinny replied. "Now le's clean up."

"I c'n knit," she offered, as she dried dishes. "I c'n make m'own stockin's."

"Good, tha's somethin' y'all c'n make a start on now." Aunt Jinny nodded. "All th' more reason ter go ter Ducktown. Iffen we go when Matt's takin' his wagon home with room t'spare, he won't mind if we brung back a bit more than I usually does. So, wool fer a skirt an' a coat, an' wool yarn fer stockin's. What'd y'all do 'bout shoon an' stockin's afore this?"

"Ma wrapped m'feet in rags," she confessed. "An' I didn' go out, so I didn' need shoon." She sighed. "'Cept fer th' Methodist Christmas Party. Then Ma wore Pa's broke shoon, an' I wore hers."

She didn't mention that going to that party was an absolute *must* for her and Ma. The Methodists had a "draw" for a turkey and other good things—though how they reconciled that with the admonition against gambling she had never been able to reckon—and gave food presents outright to families. They always came home full of a good dinner and with something for the pantry, and once they'd even gotten the turkey! It had lasted them for weeks, with every little bit of it used, even the bones, ground up between two stones patiently by her Ma and used to thicken the soup. And there were the stockings with sweets in them for the chillen—first, that was a free stocking, one that could be unraveled and knitted into a new, short pair for Ma, and second, all but one or two of the sweets got turned back into sugar-syrup to drizzle on Pa's bread and pancakes.

Aunt Jinny made a disapproving noise. "Pa must be spinnin' in his grave, that a gran-chile of his does wi'out stockings and shoon i' the winter! I'm surprised he ain't a-hauntin' me ... though, come ter think on it, he'd rightly be hauntin' Lew Jones."

But she looked so unhappy that Anna felt moved to pat her arm awkwardly. "I'm here now, Aunt Jinny. An' yore a-makin' me shoon, an' a-getting me *new* close, an' I'm a-gonna be able t'knit stockin's. Ev'thin's good."

But Jinny just sighed. "I wisht thet Lew'd give yer Ma a reason t'leave 'im. Three on us c'd live good here. But he ain't a-gonna, 'cause who else'd he git t'do fer 'im? He ain't a handsome young buck no more, an' he got Miner's Cough."

Anna sighed too, because she couldn't imagine anything making her Ma leave Pa, and because she couldn't think of any way to make their lives better. Pa already had a problem with Aunt Jinny sending potions to sell on. If they sent Ma anything like a parcel of food directly, and he found out about it, he'd probably throw it in the street.

"Wall ... le's go see what yarn I got left, an' what's left of my Ma's ol' close. Seems I 'member a wool skirt, an' iffen I does—" she winked at Anna "—tha's one thing I ain't a-gonna have t'spend on."

But she didn't go to the old clothes chest. Instead, she went to another, a bigger, blanket chest, half-hidden under piles of clean sheets they'd washed just yesterday. She opened it up to the heady smell of cedar.

Out came woolen blankets that made Anna's eyes widen. There

would be warm sleeping this winter for sure! And there, at the bottom— those folds of blue—those were no blanket!

Out came not only a blue skirt, but a brown wool dress, both with the sorts of voluminous skirts that required hoops. "Wall now," Aunt Jinny said with satisfaction. "I thunk I recollected that I niver cut these up fer rag rugs on account'a them bein' too good! Even arter y'all fatten up, they's plenty'a cloth here t'put new waistbands on, *an'* plenty left over fer—well, mebbe another whole skirt!" She caressed the wool dress. "This here's somethin' called *alpaca*. 'Twere purdy dear, but 'twas her weddin' dress, an arter thet, her Sunday best."

Tentatively, Anna touched it; it was softer than anything she'd ever touched before, except maybe rabbit fur.

"Now le's check th' bottom'f th' other chest, under th' spare sheets," Aunt Jinny said, loading her down with the skirt and dress. "I'm a-thinkin' we c'n hev us a liddle sewin' bee t'day. Git thangs cut out, anyways."

Underneath the spare sheets was another treasure. Another voluminous skirt, and not one made out of flour sack or canvas. It was a nice faded pink cotton that you wouldn't know was faded unless you looked closely at the seams. It even had a touch of rose ribbon trim around the hem. They grinned at each other over its folds.

By the time supper came around, they had three skirts cut out, extra waistbands for both, and a nice pile of pieces much too big to be called "scraps."

"I do think," Aunt Jinny said, surveying the wool pieces critically, "I do think, iffen y'all don' mind 'bout a bit'f patchwork, I c'n git that there wool coat outa what we got left. I c'n line it with fur, I'll bet. I got plenty'f rabbit, or I c'n arst the Ravens what they got t'trade. Beaver 'r otter'd be good."

"Aunt Jinny, thet'd be *fine*!" Anna beamed. "It'd be like bein' a-wrapped up in my kinfolk!"

"Why, so it would," her aunt agreed with a huge smile, politely ignoring the fact that Anna was actually not blood-kin at all to Jinny's Ma. "An' it shore is better'n leavin these thangs in them chests, where they ain't doin' nobody no good." She took the remaining lengths of wool and cotton and stowed them back in the blanket chest, then laid the cut-out pieces in the linen chest, layering them with lavender. "Thet'll do fer now. We c'n start a-sewin' when we got time an' they's light t'see by."

Anna was disappointed not to be working on that pretty cotton— but the storm hadn't blown over yet, and it was getting dark enough to make it hard to thread a needle.

"Le's hev supper, an' y'all c'n pop up on th' stove an' read a spell," Jinny said.

Back up on the stove, Anna continued where she had left off.

On hearing that all I wanted was to be a farmer again, my host shook his head. "There is no land here that is not in someone's hands," he said, "And while I would welcome you, I do not think you ever want to have anyone as lord over you again. Go to the New World, my friend. There is land for the taking there. And I will help you. This is why."

Now came a part that Anna had to read carefully, then read over again, before she properly understood it. It seemed that from Hungary westward, magicians—the ones that weren't bad, that is—organized themselves into something called "Lodges." Which didn't make any sense to Anna, because the only "Lodges" she knew about were places beavers lived … so eventually she just decided to try to stop making it make sense and just accept that was what they were called. And these "Lodges" were for the purpose of hunting down bad magicians and stopping them.

And the rich man wanted Great-Granpappy Pavel to organize one of these "Lodges" in the New World—that is, America. And if there were no good magicians in America yet to make up a "Lodge," to pass that information down to his descendants so that they could. In return, the rich man promised him money enough to get to America and set himself up when he got there, and the connections among all the "Lodges" he knew to make the trip as easy as it possibly could be.

It seemed like something he would never have dared to dream of to Pavel, and so he agreed.

"I swan, I called y'all three times now," Aunt Jinny said, poking her foot to get her attention. "Y'all done got swallered up by thet book."

She didn't want to put it up—who knew when she'd be able to

get back to it?—but she knew Aunt Jinny was not going to let a candle burn for much longer. Reluctantly, she put the book up and climbed up to the loft, to find that little mud-man waiting on the edge of the box that held her featherbed.

It nodded at her solemnly. She nodded back to it, and looked up at the rafters.

There were dozens of the little critters up there, all gazing back down at her, eyes shining.

She didn't feel any different when she woke up the next day. The mud man was gone, as was the line of observers, and she had actually awakened before her aunt did, because there was no one stirring below. So she took her time about carefully brushing out her hair, braiding it, and putting it up with her precious hairpins.

She actually had the leisure to think and wonder about a lot of things before her aunt woke up and she climbed down the ladder to wash her face and get dressed. Her aunt was a *very* good seamstress, as evidenced by her skill at unpicking everything in those three garments yesterday, rather than just ripping the seams apart—and by the careful way she had measured Anna, cutting the six waistbands— three for now, three for later, when she had "fattened up," if she ever did. How she had carefully conserved the maximum amount of fabric she could from each of the three garments when cutting the skirts. It seemed a shame that she disdained pretty clothing for herself.

Wisht I dared to arst her about thet.

The skirts were all going to be just a bit short, but to be honest that was just practical, and she had ceased to worry about how much ankle she was showing, when it came to not having to scrub her hem every night. Maybe that was all it was—Aunt Jinny didn't so much disdain pretty things, she just didn't have any use for anything that wasn't practical up here in the Holler. She certainly hadn't chopped off her hair to look like a man's—it was at least down to her waist when unbound, and she kept it braided and wrapped around her head.

I wonder if Jolene gave her hairpins too?

Jolene ... now there was a subject she longed to know more

141

about. She wasn't a "proper woman," although she looked like one. She had a *lot* of magical power, enough to be able to change her appearance in a heartbeat. And she didn't talk like anyone Anna had ever heard speaking before. In fact—she talked like Great-Granpappy Pavel wrote.

She heard her aunt stirring at last, and came down the ladder. "Aunt Jinny, why did Jolene talk so funny?"

"Because she ain't from 'round here. An' it's rude t' say some'un talks funny when they don't talk like y'all." Her aunt shot her a look from where she was dishing out mush. "Don't talk trash 'bout someone 'lessen y'all wants someone talkin' trash 'bout y'all. An' don't *never* talk trash 'bout Jolene. She gots ways of findin' thet sort of thang out."

Anna flushed, feeling as if she was five and had had her fingers slapped. "Sorry," she muttered, as much to the absent Jolene as to her aunt.

"I want y'all to trot down to th' Holcrofts arter mornin' chores an' find out when young Josh reckons t' take thet baby angel statchoo t'Ducktown, an' iffen Matt minds us comin' along an' doin' a mite of shoppin'," Jinny continued, pouring out the tea, then settling onto her seat. "Since Josh'll be gettin' paid his own self, I reckon Matt'll hev some shoppin' t'do too, an' won't mind us."

"Yes'm!" Anna agreed eagerly, any thoughts of Jolene, or even the question of whether or not she had learned Cherokee overnight, driven right out of her head by the prospect of seeing Josh again.

She didn't scant on the chores, but to Jinny's open amusement, she certainly went through them at a brisk pace. With sets of underthings drying nicely on the line, she found herself in the lane down to the Holcrofts' farm by late morning.

Without Jinny's lessons on plants and herbs going on, and since the slope led slightly downhill, she made good time, and it was certainly much less than an hour later when she emerged from the trees and onto the crossroads where the lane met the road and the Holcrofts' farm appeared on the left.

Maddie Holcroft and her eldest daughter were out hanging wash on the line. Sue spotted her first, and said something to her mother, who looked around a sheet and waved to her. She waved back and skipped the rest of the way to them.

"I'd arst if there was somethin' wrong with Jinny, but y'all don't look like a gal with a 'mergency on her mind," said Maddie Holcroft with a smile. "What brung y'all down here this mornin'?"

"Aunt Jinny wants ter know, iffen when Joshua finishes thet there baby angel an' y'all take it t' Ducktown, iffen we c'n beg a ride fer shoppin', please, Missus Holcroft," she replied, as the freshly washed laundry flapped in the breeze, mingling the pleasant scent of clean linen with green grass, and the varied scents from the garden.

"I 'spect we c'n do thet," Maddie Holcroft agreed. "Y'all's gonna hev t' sits in the wagonbed; I know yore aunt ain't a gonna mind thet—"

"I don' mind thet neither," Anna pledged.

Mrs. Holcroft's eyes twinkled. "Got yore heart set on a purdy new dress, I reckon," she teased. "An' y'all wanter pick out th' pattern yore own self."

Anna blushed and ducked her head.

"Wall, so would I," Sue piped up, with an elbow-nudge to Anna's arm. "'Cept I got a purdy new dress fer Easter."

"I'll let Matt know; y'all go 'round t' Josh's shed an' go arst him when he thanks he's a-gonna hev thet statchoo finished." Maddie Holcroft shooed her, and included her daughter in the gesture, so both the girls ran off to the barn and the shed attached to it, where steady *tink-tink-tinks* told Anna that Joshua was still working on his piece.

He had moved from the baby to the wings, which the last time she visited had only been a rough suggestion. Now each feather had been roughed out, using a chicken wing that lay on his workbench as a guide, and he was refining the details of the feathers with a smaller chisel and wooden mallet.

Sue waved to Anna to be quiet, and waited until he had straightened up to stare at the wing for a moment before speaking. "Josh! Ma wants ter know 'bout when y'all'll be a-finished with thet there statchoo!"

"Why, when it's done, a-course, goosey," he said, not turning around.

Sue stamped her right foot, which had a lot less of an effect than she likely wanted, since the sound was muffled by the straw on the floor of the workshop. "I'm serious! Ma wants ter know!"

"And I'm serious t—" He turned and saw Anna. "Wall! I'm right sorry, Miz Anna, thet I didn' know y'all was a-standin' thar. Is thet why Ma wants ter know?"

Sue tossed her head and sniffed. "'Course 'tis, blockhead. Miz Jinny wants ter go t'Ducktown fer some shoppin'. She reckons Pa won't mind iffen you an' him is a-goin' down thar t' deliver thet statchoo t' Cavenel."

"An' is Miz Anna a-comin' too?" Joshua asked. She felt herself blushing for no reason, except that he seemed very interested in the answer.

"Iffen yore Pa don' mind and they's room," she replied for herself.

"Wall then, it'll be 'bout another week," Joshua replied, combing his hair out of his eyes with the hand that held the chisel. Then, as if something had suddenly occurred to him, he looked right at her. "Say, ole Cavenel didn't give me nothin' but the name an' the dates t'put on the base, but thet jest don't feel like quite—" He groped for words.

"Quite 'nuff fer a Ma what lost her baby?" she prompted.

"Ayup, 'xactly. I don' suppose y'all c'n think of somethin'?"

"Happen I c'n ..." She didn't have to think long. "'He has gathered th' lamb in His arms.' Thet's kinda in Isaiah. It ain't exact, but it's close enough, I reckon."

Joshua beamed at her, making her blush even harder. "Say! Thet's jest right!" He took a thick-leaded pencil from the pocket of his overalls and scrawled the words on his workbench, right above the name of the baby, and its birth and death dates. "Anna Jones, y'all is a smart gal! Thenkee!"

"'Tweren't nothin'," she murmured, as Josh's sister Sue looked on with amusement. "How's it possible t' carve stone, anyways?" she continued. "I mean, it's so hard—"

"Takes th' right tools," Josh replied with authority, as Sue lost interest and wandered off. He showed her the mallet and tiny chisel he was currently working with. "I gotta keep sharpenin' the chisel, on account o' it goes dull quick, which don't happen near as fast if I was shapin' wood. An' I gotta use a soft wood mallet, not a metal hammer, on account o' a metal hammer'd make the chisel bounce in th' stone, an' might could ruin th' cut. Right now, I'm a-puttin' in the detail on th' feathers."

He bent over his work, and delicately etched in one side of the quill of one of the feathers, moving his chisel a fraction of an inch at a time, leaving dust to be blown away, rather than chips of stone. "I'd druther work on marble, which'd be a lot purdier, but marble ain't got a chance in hell in Ducktown."

She furrowed her brows. "Why not?"

"The rain," he replied, starting on the other side of the quill. "Jest makes marble melt. Eats at it. Makes it soft, too. There was a couple'a headstones that th' famblies had ter replace—good thang they had money—'cause y'all couldn't hardly read th' names on 'em no more. Whatever's in th' rain is th' same thin' as keeps things from a-growin', I reckon. So all th' carvin' I does fer Cavenel, I does in granite. Makes it a lot harder, 'cause granite's harder than marble. I needs special chisels, I gots t'keep 'em sharp, an' I gots t' re-harden 'em regular."

He finished the quill, and etched a few lines that suggested the vanes of the feather. "Now, I don' wanter put in *too* much, 'cause thet'll make it look unnatural. Jest 'nough that y'all look at it, an' say t'yoreself, 'Thet there's a feather,' an' go on. It'd be better in marble." He set the mallet and chisel aside and straightened up, shaking his hands vigourously. "I got a couple more feathers t' go, an' that'll be th' last o' the carvin'. When I'm done carvin', I'll polish her up, same as y'all'd sand wood ter make it all sleek. Then all this'll be smooth an' shiny." He picked the chisel and mallet back up, then looked at her intently. "Is y'all really innerested in this, Anna May Jones?"

She flushed, and temporized. "Wall, it's innerestin' cause y'all's the one a-doin' it. I don't reckon it'd be as innerestin' if 'twas that Mistuh Cavenel what y'all's doin' it fer."

He chuckled; the corners of his eyes crinkled up, and she suddenly feared he might pat her on the head and tell her to go help Sue or something.

"Wall, it's a sight nicer t'be workin' here with y'all watchin'," he replied. "A feller does like t'hev a purdy gal takin' a shine t'what he's a-doin'."

She felt her cheeks flame and she didn't know quite where to look.

"It's even better," he continued, bending back over his work again, "when a purdy gal likes a feller's company enough thet she don't mind when he goes on a-workin'."

"How long y'all been a-carvin'?" she asked, wrenching her mind away from the undisputed fact that he'd said she was purdy.

"Long as I been allowed t'hold a knife," he replied, etching out the quill of another of the angel wing's long feathers. "Afore thet, I was a-takin' clay when I could git it, an' mud when I couldn', an' makin' things wi' it. Reckon I was 'bout ten when I started takin' trinkets like carved stocks an' knife-handles t'the General Store t'barter, and Mistuh Cavenel seed 'em, an' wanted ter know who was a-doin' the carvin'. Next thin' I knowed, I was carvin' names an' dates an' sometimes a purdy liddle headpiece in headstones. Pay's good 'nough thet between thet an' th' liddle stuff I carve, Pa don't make me do farmwork 'lessen he has to. An' thet ain't too often, now thet Jimmie's old 'nough thet he c'n do ever'thang I can. So I ain't allus workin'. Sometimes I ain't workin' a-tall."

Now he glanced up at Anna with a raised eyebrow. "What I'm a-tryin' ter say, Miss Anna May Jones, is thet I do gots free time now an' agin, an' I'd admire yore company iffen y'all gets free time too."

For a moment she felt too flustered to answer. Then she managed to choke out—"Y'all'd hev ter arst Aunt Jinny."

He nodded, as if that was a given, which of course it was. "So I could arst her when we're all a-goin' inter Ducktown t'deliver this here liddle angel. Or on th' way back. Seems a fine plan."

"I—I'd—thet *would* be a fine plan," she stammered. And then realized that she had spent so long down here that it was almost dinnertime, and her aunt would be waiting impatiently for her. "I gots ter go—"

"It's 'bout dinnertime, an' Miz Jinny won' like it iffen y'all're late," he agreed, and stuck out his hand. "So I'll be a-seein' y'all when I comes up the Holler t' let y'all know we're a-goin' t' town, then."

"A'course," she said breathlessly, taking his hand and shaking it. She didn't remember turning to leave, but she must have, because when she finally got control of her whirling thoughts and blushing cheeks, she was about to climb the stile over the garden fence, and her aunt was waving at her from the cabin porch.

10

As they had promised, about two days after the rain, the two Cherokee came bearing mushrooms. This time when they arrived, Aunt Jinny was around the back of the cabin, and Anna was vigorously sweeping the floor and trying not to think too hard about Joshua and when he'd finally finish polishing that stone statue. It was a sultry morning; a lot of the wet from that torrential day of rain was still burning off. Her aunt was checking on the root cellar, to make sure the few things in there hadn't gone moldy or started to sprout. If the latter—never one to waste anything, Jinny planned to try to find a place to wedge the growing plant somewhere into the garden.

Anna was nearly done, had a nice pile of dirt in the center of the floor, and was actually facing the doorway, when she looked up and saw Elder Raven as he silently approached on the path to the porch. He paused on the doorstep.

She opened her mouth to greet him, but what came out was not English. "*Tohiju, Disquadisgi Kolvnv?*" she heard herself asking.

Elder Raven raised an approving eyebrow, and his son actually chuckled. "Thank you, I am very well, little sister," he said in his own tongue. "We have brought mushrooms, as we promised your aunt we would do." He set a split-willow basket on the table, full to overflowing with several kinds of mushrooms.

"Aunt Jinny's cleaning out the winter storage cave," she replied, struggling for words for "root cellar," and settling on an approximate term. But before she could say anything further, her aunt came in behind Young Raven to speak for herself.

"You brought mushrooms! I'm greatly obliged," said her aunt, also in fluent Cherokee. "Did you want more honey or jam in return, or is there something I can get for you when we go into Ducktown?"

"Into Ducktown? So, your student grows strong enough to bear the evil of that place?" Elder Raven asked in surprise.

"I expect her to be ready," Jinny said calmly. "It will be in half a moon, more or less, whenever young Joshua finishes what he is working on."

"Well then, in that case, coffee, please." Old Raven smiled broadly. "It is the one vice of the white man I find harmless, useful, and pleasurable. Especially on chilly or damp mornings, when I find it increasingly unwelcome to get out of bed, otherwise."

"It isn't much of a 'vice,' then, is it?" Aunt Jinny joked.

But Anna's mind was racing through deductions given the little bits of information she had just gotten. If he wanted coffee, then he surely had a coffee pot, or at least a pan with a handle to make it in. And if he found it hard to get out of bed, then it followed that he *had* a bed, and somewhere for that bed to be. So the Ravens probably weren't living in a cave, or a bark hut. And there was supposed to be a Missus Young Raven too. So … well, why not ask? The worst that would happen would be that Aunt Jinny would scorch her hide— verbally—for being too inquisitive. "Sir?" she said, carefully. "May I please ask you a question?"

"Hmm," Elder Raven replied, looking at her with great interest and some humor. "The fact that you ask me if you may causes me to think it will be impertinent."

"Anna May!" her aunt rebuked sharply, but Elder Raven waved a hand at her.

"I should like to hear the question," he said. "I may or may not answer it."

"How many of you Cherokee *are* there?" she asked. "Back there in the Holler, I mean."

Elder Raven and his son both laughed. "A good question," said his son, looking to his father. "Are you going to answer it?"

"I think that I shall," Elder Raven said, his eyes bright with amusement. "Several. More than a family, less than a full clan. And before you ask further, I will tell you that we have little village of houses that are much like this one; we helped your Great-Grandfather to build his home, and when we saw how your Great-Grandfather built this stove—" he used the English word, so presumably there was no easy equivalent in Cherokee "—we liked it so much we all copied it."

"The Little People are a great help to us," said his son. "They remained here when our people were Removed, so there are several clans of them here that help our small village. They confuse the trails, and make sure that no one sees our village or comes close to it. Unfortunately they were not inclined to do the same for your Auntie's father, so we had to take other measures when the Yankee and Rebel soldiers came."

She felt her eyes widen. "Little People! I've seen one of them three times!" she exclaimed, and looked to her aunt, who nodded in confirmation.

"It means they favor you and they recognize you as a medicine woman, like your aunt," Old Raven told her. "But you must not tell anyone else but another medicine person about them, or it will be a great misfortune to you."

"It would be a misfortune enough just having other people thinking I am crazy," she pointed out. "Which they likely would, if I began talking about Little People." She paused, and added, "Can I visit you some day?"

"One day," Old Raven agreed. "When you know your own way about the woods, and your aunt does not have to bring you."

"And when we're not busy, which won't likely be until winter," Jinny pointed out.

"True, and you and I both must be back to our work," Old Raven laughed.

"Thank you for the mushrooms," Jinny said. "As ever, it is good to see your faces."

"It is good," both Ravens agreed in chorus, and then left as silently as they had arrived.

As soon as they were gone, Anna turned to her aunt, who held up her hand. "Thet there was fust-rate Cherokee, so seems thet the Elemental critters larned it to y'all jest right," she said. "And afore y'all go arstin' me more 'bout Raven an' his people, y'all need t' find thet out fer yoreself. It ain't my place t'tell y'all."

"I weren't a-gonna," Anna objected. "I was a-gonna arst y'all what we're a-doin' with them thar mushrooms. Is they good in potions?"

Her aunt sighed with great satisfaction, and picked up the basket. "A-course y'all ain't niver et mushrooms," she said, as if reminding herself. "We're a-gonna et 'em. They's mighty good eatin'. An' they don't last, lessen y'all dry 'em, an' even then, it's chancy whuther or not they'll keep. We'll hev 'em fer supper." Then she blinked, and added, "But don't go pickin' mushrooms and eatin' 'em on your own. Some of 'em is pizenous, an' some'll jest make y'all sick. Wait till me or th' Ravens c'n show y'all the difference atween 'em."

With that, she got a clean pot—much smaller than the usual soup pot—and dropped a bit of bacon in a frying pan. By the time Anna got back from feeding the chickens, collecting the eggs, and feeding and mucking out the pigsty, the pot was full and simmering on the hearth, and there was a rich and tantalizing aroma filling the cabin. Anna recognized the familiar touches of vegetables and herbs and of course bacon fat, but the meaty, earthy base of the scent eluded her.

Her aunt laid out a cold dinner, since the day was already warm enough without further adding heat by fully firing up the stove. Already Anna could see the value in this kind of stove—when it was summer, you only needed to have enough fire in the hearth to cook food, not heat up that giant mass of masonry—and all that stone and mortar absorbed so much of the heat from the hearth that it didn't penetrate to the rest of the cabin. Not like a cast-iron stove, where the whole thing was either hot or cold.

"I want y'all t' go down the lane and git me some thangs," Jinny said, as they finished up the dishes. "Flares, ac'chully. Roses'r bloomin', an' lilies. Time t'make scent fer soap."

"Yes'm," she replied eagerly. This might be the best chore her aunt had ever set her. Picking wildflowers was hardly a chore at all. She listened carefully as Jinny gave her exact instructions, then sent her out with a bushel basket. The flowers weren't going to be remotely heavy, even if she filled the basket, and if there was *any* coolth to be had, it would be down the lane under the trees.

Wild roses were her first quest; Jinny had given her very particular instructions to locate a clearing off the lane where the rose shrubs had just taken over the entire place. And sure enough, within about a quarter of an hour, she pushed through bushes to find a riot of roses in various stages of bloom, bud, and developing hips. Jinny wanted things picked in a particular order—hips were as desirable as blooms, so the ripe, marble-sized hips came first, going into the bottom of the basket. Then, once she had picked as many as she could reach, a layer of leaves to keep them from moving around much. Then, carefully, the roses themselves. First buds just starting to unfurl, then another layer of leaves, then those in full bloom, picked at the height of the blossom, with just enough stem on them to keep them from wilting immediately. And she counted herself extremely lucky that this patch of roses was not only deliciously fragrant, but surprisingly thorn-free. *Not* thornless, but the thorns were small and considerably less trouble than blackberry thorns.

Getting all the flowers she could reach filled up the basket about halfway, and the scent—well she thought she could easily get drunk on it. Next, she was supposed to go to the other side of the lane to gather tiger lilies.

But as she emerged from the woods, she stopped in her tracks at the sight of someone waiting for her. There, in the middle of the lane, clearly expecting her, was Jolene.

Wearing that dress of mottled green, and her pale green apron, she looked as if someone had just set her down in the middle of the lane, rather than looking as if she'd walked here. There was no dust on her feet, and not a hair out of place. She was as cool and composed as a statue, without a sign that the heat bothered her, nor of impatience. How long had Jolene been waiting? A minute? An hour? And why was she here in the first place?

On an impulse Anna did the little twist in her mind that allowed her to see the Glory. And golden light erupted in her face, as if the sun had taken Jolene's face.

Anna fell back a pace with a gasp, nearly blinded, before she managed to shut the vision out. When she could see again, Jolene was still standing there in her pretty green dress and apron, regarding Anna with her head tilted to the side.

Better say somethin' afore she thinks I'm a-bein' rude. "Arternoon, Miz Jolene," she stammered. "Aunt Jinny sent me out fer flares."

"So I see. And your aunt showed you how to see magic as well, didn't she?" To Anna's relief, Jolene sounded faintly amused rather than irritated, or worse, angry. "I can show you how to do much, much more than she can ever teach you, you know," she added abruptly.

"I'm certain-sure y'all knows more'n Aunt Jinny ever could," Anna temporized, trying to gain some time to think, and a little breathless with what felt like rising panic. Just a few weeks ago, the worst she had to worry about was whether her aunt would be happy with how she did the chores! Now, suddenly, there was magic in her life, and an extremely powerful person interested in her. And that made her nervous, for reasons she couldn't quite articulate.

Why would Jolene make such an offer? She didn't know Anna. She wasn't kin. *Had* she actually made an offer at all, or was it just a boast about what she could do if she cared to?

Better not reckon on eggs what ain't been laid, much less hatched.

But if she had actually offered to teach Anna more magic than Aunt Jinny could, what would she demand of Anna for such learning?

"Ain't no doubt," Anna agreed, trying to draw Jolene out more. "Aunt Jinny's a good Root Woman, but ain't no doubt y'all knowed more'n her."

Jolene continued to regard her with that unsettling lack of expression on her face. "I am willing to teach you," she elaborated.

Anna felt queasy. It seemed rude to refuse. It seemed ill-advised to accept without knowing all the strings that were attached. "I dunno why y'all'd spend time doin' setch a thang," she replied, ducking her head shyly. "It'd be mighty kind of y'all, but I'm jest one liddle gal that ain't nothin' t' nobody. I cain't even pay y'all back—"

Jolene chuckled, and smiled thinly. "There is no question of payment here. I am not interested in claiming such a payment from you. It is in my own self-interest to see that magicians within my orbit are *properly* trained, and you have a potential power that I fear your aunt is ill-suited to guide. I'd rather see you schooled and controlled than ill-taught and a hazard."

Anna inwardly bristled at the implied insult to her aunt, but tried not to show it.

"But I wouldn' want y'all to waste yore time—" Anna temporized.

"But it is my time to waste," Jolene countered. "Besides, it won't take long, at least this time. And again, I shall not ask you for anything in return. I will never ask for any sort of payment for teaching you. Among my other reasons, it amuses me to do so."

"Yes'm," Anna replied, now completely at a loss for any words at all.

Jolene waited for her to say something else, then finally crooked a finger at her, in a way that suggested Anna had better not refuse. Anna put the basket down in the grass of the lane and moved closer to the woman, reluctantly.

"I am going to show you how to do something very useful," Jolene told her, as Anna looked into those startlingly green eyes and flawless face, and felt unfinished, awkward, and grubby. "I am going to show you how to find the magic of the earth, and draw it into yourself so that you can use it."

"Yes'm," Anna said, mesmerized by those eyes, which did not look at all human right now. "Thenkee, ma'am."

"Thank me by learning quickly, before I grow bored," Jolene replied. "Now—permit yourself to see the magic again—I'll make sure not to blind you this time—and watch what I do."

Slowly, and with patience Anna had not expected, Jolene showed her how to find all the sources of Glory, not growing on the earth, but *under* the earth: tiny rivulets that gathered the way rivulets of rain water gathered into thin trickles, then flowed into tiny streams, then joined into cricks and rivers. Soon she found she was able to see these things easily, and that there was a thick, rich river of the stuff flowing right down the center of the Holler and on to—well, she couldn't see that far. "But don't touch that, not yet," Jolene cautioned. "You aren't strong enough."

And she showed Anna how to connect herself with some of those trickles and rivulets and draw them up into herself through her bare feet, until she stared at her own hands, half elated and half aghast, as they glowed with the power.

Could Aunt Jinny do this?

A'course she c'n. She puts th' Glory inter things, it's gotter come from somewhere.

"Now use that power—thus—" said Jolene, and pressed the tip of her index finger to the center of Anna's forehead, bathing the inside of her skull in Glory—and making the incipient headache vanish.

Her doubts vanished. This was *good*! She felt better than she ever had in her life! And if she could learn to do that—think of the good she could do, herself!

"Kin—y'all do thet agin?" she gasped.

It took three more repetitions before Anna could work the trick herself, but when she did, the relief was not unlike the relief and release she'd felt on eating to satiation for the very first time. As if something inside her that had been starving was finally full.

"Now use the rest of the power to refresh those flowers," Jolene said, with a tiny smile of satisfaction. "Just send a bit of power into them; we've been standing here so long they are sorely wilted."

Anna held her hands over the basket and let the Glory rain down out of her hands like a gentle mist onto the roses—and to her elation, the wilted petals revived and freshened, until they looked the way they had when she'd just picked them.

"That will be how you put magic into potions, more or less, and that's enough lessons for today, I think." Jolene looked like the proverbial cat in cream. "You'll surprise your aunt, which will amuse me no end. Jinny is such a *prickly* creature. She's like that creature you have here with the spikes all over it—"

"A porkypine?" Anna ventured.

"Yes, that. When you cross her even the slightest, it's a hiss and a rattle, and she bristles all over." Jolene laughed at her own wit. "It's so amusing, and I never get tired of doing it. As if *she* could ever endanger *me*."

Anna laughed weakly, because Jolene seemed to expect it.

"Now, run along on the rest of your errand, and I shall be about mine," Jolene continued, and turned to walk away, down the lane toward the road. But then she turned back. "And mind—don't tell Virginia that I helped you. Unless she guesses it. Then you may."

And she turned back and somehow managed to get out of sight

in no time, despite taking what seemed to be a leisurely pace.

And it was only after Anna had found the patch of tiger lilies and had picked the rest of the basket full of flower heads that she remembered that Jolene had said she had an "errand"—

—and had gone off toward the Holcrofts' farm.

But Matt and Maddie didn't *have* the Glory, or Aunt Jinny would have said something.

So what could Jolene possibly want with the Holcrofts?

Cain't be. Must be somethin' else, she told herself.

Aunt Jinny greeted her harvest with pleasure, and immediately set her to pulling the petals off the roses and lilies and putting them in two big pots. She covered both with enough water to submerge all the petals completely, covered each pot with a plate, and set them at the hearth where the soup had been cooking. Then she and Anna sorted and cleaned the rose hips and carried them up to the other loft, where she spread them out on a clean sheet to dry.

By then it was suppertime, and the mushroom soup was nothing short of amazing. "Et it all, it don't keep, an' it gets mushier with cookin'. It ain't like bean soup what gets better," Aunt Jinny admonished, and Anna didn't have to be told twice. After supper, Jinny took the pots of petals off the hearth and strained petals out of the pink-and yellow-colored water through cheesecloth, pouring the fragrant liquid into bottles that she filled to the top, then corked and put away on a shelf. That meant three pots to clean instead of one tonight— though the pots that had held the petals smelled so good it could scarcely be called "cleaning." Anna just regretted that there wasn't anything left in the pots to dab on her wrists and temples.

"We'll do lavender from th' garden termorrer," Jinny proclaimed. "It's been a easy day fer y'all, so might's well do a lesson in gatherin' th' Glory an' puttin' it in potions. So, le's go outside. Works best when y'all's got your bare feet on earth."

"What'd y'all do when it's winter, Aunt Jinny?" Anna asked, as Jinny took that same split-wood bushel basket that she'd had Anna fill with flowers and filled it full of potion packets. "Cain't go barefoot on snow!"

"Th' best y'all c'n," Jinny said philosophically. "It ain't so hard. Floor's wood, an' it jest takes a liddle more strenth t'pull the Glory up through it." She led Anna down off the porch and onto the grassy verge between the cabin and the garden.

The last of the daylight gilded wisps of clouds overhead, tinging them with pink and yellow. The garden spread out below them, sloping ever so gently down toward the lane. Lightning bugs flashed here and there among the plants. In Anna's mind it was just as beautiful as a field of flowers, if not more so. That garden meant comfort and prosperity in a way no flower garden ever could.

Jinny recaptured her attention by putting the basket down between them. "Now, make that liddle trick what let's y'all see the Glory."

Anna nodded, and found that, after Jolene's tutelage this afternoon, it was literally as easy as opening her eyes. The garden glowed with magic. The "shield" over the garden was a haze of golden light. And everywhere under her feet, the Glory ran like rivulets of clean rain in the sunlight.

Without thinking, and without prompting by her aunt, she began what Jolene had taught her—drawing the power up into herself. And she only stopped when she got a look at her aunt's startled expression.

"Y'all niver larned thet by yoreself!" Jinny exclaimed. Then her eyes narrowed. "Y'all was gone a good long time this arternoon ..."

Anna bit her lip, but didn't dare say anything.

"Tarnation!" Jinny spat. "It were Jolene! Weren't it?"

"Yes'm," Anna muttered guiltily, dropping her eyes to stare at the ground.

"What'd she make y'all promise t'larn thet?" Jinny demanded. "An' look me in th'eye, Anna May Jones!"

Anna looked up—but thankfully, saw that the expression on her aunt's face wasn't anger.

It was worry. And a little fear.

"Nothin', truly!" she hastened to say. "Not one thing! She said it were her—" Her brow furrowed as she strove to remember the exact wording. "She said it were *in her interest to see thet magicians in her orbit were prop'ly trained*, an' thet it 'mused her t'vex y'all."

"I c'n b'lieve she said thet," Jinny replied, looking relieved, but in a sour tone. "'Bout wantin' t'vex me, that is. I ain't what she wanted, an' she ain't niver gonna let thet go."

That last made absolutely no sense to Anna, and she didn't even try to puzzle it out. "What'd she mean by *magicians in her orbit*?" she asked her aunt, instead. The phrase had puzzled her.

"Them of us as got th' Glory what's livin' around about these here parts. I ain't entirely sure how big thet territory is, but I knows it means at least from the Holler all th' way to Ducktown an' past th' Burra Burra mine. All'a th' Ducktown basin an' inter th' mountains." Aunt Jinny paused. "She's the strongest thang in these here parts, an' don't y'all ever fergit thet. Not for one minute. And that's 'nuff questions fer now. I reckon she larned y'all not on'y how t' draw up th' Glory, but how t' put it in thangs too. An' thet's why them roses weren't wilted when y'all come back t' th' cabin this arternoon."

Anna nodded, biting her lip.

"All right then." Jinny stood next to the basket with her hands on her hips. "Show me."

Anna spread her hands over the basket and let the Glory sift down into the basket like a rain of golden dust. Jinny watched for a moment, smiled spitefully, then said, "Stop."

Anna closed her hands and bit her lip. "Am I doin' somethin' wrong?"

"Not *wrong*, 'xactly." There was that spiteful smile again. "Jest provin' thet Jolene don't know ever'thang. Y'all's wastin' half th' Glory, doin' it thet way. Watch me."

Aunt Jinny sketched three little signs in the air, then opened her own hands and let the Glory drop into the basket. But it didn't just dust down onto the potion packets; the power made dusty little green and gold ribbons that spiraled around each other and deliberately down into the basket of packets, moving around like lazy, miniature whirlwinds. "Green fer healin'," murmured Jinny. "An' gold fer strenthenin'. These here is fer Winter Fever. Y'all cain't just sift down raw Glory on 'em, like y'all did on th' roses." She closed her hand and the little whirlwinds collapsed down into the basket.

"Was them magic signs y'all was makin'?" Anna asked breathlessly.

"Yes'n'no. They ain't magic thesselves, cause they don't do spit without y'all got the Glory behind it. But this's how m' Granny larned me t' make th' Glory do whatcher want." She nodded sagely. "Jest y'all watch. This'un here's fer healin'—"

She moved to stand beside Anna so Anna could see the figure the right way around, and traced the figure in the air, her fingers leaving a glowing line behind them. She repeated it patiently until Anna said, "Reckon I got it now."

"Then put th' Glory inter it," her aunt told her. "An' show me."

When Jinny was certain Anna could, indeed, trace and empower the sign, she moved on to the one for "strength." And then she showed Anna the third one.

"This'un's more important than t'other two, 'cause what it does, it says, 'Don't let no one meddle with what I done.' 'Tis like pourin' wax atop a jar of jam; seals in all the good, don't let no bad come in." Jinny peered at her through the deepening twilight to make sure she understood the seriousness of that last sign.

She did, of course, at least once Jinny had pointed out what the sign was for. There'd be no point in having such a thing if there weren't a need for it. And if there was a need for it—well the only reason someone would meddle in a healing thing was if they wanted to cause harm.

"Say, Aunt Jinny—can these potions *cure* Winter Fever?" she asked, thinking, of course, of her Pa.

But her aunt shook her head. "Even with all th' Glory in Tennessee, they cain't cure nothin'. They c'n on'y he'p the one y'all give it to, make thin's easier with his breathin' an' all, he'p him last. On'y God c'n cure Winter Fever, an' th' likes of y'all an' me ain't God."

She sighed. It seemed cruel that a person could work magic like this—but the magic had its limits. It was *magic*! It should just—work!

"There's rules t' these here thangs," her aunt said, as if she had read Anna's thoughts. "So, le's finish up these potions an' go inside afore the skeeters et us both up."

11

Anna had made three trips down to the Holcrofts' farm, and each time the little baby angel statue was closer and closer to being finished. What Josh was doing with the stone seemed as magical to her as what she was doing with Aunt Jinny. The angel's furled wings looked more and more like feathers, and the pink granite of the baby's head and body looked more and more like flesh instead of stone. Finally, on the last trip down, she'd seen a completed work where the stone was as soft and smooth as an egg, and Josh was finally satisfied with it. She was able to run back up to her aunt to tell her that the long-awaited trip to Ducktown would be in two days.

By this time, she'd had several lessons from Jinny in how to shield herself from the harmful effects of Ducktown and its earth, air, and water. Those lessons went swimmingly well, thanks to what Jolene had taught her—especially the part about using the Glory to heal her aching head when she had used it for a little too long. What was even better was that each time she did that, it took longer for her head to ache, and it didn't hurt as much. By the third lesson in shielding, it scarcely ached at all after working from after supper until full dark!

But it was hard to keep her mind on the lessons, however, when thoughts of Josh kept intruding.

Because by the first of those three visits to check on the progress of the statue, it had been obvious that he liked her company. And by the third, he'd been giving hints to his sister Sue—hints his sister ignored—that he would *really* have liked Sue to take herself elsewhere. Sue remained stubbornly *there*, not saying or doing anything, just braiding straw for hats. There was plenty of straw in the barn, and Sue professed to liking the shade and the relative cool of her brother's workshop.

Well, it was pretty obvious that Maddie had told Sue she was supposed to be there as a chaperone, even if Sue wouldn't own up to the fact. So all Anna could overtly do was admire Josh's work and heap praise on his carving, and all *he* could do was be modest about it while asking her about herself. He treated each bit of information he coaxed out of her—and it wasn't much, seeing as her life hadn't consisted of anything but Bible-reading, chores, and the annual Methodist Christmas party and Fourth of July picnic—as if it was of the same exotic interest to him as her Great-Granpappy's journal was to her. It was disconcerting and flattering and exciting, all at once, to be the center of such interest.

And he hinted, more than once, that if he didn't get another such commission soon, he was going to see about more visits—either her coming down to the farm, or him coming up to the cabin. The *look* he gave Sue when he said that made it very clear he'd be happy to be free of his sister's interference. The look she gave him back challenged, *Y'all jest try an' git shut of me, Joshua Holcroft.*

So by the time the day came—with Aunt Jinny laying on another layer of Glory on the shield over the cabin and garden to ensure the safety of the chickens and pigs in their absence, and asking the Domovoy to protect them while she and Anna were gone—she was nearly beside herself with excitement. She had all her "best" things on, from the skin out, and a nice new straw hat she had braided and pieced together herself, with "ribbons" made of the carefully joined scraps from her new underthings. With a lot of scrubbing and a long bleaching in the sun, the skirt and apron she had arrived in were in what she would have considered a fit state to go to church in, and the best of the salvaged shirts had been made a little prettier with a couple rows of pintucks down the front, and a faded pink ribbon tied into a bow under the collar. She'd taken a bath the night before and washed and dried her hair, and as usual she had put it up carefully with Jolene's hairpins. And while she was out this morning feeding the hens, she'd snitched a bit of lavender, and rubbed it into her wrists and behind her ears.

Her aunt either didn't notice these preparations, or had decided to act as if she hadn't. And as for Aunt Jinny—well, she'd taken a bath as well, and put on a clean shirt and set of overalls, but she had scraped her hair up to the top of her head so tightly that Anna's eyes watered in sympathy, bound it into a hard knot, and jammed her straw hat down over the top of it. Anna had thought that she would at least make the concession to other people's ideas of what was proper by putting on a skirt—but no.

Wall, she's been here a long time. Mebbe them folks in Ducktown're useter her ways by now.

She somehow managed to keep herself from running down the lane to the Holcrofts', but it was with a supreme effort, and her heart actually felt as if it stopped for a moment when she saw Josh standing in the bed of his father's wagon, doing something back there, while his father checked the harness on their mule.

When they got to the wagon, she saw what it was he was doing. They'd put straw in the wagonbed, and a hessian sack over the straw, and the angel-baby was cradled in both. Josh was just making sure there was no way the statue could move around back there. He glanced up—when the mule reacted to their presence by looking at them and snorting loudly—smiled, and waved.

"Pa says y'all should ride up front with him, Miz Jinny," he said, when they were within conversational distance. "Anna an' me'll ride in back and keep this here statchoo steady."

"Better yore behinders than mine," Jinny replied, with a glance at Anna that said, as clearly as speaking, *Y'all ain't foolin' me one bit, chile*. Anna flushed, but was more than happy to have Josh lift her up into the wagonbed and show her where to sit, while Matt Holcroft came around and took his spot on the driver's side of the bench, and Aunt Jinny hoisted herself up beside him.

Matt clucked to the mule and slapped her back gently with the reins, and off she went, at a sedate pace.

"Rosie don't much like a-goin' inter Ducktown," Josh said, as if to excuse the mule's reluctance to move any faster. "Don't rightly blame her. Ev' time I go down there, m'nose an' eyes start a-burnin', an' m'throat gits raw. Reckon they's plenty wrong with the place, like yore aunt says. Think I tol' y'all it ain't no use makin' stuff in marble cause it don't last down there?"

Anna looked over the statue that lay between them. "Aunt Jinny says thet too. Not 'bout the marble, but she says the pizen goes up from the smelters, inter th'air, then down as rain."

"Ain't no doubt," he agreed. "It's pizened from one end've the Ducktown Basin t' t'other. I dunno how anybody c'n stand t'live thar. I cain't get outa thar fast enough when I gotta go." He sighed. "Makes me wisht there was a faster way there an' back. I mean, there *is*, iffen I had a hoss, but I cain't carry stone an' finished pieces on a hoss, so hevin' a hoss wouldn't do much good." He scratched his unruly hair and grinned sheepishly at her. "Reckon I made a muddle of 'splainin' thet."

"I unnerstood it jest fine," she assured him, acutely aware that her heart was beating just a little faster, and she was feeling just a trifle breathless around him. But not the kind of "breathless" she'd been when she'd been so sick. No, this was a distinctly pleasant sensation. "Whatcher do when y'all ain't carvin' headstones?"

"Pa don't arst me t'do nothin' thet'll harm my hands," he said, as the wagon rolled through a crick bed, and they braced themselves against the sides. "So it's whatever chores what don't come with th' chance of choppin' 'em off, or sechlike. So, no choppin' firewood. No usin' a scythe or a sickle. Thet leaves plenty, though. I c'n still hoe an' chop weeds with th' hoe in th' garden. I c'n drive Rosie on th' cultivator, or th' plow, or th' harvester or the mower." He laughed. "Pa finds me plenty t'do."

"Devil finds work fer idle hands," his father said over his shoulder.

"Plus, like I tol' y'all when we fust met, I do other carvin' when I got th' material. I'm plumb outa pearl shell though, so I cain't do knife handles, nor gun grips right now."

"Wonder iffen they's anybody 'round Ducktown that'd pay fer a fancy cane?" she wondered aloud, having vague recollection of seeing a cane with a dog head at a Christmas party one year— had the mine owner been the proud possessor of the thing?—and being fascinated by it. It had been so realistic that child-her had wanted to pet it. "Y'all could do thet in wood."

"Say!" he exclaimed. "Reckon yer right! I'll arst—no, I gotter better ideer. I'll go ahead an' make one, an' put it with Mistuh Clay what runs th' gen'ral store. I put stuff with 'im all th' time, an' we see iffen anybody'll pay. Yer a smart gel, Anna May Jones!"

She blushed with pleasure, and his grin broadened to see it.

"Reckon a dog head'd be nice," she offered shyly. "Or mebbe a eagle."

"Wood carves easy," he pointed out. "Quicker'n stone. Reckon I might as well do both."

"But what if this baby's Ma wants y'all t'make another statchoo fer her parlor?" she continued.

"Iffen it's a-goin inter th' parlor, I c'n make it smaller, an' make it outa marble," he said. "They's plenty marble 'round here, jest lyin' about. I c'n hack th' rotten bits off a bigger piece an' hev 'nough good marble t'make a liddle life-sized statchoo 'bout yay so big." He measured out a length of about a foot with his hands apart. "Thet won't take near as long as th' headstone did, an' marble's softer an' easier t'carve an' polish. An' it'll be good money!"

"An' it'll fit inna parlor better'n this," she pointed out.

"Donchew count yore chickens afore they's hatched, Josh," his father said, looking over his shoulder.

"Ain't a-countin' chickens, Pa," Josh replied, as his father turned his attention back to the road. "Jest speculatin' on how to do her, if she's wanted." He laughed. "Now, speculatin' on how ter spend the money, *that'd* be countin' chickens."

The straw hat nodded. "Point made," Matt Holcroft replied easily.

Anna marveled at how Matt Holcroft spoke to his son as if he was a man grown, and nearly Matt's equal. Certainly her Ma and Pa had never spoken to or of her, as if she was grown, nor had Aunt Jinny. But then, Josh *was* bringing good cash money into the household on a very regular basis, so probably his father figured he'd earned the right to be treated as grown. She tried not to think too hard about the fact that she was doing the opposite, pulling money out of Jinny's household rather than bringing it in.

'Cause I am *helpin' with the chores, and I am helpin' with the potions*, she reminded herself. *And the more I larn, the more I c'n he'p.*

Maybe one of these days she could actually do something her aunt couldn't!

Josh was looking down at his statue, which looked perfect to her, but the discontent on his face suggested he thought he could have done better. "Iffen I gits th' chance t'do a liddle one in marble, there's a passel I could do t'make it purdier," he said, looking up at her. "The wings ain't quite right. Feathers don't curve, they's straight. The mouth ain't right, neither. Face looks flat."

Well, she didn't see any of that. But maybe that was because he was an artist and she wasn't?

She caught a little movement out of the corner of her eye, just as the wagon hit a section of rutted road and Josh reached out reflexively to steady his creation. To her amusement, a couple of the little Elemental critters, a mud-man and a thing made of chestnut leaves, nuts, and twigs, emerged from the straw. Had they been there all along? Or had they somehow just spontaneously generated from the straw? Or had they just appeared "by magic"?

The mud-man clambered over the straw and her ankle to come stand on the hind end of the statue, looking down at it, as if examining it critically. The other one climbed her skirt to tug at her hand. She opened it obediently, and it climbed into her palm to survey the statue from this loftier perch. She repressed a giggle—held it back because Josh would have no idea what she was laughing at—when she heard a snort from Josh.

She looked up to see he was staring at her hand, grinning, as if he could see the Elemental too.

Then he looked up to meet her astonished eyes.

You seed 'em too? she mouthed at him.

He nodded.

What 'bout yore Pa?

He shook his head, then mouthed back at her, *We'll talk later.*

Well, she durned well hoped they'd talk later! The fact that he could see the Elementals too made her so excited she wanted to bust!

But the two critters evidently had seen all they cared to. The one in her hand hopped down and buried itself in the straw, followed by the mud-man. And when she cautiously parted the straw where they had vanished, there was nothing there.

She looked up at Josh again. He shrugged, as if he was quite used to Elementals appearing and vanishing before his eyes.

"What I'm a-hankerin' fer, more'n anythin' else in th' world," Josh said aloud, as if picking up a conversation in the middle, "is somethin' I cain't git in Ducktown, an' I ain't sure where I can git it. I only knows it'll be purdy dear iffen I c'n find it, so I gotter save fer it."

"What's thet?" she asked, going along with this line of conversation.

"Carvin' tools. The kind what *real* artists use. Every size'a stone chisel there is, an' I know they's liddler ones than I got, fer carvin' agate stones inter cameos. An' I want wood carvin' chisels too, on account'a they's some carvin' easier done with a chisel than a knife. An' I want real wood carvin' knives, not jest a penknife, nor a claspknife, nor a pig-sticker." He sighed. "None'a thet's at th' gen'ral store, an' I don' reckon they knows how t'git setch stuff. The stone chisels I got now's on loan from Mistuh Cavenel. I want m'own."

Then his eyes got a distant look in them. "I wanter learn how t'cast metal, too. I c'n make stuff in clay, but how d'ye go from a clay statchoo to a bronze one?"

"I dunno," she said into the silence, impressed by his ambition, his hunger to learn things. Clearly there were visions of works in his head that he was itching to get out and into material form—but he didn't have the knowledge or the tools. And that frustrated him.

Then he shrugged and smiled at her. "Might's well wish fer the moon, aye?"

"Wall, Cavenel gots his chisels from *somewhere*, so he oughter know where t'start lookin'," she pointed out. "And ain't they moo-seums jest fer art?" Where had she heard that? She wasn't sure. Maybe it was her Ma?

"Aye," Aunt Jinny said, turning around. "Your Granny set a powerful store by readin' 'bout th' doin's in th' big cities. She useter git nooze-papers sent to 'er from all over arter th' War. I allus thunk it was useless hankerin' arter thin's she'd niver see, but iffen it kep' 'er happy, thet kep' Pa happy, so it weren't no skin offen my nose. An' there was plenty in them papers 'bout ar-teests an' moo-seums, an' somethin' called galleries. She useter read thet stuff out loud arter dinner, so I know Maybelle heard 'bout thangs like thet."

"So iffen I got a-hold of one o' them papers, I could find out about sech places, an' I could write to 'em, an arst 'em where t'get sech tools!" Josh exclaimed.

Aunt Jinny shrugged. "Reckon y'all could. Reckon they's folks in Cleveland what gits them papers sent to 'em regular. Reckon y'all could git someone t'give y'all th' old ones. Reckon th' man ter arst'd be Jeb Sawyer in Cleveland, since he does cartin' work all over Cleveland, an' I reckon he knows th' rag-an'-bone man. So there's yer start." Anna could tell that her aunt was highly amused by the way Josh was about to bust; that was why she was doling out the information a little at a time. "An' I reckon I c'n send along a note fer him next time I sends a batch'a potions t' Anna's Ma."

"Miz Jinny, I swan, I could kiss y'all!" Josh burst out.

"Here now, ain't no call fer thet," she objected mildly. "An' don't fergit what y'all said at th' beginnin'. Them things is gonna be purdy dear. So y'all'll prolly know where t' git 'em long afore y'all's got the money t' *buy* 'em."

"It's easier savin' when I knows what I'm a-savin' *fer*," he pointed out.

Aunt Jinny just smiled very faintly and went back to her conversation with Josh's father, which seemed to be about some small trades for butter and cheese.

They had been traveling for about an hour when the mule suddenly slowed down and began shaking her head. Matt slapped the reins on her back and made encouraging noises and she picked her pace back up to a brisk walk, but clearly was not happy about something up ahead of her.

"Ducktown Basin's over thet ridge ahead," Josh observed. "Mule c'n already smell it, and she don't like it one bit."

Anna had started out the day under her shield, so she wasn't feeling sick, but she did detect a faint, unpleasant tinge to the air. And that was when she got an idea.

She put her finger to her lips to warn Josh to be quiet, then gathered the Glory to herself and with a push of her hands, sent it toward the poor mule. Drawing the four signs in the air that Aunt Jinny had taught her for this Work, as her aunt called such things, she set the same sort of shield on the mule as she had on herself.

But smaller. Focusing on the mule's head, because she reckoned what bothered the beast the most was the poison in the air. And it wasn't as if the mule was a fellow Earth Magician who would feel sickened by the poisons around her. She only needed to be shielded from what bothered her in the air.

As soon as she had completed her self-appointed task, her aunt turned slowly—and far too casually—to look at her. But the look she gave Anna was one of approval. Then she turned back to Matt Holcroft, and made some inquiries about his other children. The mule, meanwhile, gave a surprised snort in reaction to sudden liberation from the noxious smell.

The wagon topped the ridge—and Anna gasped at the devastation spread out in front of her.

For as far as the eye could see, the landscape consisted of bare red earth that looked as if it had been blasted by the hand of God. Naked mounds of clay, furrowed with erosion fissures, rose between gullies created by rain that had no vegetation to hold it. It was not entirely fair to say that *nothing* grew in this nightmare landscape—here and there a struggling tree or clump of bushes attempted to survive, and there were a few scattered patches of weeds, but all their leaves were yellow and burnt at the edges, the branches spindly and failing utterly to thrive, and not even insects were trying to make a meal of them.

In the middle distance was Ducktown, its homes and businesses clustered around the smelter and minehead of the Burra Burra copper mine. The mine and smelter stood on a hill above most of the town. There were a few—a very few—trees there. Many fewer than were inside the Soddy town limits. Ducktown did not have Soddy's soot and black smoke, but the white smoke that billowed from the smelter's chimney must be the source of that harsh, sulfurous stink that got through Anna's shields. For a moment she wondered if her shields weren't working—but Josh's tearing eyes told her that those shields were successfully protecting her from the worst of it. And she realized when she saw him go pale—he probably wasn't as sensitive as she was, because if he'd been strong in the Glory, he'd have been able to shield himself, but nevertheless, he was sensitive enough to be sickened by the poisoned earth around him.

Although the energies of the earth were distinctly skewed here, she quickly mustered enough to shield Josh as well, and the look of gratitude he gave her as he wiped his eyes with the back of his hand made her flush with pleasure.

"Iffen I didn' hev t' pick up thin's fer Maddie, I swear, I'd tell Cavenel t' come git his own statchoos an' headstones," Matt mumbled, as the mule picked her way along the rutted road. "Whenever Preacher talks 'bout Hell, this's what I think of. 'Cept with lakes'a fire."

"Iffen they's a Hell on earth, this's it," Aunt Jinny agreed sourly. "I promise y'all, Matt, me an' Anna'll be quick. We'll prolly be done afore Josh gits done talkin' t' Cavenel."

"I'll jest let y'all down at th' gen'ral store, then," Matt replied. "I got some scrip t'be rid of at th' Company store, an' they's a water trough there, so I'll leave th' wagon an' mule hitched there. When y'all's done, jest bring yer stuff thar an' come wait with the wagon."

The mule actually seemed eager to get to Ducktown now. Possibly it was thirsty; besides being unpleasant to breathe, the air was terribly dry. It picked up its pace to a fast walk, and they were passing between rows of Company houses sooner than Anna had anticipated.

In Soddy, all the houses had been a soot-stained gray. Here they were all bare wood with little flecks of whitewash, as if the rain had eaten away the paint. But they were just as depressing, because the wood had weathered to a silvery gray not far off in color from the gray of the Company houses in Soddy. The big difference was the lack of soot and smoke.

She wondered what on *earth* people burned in their fireplaces and stoves here. You'd have to go miles to get firewood. And unlike in Soddy, what came up out of the Burra Burra mine could not be burned. Another crippling expense then, as if miners didn't have enough of those already.

An' Pa thinks bein' a miner's better'n bein' a farmer! The more she saw of the world, the lower her opinion of her father's notions got.

There was a cluster of businesses on a street with a sign that optimistically declared it to be "Main Street." Anna spotted a barber's pole and the three balls of a pawn shop before Matt Holcroft pulled up in front of a red-painted building with a fancy sign over the door that announced it as "Clay's Main Mercantile."

She scrambled out the back of the wagon to join her aunt on the dusty red-dirt street. Matt drove off, and they went inside.

This was literally the first time Anna had been inside a store of any kind in her entire life, since her Ma had made her wait outside and all she'd ever been able to see was the counter where you paid for things, and where the candies were in their big jars, and the sheer amount of *things* for sale took her breath away. The walls were lined with shelves all full to bursting, from the floor up to the rafters. There were barrels and bags piled high in every space where they could be piled. There were two counters running the length of the store; the one on the right had canned and bottled and boxed food and the like behind it and piled in pyramids on it, with a big jar of peppermints beside a large brass contraption. The one on the left had everything that *wasn't* food behind it, from fabric to chinaware. A balding man with a handlebar mustache and a spotless white apron tended the right-hand counter; a round, brown-haired woman in a brown dress and a similar apron tended the left-hand one. Each of them had a boy, also in a white apron, beside them, and two more boys sat in chairs next to a pile of baskets in front of the right-hand counter. At the rear was a stove—cold—with a cluster of ladderback chairs—half of them occupied with men smoking. Two of the men at the stove were playing checkers on the top of a barrel. Despite the stink of sulfur, the air was still full of interesting scents she couldn't identify, though they were all pleasant.

"Mornin', Jim, Abby," said Aunt Jinny—and to Anna's relief, her aunt's overalls and shirt did not occasion as much as a raised eyebrow. Aunt Jinny put the basket she was carrying down on the counter in front of the man. "Here's them potions y'all arst fer, Jim."

"And glad t'hev 'em, Miz Jinny," the man said. "Am I a-gonna git back any of what I owes y'all fer the last batch terday?"

Aunt Jinny laughed. "Reckon so, Jim, but it'll be Abby doin' th' honors. This here's m'niece, Anna Jones. We aims t' make her a 'Sunday best' with all the gewgaws and frou-frous."

While Jim unpacked the basket, Anna's aunt engaged the services of Abby at the "dry goods" counter. A long and serious discussion ensued over lengths of printed calico and muslin, with several being held up to Anna's face to see if they "would suit." Eventually several yards of a soft pink covered in sprigs of white roses were selected, followed by thread, matching white ribbon, pearl buttons, and even, to her astonishment, a white lace collar.

On'y thangs with lace Ma had were thangs from afore she married Pa ...

Then the two older women suddenly went into a whispered conversation over the counter while Abby wrapped up their purchase in brown paper and wrote what they had bought on the outside. As this transpired, they took covert looks at her. She found herself blushing without knowing why.

"Come along, missy," Abby said, crooking her finger at Anna, and taking a white pasteboard box from underneath the counter. When Anna looked at her aunt in confusion, Jinny nodded.

"While y'all are busy, I'll jest git th' rest of the shoppin' done," Aunt Jinny said blandly, and moved over to the other counter. Obedient to a fault, Anna followed Abby.

Abby ushered her past the loungers and checker-players and whisked her through a door-curtain, into a kitchen, then up a set of stairs and into what, in Anna's eyes, was a *beautiful* bedroom that was the utter acme of luxury and good taste. There was a brass bedstead with no sign of a trundle, braided rugs on the floor, and varnished bureaus and a wardrobe. The bed had a white and pink quilt, white and pink ruffled curtains were at the window, and a white and pink china basin and matching pitcher stood on the varnished washstand. Everything was completely neat and spotless.

But she quickly lost interest in the contents of the bedroom, because Abby had opened the pasteboard box, revealing—

—a corset!

Now, the one thing that Anna had longed for as a sign of being a grown woman—besides proper hairpins—was a corset. Of course, being as they couldn't afford hairpins, her Ma and Pa certainly had not been able to afford a corset. They couldn't even afford the fabric sturdy enough to make into a handmade one with goose or turkey quill boning. "Slip off yore thin's, chile," ordered Abby as she sorted out the laces. Anna had to slow down her fingers, lest she pop buttons off her waist in her haste to disrobe. Within moments, her skirt and petticoat were in a puddle around her feet, and her shirtwaist was in her hand, leaving her standing there in her drawers and chemise. And she was very glad she had dressed in the best of those that she possessed today. Her underthings might not be new or stylish, or even decorated, but they were clean and neat.

Abby fitted the garment around her torso and hooked up the front, then went around to her back and began tightening the laces. "I ain't a-gonna tight-lace y'all now, chile," she said in an admonishing tone, as if she expected Anna to demand that she pull the laces so tight Anna could not take a breath. "Jest 'nuff fer good support. I don't hold with tight-lacin', specially not fer a young gal, or a gal like y'all an' Jinny, what's gotter work like a man. Y'all gotter get inter this thang by yerself ev' mornin', an' y'all gotter be able t'move an' work. This'll make yore close lie neat, an' he'p yore back."

"Yes'm," Anna said, flushed with excitement, as she felt the garment close around her like a gentle hand.

"My land, y'all's tiny 'nuff," Abby exclaimed, as she pulled the laces until the two halves of the back met. "This's the liddlest model we got!" Abby came around to the front and surveyed her with a critical eye. "Aye, thet'll do, thet'll do. Y'all c'n jest unhook it in th' front ter lay it aside an' sleep, an' hook it back up in th' mornin'. Wash it reg'lar, but gentle, jest sponge't like yore skirt hem. Iffen y'all thank it's gettin' shabby, give't a good scrub an' bleach but dry it quick. Thar's jest a liddle steel bonin' innit, an' thet'll rust iffen it don't dry in a hurry. An' make a purdy cover fer it; thet'll make it last twice as long."

"Yes'm," Anna said, making careful mental notes.

"Don't be afeered t' arst yore aunt 'bout dressin' up. She goes her own way, but she knows how t'tend t' ladies thangs t' keep 'em clean an' make 'em last." Abby took her shoulders and turned her around in place, then nodded in satisfaction. "Aye, thet'll do. Y'all c'n put yore thangs on now."

Anna put her waist back on, and had no trouble bending over to retrieve her skirt and petticoat. She was tickled to see how much nicer her clothing lay over the corset, and vowed to make a really nice corset cover to save it from getting dirty as Abby had advised. "Y'all look like a proper woman now," Abby said with approval. "Ain't nobody gonna mistake y'all fer a liddle gel."

Since this was precisely the effect Anna had hoped for, she beamed with pleasure and started to thank Abby Clay. But Abby just picked up the box—which looked to hold several more corsets—and shooed her downstairs and back into the store.

The loungers and checker-players didn't even look up from their jawing and game, which was a *little* disappointing, but only a little. Her aunt smiled wryly—with the sort of expression that said *I think yore plumb crazy, but I knowed this was what y'all wanted*. And she *did* want this. She did not for a moment regret wanting it.

Among other things, Aunt Jinny had ordered flour, in sacks printed with patterns Anna could not imagine Jinny ever wearing—a tiny blue gingham check, and a pink with flower sprigs. There was no doubt the fabric of those sacks was destined for Anna, and she flushed with pleasure at the thought—and then started to worry about the cost. Her aunt hadn't had much flour in the house, because she clearly preferred to save the money and just eat cornbread. And now there was the material for the dress, and a corset, and a lace collar and all. "Aunt Jinny—!" she began, but her aunt cut her off.

"Hush. We gotter eat. Reckon I was gittin' a might weary of cornbread an' johnnycake all th' time, an' with two on us up at th' cabin, 'tis wuth makin' bread an' pie, cause we'll et it afore it spoils." Jim Clay nodded wisely as he totted up Jinny's purchases.

"Wall, this's a fust," he said. "Y'all owe me three dollars, Miz Jinny. I cain't recall th' last time y'all owed *me*."

Anna gasped and went pale at the enormous sum, but Jinny just laughed. "With m'niece here t' he'p with the potions, reckon shoe'll be on t'other foot agin next time," she smirked, and pulled a cloth pouch out of her overalls pocket, counting out quarters and fifty-cent pieces.

Then four of the boys were loaded up with purchases, and the little parade marched out the door and down the street to the establishment marked "Burra Burra Company Store," where Susie, the mule, was tied up next to a water trough. The boys loaded the wagonbed with the goods and marched back to the mercantile, while Aunt Jinny took another basket out from under the wagon seat, and went into into the Company store. She came right back out again.

"Matt an' Josh ain't there," she told Anna, "which means they's prolly still jawin' with Cavenel, or the like. I'll mosey over an' jest put m'ear in the door. Y'all should stay here, keep an eye on th' wagon. No point in puttin' temptation in th' path'a the weak."

"Yes'm," said Anna, who was more than willing to sit on one of the benches in front of the store and watch all the people going by.

"I'll be back quick," her aunt said, with an odd glance up and down the street, as if she was expecting to see something or someone unpleasant. "But iffen someone comes a-botherin' y'all, don't be afeared t' run in th' store. Thomas Cooper's a good man, even iffen he do work fer th' Company, an' so's ev'body thet works fer 'im. They won't let nobody pester y'all."

"Yes'm," Anna replied, wondering what on earth had prompted this pronouncement from her aunt. But she didn't get a chance to answer, as her aunt went hurrying up the street and turned a corner, out of sight.

12

Whatever it was that Jinny was worried about, it didn't materialize while Anna sat there. And if the air hadn't been so nasty, even with her shields, she'd have been willing to sit there all day and watch the people going by. This wasn't like sitting on her porch in her raggedy old clothing, looking at the dirt street in front of her Pa's house, near to invisible as a human being could have been. No, she sat carefully upright, legs crossed at the ankle, hands settled in her lap, and nodded "hello" to people who noticed her and saluted her. It was nice to be noticed. It was even better when they didn't look at her with expressions that told her they felt sorry for her because she was so sickly, or so raggedy.

She wondered if Jolene ever came here. She was surely powerful enough to shield herself from any of the effects of the poisons in the earth and air. But there was no good way to find out if they knew about her here in Ducktown—she couldn't exactly go up to random strangers and ask about her by name. On the one hand, she could easily imagine Jolene strolling down Main Street, taking great pleasure in all the admiring glances (or jealous ones) she'd get simply from being such a beautiful woman. But on the other hand— it was hard to actually predict *what* she'd take pleasure in, given she didn't act like anything or anyone Anna had ever met before.

Not that she actually knew more than a handful of people—so maybe she didn't have enough experience to—

And then, as if thoughts of her had called her, along came

Jolene, sauntering around the corner Aunt Jinny had gone around, and onto Main Street.

She was not wearing the strangely patterned dress she had been when she'd given Anna her lesson—nor the extravagant gown Anna had first seen her wearing. This was a simple pale green with darker green gingham pattern, and her apron was the same pale green. She wore what could only be a store-bought hat, since no amount of careful stitching was going to produce that perfectly flat brim and perfectly circular, flat crown, particularly not with handmade straw braid. It was adorned with a dark green satin ribbon band and large, green satin ribbon roses. Her abundant hair had been gathered on the top of her head in a fashionable pompadour style. And she moved as if she was aware that every eye on Main Street was on her, though she gave no outward indication of this. She carried a shopping basket loosely in one hand; it was empty, and seemed more like an excuse, rather than a reason, for being on the street.

"Mornin', Miz Jolene," "Nice day, Miz Jolene," "How do, Miz Jolene?" Every man on the street seemed determined to salute her, much to the annoyance of every woman they happened to be with, and she acknowledged these salutations with simple nods of the head, rather than in words. And all this was so exactly as Anna had imagined it, that if it were not for the fact that the people of Ducktown very clearly saw her, she'd have suspected she was daydreaming.

She did that little mental twist that allowed her to see the Glory, but made sure to be very cautious about it, remembering what had happened the last time she'd "looked" at Jolene in that way. It was just as well that she'd exercised that caution, because Jolene blazed up to her inner sight. But this time with a difference. She was surrounded by a shield so strong and so opaque that nothing of "her" was visible behind it.

Exactly as Anna had speculated.

Jolene ambled past, a sinuous gait that owed absolutely nothing to any corsetry ever made, and Anna didn't call out to her. This was partly because she really didn't want to attract the animosity of every female within earshot, but also because she didn't want Jolene to ignore her salutation either.

But just as she came even with where Anna sat, Jolene cast a sidelong glance at her and winked, as if to say, *Look at all these ridiculous people! Men acting like puppies eyeing a treat, and women acting like dogs defending a bone!*

Then before Anna could respond, Jolene glided past and around the next corner and out of sight again.

Anna almost got up to see what was around that corner that might have some sort of attraction for Jolene, but then she remembered her promise to watch the wagon and its contents, and stayed where she was.

But she couldn't help but notice it was becoming uncomfortably hot down here, as the sun climbed closer to noon, where there were no trees, and the bare dirt of the street did nothing but reflect the heat back. She took off her hat to fan herself with, and wished there were someplace to get a drink of water. She was, in fact, giving serious consideration to cupping some water in her hand out of the dubious depths of the horse trough—not to drink, but to splash over her head and neck—when Aunt Jinny and Matt and Josh Holcroft rounded the corner at long last. They all three waved at her, and Matt and his son went into the Company store, while Jinny joined her on the bench.

Her aunt leaned over as if to offer a confidential thought. "Th' earth's nice'n cool deep down. Jest reach on down thar an' let it pull th' heat outen y'all."

Then she straightened up. She pulled off her own hat and fanned herself with it—but her face wasn't flushed at all, and there wasn't even a hint of sweat on it. Anna closed her eyes and tried to do as her aunt had suggested.

She let her awareness sink down beneath her ... and her aunt was right! She sensed a coolth, and then found the earth itself pulling all the heat out of her! In fact, she had to cut it off before too long, before she started to shiver!

She wasn't sure how long she'd been sitting there, wrapped up in this new application of magic, but when she opened her eyes, Matt and Josh were just coming out of the store with their arms laden with purchases.

"Le's git loaded up an' outa here," Matt said to her aunt. "By noon this town'll be a oven."

"Got no argument from me," Aunt Jinny agreed, and got to her feet. Anna followed a moment later.

And that was when the strange man came around the corner that Jolene had vanished around.

He was big and strong and surprisingly healthy for a miner—for a miner he certainly was, given his massive physique, in a town where the only real employment was mining. Black-haired and blue-eyed, he strode down the middle of the street as if he owned it, as if he was wearing a "flash" suit and smoking a big cigar, not a collarless linen shirt, brown moleskin trousers, and bracers and smoking an old cheroot. Urged by instinct, Anna looked at him with that inner eye—

And sure enough. There was the Glory.

Except he had no shields, and the Glory was wrong ... twisted somehow. Not a glowing gold, but a muddled, ugly color that actually seemed to take its strength from the poisoned earth.

"Go in th' store, Anna," her aunt ordered in an undertone. Anna did not argue. She felt a fear of this man she could not rationalize but did not care to fight. She whisked just inside the Company store door and peeked around the edge of it.

"Wall, Miz Jinny!" the man boomed. "Didn' 'spect t'see y'all here t'day!"

"Josh and Matt had bizness, an' I tagged 'long," Jinny said shortly. "Got weary of hoecake. Reckon on bread an' pie fer a while. An' afore y'all ask, left yer potions with word fer Cooper in th' Company store."

"Good," the man grunted. "I'll fetch 'em later." He moved a little, as if he was going to examine the load, but Matt moved casually to the side of the wagon, intercepting him. Matt didn't say anything, and he wasn't rude, but the action made it very clear he didn't appreciate the man's attempt to snoop in his business. "Wall, howdy, Matt," the man said. "Josh been doin' some work fer Cavenel?"

"Jest delivered it," Matt said shortly.

The man laughed, which was scarcely an appropriate reaction to someone deliving a grave marker. "No lack'a work fer yer boy in this town, aye! Reckon plantin' stones is easier'n plantin' corn!"

"Not really," Josh replied to this singularly tactless statement.

"Wall, wife's expectin' us fer dinner," Matt interrupted.

The man laughed again. "Niver took y'all fer hen-pecked, Matt Holcroft," he jibed.

"Thet's 'cause I ain't. What I *am* is hungry." Around the corner of the door, Anna saw Matt motion to Josh. "An' y'all'll haveta pardon me, but I wanter get t'thet dinner."

The man laughed again, tossing his head back, but moved out of the way and down the street without so much as a word of farewell. After a moment, Aunt Jinny gestured to Anna, who ran out and hopped into the back of the wagon with Josh.

Because everything about that man made her want to get out of Ducktown as quickly as she could.

And not much longer after that, they were on their way out of town, the mule moving considerably faster than she had on the way in.

She and Josh had made themselves tolerably comfortable seats with the straw, the bags, and the parcels. Josh cradled a blue and white pitcher in his lap with great care. Anna eyed it.

"She's called th' Blue Willow pattern," Josh said, noticing where she was staring. "Ma sets a lotta store by it. I got it fer her as a present. It's got a purdy liddle story in the pattern. Wanter hear?"

"A'course!" she said instantly, and he rolled the pitcher to the side so she could see the design.

"It's Chinee, see?" he said. She *didn't* see, since this would be the first time she'd ever seen anything Chinee, but nodded. "See, here's a palace, an' here's th' willows all 'round, an' here's a bridge an' th' island it goes to. So th' story goes, here in this palace was a Mandarin. Thassa kinda rich man like a prince. His name was So Ling. An' he had a be-yoo-tiful daughter, name'a Kong-see, an' he promised her as a wife t' this fat ol' rich man. But she went an' fell in love with her Pa's servant Chang. Her Pa found out 'bout it an' built a big ol' wall around his house t' keep her in. Here's th' wall. Then he sent fer the rich man—see, there he is, a-comin' on his boat. But Kong-see an' Chang ran away on th' rich man's boat while her Pa was givin' him dinner, an' got t' the island there, where my finger is, an' they lived happy fer a while. Then her Pa found out where they was, an' he sent them three sojers, here on th' bridge, to cotch 'em, an' kill Chang, an' drag Kong-see back

from her fingers. They'd both just scraped a thin layer of it over their cornbread, making it serve as a treat at the end of the meal. "I got inside when y'all tol' me, but I seed 'im. I reckon he didn't see me none." She nodded in agreement with what her aunt had ordered. "Y'all's right, Aunt Jinny. He's pizen. He's got th' Glory, but it's all twisted wrong."

Her aunt pursed her lips before she spoke. "I'd'a thunk it was him as pizened Ducktown in th' fust place, but it was pizened afore he got there. He thrives on th' pizen, though. His heart's as black as his hair. He *needs* me, on account'a th' way he thrives on pizen. He cain't grow nothin'. An' he needs m'potions. So he won't cross me. But y'all—he'd et y'all up and spit y'all out, jest 'cause he kin." She thumped on the table with her knuckle to get Anna's full attention. "Hear me, now! Y'all's a purdy liddle gal. Y'all know what happens t' purdy liddle gals with men like thet?"

She shook her head.

Her aunt *tsk*ed, briefly cursed her Ma for a fool and an idiot, and then told her.

"Likely, he'll try an' beguile y'all. Use thet there twisted power of his t'git y'all so tangled up in his wiles thet y'all's as bad 'bout him as yore Ma is about yore Pa. On'y, there ain't a-gonna be a weddin' an' a ring; there's gonna be a beddin', with no weddin'. Then he'll git tired of y'all, an' boot y'all out, an' there ain't gonna be a honest man or woman thet'll so much as look at y'all arter thet. But wust is, he'll beguile y'all jest enuff that yore guard is down—then he'll take y'all howsomever he fancies, an' mebbe wust of all, they'll be a chile out of it."

By this time, Anna was feeling sick and terrified, no longer *strong*. If the cost of staying here, if the cost of having the Glory was she had to be afraid of the likes of Billie McDaran—maybe she didn't want to be here at all anymore!

But that was when her aunt slapped her lightly on the cheek. "Stop thet," she said, harshly. "Yer frettin' afore anythin' has happened. Now y'all listen t'me. Mebbe he knows y'all's here, mebbe he don't. He mighta heered somethin', but he don't know what y'all looks like, so right now he ain't innerested. He's as lazy as a hog with a full belly. So he ain't gonna come all this way jest t'hev a gander at y'all. As long as he don' know what a purdy liddle thang y'are, as long as he thinks y'all's jest as homely as me, he ain't gonna care 'bout y'all. So stop a-shakin'."

Anna took several deep, shuddering breaths, which didn't help as much as she would have liked, but nodded.

"T'other thang—y'all ain't stronger than him *yet*, but y'all *will be*. Iffen I git my way, by th' time he lays eyes on y'all, there won't be a thang he c'n do t' y'all, an' y'all c'n snap yore fingers in his face. I aim t'make y'all inter a woman what ain't afeerd of man nor beast."

Her face took on an expression of icy bitterness. "I'm a-gonna tell y'all a story I ain't niver told no one but my Granny an' Old Raven. Them troopers weren't th' on'y ones what come a-sniffin' round our farm in th' war. We got drifters an' deserters sneakin' through, lookin' fer whatever they could steal. One on 'em caught me all alone i' th' woods. I shouldn't'a been there alone, but—" she shrugged. "I wanted nuts, an' my brother wouldn' go with me an account'a he was a workin'. I dunno iffen the rat was Yank or Reb, or jest plain trash—he had a blue coat an' gray trousers and stunk like a skunk, he caught me off-guard, an' he had me on th' ground an' my skirt up afore I knowed he was even there."

Her knuckles were white as she clenched her knife, and she looked down as she paused, and slowly put the knife down.

"I weren't gonna abide thet. He didn' even git as far as gittin' his trousers down. An' I killt him," she said flatly. "Or, the stag I called did. Ten points through the lungs. He was a long time dyin', an' I watched, all of it, t'make sure he was dead. Then I called in the wild pigs, an' left 'em ettin' him. Thet is the kinda woman y'all's gonna be. Y'all c'n do better'n me, iffen y'all have to, once y'all learn enough t'be in yore full power."

Silence for a very long time, as Anna thought this over. This was a side of her aunt she had never seen—but hadn't she kind of ... guessed at it?

Do I want t'be thet kinda woman? One what don't need a man ter keep her safe?

"How?" she asked, finally.

"Them liddle critters y'all been seein'? They ain't nothin'. They's thin's out there what y'all c'n call thet I cain't, what makes a bear look like a pup. Once y'all knows 'nuff, an' y'all makes yore alliances, ain't nothin' an' nobody c'n bring y'all no harm." She looked down at the remains of her dinner, and ate it. It seemed to settle her, since she looked back up at Anna and nodded. "Mostly I want y'all t' stay as clear'a thet snake Billie McDaran as y'all possibly kin till y'all knows thet stuff."

"I don't want nothin' t'do with him," Anna protested. "He makes my skin crawl. When I seed him in Ducktown, what I seed make me purt near sick."

"He should make y'all sick. But I need y'all t' *shield* 'gainst him too. An' don' lissen t'anythin' he says. He's got some hoodoo I ain't niver seen afore, what beguiles folks. Even them as should know better." Aunt Jinny shook her head. "Even me fer a liddle bit, afore I woke m'self outen it. It works without potions, an' he don't seem t'call on nothin', he jest does it with his voice. Might be part'a thet there twisted sorta Glory he got. I'll swear thet's how he got the Mine Foreman job, an' how he keeps it, given thet he don't spend half th' time at the mine thet he should."

Then she laughed sardonically and added, "An' I guess I should be grateful, seein' as how the less ore comes outa thet mine, the better off everybody in th' Basin is."

They did the few dishes there were, then went off to the garden for harvesting, and following the harvesting, some preparation and preserving. Aunt Jinny did a lot of drying of her vegetables and fruits, especially things like corn, which she took off the cob, dried, and "parched," and beans. But she had other ways of preserving things too—potatoes and sweet potatoes and winter squash were still holding from last year's harvest in the root cellar, and onions stayed sweet and sound for quite a long time—so Aunt Jinny said— when you braided the leaves and hung them up in the shadow.

That would not have been enough to distract Anna from the terrible things her aunt had told her—except that the afternoon turned out to be another lesson in magic. First, though, she partly disrobed and took off her corset, with a guilty look at her aunt, who had paid so much for it.

But Aunt Jinny just chuckled. "I druther y'all kept thet for Sunday best, an' even then, not till y'all sew a cover fer it," she said. "Abby's a good woman, but she got no notion what farm work's like. It ain't like standin' behind a store counter all day, which is all she does, on account of I know she's got a maid a-doin' th' heavy housework."

Anna carefully folded her treasure in a bit of leftover petticoat and put it with the unsewn pieces of her winter skirts and coat. She was looking forward to sewing a cover for it, though.

They had an overabundance of tomatoes, and Anna didn't see nearly enough jars to preserve them all. But Aunt Jinny instructed her to quarter enough to fill the sieve and leave the pieces to drain into a bucket. When enough juice had been drained, her aunt poured the juice into a pitcher, replaced the bucket, and sat down next to the bucket on one of the stools.

"Watch," she said, and sketched two signs in the air over the sieve full of quartered fruits, and let Glory drift down onto the sieve. And the quartered tomatoes began to shrivel.

Within moments they were hard little nuggets, as dry as rocks and the color of dried blood, and the bucket beneath them had a couple of inches of water in it. Aunt Jinny tipped the tomato nuggets out into a basket and told Anna to quarter up some more tomatoes, while she poured the water into the water barrel next to the sink. "This here's the purest water y'all ever will find," Jinny said. "There jest ain't nothin' in it, 'cause I kept ever'thang else in the 'maters. It's wuth savin'."

"What'd y'all jest do?" Anna asked, industriously quartering fruit.

"Simplest thang we c'n do. I tol' the water t'leave." Her aunt chuckled at Anna's expression. "Water don' like earth. Wall, thet stands t'reason. Even mud, let it set even without usin' th' Glory, an' th' water'll rise an' th' earth'll settle. I jest made thet happen fast an' completely. Same thing'd happen iffen we sliced them 'maters thin an' left the slices t'dry in the sun, but these nuggets store easier, an' nothing I make in th' winter needs sliced 'maters."

Anna watched her aunt repeat the action three more times before Jinny turned the task over to her. Jinny used the juice initially drained from the tomatoes as the base for their soup, then, when there was more than she needed, directed Anna to pour it into the slop bucket for the pigs.

"C'n we do this with ever'thang?" she asked.

Jinny nodded, her back to Anna while she cut up more vegetables for the soup. "Some thangs it don't pay t' waste th' time an' Glory, though," she pointed out. "Most stuff might's well let the sun do th' work. Peas 'n beans. Corn. I like t' sun-dry apples. Mostly, y'all wanter do this with anythang what's real juicy an' cain't hold in a barrel or bag an' cain't be pickled—which ain't much. Mushrooms, iffen y'all got 'nuff, though mushrooms mostly don' last long 'nuff 'round me t'git dried."

"Strawbs?" Anna asked hopefully.

To her regret, her aunt shook her head. "Naw, strawbs don' hold up well t'dryin'. Most berries don't, jest deerberry an' blueberry. Some thangs we jest gotter enjoy in jam an' in season."

Mastering this drove most of that uncomfortable conversation out of Anna's head, and the novelty of having wheat bread instead of corn bread for supper further distracted her. Her aunt had made up the dough into four little round loaves rather than one big one; when time came for supper, she sawed the bottom off two of the loaves, dug out the soft insides, set the pieces aside, and filled the bread "bowls" with soup, with the soft bits on the side to sop up the broth. The bottoms got spread with strawberry jam for dessert.

"Go sit on th' stove an' read yore book," her aunt directed, when the little that needed to be cleaned was done. "I gotter go talk to some'un." And she took down that piece of black glass Anna had seen her staring into once before.

"W-w-wait," Anna stuttered. "What?"

"This," her aunt told her, "was my Granpappy's. 'Tis called a *scryin' plate*. Thet means I c'n use it ter talk ter other people what gots th' Glory, an' iffen I had the power ter look inter th' future— which I don't—I could see what was a-comin'. Or iffen I had the power t' see what's a-goin' on fur away, I c'd do thet. My Granny showed me how t'talk to 'bout a dozen folks up Nawth a-ways, 'cause them's who she knowed. An' they innerduced me t'their kin, which's who I talk to now. An' iffen y'all wanter know more 'bout thet—read yer book."

With that she took the black plate and went out onto the porch, where the westering sun was turning everything a deep gold.

So Anna got a candle and her book, and climbed up on the stove, where she shortly had company. But the three little leaf-

and-stick critters didn't seem inclined to do anything other than share the warmth and twitter at each other, so she settled into the book again.

Pavel was passed from Master to Master, right across Germany and France and all the way to England. Most of the time he left with more money in his pocket than when he'd arrived, because the Earth Masters he was sponsored by all seemed to be prosperous, some extremely so. And England was where he settled for the winter months with a "squire," which seemed to be a sort of rich man whose money came from his land, rather than a mine or a factory. Not as important as a "lord," but more important than a farmer.

It was this "squire," living in a place called "Devon" (which she gathered was something like a state even though it was called a "shire"), who also advised him to go to America, reinforcing what the Hungarian Master had said. Or as Pavel put it, "The New Territory of the United States." It hadn't *been* a country for more than thirty years at that point, maybe less, which was something of a shock to Pavel, whose home country had been a nation "forever" as far as he knew.

And it was there, at the home of Squire Thomson, that he met Sally Lacey, who was both the daughter of the fellow in charge of all of Squire Thomson's cows, and a very skilled magician who was well known for her healing ways.

Now, Sally had got her powers from her Ma. And things were changing in England. People weren't going to "herb-wifes" anymore; they were going to doctors. Only the poorest were resorting to Sally's Ma for help. And Squire Thomson was a bit concerned that at some point in the near future, it might actually be *illegal* for people like Sally to help others with their ailments. Certainly all the newly minted doctors were complaining to people like Squire Thomson and other "members of Parliament" that "medicine should be taken out of the hands of the unwashed and ignorant peasant midwives" and entrusted solely to them.

So Squire Thomson had a notion that Sally ought to go to America, where she'd be more than welcome. Sally had been pretty dubious about this notion. Until Pavel arrived.

Pavel was educated, her equal in magic, and also an Earth Magician. Pavel was blond and handsome and—thanks to his difficult life in his homeland—modest about his abilities and his looks. Pavel for his part fell head over heels for pretty, brown-eyed, brown-haired Sally the moment he saw her. And Pavel was going to America in the spring, his pockets full of gifts from other Earth Masters who were eager to see an Elemental Master well established in the New World, where he could relay reports about how Elemental Magic was practiced there and help find and educate new Masters.

Sally's Ma and Pa were very much inclined to like Pavel from the beginning, as he put on no "airs" with them. They liked him even more for his deference and gentleness with Sally.

And as for Sally—well, if Pavel was to be believed, and Anna saw no reason why he shouldn't be—it was love at first sight for both of them.

It was during that winter that the squire taught Pavel how to "scry," and gave him that black glass plate, which was not glass at all, but a stone called "obsidian," which was something Anna had only heard of, never seen. Pavel gave a long and detailed description about how to use this plate, but made it clear that it didn't *have* to be an obsidian plate, it could be any shiny, black surface. A black bowl full of water, for instance—though that would be better suited to a Water Magician. Or a ball of black or clear glass. Or a ball or plate of some other black stone. Why, it could even be polished coal! First, you filled the plate with the Glory. The first time you used it you had to "seal" it to you with a couple of signs. After that, all you had to do was fill it with Glory and think of the person you wanted to talk to. The critters on the other person's end would let him know he was wanted, and he'd get his plate or bowl or whatever, and talk to you through it.

It was more complicated than that, but that was the short tale. And the thing was, since Pavel had the power, and so did Sally, it wasn't like it was with most folks, which meant that her parents were fine with her going off across an entire ocean away from them. For most people, if a child went off to America, they'd be lucky to get a letter or two a year, if that. Sally's Ma could talk to her every night if they wanted.

So as soon as shipping began after the end of the winter storms in the Atlantic, Pavel and Sally were on a stout sailing vessel, a trading ship full of household goods on the way to make profit from the former colonies, Pavel traveling only with his precious set of carving tools and clothing, and Sally with an equally precious stock of herb seeds, her healing powers, and enough herbs to be useful on the voyage.

And that was when Aunt Jinny touched Anna's foot and jerked her out of the book.

"Larn anythin'?" she asked. "Y'all was so deep in thet book I called y'all three times an' y'all didn' stir."

"Great-Granpappy wrote 'bout that there scryin' plate," she said, then unexpectedly yawned.

"Good. Then I c'n start larnin' y'all how t'use it. Termorrer. Y'all jest 'bout split yore head with that yawn," Aunt Jinny chuckled. "I's been a long day. Git t'bed."

13

"So now you can scry?" asked Jolene, when Anna finished telling her what she had been learning from her aunt.

This morning her aunt had expended quite a bit of Glory bolstering the shield around the farm, and Anna hadn't had to ask to know she'd been specifically doing it to protect against Billie McDaran. Anna had watched closely, and helped where she could, but it was clear when Jinny was done that the task had taken a lot out of her physically, as well as the expenditure of Glory. After dinner, Jinny had admitted to being "a mite tuckered" and that she needed "a bit of a lay-down." Armed with a list of the wild plants Aunt Jinny wanted and strictures not to wander so far from the lane that she couldn't see it through the trees, Anna had gone off in search of more ingredients for potions.

And as she had half expected, Jolene met her on the lane. They settled in, at Jolene's insistence, beside a little thread of a stream where Anna could cool her feet. Jolene didn't seem to need or want any such thing, but Anna was glad of it. Her basket was more than half full and it was a warm day. Her hair was coming down from its neat bun, making little draggles around her face, and she was pleased to have the chance to put it back up again.

"Yes'm," she replied. "I ain't too good at it."

Jolene laughed softly. "Perhaps that is because you are trying the wrong people. You have no real connection with these acquaintances of Jinny's. Try someone you know, first. Like Younger Raven."

Anna furrowed her brow. "But Younger Raven ain't got th' Earth—"

"Master can speak to Master regardless of the Element," Jolene told her. "It's only the ordinary magicians like your aunt who are restricted to speaking to those of their own kind."

Anna blinked at that.

"But this is boring," Jolene continued, her eyes alight. "There is nothing exciting about staring into a bowl or an obsidian plate. Would you like to learn something exciting instead?"

"What d'y'all mean?" she asked, looking into those eyes and remembering that Aunt Jinny had warned her over and over that Jolene was dangerous.

"Like summoning creatures!" Jolene laughed. "Wouldn't you like to know how to summon creatures?"

Well ... she *would*, actually. That was certainly more exciting than Aunt Jinny's scrying. But ... but ... but. "What kinda creatures? An' fer what? An'—" She paused to put some of her whirling thoughts into a more concrete form. "An' what d'y'all mean when y'all say *summoning*? Is it like arskin' 'em t'come? Or is it like *makin'* 'em come?" Because if it was the latter ... well, even though the Joneses were poor and Anna didn't have much real time or more than casual friends, that didn't mean Anna had been left out of invitations to parties. Especially when she had been younger. There wasn't only Christmas, which was a traditional time for ghost stories, there was also Halloween. Pastor might've frowned on it, but girls *would* get together and tell fortunes and try to scare each other. And there were lots of stories about people who *summoned* things and couldn't control what came to their summons.

"Either. Both," Jolene said, with the carelessness of someone who knows she is powerful enough to control anything she cared to call. "Does it matter?"

Anna didn't answer immediately. And when she did, she picked her words slowly and with great care. "Arskin' is one thing. But it ain't perlite t' jest drag somethin' in without a 'please will y'all.' My Ma allus says y'all ketch more flies with molasses than vinegar."

Jolene looked at her oddly, as if her words made no sense, then shrugged. "If you insist," she said, with impatience. "So, do you want to learn how to summon?"

"Yes'm, please," she replied, ducking her head. Jolene chuckled.

"It's simple. Just draw up the power as I showed you, then cup your hands together, like *so*." She held her hands a little apart, as if she was holding a large ball between them. "Then fill the space between them with the power. Go ahead, do it—" she urged, and Anna carefully did as she had been told.

Between her hands, a sort of ball of that lovely golden glow formed.

"Now put your intention on it. Tell it the kind of creature you want to summon," Jolene continued.

"Kin it be anythin'?" she asked.

"Anything you have seen. Earth Elemental, or actual animal, that is. *You* cannot summon any Elementals but your own. I can, of course, summon anything I care to," Jolene replied with unconscious arrogance. "What would you like to see?"

"Liddle People," she said, without a second thought, and turned her attention to the glowing ball in her hands. *I'd take it right kindly*, she thought, as hard as she could, *if any of y'all Liddle People'd come an' palaver a bit with me*. And she pictured the tiny Cherokee in her mind as vividly as she could.

She was conscious of Jolene's intent gaze on her the entire time, but she didn't allow it to distract her. "Now squeeze the power between your hands, as tight as you ever can," Jolene instructed her, after what seemed like forever. "Because when you release it, you want it to explode, like dynamite, and scatter itself and your intention far and wide."

Well, that, at least, was something she could easily picture. Except she wasn't going to think of it like dynamite. She was going to think of it like a beautiful firework, the kind of thing the mine owners would send up into the early evening sky at their Fourth of July parties. Not that miners or miners' children were invited to such things—but if you went out on your porch, you could see the rockets and roman candles exploding over the houses at the rich end of Soddy.

So she squeezed ever so hard, with her hands and her mind, feeling the power building in strength the more she compressed it, until the moment when Jolene said "*Now!*" and she cast her hands wide and tossed it up and it *did* explode just like a Fourth of July rocket up above her head.

"Now we wait, and while we wait, I show you what *I* can summon," said Jolene. And she made a little swirl of her right hand in the air, and something infinitely more powerful than anything that Anna could conjure spun up and then exploded like another rocket.

She heard it before she saw it: great, slow *thuds* that shook the earth she sat on, and made the leaves tremble. At first she heard and felt the thuds with puzzlement; it sounded a little like distant thunder, but it wasn't overcast, and anyway, the sound was too abrupt to be thunder. Was it explosions? Had Matt decided to use dynamite to blow up some stumps on his land? But that didn't make sense, the sounds were too close together. What could it possibly be?

The trees across the lane shook, and birds flew up from them, as the thuds grew closer. Her heart beat faster, and she glanced over at Jolene, who looked as calm as a statue. What was going on?

And between one breath and the next, a *thing* came lumbering out of the forest across from them.

Anna felt the paralysis of sheer terror strike her as the thing pushed its way through the trees. It was taller than the cabin, a manlike shape covered in long, shaggy green hair, long enough to completely cover a body that was otherwise unclothed. And it carried a club that looked to have been made out of an entire tree trunk over one shoulder.

The creature lumbered up to the crick, and stood above her. It gazed down at her, and she trembled all over, expecting it to strike her with that massive club at any moment.

But what struck her was Jolene—Jolene smacked her lightly on the shoulder, with impatience. "Didn't I say I was going to show you the sort of thing I could summon? Don't be afraid, you little fool! This is a Borovoi. He won't hurt you."

She managed, somehow, to turn her head to look at Jolene, who seemed to be torn between amusement and exasperation.

I cain't let her think I'm lily-livered ...

Somehow, she managed to muster the courage to stand.

Somehow, she got one foot in front of the other and took a step. Then another. Then another. Until finally she was standing at the monster's feet, looking up at it.

It looked down at her, face unreadable under all that hair. All she could see were a pair of eyes like distant stars, glowing with a dim, white light. She reached up her hand, somehow, and managed to choke out words.

"Pleased t'meetcher, Mistuh Borovoi," she said, even though her voice quavered with fear.

The Borovoi reached down with its free hand and delicately took her hand between its finger and thumb, with no more pressure than if it was trying to hold a delicate feather. It shook her hand politely. "*Privyet, sestra,*" it rumbled, and looked up at Jolene. "*Ya tebe nuzhen seychas?*"

"*Nyet, spi dal'she,*" she said dismissively.

The creature looked down at her again. "*Do svendanya, sestra,*" it rumbled. Then it let go of her hand and thudded ponderously back into the forest again.

Her legs felt as if she had no bones in them at all, and threatened to collapse under her. Somehow she managed to walk back to Jolene, who looked more approving now. She sat back down in the grass of the crick bank, then scooped up a handful of water and dashed it against her face. Distantly, a part of her wondered what on earth that language that Jolene had spouted was. It didn't sound like *anything* she'd ever heard before. But—

Hadn't Jolene said the thing was a "Borovoi"? That sounded like "Domovoy." Was this creature from Roosha too? Had it come with her Great-Granpappy like the Domovoy had?

He was s'pposed to be real powerful. If Jolene c'n control thet thang, reckon he could.

But did that mean Jolene was Rooshan? Or did it just mean she knew some Rooshan palaver?

If she was Rooshan, that might have accounted for the outlandish— but beautiful!—dress that Anna had seen her in, that first day. Foreigners— well, you never knew what they'd wear, or not wear. Like that little bit of a petticoat that Pharoah's daughter wore in that picture in her Bible, or the robes other people in her Bible wore.

She was so caught up in her thoughts that it wasn't until she felt a tug on her sleeve that she realized there were three of the Little People—all male—standing next to her, waiting patiently for her to notice them. Unlike Elder and Younger Raven, these doll-sized men had heads shaved except for a single strip down the middle, and wore only leather breechcloths and leggings.

Jolene had on an expression of amusement again, but Anna was too pleased to see the Little People to take any offense at the fact that Jolene found her funny.

"You came!" she said joyfully in Cherokee, surprising shy smiles out of them. "Thank you for coming—" her mouth seemed to know the right honorific, even if her head didn't, "—grandfathers. I hope I was not rude in calling you."

"All was as it should be," the one that had tugged her sleeve said. "What is it that you need, granddaughter?"

And they waited patiently while she gathered her thoughts, and considered each word carefully.

"I have just come into my power," she told him. "I am unlearned, and I have many questions. Some of them my aunt does not know the answers to. I know that I may call upon the spirits of the earth, but I do not know which ones. *May* I call upon the spirits of the earth known to the Cherokee?"

"You may, if you call, and not summon," the little man said, with a gravity worthy of Elder Raven. "Your best ally at most times will be Bear, and if you cannot think upon whom to call, call Bear. For every forest animal, there is a clan of Spirit Animals that can speak to you and aid you. Grandmother Spider will tell you about all of them; she is the wisest of us all, and the best teacher. You may summon the ordinary animals of the forest, as your aunt does, but they may not come when you call upon them unless your summons is very strong. Grandmother Spider can teach you about all that may be taught to you. Some, you may not learn, because you are not of the Cherokee People."

Anna cast a glance over to Jolene, who nodded slightly, as if all of this was completely expected. But—Grandmother *Spider*? She didn't much care for the sound of that; she didn't like spiders at the best of times. And at the worst, like the times she had run into webs on the way to the privy? Ugh! Ugh! Ugh!

It made her skin want to crawl right off her body!

But she wasn't given a chance to object, as suddenly, right before her horrified eyes, a gigantic spider came sliding down out of the tree above on a strand of silk, to dangle mere inches in front of her nose!

"There is Grandmother Spider now," the Little Person said conversationally. "She is ready to instruct you."

All that Anna could do was stare at the thing, rigid with fear.

"Let us tell you why Grandmother Spider is such a great teacher," the tiny man continued. "It is because she is clever, she thinks things through carefully, and she always does what she sets out to do. My grandfathers told me this story when I was a boy, so it must be true. In the Before Times, this world was covered in darkness, and all the Peoples of this world kept getting hurt because they bumped into each other in the dark. Fox, who had been everywhere, looking and spying with his long, sharp nose, said, 'I know where there is light all the time, but the people over in that place won't share it because they are greedy.' He was speaking of the world of the Thunders, who had the Sun all to themselves. Raven said he would go and steal some of the light and bring it back. And everyone thought he would do it because he is so strong. But he got too near the Sun—because that is what it was—and his feathers were burned black and he got frightened and flew home. Possum said, 'I have a big bushy tail, I can hide a piece of the Sun in my tail and the people over there won't see me take it.' So Possum went, and stole a piece of the Sun and hid it in his tail. But the Sun was so hot, it burned off all his beautiful tail fur, and the Thunders saw it shining and took the piece of the Sun back. And that is why Possum has a bare tail now. And Vulture said, 'I will go and steal it, and fly high with the piece of the Sun on my head so I can see where I am going.' And he took the piece of the Sun and did that, and it burned all the feathers off his head, and he dropped it, and this is why his head is bald now. But Grandmother Spider had been studying and watching, and she said, 'I think I know how to bring back a piece of the Sun.' And she made a little pot of her web, lined with clay, and she went to the place where the Sun was, spinning web behind her all the time so that she could make her way home in the dark, until she saw the Sun hanging in a tree. And she stole a piece, and put it in her pot and closed the lid. And the clay kept the Sun from burning up her web, and the lid kept the Thunders from seeing that she had stolen it. And she followed her web through the darkness back to this place, where she hung the Sun in the sky for all the Peoples to see by. And this is why she is the wisest of us all, and meant to be a teacher. The old men told me this story when I was a boy, so it must be true."

Anna could only stare at the spider dangling in front of her face. And then—it—she?—chuckled. She had a lovely voice, deep and kind, and Anna relaxed a very little.

"That is a good story. You may go now," the spider said. "I shall undertake to teach my granddaughter."

"Thank you, Grandmother," chorused all three of the Little People. And then they slipped into the reeds beside the crick, and were gone.

"Look at me, child," the spider ordered. "Put your fear aside. Try to imagine that you have never seen a spider before and *look* at me. Look at me as if I were one of Jolene's pretty baubles. Imagine that I am a beautiful brooch."

Somehow the spider seemed to grow until she filled Anna's entire range of vision … and the first thing that she realized was how delicate and elegant the legs were, each one tipped with a neat little claw. Then, as her mind calmed, she actually paid attention to the beautiful red and black patterns on Grandmother Spider's body, and lastly, she gazed into the four black, black eyes of Grandmother Spider, two big and two little. They were like four beautiful black beads, and even though they looked nothing at all like human eyes, Anna sensed that there was kindness behind them. And Grandmother Spider gazed back at her, and said, "Now, you see."

And she did. The spider was a beautiful, elegant creature, and nothing to be afraid of. In fact, there was much to be grateful to her for, because she ate insects that really *could* bring harm to people in the form of sickness.

She blinked, and the spider no longer filled her eyes; she held out her hand, no longer full of fear, and the spider spun down her strand of silk and landed gently on the back of it, her touch lighter than a feather.

"I will teach you first about Bear," Grandmother Spider said. "For as the Little People told you, Bear is the spirit that you are most likely to need if you are in danger. Bear can run, and swim, and climb, and fight; Bear is fearless when that is called for, but does not lose himself in rage and will run when that is needed. And Bear is near to the Cherokee peoples. This is how you call Bear, and how you summon the lesser bears."

With Jolene looking on in approval, Grandmother Spider taught her about Bear, and Deer, and Badger, and Panther. "And that is enough for today," she concluded. And that was when Anna realized that they had been sitting there all afternoon, it was getting late, and she hadn't actually gathered any ingredients for potions—

As Grandmother Spider reeled herself back up into the tree above, Anna looked frantically for her basket.

And that was when she saw the little green lizards; she had been listening so hard to Grandmother Spider, and the lizards were so quiet, that she hadn't even noticed them until that moment.

There must have been two dozen of them, scurrying around the basket, bringing neatly cut-off stems of the plants she had been asked to gather, carrying them in their mouths, dropping them in the basket, and scurrying off again. They were beautiful little things, with scales that glimmered like polished gems and copper-colored eyes. She'd never seen lizards like these before in her entire life.

And she had certainly never seen lizards working together like this.

As she raised her eyes to Jolene's amused face, she knew without asking that this was Jolene's doing. "Don't think to summon these, ever," Jolene admonished her, with a lizard on each shoulder and one being stroked by those beautiful, white hands. "These are mine, and mine alone."

"I niver would!" Anna promised. "How did y'all know I was worritin' 'bout not gitting Aunt Jinny's her-ubs? How did y'all know which ones I was s'posed t'git?"

"I have eyes everywhere," Jolene replied, with a slightly mocking smile. "And ears too. I couldn't let you go back to Virginia empty-handed. Not—" she added, "—that Virginia would fault you for neglecting her task in order to get a lesson from Grandmother

Spider. But you did promise her that you would bring the things she needed, and I don't like to be the cause of you breaking a promise. You both need these plants for your cures, they were easy to find, and my pets didn't mind. And now that you don't need to tell Virginia why you didn't have what you set out to gather, you needn't say we met unless you choose to."

Anna hesitated a moment, then asked one of the questions she'd been worrying over in her head. "What's Aunt Jinny got 'gainst y'all?"

"Ah … partly that goes back to things her Grandmother told her, I think," Jolene replied, thoughtfully. "And partly that she misunderstood something I told her. And mostly that she does not understand what I am. Everything is black or white with her. Good or evil."

"And—" Anna dared to prompt.

"And that is a very simple way to think of—those like me." Jolene shrugged. "Too simple. And really, Virginia should know by this time that nothing is ever that simple. Your Great-Grandfather knew better than that."

That seemed to be all that Anna was going to get out of Jolene, because with a wave of her hands, Jolene sent her lizards scattering into the underbrush and rose. Anna did the same, stooping to pick up her basket.

And when she rose again, Jolene was gone.

Aunt Jinny was so pleased with the quality of the cuttings Anna had brought back that she didn't even comment on the fact that Anna was a little late, and Jinny had already fed the pigs by the time she climbed over the fence and headed for the cabin. Over supper of bean soup, she decided to tell part of the truth. "I done seed the Little People, an' Granny Spider is a-larnin' me now," she said.

Aunt Jinny looked up at that. "That so! Wall, good. What I cain't larn y'all, Granny Spider shore can. Mind yore manners with her, she ain't t'be trifled with."

Which was almost exactly the same thing that Aunt Jinny had said about Jolene …

"Granny Spider ain't 'xactly a Earth Spirit, is she?" Anna hazarded.

"Not 'xactly," her aunt agreed. "Y'all don' call or summon her, y'all arst perlite, an' iffen she don't come, say thenkee anyway. She's what my Granpappy called a *Great Elemental*. Did she tell y'all 'bout Bear? Not just any ol' bear, but *Bear*?"

Anna nodded.

"Bear, an' Wolf, an' Fox, an' all o' them, they's *Great Elementals* too, by Granpappy's reckonin'. Critters what might he'p y'all, an' might not. An' don't go gettin' hoity toity an' thinkin' y'all c'n boss 'em around, or—well iffen y'all's lucky y'all *might* get a mighty setdown an' th' wust day of yore life, an' iffen y'all ain't lucky, they might be a-pickin' pieces of y'all outen th' crick." Aunt Jinny finished her tea and picked up her dishes to take them to the sink. "I ain't niver seed nobody what was thet stupid, so—" She shrugged.

"Yes'm," Anna agreed, taking her own dishes to the sink. As usual, Aunt Jinny washed, and Anna dried.

Aunt Jinny immediately set to work sorting and bundling Anna's harvest and hanging it to dry. Since her aunt didn't give her any directions, Anna got the cut-out pieces for the corset cover and set to work on them on the front porch, with her Great-Granpappy's book open on her knee. The sun still hung over the mountains to the west, and the light was the same color as the Glory. The hens were still out, but gathered up at the henhouse, ready to be shut in for the night, scratching away at the feed Anna had scattered up there for them. A few birds twittered sleepily under the eaves where they had a nest, and swallows swooped and darted everywhere, catching the 'skeeters that were injudicious enough to come out early. In a little more time, they'd be joined by, then replaced by, the bats.

She was impatient to get to the part where Pavel and Sally arrived *here*, and first met Eagle Sight, and made their home—but she got the sense that it would be a much better idea if she kept reading steadily and didn't skip ahead. *Reckon maybe the reason Aunt Jinny don't know some things is because she just skipped around, and didn't read the whole book*. Since this book and the receipt book were the only two books in the entire household, she was beginning to think that her aunt was one of those people who just didn't like reading.

It was a good thing that she did just that, too, because it was in the parts about the sea voyage that Pavel revealed the trick of scrying someone that you didn't personally know.

You used a map.

A map is an example of how the ancient laws of imitation and correspondence operate. A map is an imitation of a place. Spots on the map correspond to the actual places. If there is a Master known to be in a particular place, having a map of that place and putting one's hand on it will link one closer to any Masters in that place and make the connection with them surer.

But what iffen I ain't got a map? she thought with frustration, feeling as far from the answer now as she had been before she began to read. She was just about to close the book and put all her mind to her sewing, but there was still good light—so she carried on.

But what if one does not have a map? Pavel wrote, startling her with how that echoed her thoughts. *Then one uses the scrying bowl to attain the view from above like that of the eagle, and moves that view steadily in the direction of the person that one wishes to scry. The landscape will roll beneath at a fearful pace, until the view is that of the place where the Master resides. Then one makes one's own map. From there, one can even use a pendulum to pinpoint the Master's location on the new map down to the actual house. From that, contact is but a trifle.*

By this time her head was spinning. *But a trifle—!* First Pavel said to somehow make the mirror show you everything from the air, like a bird. Then you were supposed to know what direction to "go" in to find the place where the person you wanted to see lived. How did you do that? And then you were supposed to draw your own map—she didn't even really know how to draw!—and *then* you could, maybe, use that map with a pendulum—what was a pendulum?—and—and—and—

Now she truly got some idea of the scope of her Great-Granpappy's knowledge. All these things were second nature to him! And as easy as making a neat line of stitches was for her!

Now she shut the book, and devoted the remaining light to finishing her corset cover, trying not to feel absolute despair. Today had been a good one, after all. She'd managed to call to the Little People. And the Little People had introduced her to Granny

Spider. And Granny Spider was willing to teach her. So, maybe she couldn't learn all of Great-Granpappy Pavel's ways, but she could at least learn some of the ways of the Cherokee along with what Aunt Jinny, and maybe even Jolene, could teach her.

So that wasn't so bad.

She set the last stitch just as the light went all blue, and it became too dim to see anything. She carefully set the needle in her needle-book and went to put the hens up.

When she came back, Aunt Jinny was done with the basket of cuttings. "Y'all gonna set a spell an' watch them fireflies?" her aunt asked her from the door.

"C'n y'all larn me what them liddle Earth critters that y'all know are? An' mebbe how t'call 'em?" she countered. "All I knowed so far is what Granny Spider showed me. Please?"

Aunt Jinny laughed. "They's a powerful lot o' 'em!" she exclaimed. "But y'all don' need t'call each one separate, gen'rally, lessen y'all wants a particular one. Y'all jest call. Like this—"

Anna sat down on the stool, putting aside the corset cover with the book on top of it and the needle-book inside of the front cover. Aunt Jinny sat down in her chair on the porch. As she watched, Jinny sketched a glowing glyph in the air between them, then let the sign dissolve into little motes of Glory and drift off. "Now, iffen they's any critters close by, they'll know I'd admire t'see 'em—wall, see, there they is—" She pointed at the edge of the porch, and there were some little faces peering up at them. "Now, that there's what m'Granny called a gnome." This was a little wizened old man with an odd red cap that flopped over to one side, and a beard. "That one's a piskie." This was one of the creatures that seemed to be made out of leaves and twigs. "That one's a hob. His name's Coby. Me'n him's old friends. He come with my Granny, an'—wall, tell 'er, Coby, y'all c'n speak fer yore own self."

This was another wizened little old man, without a cap, who hopped up on the porch and looked up at Anna from beneath enormous, shaggy eyebrows.

"I be a Hob, right enow," he said, in an accent so strange she had trouble understanding him. "And Hobs be crathurs what tends to housen, mostly. Thy Great-Grandam's Papa asked me t'come along of her and see to her house. But thy Great-Grandsire had yon Domovoy wi' 'im, sure he did, an' there weren't no room for two housen-minders in th' same house. So, bein' as the Domovoy don't tend t'farmyards, an' Hobs do, I do be tendin' t'yard."

"This here's why I weren't worrit iffen I got sick or hurt," her aunt said with a sly smile. "Domovoy'd tend th' house, Coby here'd put the hens up an' let 'em out, muck th' pigs and feed 'em till I got better. Not that I ever needed 'em t' do'it, but they was there iffen I needed 'em."

"Don't thee be a-thinkin' canst be slatternly," Coby said sternly. "Hob won't stay! Nor will Domovoy!"

But Anna had something else in mind than wondering why she and her aunt were doing all their own chores if the Hob and the Domovoy would tend the house and yard—she was wondering why her aunt didn't rely on them so they could go to church on a Sunday. Surely these creatures would take care of things for a good reason like that!

It was surely too dark for her aunt to read her expression, but Jinny must have known her well enough to figure out what she was thinking.

"Billie McDaran," she said, shortly.

"Oh!" she said, knowing immediately what Aunt Jinny meant. "Do he go to church?"

"Dunno," her aunt said. "Don't matter. He'd'a seed y'all a-comin' or a-goin', no matter what. Ain't much in Ducktown he don't know 'bout."

She sighed with disappointment, and a little guilt. "It don't seem right," she said reluctantly.

"Fust settlers here didn' hev no church. Cherokee don't hev no church," her aunt pointed out. "By my reckonin' God don't give two hoots iffen y'all goes an' sits in a pew twice on Sunday, long as y'all obeys the Golden Rule."

"But wouldn' it be a brave thang t'face down Billie McDaran an' go t' church, like facin' down th' Romans?" She actually had only a vague idea what that meant, formed from sermons, but when the preacher had talked about it, it seemed a great thing.

Aunt Jinny snorted. "Don't reckon God'd thank y'all was bein' brave. Reckon He'd thank y'all was bein' stupid, fer puttin' yoreself in thet man's way. An' it's not like other folks'd *know* y'all was doin' it jest t'git t'church, neither, so y'all wouldn't even be a good 'xample."

"Oh."

"'Specially when there's been plenty of folks that done without goin' t'church an' was good, Godly people," Aunt Jinny persisted. "Hermits don't go to no church, now, do they? An' they're in the Bible as bein' some of the Godliest of all!"

She had to admit that was true.

Her aunt sensed her defeat. "So, no more persterin' me 'bout goin' t'church?"

She sighed even more deeply. "No, ma'am."

Her aunt chuckled. "Then I'll tell y'all what I done decided this arternoon. Iffen y'all git yore chores done, an' whatever else I arst y'all t'do in the mornin', y'all c'n hev ev'ry arternoon to yoreself. Git a lesson from Granny Spider, or run all th' way down t'Holcroft's farm an' palaver with Josh an' his sister, though y'all ain't foolin' me, an' I know it's Josh yore hankerin' t'see."

She gasped. "*Really? Truly?*"

"Ayup," her aunt agreed. "I reckon cain't hurt, 'cause Josh ain't a-gonna take his eyes an' hands offen his paid work. An'—" She paused. "Wall, niver mind. Jest be back by supper, or I'll feed it t'the pigs, an' y'all c'n go ter bed hungry."

She felt as if she was going to burst with happiness.

The moon rose. Coby sat down at her aunt's feet. The other two critters sat on the steps. The piskie produced a length of thread and laced it on what passed for its fingers. It and the gnome began playing a game of cat's-cradle. "Is hevin' Coby an' th' Domovoy why y'all don't got a cat?" Anna finally asked, "cat's-cradle" having led her wandering mind to "cat" and then to the realization that despite her aunt taking precautions against their depredations, she hadn't actually seen so much as a trace of a mouse around the cabin or storage areas. "Do they chase off varmints?"

Coby snorted.

"Nope. I don't got a cat, on account'o cats go a-wanderin' an git thesselves killt, an' I cain't go gettin' fond'o somethin' an' have it run off t'git itself killt." She jerked her head into the house. "Domovoy knows thet, so he runs off th' varmints what gets inside th' shield." She chuckled. "Coby'll tackle a fox or a weasel, but he's above chasin' mice."

Coby sniffed.

"Wouldn't the shield keep the cat in?" Anna wanted to know. "The way it does the hens?"

Coby laughed. "Ah, lass, thee don't know cats, does thee?"

"Reckon not," she admitted. "We ain't niver had one." *On account of we niver had 'nuff food thet there'd be mice fer a cat t'et.*

The night filled with sound. Crickets by the hundred, bullfrogs, small frogs, and the little green tree frogs. The skeeters came around, but Aunt Jinny made a glyph that kept them off, and taught it to Anna, so the skeeters were frustrated and the bats were pleased that the skeeters were now hovering, frustrated, above their targets. That made a little cloud of prey for them, and they sometimes swooped close enough to Anna that she felt the wind from their wings on their way out of a dive.

With the moon rising above the garden, and everything so pretty and peaceful, Anna couldn't help but think it would be even nicer if Josh was up here on the porch with her, instead of Aunt Jinny. Maybe sitting close, and holding her hand …

"Aunt Jinny," she said finally. "Did y'all know Josh Holcroft's got th' Glory?"

She heard her aunt's nightdress rustle a little as Jinny turned her head. "I did not!" her aunt exclaimed. "How do y'all know thet?"

"When we went t' Ducktown," Anna explained, "there was a piskie an' a liddle mud-man in th' wagon-bed. They wanted ter see the liddle angel baby. Josh seed 'em."

"Huh," Jinny said. "Reckon he got much?"

"Dunno, but iffen he did, wouldn't Elder Raven know it an' tell y'all?" Anna pointed out.

"Reckon yore right." Jinny seemed to be pondering that for quite some time. "Y'all oughter see how much of th' Glory he got," her aunt added, finally. "An' y'all c'n larn him what I done larned y'all. Jolene's got one thang right; anyone with th' Glory's gotta be taught."

Anna decided to ask another question.

"Aunt Jinny, what's them liddle rock and stone critters?"

"Jest Earth Elementals. My Granny said they could be liddle or big, but I'd likely niver see a big 'un, since th' bigger they gets, the less they wants t' be anywhere near people."

"They also become sleepy, lass," Coby said. "Sleepy enough that they buries themselves into th' earth and are mortal hard to rouse."

"Innerestin'." Her aunt chuckled. "See now, thet's what happens when I get a young'un about what arsts questions. I larns thin's too."

Her aunt seemed content to sit there for the next hour or more, but Anna soon found herself yawning. There was only so much fantasizing about Josh being here beside her that she could manage, particularly with the Hob and her aunt plain as plain in the moonlight. So finally she excused herself, picked up her things, and went back into the cabin to put them away safely and climb the ladder into her bed.

But she did wonder why her aunt had gone so quiet on learning that Josh had the Glory too.

14

The marble had been delivered and Josh was chiseling out the rough outline of the smaller baby angel when Anna arrived at the Holcrofts' farm that afternoon. She heard the *chink, chink, chink* of his hammering almost as soon as the farmhouse was in sight.

While she had sped through her chores and made quick work of the potion lesson Aunt Jinny had set her, it had not been sloppy or slip shod, and her aunt had acknowledged as much over dinner. "An' if I'd'a known I could light a fire under yore feet jest by lettin' y'all see Joshua, I'd'a done it afore this," she'd laughed teasingly, as Anna blushed. "Jest do the warshin', an' off y'all go."

Anna had finished the dishes and the day's washing, hung her things on the line, and practically flown down the lane, marveling at how easy it was to run now, and how long it had been since she'd have been out of breath from mere walking.

When she trotted out of the green shade of the lane into the open, the sun hit her with a flash of heat that made her wish she had worn a hat. Neither Maddie Holcroft nor her daughter Sue were in sight when she arrived—and although she didn't exactly *sneak* into the barn and the workshop, she didn't go out of her way to find them, either. She had the feeling that if she did, Maddie would find a way to set Sue as a chaperone, and that would put paid to about half of what she wanted to talk to Josh about.

So she headed straight for the barn, staying out of visual range of the kitchen door and the kitchen shed. And she was very glad to step back into the relative cool of the shady barn. They must have just brought in a harvest of hay and spread it up in the hayloft, because the building was full of the sweet, dusty scent of it. She waited a moment for her eyes to adjust to the darkened interior, then made her way to the rear.

The windows were open wide to a fresh breeze, and Josh had his back to her. Josh was very much engrossed in his work, and the ringing of hammer on chisel covered the sounds of her footsteps, so she waited patiently until he stopped chiseling off pieces of marble for a moment, wiped his forehead on his sleeve, and turned to get a drink of water from the bucket behind him. That was when he saw her standing there, waiting for him to finish what he was doing.

"Anna!" he exclaimed, eyes lighting up and generous mouth immediately forming into a grin. "How long y'all been a-standin' thar?"

"Not long. I weren't a-gonna innerupt y'all," she said, gratified at such a positive reaction to her presence.

"Didjer aunt send y'all down here?" he asked, offering her the dipper full of water first before draining it himself.

"Sorta. She tol' me she's purt pleased with what I been a-doin', so as long as I git all m'work done in th' mornin' she give me leave t'go do what I want ev'ry arternoon now. An' I wanted t'come down here." She didn't add *to see you*, because that would have been awfully forward of her, but from the way his grin widened, she got the feeling he understood it.

"Wall, Cavenel sent th' marble, like he promised. I got all th' rotten stuff hacked off, an' I 'bout got the statchoo roughed in." He gestured to the ovoid on his workbench, which was just about the size of an actual baby plus the angel wings, so far as she could tell. "It gits more finicky from here. But leastwise, we ain't a-gonna need a cart t'git this back ter Ducktown. I might could take her m'self ridin' th' mule with a saddlebag."

There wasn't much to admire, but she admired it anyway. "Reckon y'all c'n stop fer a liddle bit?" she asked, hopefully.

He made a show of shaking out his hands and arms. "Reckon I better, or I might start missin' what I aims t'hit," he laughed, and set hammer and chisel aside. There were several tall stools here in the workshop; he pulled one out for her to perch on, and dropped himself down atop another. The breeze picked up a bit, and she gathered herself some straw from the floor and started finger-weaving it to make a flat bit she could fan herself with. "Wall, this does give me a chance t'arst y'all iffen y'all *really* saw them liddle critters in the wagon t'other day."

Well that wasn't *exactly* what she wanted to hear from him—but it was one of the subjects she had determined to talk to him about.

"Plain as plain," she assured him, on second thought relieved that he had been the one to broach the subject so quickly. "Tha's parta why I come down here. See … seein' them thangs … it means y'all got *magic*. Like me, an' like Aunt Jinny."

She waited, a little apprehensively. How was he going to react to *that*?

The prospect did not seem to alarm him in the least. He nodded. "I been a-wonderin' 'bout that. But—I got magic?"

"It's th' on'y way y'all c'n see 'em," she said. "Aunt Jinny, she says thet's the fust sign y'all got magic, is seein' 'em."

"Huh." He scratched the back of his head. "I thunk mebbe they was some kinds o' hants, mebbe somethin' Cherokee."

"They ain't hants. Some on 'em's Cherokee, some ain't," she said. "Leastwise thet's what Aunt Jinny says. When'd y'all fust see 'em?"

"Started seein' 'em this spring, when I started workin' on th' angel-baby. Figgered at fust I was mebbe lettin' my 'magination run off, on account'a this's the fust time I ever done a death-piece fer a chile, but then they started helpin' me."

She blinked. "Helpin' y'all? How?"

"Findin' stuff I'd lose. Or not *lose*, but drop in th' straw." Since the straw underfoot here in the workshop was at least a couple inches deep, she nodded. It would be very easy to lose a small dropped tool in here.

"I'd drop a chisel or som'thin', lean over, an' the liddle critter'd be there, holdin' it up fer me." He scratched his head. "I figgered at thet point it weren't no fever-dream, and weren't somethin' I was maunderin' over. So, what *are* they?"

She was only too happy to explain, and he listened intently, nodding from time to time, but didn't interrupt her. About the Elementals, and magicians. About the magic that her Aunt Jinny called the Glory. About how that was why *she* was here with her aunt in the first place. About Aunt Jinny and her Great-Granpappy and Great-Granny.

She hadn't really thought about *how* he would react when Aunt Jinny had told her she should tell him all about magic. And it wasn't until she'd started in on it that it had occurred to her that he might not take it all in stride—

But he did. In fact, he acted as if this was something he might could have been thinking and wondering about for some time.

"But they ain't *yore* Great-Granpappy an' Great-Granny, right?" he asked. "'Cause they's yore Aunt Jinny's, an' she ain't yore Ma, an' yore Ma's on'y her half-sister. So how's come y'all got thet there magic?"

"Dunno," she admitted. "I don't unnerstand a lot of it. I was afeerd there was somethin' bad 'bout it, on account'a it says in the Bible thet 'thou shalt not suffer a witch t'live,' so I arst Jesus fer a sign, an'—" She hesitated. "An' it seems like Jesus don' think it's a bad thang t'hev magic, long as y'all does good with it."

"Seems t'me it's jest another thang folks c'n do," he observed, looking earnestly into her eyes, as if he was trying to reassure *her*. "Like havin' a silver tongue, that's somethin' Pa talks 'bout sometimes. It means y'all c'n talk a body inter almost anythin'. Y'all c'n—oh, I dunno. Be a good preacher! Or y'all c'n use it t'swindle folks." He grinned at her. "I purely cain't think y'all would ever do nobody no harm, even iffen y'all was mad as hops at 'em."

She nodded, amazed and thrilled that he seemed to understand it all and accept it so easily, without even asking for proof. "Reckon yore right. Aunt Jinny uses it t' stren'then up her potions, so they work better."

He flexed his fingers and stood back up. "I'm a-gonna get back t'chippin', an' yore welcome to set by me. I prolly won't talk much, but iffen y'all wanter go on a-talkin' 'bout this magic stuff, I'll be a-listenin' purt hard. This's jest answerin' a whole lotta questions I didn't even know I had."

"I don' mind," she said, and she didn't. And for a while, she just sat there and watched him work. It was interesting to watch how he considered the stone before he set the chisel on it, and hit it with the hammer just *so*, then set to considering again.

"Yore a-takin' all this 'bout magic purdy well," she observed after a while.

"On account'a I allus knowed magic was out thar," he said, between chips. "Never reckoned *I* had it, but figgered someone did. All'a the tales 'bout hants an' curses, an' witchery, so many on'em there had t' be some truth there. An' ain't all the stories 'bout bad stuff, neither." He turned his head slightly to give her a little grin. "My Granny was jest *full* of stories afore she passed, an' she tol' 'em like they was the gospel truth. Granny niver lied t'me, not once. When somethin' was jest a story, she come out an' said so afore she told it. But when she told me 'bout people she knowed with magic, it were jest like she were a-tellin' me straight up. Now I come t'think of it," he continued, returning his gaze to the statue, "she had some stories 'bout liddle critters, like we been a-seein', on'y they was things with wings. An' most of her stories 'bout magic was about them as can whistle up storms an' shut 'em down agin. So—reckon thet'd be Air Elementals?"

Anna considered that. "Dunno what else it'd be," she admitted. "Ain't never seed them, an' Aunt Jinny cain't whistle up no storms or nothin', but she says we-uns is got Earth magic, so stands to reason we ain't gonna see no Air nor Water nor Fire."

"Reckon thet's where I got th' magic from, then, was Granny." He took a few more chips. "Though hang if I know why it'd matter where I got it from. Ain't no cause t'wonder where it come from iffen I got it. Jest gotter figger out how t'use it."

"Gotter see it afore y'all c'n use it," she told him. "I could see the critters afore I could see the magic."

"Reckon thet's where I oughter start, then," he observed. "An' right now, tryin' t'see magic ain't gonna get no stone cut."

"Mebbe it *could*, but I dunno how," she admitted. "An' Aunt Jinny says usually it's harder t' do thangs with magic than it is t'do 'em with yore hands."

"Durn pity," he chuckled. "Here I was hopin' I c'd jest sit back an' let magic dry th' dishes an' muck out the mule when it's my turn!"

She laughed at that, picturing the dishes floating in the air, and then laughed even harder, trying to picture the poor little Earth critters trying to juggle dishes that were their own size or bigger.

"Naw, I wouldn' do thet t' the pore liddle critters," he agreed. "Not even if they'd let me, which they prolly would not." He worked the stone a while more. "How hard's it t'larn this stuff, anyways?"

"Reckon it's different fer ev'body," she said, after a moment of consideration.

"Wall, then, we'll wait till I needs a liddle rest fer m'hands, an' y'all c'n see iffen y'all c'n larn me," he said reasonably. He cast a grin at her over his shoulder. "I dunno why, Anna May, but I kinder feels like I knowed y'all all m'life. Y'all's plenty easy t'talk to. Like I could tell y'all anythin', anythin' a-tall. Like I could trust y'all *with* anythin'."

She got blushing and a little flustered then, in no small part because she felt exactly the same about him, and she couldn't account for it. She knew why she felt all kinds of *other* things about him, most of them exciting and fluttery, and not the way she'd ever felt about any boy before. That was just simple to reckon the reasons for. He was the first boy who'd ever paid her a lick of attention, and he was good-looking on top of that, and she knew very well she was spoony about him. She'd been on the outside of that, at those Christmas parties and July Fourth picnics, and Halloween gathers; she'd seen plenty of girls get giggly and goo-goo-eyed over boys, and she recognized some of that in what she was feeling. But there was something deeper there, a sense of connection that wasn't fluttery and giggly at all. On the contrary, it felt like a deep, slow river, moving at its own pace, but powerful, and something that would endure regardless. "I guess I kinder feel like thet too," she confessed. "Mebbe it's on account'a the magic?"

"Thet don't seem right." He shook his head, and took a couple more hammer taps. "Wall, y'all got more sense than m'sis Sue. An' y'all ain't as flibberty-gibbet as the gals down in Ducktown. An' thas a fact. But they's a lot more to it than that. It ain't fair t'compare 'em to y'all, cause y'all's special, and it ain't jest the magic. I cain't put it inter words, but it's like something I *know*, like I know what m'own hand'll do when I want it ter do somethin'." He nodded, as if that settled it. "I know we ain't knowed each other fer long, Anna May, but I'd admire iffen y'all wouldn' mind iffen I arst Miz Jinny t'let me court y'all."

She felt as if she'd been struck by lightning, and sat there for a moment, gasping like a landed fish.

In fact, she sat there so silent for so long that he put down his hammer and chisel and turned around to face her, expression one of dismay and concern.

"Iffen y'all don' like thet, we c'n jest be friends—" he stammered, for once, obviously, just as flustered as she was.

"No!" she managed. "I mean, yes! I mean, I mean, I'd *really truly* like it iffen y'all'd talk to Aunt Jinny!" She became suddenly aware that she had clasped both her hands tightly under her chin as if in prayer, as he grinned again, reached out, took her hands, pried them open, and leaned forward to kiss her chastely on the cheek.

"Y'all had me plumb skeert there, a minnut," he said, and picked his hammer and chisel back up again, turning back to his work.

It was a good thing that he did, because she was utterly speechless for quite some time, her right hand held to her cheek where he had kissed her, almost unable to breathe.

"So," he said into the silence, quite as if he hadn't asked her that incredible question, and hadn't just kissed her. (Her first kiss from a boy!) "What's thet magic look like?"

She managed to gather her scattered wits. "It looks kinder like foxfire," she said, after long consideration. "'Cept I c'n see it by daylight, an' it's a purdy gold, kinda like the way sunlight gets real late afore the sun ac-chully starts t'set. When *I* look at them liddle critters, *I* see thet kinda glow a-haloin' them. And afore I sets the magic loose to do what I done told it to, I kinda gather it inter a glowin' ball a-twixt my hands. Thet might be the easiest t'show y'all."

It was something of a relief to her that after asking if he could court her, he went right back to asking about magic. She had much rather get a chance to get her insides settled down again before he started acting sweet on her; much rather they acted like ordinary friends and not sweethearts, not just yet. It was a big thing to consider!

And after all, they didn't have permission to be any such thing as sweethearts yet. He hadn't asked Aunt Jinny, and while she doubted that his parents would object—they were clearly good friends with her aunt, and on top of that, they knew she was being taught a trade that was respectable for a woman to be in, and would bring in steady income to augment what came from Jinny's little farm—he still would probably have to get their blessing before he took things any further.

Don't count yore chickens, Anna May Jones, she told herself. *They's all kinder thangs that can interfere.*

"All righty then." He put the chisel and hammer aside, and shook out his hands and arms again. "Is thet somethin' y'all c'n show me now?"

"Easy as pie," she assured him. She half-lidded her eyes and unfocused them, searched around for those rivulets of power, found one running right under this very workshop, and gathered the Glory to herself. She felt more than saw the power coming up her legs and down her arms, into her hands; it felt like a subtle tingling, and her skin felt more alive somehow. It began to collect in her hands. She frowned as she focused her intent on it, and concentrated it into a glowing sphere that hovered between her palms. "It's thar," she said, holding her cupped palms out toward him. "See?"

She fully expected him to exclaim at the sight of it and say "yes." But he frowned. "Nope," he replied with obvious disappointment. "Don't see nothin'."

She gathered more of the power, concentrating it further, until it glowed like a little sun, hoping more power would make it easier for him to see, and looked back up at him with expectation. He shook his head. "Still don't," he admitted.

"Mebbe don't try so hard?" she suggested. "When I kinda stopped tryin', thet's when I seed it fust."

He closed his eyes and stood there, shaking his hands to get all the cramps and numbness out of them, she supposed. Then he slowly opened his eyes again, and fastened them on the space between her hands. "Still nothin'," he said with disappointment.

She sucked on her lower lip. *I wonder. Aunt Jinny says doin' a "spell" is jest making th' Glory do what you want it to. So can I make it fix things so he can see it?*

Worth a try.

She concentrated on the little orb of magic power between her hands, telling it fiercely that she wanted Josh to be able to see it the way she could. She didn't have a particular glyph to write in the air to make it do that exact thing, so as she released the power in a shower of golden sparks, she wrote the one for "as I will it" between the two of them, keeping her intention firmly in mind—and hoping he might be able to see the glyph anyway.

The sparkling motes of power gathered to form the glyph, which hung there between them for a moment, then burst like a firework.

He blinked and stepped back a pace. "Did y'all see what I wrote?" she asked hopefully.

"Wall, no," he said cautiously, "but I shore *felt* somethin' jest then."

She cupped her hands and gathered power for a second time, and the moment the little orb began to form, he jerked his head up and stared.

"By gum!" he exclaimed. "I see it! Like a liddle ball o' light!" He stared at the space between her hands as if he had never seen anything so fascinating in his life.

Well, it is magic.

"Can y'all see thet glow anywheres else?" she asked. "Y'all might not. Aunt Jinny cain't. She says I got more of the magic than she do."

"Like where?" he asked.

She released the power gently to go back to its source, and pointed to the tiny rivulet of magic that was practically at her feet. "Thar, fer one."

He shook his head. "But I c'n see sorta—" his face twisted a little as he sought for words to describe what it was he was seeing, "—it's kinda like a glowy dust over y'all. Lots on your hands," he added. She looked down at her hands, and sure enough, they were still aglow with residual magic.

"So y'all cain't see it as good as me—" she began.

"But at least I c'n see it a-tall!" he interrupted. "An' now I know what t'look fer. Thet'll do fer—wall, howdy, liddle feller—"

She glanced down and saw one of the piskies at his feet. The piskie waved a twig-like arm at him, and scrambled up the leg of an empty stool to perch on the seat.

"Huh. He *do* got thet glow 'bout him, like y'all said. What y'all call a critter like him?" he asked, looking up at her again.

"Aunt Jinny calls it a piskie," she replied, pleased that she was able to put a name to the critter for him.

"Wall, yore welcome t' watch me work, liddle piskie," he told it gravely. "But there ain't much t'see right now, I reckon."

He went back to work again, and the afternoon passed *much* too quickly for her liking, what with telling him what she knew about how magic worked, and the kinds of critters he was likely to see. She didn't get into the Cherokee critters, nor the Cherokee magic. Partly, that was caution—she had no idea what the Holcrofts knew about the Cherokee living in the Holler. Partly, it was because she didn't know if he'd be *allowed* to know about them, or about Cherokee magic. The Ravens might not cotton to that notion. And partly it was because she didn't know if any of the Cherokee spirits would be inclined to show themselves to him, being as he was a white man with no connection to them. She wasn't quite sure why *she* had been seeing the Little People even before she came here and met her aunt and the Ravens, but Josh didn't describe anything like the Little People, so she elected to keep their existence to herself for now.

She also didn't tell him about Jolene.

And that was just pure selfishness. If he knew Jolene—that is, the Jolene that the people of Ducktown clearly knew—she didn't want him approaching the woman to ask about magic, which he might. He was friendly, and open, and honest, and she could give him no good reason why he *shouldn't* ask Jolene about magic if he had the chance.

And once he approached her, that was where the trouble might start. How could she ever compete with someone as beautiful as Jolene, if Jolene took an interest in him? And she surely, surely did not want Jolene taking an interest in him.

Never get between Jolene and something she wants.

So, best to leave Jolene out of this discussion altogether.

Finally the westering sun told her that she was going to have to take her leave of him if she wanted to get back to the cabin without running afoul of her aunt. "I gotta go," she said reluctantly.

"Or yore aunt'll hev a conniption, an' y'all will be late for supper. Not in thet order," he agreed, and put down his hammer and chisel again to turn and take her face in both of his dust-covered hands. "I meant what I done said, Anna May Jones. All of't. Y'all's th' best thang t'come t'Lonesome Holler, ever, an' I don't intend t'let m'chance with y'all slip away." And with that, he very gently kissed her on the lips, and quickly let her go. "Now y'all better skedaddle. I'm a-gonna go find Pa, an' let him know what we're a-thinkin'."

Then he turned her bedazzled self around by the shoulders, faced her toward the opening into the barn, and gave her a gentle push.

She absolutely did not remember a single moment of the trip up to the cabin, because the next thing she knew, she was washing up at the well alongside her aunt. Thankfully, either Jinny hadn't said anything, or she had somehow managed to respond intelligently, because her aunt said nothing until they were both sitting down to supper, with the light gilding the landscape outside the door.

"Y'all seem a bit mazy," her aunt remarked shrewdly, as she dished up soup and cornbread. "Anythin' y'all see fit t'tell me?"

She blinked, forced her head to clear, and took a deep breath. "Josh aim's t'arst y'all fer leave t'court me," she said, deciding to get it out all at once and have done with it.

She waited for the storm. She knew exactly what her Ma would have said after such a revelation as that, and there would have been thunder and lightning. And as for Pa! Given how much he'd been against her coming here in the first place, she could well imagine the avalanche of disapproval.

Or—on second thought, maybe her Pa would take such a thing as an opportunity to get her off his hands.

Her aunt put down her spoon. "My land," she said, which was a sight milder than Anna had expected. "That was a leap. Care t'tell me how this come about?"

Relieved that there had not been an outburst of anger and opposition, she poured out the words. Exactly what had happened and, as near as she could remember, exactly what had been said. Her aunt listened patiently, with no sign of disapproval—in fact she continued eating through the whole recitation—until Anna finished.

"So—how d'yall feel 'bout him?" she asked. "An' I don't mean all the stuff'n nonsense. I mean at bottom."

"Like we been friends always," she said carefully. "Like I c'n count on him, an' he can count on me. Like when trouble happens, we'll both put shoulder t' the wheel and git the cart back on th'road. Am I a-makin' any sense?"

"Better sense than I reckoned," her aunt admitted. "S'pose I tell him yes, he c'n court y'all, but I ain't lettin' y'all marry till yore eighteen? 'Cause I ain't. It'll take y'all thet long, at least, t' larn all I got to show y'all."

"Then that's how it'll be," she agreed.

"An' what iffen I tol' him *no*?"

"Then I'd wear y'all down," she replied, daring a bit of sauce. "Reckon I c'n be as stubborn as y'all, an' I'm younger. I got time."

Aunt Jinny laughed softly. "Good. All right, then. When he comes up t'arst me proper, I'll tell him it'll be a long courtin', but Jacob'll git his Rachel in th' end an' he won't have ter take no toad-faced Leah fust."

Anna actually leapt up from the table and kissed her aunt.

"Oh, hush now," Jinny said, snorting, but pleased. "It wouldn't'a been so easy iffen I hadn't known thet boy an' his fambly since Hector was a pup. He's a good young feller, an' he ain't a-gonna waste his life down a hole in th' ground. *And* he's got th' Glory, which is kinder important, since y'all got it strong. Any man y'all married up with'd either have ter hev it his own self, or be easy with it like my Pa was with my Ma, or y'all have ter hide it from him. Most fellers don' cotton to it when their woman's got somethin' powerful they ain't got an' cain't hev. An' thet hidin' part ain't easy."

"Y'all didn't say give it up—" Anna ventured.

"Thet's on account of now that y'all's got the way of it, the Glory's got its hooks deep in y'all, an' givin' it up'd be like givin' up a arm or a leg," her aunt replied soberly. "Think on it a minnut. Y'all'll know it's truth."

She didn't even have to think about it for a minute to know that her aunt was right. Giving up magic now was as unthinkable as *having* it had been before she came here.

"Finish yore supper, he'p me clean up, an' go do whate'er y'all's gonna do afore y'all sleep," Aunt Jinny told her, with a half smile. "Which, I reckon, is ter go hang out the winder up by y'all's bed, stare at th' moon, and daydream 'bout thet boy."

She was awfully glad that the deepening gloom of the cabin hid her blushes, because that was exactly what she most wanted to do.

15

Thunder shocked her awake with a gasp and a pounding heart. Her eyes flew open in time to catch the flash of lightning that turned the entire loft white, and another crash of thunder that occurred simultaneously. She shrieked before she could stop herself. Not that anyone could have heard her in that noise!

She scrambled to the window to shut it when a gust of icy wind drove in, carrying with it stinging rain that pelted her face before she slammed the window shut. Then she sat on the floor beside the window, looking out at the glimpses of the garden offered by the lightning, waiting for her heart to stop pounding. This was the second huge storm that had come in the night since she moved here. How often did these things blow in, anyway? She just wasn't used to weather like this.

It wasn't as if there hadn't been storms back in Soddy ... but they seemed so much *bigger* here.

The garden—how was the garden going to fare? She thought of all the half-ripened vegetables out there with a stab of apprehension. The root vegetables would probably be all right, but what about the rest?

She expected to hear a torrent of rain pounding on the roof just over her head, but despite the violence of the lightning and thunder, it appeared they weren't going to be drowned any time soon, nor were they going to find the garden flattened. There was rain, she could see it in the lightning flashes, and hear it between the thunderclaps, but it wasn't the sort of toad-strangler she had expected from the aerial violence outside.

Downstairs she heard her aunt slamming the windows—and then slamming the door, which must have been blown open—shut against the storm. But her aunt didn't call up to her to ask for her help with anything, so after a little, she went back to her bed. The thunder receded into the distance, and she slept again.

She woke again, around the usual time, to realize that although the lightning and thunder had subsided somewhat, the rain certainly had not. It was still drumming on the roof overhead, which suggested that this storm was going to last the day.

So we ain't going out today, she thought with a moment of pleasure, which vanished when she realized that she had a lot of reasons to want to go out now.

She bit her lip in dismay. Would Aunt Jinny allow her to make the trek down to the Holcrofts' farm and back in a storm?

She heard her aunt moving around downstairs, and hurried down the ladder to make her case. She turned to face her aunt, who was just setting the table, and opened her mouth only to have her aunt give her a gimlet stare.

"No," Jinny said flatly. "I know what y'all's thankin'. Not terday. I ain't a-gonna let y'all git lightnin'-struck, nor soaked an' chilled an' git sick, nor take a slip an' mebbe sprain or break somethin'. Th' boy'll be there termorrer, an' th' day arter thet, an' th' day arter thet."

She *almost* started to argue, when Jinny put the cap on it. "Y'all needs ter show Matt and Maddie that y'all's responsible afore they're gonna let their boy come a-courtin'. Y'all thank it's gonna look responsible t'show up on their doorstep soaked through an' needin' t' git put up by th' fire an' fussed over? They'd be a-wastin' their time, all 'cause y'all couldn't wait a day. Thank it's responsible t' go courtin' a fever? Y'all might thank it's romantical thet y'all ain't gonna let a little thang like gittin' sick keep y'all apart, but know what Matt an' Maddie are gonna thank? Once the fuss is over, they're gonna thank how y'all put 'em out, confusticated their day, an' caused a ruckus." Her stern gaze grew even sterner. "They'll be a-wonderin' what kinda gal is gonna leave me all alone up here when lightnin' could hit th' house, or the pigs or hens could git loose, or th' roof could spring a leak. What d'y'all thank they'll be thankin', thet y'all cain't bear t' be away *one damn day* when wimmin 'round these parts sent their men off 'n niver saw 'em fer *years* t'fight the war not thet long ago?"

She shut her mouth. Because, of course, Aunt Jinny was right. She *hated* it, but Aunt Jinny was right. She wouldn't look like someone who could be trusted with a household. She wouldn't look like someone who could be trusted in a crisis.

In fact, she'd look like her Ma, and her Ma's Ma, at least if Aunt Jinny was to be believed. A flibbertigibbet. A girl with more hair than sense. Too lovestruck to think straight. Not to be trusted to act sensible any time her man was concerned.

Someone who needed to be taken care of. Not someone who could take care of others.

So instead of objecting, she heaved a long, tragic sigh. Aunt Jinny snorted. "Y'all oughter be a actress in a mellerdrama. Come stir th' mush," she ordered, and gestured at the pot on the hearth. "It'll be ready ina minnut. I'm already dressed, so I'm a-gonna run out t' th' hens and pigs, an' let y'all stay dry fer once."

Jinny didn't have skirts to tie up, but she rolled up her overall cuffs to the knee and threw that piece of oilcloth over her head and ran out the door, leaving Anna feeling just a bit guilty that she had taken the chore.

The rain showed no signs of slackening all through the morning, no matter how many times she went to the door and glared up at the clouds. The continuing downpour curtailed their usual chores by a considerable amount.

At least the garden looked intact from the front porch. And being as everything was on the easy slope, it wasn't going to get waterlogged, so there was not much chance they'd lose any produce. No point to run out into the rain to save what they could, as they might have had to do if damage had been done.

So they tidied up with a vengeance, and not only swept the floor, but gave it a good scrub with a rag mop. They did the washing and strung it across the cabin on a line, and by then it was time for dinner, which Anna ate with a seasoning of gloom.

"I swan, y'all's face is more stormy than th' weather," her aunt said, with a touch of both humor and exasperation. "Y'all c'n git lost easy enough in Granpappy's book, why don't y'all try thet this arternoon?"

"I wish't I was Air an' not Earth," she replied, crossly. "I c'd make thet there storm blow clean away!"

"An' send it a-pilin' up on Ducktown, an' mebbe make a flood what'd kill folks?" her aunt demanded unexpectedly.

Startled, she stared at Aunt Jinny in disbelief. "I—could'a done thet?" she faltered. "Iffen I was Air?"

"Thet's why Air's one'a the dangerest powers there is," her aunt confirmed. "Iffen y'all ain't *extree*, *extree* careful, an' y'all jest *does* stuff wit'out thankin' an' plannin' it over fer days and days, thet's what c'n happen. Earth's a slow power, an' forgivin'. Water, Air, an' Fire c'n get y'all in trouble afore y'all c'n blink. Afore y'all so much as ponders a-changin' somethin' as big as weather, y'all damn well better hev a long talk with whatever Marster's downwind, or y'all'll hev a magic fight on yore hands. 'Lessen y'all c'n keep what happens in yore own land an' yore own hands, y'all better figger out who *else* is a-gonna be in the path of it, an' what they're gonna git in they teeth, 'cause y'all'll be called to account fer all of it."

"Oh," she replied in a small voice, getting a mental flash of flattened crops and houses knee-deep in muddy water. She swallowed hard, and went to get the book.

As usual, she climbed up on top of the stove to read it, and despite wishing with every other word that she were down at the Holcrofts' watching Josh at work, all cozy with him in the workshop—maybe helping out by keeping that little stove tended—talking and learning more about him—

Well, Pavel's words eventually worked their own sort of enchantment on her, and she fell back into the story.

On reaching new shores, Pavel and Sally found that they were by no means the only Elemental Masters in the new United States.

Initially, they disembarked in New York City, but neither of them could bear the place. In fact, it had the same effect on them that Soddy had on Anna, and having to shield all the time nearly wore them away to nothing in the course of a single week. They could have been in a bad situation, but they were saved by

Pavel's scrying; he spoke to his father-in-law, who spoke to folk in London, who got them the name and address of a Fire Master, and told him they were coming and in need of help.

The Fire Master, like so many Masters Pavel had met on his travels, was prosperous—though it was by his own efforts, rather than inherited wealth. It was beginning to look to Anna as if being able to practice magic gave you an edge on prosperity.

When she paused to think about that, it all began to make sense. If you were an Earth Magician, you could virtually guarantee the success of your crops and animals. Presumably Fire, Water, and Air brought with them their own means of making you prosperous, or even rich, as long as you were willing to work at it.

She returned to the story of the Fire Master that Pavel and Sally took shelter with. Fortunately, he lived in a rural area outside the city limits, and he willingly had them as guests, which took them out of the poisonous atmosphere of the city itself. Having begun as a blacksmith's apprentice, he now was the owner of his own ironworks, and unlike the more altruistic of his European brethren, he expected to get value for value given when he offered to host them and help them on their way.

I soon learned why "Yankee trader" signifies the height of sharp dealing, Pavel wrote. The Master got full value out of both of them: a fully stocked cabinet of treatments and medicines from Sally, and expert supervision of some stonework and installation of a "Rooshan stove" in his own home from Pavel. Only when these conditions had been satisfied was he willing to pass them to a coastal trading vessel captained by a Water Magician he knew.

He advised that we sail further south, Pavel wrote. *He told us that we would not find land "for the taking" until we got further south and then into the interior. I did not know what "land for the taking" meant at that time, and naively thought it meant there was open wilderness that belonged to no man. But in his defense, perhaps that was his impression too. I certainly saw nothing at the time, nor have since, to think he was trying to deceive us.*

So sail south they did, as slowly as if they had been walking, for the trader stopped at every tiny settlement of more than a few houses, and the further south they got, the more often he was trading his goods for tobacco, which he compressed into tight bales with a machine he had on board for the purpose, and stowed in the emptying hold. Pavel was fascinated by this process; the trader bought the loose, dried tobacco from small farmers once they had cured it, loaded it into this ingenious device, which used a screw, like a printing press, to create compact bales, then weighed the resulting bales and paid the farmers by the pound. None of these farmers raised enough tobacco on their own to bother with owning such a thing, but the money they got from their small crops was enough to make a real difference in their lives. Not unlike Aunt Jinny and her potions.

For the first time I began to see the Negro slaves I had heard about in New York. It seemed that every farmer had at least a few. We were appalled to see people in a condition that was worse than that of a serf under a cruel boyar, but what was I to do? With a heavy heart we kept quiet.

The trader was a good host and a good companion, full of stories, and they were sorry to say goodbye to him when they reached North Carolina.

But there, he left them in the care of yet another Fire Master, who was also a blacksmith, in Wilmington, a coastal city in North Carolina. The city proper did not cause them much discomfort even without shields, and they learned that they could enjoy the amenties the place offered without much difficulty. There was a great deal of farmland available for purchase at prices Pavel did not consider extreme. Many of those who had settled there came from the same part of England as Sally, a few generations back. In short, they began to think about settling where they had landed.

And we liked the climate and the land, wrote Pavel. *Or rather, we liked the farmland outside of the city, and it seemed to welcome us. It seemed to us that this would be a good place to make our home. Until the storm … which changed our minds completely.*

It began with a sultry and oppressive morning, and as we all rose early in the household, we all took note of the blood-red morning skies. "This ain't good," said our host, and proceeded to direct us, his apprentices, and all his "hired hands" and his two slaves to make the house and forge ready for "a blow." All fires were put out and smothered. Doors to the forge were closed and barred by stout lengths of wood, and wooden shutters nailed shut over all the windows. Anyone who had left horses at the forge to be shoed in the morning got their beasts back unshod. "I'm lucky I ain't got no stock, not even a chicken," said he, and he gathered his household and slaves and us and his two hunting hounds into a single room on the westward side of the house, sent those of his men and apprentices who had homes elsewhere in the city back to their families, and directed us to provision the room that would be our shelter with bedding, two barrels of fresh water, and all the food from the kitchen that did not need to be cooked. The rest, we either hastily cooked and added to the storm provisions, or he had us pack inside as many barrels and casks as he could find. These he sealed, and stacked around the walls of the room. Then everything of value in the house was added, until there was scarcely room to move. I had no idea what all this meant; it seemed a most peculiar sort of preparation for a mere storm.

But as the "blow" approached, and the winds began, I quickly changed my mind.

"Reckon it's a cyclone," he said, as we looked out from the porch of his home and saw the trees bending nearly down to the ground, in winds so strong I could scarcely believe my own eyes. "Time to hunker down."

We retreated to the room, and barred the two doors to the house from the inside.

Then the winds and rain began in earnest. His powers were useless—but Sally's and mine proved to be of some utility, as we bent our magic to desperate measures and managed to find ways to strengthen the wood and stone of the house against a wind that tore at it as if it had been a helpless lamb and the storm a starving lion.

That day and night I envied those who were able to sleep through this. They, at least, could snatch an hour or two of rest. Sally and I dared not sleep, and only ate and drank when someone put food and water into our hands. Although the servants and slaves had never been told what we were, somehow I think they intuited that we were working to their safety, for they cared for us most tenderly.

Then there was a sudden calm, and Sally and I started up, intending to rejoice, but our host disabused us of the notion that we were safe. "This's just a cruel, hard trick of the devil," said our host. "But come outside an' I'll shew y'all."

By now, it was sunset. We unbarred the doors and stepped out onto the porch into a landscape of utter destruction. We stood in the middle of an island of calm, and around us—all around us—the storm raged, a gigantic wall of wind and rain and fearful lightning that ringed us perfectly. Our safety, as our host had said, was an illusion. In mere hours the storm would be upon us, this time the winds howling around us from the opposite direction. I have never seen the like. Not even the worst that a winter in Mother Rus could bring could match anything so fierce as this. I hope never to see such again.

Once again we retreated into our safe room, Sally and I mustered our powers, and the storm began anew.

It was an untold number of hours of desperate work and terror before the winds began to drop again, our host told us that the worst was over, and we fell into a sleep of exhaustion of the sort I have never needed before or since.

When we emerged again, and saw the utter destruction, the houses and barns blown to pieces, the herds of drowned livestock, trees felled and the bodies of the dead being laid out by the survivors, Sally gave me such a look as told me she would be dead before she consented to live in a place that spawned such terrors.

Well, this was nothing like anything *she* had ever heard of before. Was this just exaggeration on Pavel's part? "Aunt Jinny—" she began. "When yore Granpappy was in North Carolina—"

"Thet'd be the cyclone he went through. They got them thangs on the coast. Most times they ain't thet big, but the one he saw was a whopper. There was another like it jest a few years ago," her aunt said, as usual, anticipating her question. "He weren't talkin' thangs up, it were thet bad. An' they was inland a good piece. It were worse on th' shore, the sea done run up till a lotta them houses on the coast was so deep in water they was washed off clean away. Sensible folks git th' bejabbers offen th' coast when one of them thangs comes in." Then she snorted. "But sensible folks wouldn' be livin' thar in the fust place, iffen y'all arst me."

She tried to imagine it, and couldn't. And she could not blame her Great-Granny for refusing to live where such things could happen.

After that dramatic incident, Pavel and Sally *did* stay the winter, however. They stayed to help with the recovery after the cyclone, winter set in, which would have made hard traveling, and then there seemed no good reason to move on until spring, not when their host was so grateful to them that he gave them the best room in his house and feted them all winter long.

Then, in the spring, they bought a stout wagon, provisioned themselves, and headed west, into Tennessee, where everyone said there was cheap land for sale. This, Pavel noted, was a far cry from "land for the taking," but it was land that was in the midst of settlements, villages, towns, and even cities, and they had already discovered that the money they had brought with them was worth more in the United States than it had been at home.

And so, we traveled without incident through the spring, until we arrived at a spot that was for sale by the government that called to both our hearts.

Little did we know it was not the land that was calling to us. It was the Cherokee chief, Eagle Sight, who became my dearest friend in this country.

She became aware that her aunt was gently poking her foot. "Supper," Jinny said. "Told y'all thet y'all'd git lost in thet book agin."

Rain still drummed on the roof, and much as she hated to admit it … Jinny had been right. If she'd been given leave to go to the Holcrofts, she'd have arrived soaked and shivering. Maddie probably would have insisted that she at least sit by a fire until she got dry. Then she'd have had to *build* a fire for Anna to sit by. And she'd make hot tea. All of this would have put Maddie out, and none of it would have allowed her to be alone with Josh.

And conditions would have been worse when she returned, because the trek was uphill. Longer, more chance of slipping and falling, and certainly more time in the rain. Why did Aunt Jinny have to be so very right?

And poor Josh … would he have been working away over his statue, hoping she would be able to get away and join him, not knowing Aunt Jinny had forbidden her to leave? He'd have understood, of course. In fact, he probably had already thought of all that. But he might have been hoping anyway.

If only there was a way to send Josh messages!

Wait— "Aunt Jinny?" she said, as she climbed down from the stove. "Would one-a them Elemental critters take a note t'Josh fer me?"

Aunt Jinny looked taken aback, as if the thought had never occurred to her. "Wall ... prolly," she admitted. "I ain't niver arst one."

She didn't wait for permission; she gathered magic and sent out a call for a piskie. And almost immediately, one appeared out from underneath Aunt Jinny's bed. It was completely dry. Had it been there all along?

Never mind that. "Iffen I give y'all a thing fer Josh, the feller down the Holler what carves stones, c'n y'all give it to him, an' mebbe bring me back another from him?" She didn't want to confuse it by referring to a "note," which it might not understand, so she just said "a thing."

The little critter cocked its head to the side, then nodded. Aunt Jinny sighed and rolled her eyes, but rummaged for a scrap of the paper that had been wrapped around their Ducktown purchases, and gave her a stub of a pencil.

Storm 2 bad, she wrote. *Sorry. Sad!*

She folded it tight and handed it to the critter, which ran away under the bed and did not return.

"Eat," Jinny ordered, as she stared at the empty floor. "Thang ain't gonna give it to him till he's alone. No point in y'all starvin' whiles y'all wait."

She didn't feel as if she *could* eat, but with Jinny staring at her as if her aunt was willing her to eat, she picked up the spoon and made an attempt, all the while keeping her gaze fixed on that spot under the bed where the piskie had gone.

They finished dinner and had cleaned the dishes when it finally trotted out from beneath the bed again. When she saw it was carrying a folded paper, it was all she could do not to grab the note and the critter together in her eagerness to see what it said. It held the bit of paper up to her, and she took it, with a nod of thanks. It giggled and rocked back on its heels.

Figgered. Sad 2. Pa and Ma said all right.

For a moment she couldn't make out what that last sentence could mean. Then it suddenly struck her. He'd asked Maddie and Matt if he could court her, and they had said yes!

Wordlessly she held the scrap out to her aunt, who scrutinized it, and smiled and shrugged. "Like I tol' y'all, it's gonna be a long courtship. Plenny of time fer one or both of y'all t'figger out thet mebbe marryin' th' fust person near yore age that y'all lay eyes on what ain't yore relative ain't the best ideer."

"I've seed boys afore!" she objected.

"But did they see *y'all*?" her aunt asked shrewdly.

She bit her lip, because she knew very well what the answer was.

But her aunt took pity on her and patted her hand. "An' mebbe y'all will suit. He's got th' Glory, y'all got the Glory, an' there's been wuss thangs to git hitched over."

Then she changed the subject. "Send 'im 'nother note thet I reckon it's gonna keep rainin' temorrer, which I do, an' y'all will see 'im on Monday."

She almost cried in dismay. But there wasn't anything she could do about the rain, and if Aunt Jinny was right (and why wouldn't she be?), it would be better to let him know.

The little piskie was still just standing there waiting, as if it had figured there was going to be another exchange of notes. She rubbed out what she had written as best she could, wrote a new one, and folded the note and handed it to the critter, which ran off, just as before. In a much shorter time than she had expected, it returned. *Sad!* read the note. *Miss U already.*

So that was all right.

Even if it was all wrong.

"Thenkee kindly," she told the piskie, who took that as the dismissal it was, and skittered away.

Aunt Jinny seemed to take pity on her then, because the next thing she knew, her aunt had taken out some corn from a bag she kept separate from the parched corn she often used in meals. "Y'all know what this is?" she asked, holding out a handful.

It was—odd. Round in shape, and hard and shiny, nothing like the rectangular, matte flint corn Jinny grew and dried to have ground into meal. "No, ma'am," she said, baffled.

"It's poppin' corn. An' we're gonna et some." Before she could ask any questions, her aunt had dropped a little bacon fat into the stew-pot, dropped a couple of handfuls into the fat, and clapped a lid on it. Then she put it by the fire.

The first explosions took Anna by surprise, but the delicious aroma coming from that pot surprised her even more. It didn't take long after the first explosions for the last to die off. Jinny had pulled the pot away from the fire as soon as the popping began, and now she took the lid off, grabbed the pot with rags wrapped around her hands, and tilted the contents out into a bowl. She set the pot back down, sprinkled salt over the fluffy white and fragrant bits, and set to eating. Anna got a handful and tasted it, and was won over immediately.

"I c'n see there's gonna be a lot o' letter writin'," Jinny said between bites. "Leastwise, 'lessen we c'n larn th' both of y'all how to scry." She was silent for a moment, as she seemed to roll that notion around in her mind. "Happen I ain't got a lot o' paper t' spare. Josh might hev more; he got proper schoolin' till he started workin' fer Cavenel. We'll arst him 'bout thet when he comes up t' arst fer my blessin'. An' we'll see iffen he c'n larn scryin'." She sighed. "Then I'll hev t' figger out a scryin' bowl or somethin' fer y'all."

"What 'bout Josh?" she asked.

"He c'n figger thet out fer his own self," Jinny said. "He works with stone, likely he c'n make somethin' outa flint."

But the notion that Josh *might* be able to learn to scry and then the two of them could talk to each other every single night before bed made her so happy that it completely washed away the *un*happiness she'd felt when Jinny had said tomorrow was going to be rainy.

It was no night to be hanging out the window, looking at the moon and wondering if Josh was looking at the same moon, wondering if she was looking at the moon …

Instead, she tucked herself properly into bed, and although she *intended* to lie there and think about Josh and wonder what he was doing, no sooner had she settled in, listening to the rain drum on the roof, than it was morning.

Jinny was stoking the stove, so there would probably be baking today. And it was Sunday, which meant a full bath. When she climbed down the ladder, Jinny greeted her with, "We'll be hevin' our bath in th' rain, so I'm a-warmin' up th' place. An' since we'll be a-hevin' our bath in th' rain, we'll be gettin' whatever in the garden looks like it's gettin' puny afore thet, 'cause it won't matter a hill o' beans how wet an' muddy we gets."

She sighed. Wet, cold, muddy, and Aunt Jinny was still not going to let her go see Josh, most likely. No point in putting up her hair with those pretty hairpins—she just took both braids and pinned them in a sort-of bun with a splinter of wood. Then she got dressed, leaving off the petticoats, tied her drawers up above the knee, tied her skirts up, and went out to take care of the hogs and chickens.

By just before lunchtime, she and her aunt were filthy, soaking wet, and half frozen, but they had a good lot of produce gathered that would otherwise have gotten ruined. It wasn't until they were both clean and dry and Jinny was dishing out dinner that it occurred to her that if she were stupid enough to insist on going down to the Holcrofts—by the time she got there, she'd be just as soaked-through muddy and mucky as she had been after working in the garden. And never mind all the other things Aunt Jinny had reminded her of—she purely didn't want Josh to see her looking like a drowned cat!

"I reckon y'all's a-pinin' fer young Holcroft," her aunt said with a smirk, passing her cornbread. "Wall, it come t'me thet we c'n kill two bird with one stone. Y'all hev been havin' trouble scryin', but I reckon scryin' someone y'all know will come easier, an' y'all got motivation t'try an' see the boy."

Her jaw dropped. "I c'n do thet?" she demanded.

"It'll jest be a-seein' him," her aunt cautioned her. "Unless he larns how t'scry back, y'all won't be able ter talk. But I'm thanking we jest needs t'git y'all over that stile of not bein' able to see. Once y'all c'n do thet, I reckon we c'n get y'all a-talkin' t' th' Marsters I know."

Anna could cheerfully have seen all of those unknown "Masters" to perdition. It was seeing Josh she wanted to do!

Aunt Jinny didn't say anything more about it, but for once Anna didn't linger over the good food. She was on fire with impatience as she and Jinny worked through all the produce they had brought in from the garden, preparing some of it for storage and the rest for meals for the next few days. She knew very well that Jinny was aware of her impatience, and was amused by it.

She ain't never been in love, Anna thought resentfully, using that loaded word "love" for the first time even in her own thoughts. *So she thinks it's funny.* But it wasn't funny. It was exhilarating and scary, and had her insides and sometimes her thoughts buzzing around like a hive of disturbed bees. And right now the only thing that seemed to make those bees settle was the idea of seeing Josh.

Finally, they finished drying the last nugget of tomato, shelling the last pea. Finally, Aunt Jinny got out her black glass plate and directed Anna to settle herself down on a stool beside the stove.

"All right," she said, as Anna fixed both eyes on the plate. "Fill thet there plate with th' Glory. Make the sign I showed y'all over it. An' concentrate on seein' Josh."

Carefully, she gathered the power to her, blocking off all the distractions around her, like the feel of her hair drying, the warmth of the stove at her back, the cold of her bare feet. She brought up the power from the earth under the cabin, and it answered to her easily; she directed it into the plate, and it flowed there with docility. When it felt as if the plate was humming in her hands and was drinking all the light in the room, she took one hand away from it briefly, and made the glyph Aunt Jinny had showed her the last time over the pool of blackness in her hands.

And she didn't even have to do anything more. The black void became a window, a window that showed Josh in his workshop, shaping the stone on his workbench with a smaller chisel than before, the little stove showing a good fire through the slits in the door.

None of the little critters was nearby—evidently they didn't find carving stone as enthralling as Anna did—but one of the calico farm cats sat on the toolbench, drowsing in the heat.

The sense of triumph she had for finally conquering the task was almost as sweet as being able to see Josh—even if he was unaware of her.

"Good," was all Aunt Jinny said. "Now we see if y'all c'n talk to Young Raven. Then we'll try for Rufous Taylor over to Asheville."

Anna just sighed.

16

Anna had lost track of the days and the weeks; it was easy to do that when every other afternoon was full of Josh. He wasn't "absent-minded" anymore during their afternoons; in fact, he took great pains to show her what he was doing with the little angel, even going so far as to have her hold the chisel and use the mallet, and carve away bits of the marble where it didn't count. He explained everything to her in great detail, eagerly, offering her his knowledge as some other boy might give her a flower. He was unconsciously kind—that is, he was kind without even having to think about it— things like making sure all the kittens in the barn cat's litter were being fed by their mama, and not losing his temper with Susie even when she deserved it. It inspired Anna to be the same. Everything about her feelings for him had deepened, until she thought she understood (and completely forgave) her mother's obsession with her father. There were times she was so happy with him that she'd even forget to breathe.

Her aunt got a letter from Ma that made Jinny *tsk* with disapproval. Ma, it seemed, had lost faith in Jinny's potions, and was now relying on patent medicines from the Company store, since they eased Pa's cough and the "potions" didn't. "Thet's on account o' they's opium in thar," Jinny said darkly, but said nothing more, and Anna dismissed it from her mind. They still sent the baskets anyway, since Ma hadn't said a thing about not wanting the potions to sell on anymore, and Jinny added what she thought would slip by Pa's eye in the way of foodstuffs.

The summer came to an end. The summer vegetables had all ripened and been harvested, and all but one of the pigs and the sow— now almost large enough for slaughter—had been driven down to the Holcrofts' farm, where they joined others in a larger sty until it was cold enough to slaughter them. Jinny planned to slaughter their own pig, and of course the sow would be kept for breeding next February. All the autumn vegetables were nearly ripened. And frost was on the grass and leaves nearly every morning, except in Jinny's garden, where her magic (and Anna's) kept it off, lengthening the growing season for as long as they possibly could, because fresh vegetables were so much better than preserved.

Jolene continued to appear at irregular intervals, teaching Anna bits of this and that.

In her turn, with Josh as the example at the front of her mind, she was trying to be kind and befriend Jolene, who surely could not have many woman-friends. It had occurred to her that the one thing Jolene probably wasn't able to provide for herself was … baked treats. Remembering the greed of the Little People, the piskies, and all, Anna took to carrying a carefully wrapped square of honey-soaked cornbread or a bacon sandwich with her. It wasn't as if this was in vain—if Jolene didn't happen to intercept her, Josh was always going to welcome a gift of food. Jolene certainly did respond to the homely gifts—and to Anna's other overtures of friendship.

She began teaching things to Anna that not even Great-Granpappy had mentioned in his book. The oddest of all, in Anna's mind, were the illusions, which, to both their surprise and delight, she was particularly good at. "What d' I need them fur?" she asked, astonished. "They ain't real!"

"Because, silly girl, illusions take less power to make and hold than the real thing—and you might not be able to get the real thing when you need it," Jolene said lazily, creating the illusion of a massive, copper snake that rose above them, then vanished into sparks. "What if, despite what the Ravens say, there was a bear?"

Anna no longer feared bears, thanks to the Ravens, but she held her tongue.

"You create the illusion of something the bear fears, and while it is staring at it, you flee. What matters is not if it is real, but if you persuade someone or something else that it is real."

Old Raven—and often, Grandmother Spider—also appeared from time to time to teach her the Cherokee Earth Magic, which could not have been more unlike Jolene's, and yet sprang from the same power. It was a contradiction she finally just accepted, and kept the two separated in her mind.

And with the shortening daylight, Josh couldn't work as late. So sometimes he came up to Jinny's cabin to share supper, and afterward he would sit on the porch with his arm around her while they watched the night, and the magic in it.

Those hours made Anna so unspeakably happy she thought she might float up to heaven.

"And where are you going so fast, on this warm afternoon?" called a lazy voice from the side of the lane to Anna's right.

Since Anna hadn't been paying attention to anything except how quickly she could get to the Holcrofts' farm, Jolene's question, coming without any warning at all, startled her so much that she yelped and tripped, flailing to keep herself from falling.

Jolene laughed, and seemed to *separate* herself from the undergrowth, her green gown and apron had blended into it so well. Today she had three of those little jewel-like lizards arranged around her, one in an apron pocket, one on her shoulder, and one draped in her hair, like an unusual comb.

"Not only hurrying, but paying no heed to what is around you." She *tsk*ed. "That is likely to get you into trouble. What if I had been a panther?"

"The Ravens done promised there ain't no panthers 'tween here an' the Holcrofts," she replied, and could have bitten her tongue for revealing where she was going. She had, thus far, managed to keep the fact that Josh was courting her a secret from Jolene. Or at least, she thought she had. Certainly no one else knew about it but Aunt Jinny and the Holcrofts. Aunt Jinny wouldn't tell Jolene *anything* if she could help it, and the Holcrofts wouldn't have thought it something appropriate to tell a stranger.

"The Holcrofts?" Jolene's eyes gleamed. "Let me see—you are

traveling on swift feet, you are so preoccupied that you pay no attention to what is going on around you, and you are flushing with something other than the heat. I very much doubt that Susan Holcroft is the cause of this. So—it must be Joshua!"

Anna felt her cheeks flushing violently, and Jolene clapped her hands in glee at having had her guess confirmed. "So it *is* Joshua!"

Anna did not ask *How do you know the Holcrofts*, because it was perfectly evident that Jolene knew just about everyone between here and Ducktown. It was perfectly evident at this point that everyone, in turn, "knew" Jolene. She was not the sort of creature to go overlooked.

And I still don't know what she is. Aunt Jinny still just pursed up her lips when Anna asked. Powerful witch? Mythic being? Something else? The only thing that Anna was sure of was that Jolene was no ghost. No ghost could ever make the people in Ducktown react to her the way that Jolene could.

"But there is something more here than just a girl flying to her lover," Jolene continued, narrowing her eyes with speculation. She paused, then ordered, suddenly, "*Tell me what it is.*"

A wave of pure power washed over Anna's unshielded self— because she had never thought she would need to shield against Jolene. Anna tried, she really *tried* to stop herself from telling. But the words came out of her mouth anyway. "Josh has magic. I'm helpin' t'larn him how to scry, so's we c'n talk ev' night." So far, it didn't appear that Josh had enough magic to make the trick work, but Anna had no intention of giving up without a good fight. Much as she liked using the little "black mirror" that Josh had made for her (with black enamel paint and a hand-sized picture frame and its glass) to see him before she went to bed at night, she would much rather have been able to *talk* to him as she could with Aunt Jinny and two of the Elemental Masters her aunt knew.

And she clapped both hands over her mouth, but it was too late.

"Oh, *really*?" Jolene's lips curved in a little smile. "I knew that Joshua is a stone craftsman, but he is also one with power? How very interesting."

The hair on the back of Anna's neck rose. *Niver get a-twixt Jolene and somethin' she wants*, Anna heard, ringing in her memory.

"Still! The hours are passing, and you have much to teach him, and it is clear that your mind would not be on what I was going to teach *you* today." Jolene made little fluttering motions with her fingers. "Run on, Anna May! But watch what is around you."

She laughed and took a few steps backward, allowing the vegetation to somehow absorb her. And in a moment, she was gone.

Anna ran.

Josh worked away at his statue with single-minded intensity; he acknowledged her presence with an absent-minded peck on the cheek, but turned back to his statue immediately. It was clear that she had arrived at a critical time in its creation, so she took her usual seat on a stool and tried to calm her nerves, which had been badly rattled by the encounter with Jolene.

"Y'all know Jolene?" she asked, when at last he paused to study what he had done.

He snorted. "Ain't a man in th' Ducktown Basin thet *don't*. She could hev ary a man she wanted. Not—" he added hastily, "—thet I'm a-sayin' she's *loose*, 'cause she ain't. Hasn't nobody, nowhere, iver said he got more'n a 'howdy' from her. But y'all'd hev t'be blind not t' *see* her what with thet fire-hair and her purdy green dresses, an' she seems ter make a point o' knowin' ev'body's names at least."

Well, she was at a loss of how to ask what she wanted to know next. Like how *well* did he know her, and did she ever come to the farm? And if so, why? She already knew that Josh was a stone carver—was that what interested her?

Niver get a-twixt Jolene an' what she wants.

"She comes by here irregular, t'see what I'm a-workin' on," Josh replied to her unspoken questions. "Been doin' it since I started. Reckon she saw somethin' I carved fer sale in th' mercantile a while back an' arst who done it. She do know her stone!" His voice took on a brightness that made Anna's heart twist a little with jealousy. "She knew right well how I could git a better finish on granite an' marble, an' she's th' one what tol' me where t' git the par-ti-cu-lar sorta sand I use t'polish with now."

Is that something she knows because it's an Earth-Magic thing? Anna wondered. *But why wouldn't Aunt Jinny know that sort of stuff?*

The answer was obvious in the next moment. *Because Jinny*

don't care 'bout it. She cares about plants an' growing an' healing.

But Josh had fallen silent again, in a way that suggested he wasn't all that interested in talking about Jolene. Not in the "I'm avoiding the subject" way, but in the "I'd rather concentrate on what I'm doing" way. Anna took the hint and fell silent.

Aunt Jinny had suggested—in that way that made it an order rather than a suggestion—that if she was going to be spending her afternoons down in Josh's workshop, she really ought to be doing more than just watching Josh work, gazing on him like a devoted hound. So she picked up straw and the narrow plait she had begun a few days ago, with an eye to sewing the straw into another sun hat. She wanted a hat with a broader brim than the hat she'd arrived with. That hat was scarcely more than a narrow-brimmed bonnet. And after all the money Aunt Jinny had spent on her, she felt that the only way she was going to get one was to make it.

Besides—men and women both used the same kind of wide-brimmed straw hats. If this one turned out, she could make another, and it would be lovely to have something useful to give to Josh.

She hoped that keeping her fingers busy would get her mind off Jolene's sudden interest in Josh. It didn't work. All she could think about was that time in Ducktown, when she'd seen for herself how the fellers all lit up when they saw Jolene.

... and when I lost sight of her in Ducktown, Jolene was a-headin' around thet corner Billie McDaran come from!

Billie McDaran ...

Now Billie McDaran was no spirit, that much she was certain of. Where Jolene seemed utterly indifferent to, or was at least amused by, the evidence that she was very attractive to every man that saw her—well, Billie had been the opposite. When women peeped at him out of the corner of their eyes, or gave little flirtatious glances, or even stared at him openly, he had preened under their gazes. And when a few of them had looked at him in alarm or apprehension, well, he seemed to like that just as much. And though he had pulsed with a twisted form of the Glory, he had not had the overwhelming power that Jolene did.

He was almost certainly an extremely powerful magician—and certainly as human as she was.

And surely Jolene knows McDaran.

Ducktown wasn't that big. There couldn't have been much in town once you got off Main Street. Had she been going to meet McDaran? And if so, why?

She's purdy innerested in everybody what's got magic around her ...

She waited for Josh to pause again in his work. "What'd y'all know 'bout Billie McDaran?" she asked him.

"Thet he's a no-good snake, an' y'all better stay fur away from him!" Josh replied, sounding surprised and anxious all at the same time.

"Wall, Aunt Jinny says th' same, but what d'y'all *know* 'bout him?" she persisted.

Josh put down both his hammer and his chisel, which demonstrated just how seriously he was taking this conversation, and turned toward her, giving her his full attention. "He come t' these here parts 'bout six, eight years ago. I dunno where from. I'm thankin' thet the mine owners brung him here, but I dunno fer sure. I was purt little then, an' there weren't much room fer anythin' in my fool haid but fishin' an' tryin' t' git outta chores an' school lessons."

"Y'all went t' *school*?" she said, surprised, thinking about how far from Ducktown the farm was.

But he shook his head. "Ma larned us. She'd larn us till it were purdy plain we weren't gonna larn nothin' else, an' she'd let us quit. Me an' Sue an' Gertie, thet is. She's still larnin' Seth, Becky, an' Ned. Sue an' Gertie an' me don't need no more o' thet stuff. We got readin', writin', an' 'rithmatic, an' thet's all we need."

He looked as if he was more than happy to go off on that tangent, so Anna hauled him back. "Billie McDaran," she reminded him.

He made a face. "All *I* know fer sure is he's a scandal. He's got two wimmin as he says does housework an' cookin' fer him what lives in his house, an' Pa said to Ma when he thunk I wasn't listenin' thet he reckons McDaran's a-livin' in sin with the both of 'em. *I* ain't never seed 'em, but they's supposed t'be real purdy, iffen you don't mind a woman lookin' like a whupped dog. Cooper at the Company store cain't hardly stand him, but he's gotter be nice on account'a McDaran's the mine foreman. Cooper's the one tol' me them wimmin look like they's askeert alla time. He says they don't hardly never come outa thet house 'less McDaran sends 'em t'the store on a errand. The mine owners *gotta* know 'bout them wimmin, but they don't say or do nothin'." Josh scratched his head in perplexity. "Mebbe they don't do nothin' on account'a Cooper says they's quadroons, an' some folks reckon … wall, thet they don't count. Not like a white woman, anyways."

That was a lot to digest. "So does ev'body in Ducktown gotter act nice to him?" she asked.

"Purdy much, on account'a ev'body either works in the mine, or needs miners' money. Like the mercantile. An' even iffen they don't gotter, it don't pay t'git acrost him, 'cause he'll lay a man out with one punch, an' swear t'other feller started it. Thet's partly how he keeps th' miners workin'. I knowed fer a fact thet he's laid more'n a few out, an' some was seein' stars fer a week arter." Josh shook his head. "He's mean, he's bad, an' he's a bully."

"An' he's a magician," Anna told him. "On'y his magic's all twisted up wrong, somehow. I seed it 'round him when we was in Ducktown an' he was a-plaguing yore Pa."

"He is?" Josh scratched his head again. "Miz Jinny knows?"

"She knows. She says he c'n use thet magic t'git inside yore haid an' make y'all do what he wants and thank it's reasonable on top o' thet." What would Jolene want with a man like that? Did he "amuse" her too?

"Wall, thet 'splains a lot. Sure-e-ly 'splains why the mine owners ain't fired him, an' mebbe 'splains why they hired him in the fust place."

She nodded, but she was still trying to think of reasons why Jolene would want anything to do with someone like McDaran. Surely his twisted form of the Glory revolted her the way it revolted Anna …

But she's more powerful than he is. Mebbe it don't bother her none.

This was leaving her head all of muddle, and she was no closer to sussing out Jolene than she had been when she first met the— what was she, anyway?

Now Anna was back to where she had begun. She was sure Jolene was no human woman, just as Aunt Jinny claimed, but what could she *be*? And what could Anna do if she decided she was interested in Josh?

When she reluctantly left Josh, it was with a mind full of doubt and fear and confusion. She trudged up the lane in a kind of fog, so much so that she almost didn't hear the sound of hoofbeats on the sod behind her until it was too late.

And in fact, it wasn't the sound of hoofbeats that alerted her. It was the sudden feeling of *wrongness* behind her that sent her scurrying into the bushes beneath the trees, throwing up a shield at the same time. Then she waited, crouching there, hidden, until she could see who it was that had given her that gut-twisting feeling.

As if merely thinking about him had somehow conjured him, to her horror, it was …

Billie McDaran.

Billie McDaran, riding in the sort of awkward, off-balance way that told her he really didn't know how to ride, on a poor horse that was literally foaming with fear-sweat and clearly did not want to be carrying him. It was impossible to tell what color the poor beast was, it was so soaked with its own sweat.

He was paying absolutely no attention to anything on either side of him, and she thanked Baby Jesus that she had put the shield up when she had. He *shouldn't* sense another magician here, and hopefully he didn't even know she was one. But if he had managed to tell there was one here, before she had detected him, it would have been—ahead of him, where he would have expected Aunt Jinny to be, and not down here in the lane. *She* couldn't tell exactly where someone was, or (more importantly) how far away they were, and she doubted that he could.

Why was Billie McDaran riding up this lane? There was only one thing at the end of it, and that was Aunt Jinny's cabin.

Well, she surely did *not* want to encounter him. There was only one thing to do. Take some of the game trails instead of the lane, and come out at the back of the cabin rather than the front. Then what? *Wait, I guess. Watch and listen?*

Thanks to all her hunting for plants for Jinny's potions, she knew the forest on either side of the lane intimately. She couldn't exactly eel through the underbrush the way the Ravens could, but—

A hand touched her shoulder from behind, and she nearly

shrieked aloud, stuffing her fist into her mouth to muffle it as she whirled, ready to—well, she wasn't sure *what* she was going to do, but she had every intention of defending herself if she had to—

But it wasn't an interloper, it was Young Raven, an uncustomary expression of deep concern on his face. "Come with me," he said quietly. "It is not safe for you at your home for a while."

"But how—" she began.

"Jinny was warned by the Little People, and to be certain they were right, scried the road from Ducktown. She saw the man McDaran on his horse, and knew there was likely only one place he would be coming. She does not want him to see you. She believes it would be very dangerous for you if he did. She sent to me to find you and bring you where you can be safe. Now follow," he concluded, giving her no chance to ask any more questions.

Soon they were entirely off the trails she knew, and going deeper and deeper into the Holler. It would not be fair to say that this part of the woods had never had man set foot in it—because obviously the Cherokee *did* make free of its game trails—but they certainly had left it all fundamentally untouched. If there was any sign that anything other than animals used these thread-like paths through the woods, she certainly couldn't read it.

Old trees grew here, trees that never saw an axe, but had been left to die in their own time. Some were big enough that it would take two or even three people to encircle their trunks. And the growth was so dense that she couldn't see more than ten or twenty feet in any direction. Only where the giants had fallen, or where tiny cricks wound through the vegetation, were there places for younger trees to seek the light, but that did not mean the forest floor was barren. On the contrary, shade-loving bushes as high as her head and ferns as tall as her waist thrust their way to the dim light through a floor so carpeted with damp, dead leaves that their footsteps made scarcely a sound. Streaks of red, orange, yellow, and brown showed where frost had already touched some parts of this forest. It was actually *cold* under those branches, and all she could smell was the bitter scent of falling leaves.

Bright sunlight ahead warned her that they were coming to a clearing, but when they passed through the thick bushes that took them inside it, she found herself blinking in surprise. Before her astonished gaze were eight cabins virtually identical to Aunt Jinny's place, one much bigger one in the center, and one smaller, off to the side of the others, all surrounded by a ring of productive gardens. And there were people everywhere. She had suspected that there were more Cherokee than just the Ravens and Young Raven's wife deep in the Holler, perhaps as many as a dozen, but she'd had no idea there was an entire tribe back here.

"This is not what a traditional village would look like," Young Raven said, as she stared at more people than she had ever imagined were hiding back here. "A traditional village would have summer and winter houses for each family, and a sweathouse for the sick for each family as well. But there was no point in building summer and winter houses, when the kind of cabin we knew how to build at the time of the Removal was much better in both halves of the year, especially after your great-grandfather showed us how improve our own, and how to build his wonderful stove. The center building is the Council House. The little one is the sweathouse we all share, because thanks to my father, my grandmother, me, and my wife, we are all seldom sick."

There were children everywhere, from toddling babies to ten- or eleven-year-olds. Some were doing chores; some were just playing. There didn't seem to be any men around; the women were dressed in a practical outfit of a kind of long smock with a belt or sash and leggings, often in a mix of leather and colorful calico, and were mostly engaged in all manner of work. Except for the oldest women, who were supervising the children. The boys wore outfits like Young Raven's, the girls like their mothers, the toddlers wore nothing at all—which, after a moment of shock, seemed eminently practical to Anna. Given how dirty very young children liked to get in play, what could be more sensible than just leaving them in their skin as long as the weather allowed it? After no more than a glance or two at her, the adults went back to their work, which was everything from working in the garden to smoking meat in racks over smoldering fires, to working on hides stretched over curing frames, to what she presumed was grinding corn the hard way—by hand. But the children came pelting over to stare at her as soon as they spotted her.

Reckon I'm a reg'lar circus, she thought wryly. "O'siyo," she said, politely, as all those grave little faces looked up at hers.

"This is Anna," Young Raven said. "She is hiding from an enemy of hers, and ours. You must all be very careful and stay within the boundary until she leaves. Only then will you know the enemy is gone. We do not want to discover you have been stolen away from us and sent far away as our brothers and sisters were."

All those big, dark eyes grew much bigger when Young Raven said that she was hiding from an enemy, more so when he spoke about Removal, and all the heads nodded instant agreement. But one little girl was less impressed with that than with Anna's hair.

"Why is your hair the color of corn?" she asked, staring as if she wanted to touch it.

"Why is your hair the color of a crow's wing?" Anna asked back. "Mine is the color of corn for the same reason." It seemed the most diplomatic way of answering. Despite the seriousness of the moment, Young Raven seemed amused by the exchange, and the little girl's face puckered with thought for a moment.

"All right," she said at last, simply accepting the answer. Young Raven made a slight shooing motion, and the children scattered again, going back to what they had been doing before her entrance interrupted them.

She looked over at Young Raven, astonished. "How do you keep so many people a secret?" she asked.

He shrugged. "The Holler is big enough that as long as we do not have more people than this, it can sustain us. Most of us never go past your aunt's cabin. Those who choose to leave, to look for husbands or wives, for instance, simply never talk about where they are from to anyone but other Cherokee. We are not the only band that is in hiding— and there are Cherokee in the Removed lands who had proper title to their land and farms as the white man deemed legal; they remained when the rest were forced to depart. Not many, but enough that the young men and women can go find mates among them, and bring some of them here, as I did. Hunters and trappers are unlikely to trespass for fear of your aunt. And my father and I keep the village from being discovered with a barrier of power, which makes those who are not permitted here go around us without ever finding us. And the little people help with that."

That sounded even more effective than Aunt Jinny's shield. *I need to larn how to do that.*

"Now we will go to my family's home and see what Billie McDaran wants," he continued, and strode off into the circle of houses, with her trotting after him to keep up.

Aunt Jinny had been right; aside from a few oddities, like stuffed animal skins on the floor to sit on, colorful patterns painted on the side of the stove, not much furniture, and more furs than blankets, this cabin could not have been told from the one she lived in. The walls were as full of shelves with things stored on them as Jinny's walls were. Except that none of the windows had glass. But then, she knew plenty of houses in Soddy that didn't have glass either.

In fact, now that she thought about it, she should have been surprised that Aunt Jinny's cabin did.

The cabin held five people: Old Raven, a woman who looked about the same age, a young woman who Anna assumed was Young Raven's wife, and two children, a toddler and a baby. The old woman was fixing something at the stove, the young woman assisting her with the baby slung on her back, and the toddler was being amused with a carved figure of a horse by Old Raven, with both of them on the floor on a bearskin. Anna paused in the doorway, not exactly sure what to do now, and not wanting to offend anyone. Because suddenly that seemed to be the most important thing, that she not offend any of these gracious people who were hiding her from someone who was dangerous to them all, not just her.

"Be welcome to our house," said Old Raven. "Please come in, and sit down. If your aunt does not manage to rid herself of McDaran in a reasonable length of time, we would be pleased if you would share our evening meal and rest with us through the night. And, indeed, you may stay as long as it takes your aunt to be rid of the wretched creature."

"Thank you, grandfather," she said. She came in and gingerly took a seat on a stuffed deerskin. The toddler turned to look at her, but found his horse much more interesting.

Young Raven went to a shelf and came back with an actual glass mirror. "This will do reasonably well for all of us to watch with the eyes of an eagle," he said, laying it on the floor where all three of them could look at it. "It is made of sand, which is earth, forged in fire, which is my power, and Father can use anything he cares to. So let us all see what we can see."

She assumed that meant she was to contribute to the effort by using the magical tools *she* knew to add to the scrying session. So she felt for one of those lines of power—and without any surprise found one running right under the village. She felt the shield that Young Raven had spoken of, and that it was using some of that power, but there was plenty more to spare. She teased a little magic away from it, drew it up through the earth into her hands, let the power fill the mirror, then wrote the glyph for "seeing" over it, keeping her Aunt Jinny firmly in her mind as she did so.

The mirror misted over, and then suddenly filled with an image. It was as if she was a bird above her aunt's cabin; her aunt was down at the stile, and facing off against her, on the other side of the stile, was Billie McDaran.

He had dismounted and was holding his horse by the reins, but tightly, just under the poor thing's mouth, grinding the bit down into the lower jaw. As Anna concentrated on them, it was as if the "bird" swooped closer to land just above her aunt's head, and thin voices came into her head in such a way that she couldn't tell if she was actually hearing them or if they were in her mind. Her excitement at *finally* being able to master scrying to this extent was tempered by what they were saying.

"... we both know y'all didn't come up here fer *potions*, McDaran," her aunt was saying.

McDaran laughed. It sounded mocking, and it grated on her nerves. "A'course not, ole woman," he replied rudely. "I heerd y'all got a visitor. Damn shame y'all didn' let me know so's I could pay a visit. Reckoned as how I'd make her welcome anyway."

"Iffen y'all mean m'half-sister's gel, she ain't here," her aunt said shortly.

"Oh, be careful, Virginia," Old Raven muttered. "A word of falsehood and he will have power over you."

"Where is she, then?" McDaran countered.

"Dunno." Aunt Jinny's face was giving nothing away. "Had her here t'mend her up. She was sickly. Now she's well, an' she ain't here."

"Wall, thet may be true," said McDaran. "But I heerd y'all was a-settin' her up like y'all was her own Ma."

"Her own Ma ain't got a pot t'piss in," Jinny said rudely. "Am I s'pposed t'let her look like a scarecrow? What would folks thank iffen I didn't do right by my kin? So while she was here, I set her up with some stuff fer new close, on account'a she ain't niver been provided for proper. Gel did her own sewin', so it weren't like it was work fer me."

Old Raven let out a sigh of relief. "The exact truth, and just enough of it," he breathed.

"Reckon y'all heerd about it from Abby at th' mercantile," her aunt continued. "Wall, let me tell y'all, Billie McDaran, this is the damn truth. Her Pa was dead set against her comin' here in the fust place. He figgers a gel b'longs with her own fambly, helpin' her Ma as God intended. Must'a taken her Ma movin' Heaven'n earth t' allow her t' come in the fust place. An' he wanted her back soon's she was well."

That was all true too. Anna found herself nodding her head. The fact that she *hadn't* returned home had no bearing on what Pa *wanted*.

"So, 'fraid y'all come all this way fer nothin', McDaran," her aunt said, sounding very final. "She ain't here. Y'all might as well go back t' yore dinner."

"Somehow I don't b'lieve y'all is tellin' me the whole truth, Jinny," the big man replied, eyes narrowing. His fist tightened on the poor horse's reins, and it froze in pain. He looked at Jinny as if he would have liked to beat her, if he could just get the chance.

"Ain't one word I tol' y'all thet's a lie," Jinny said flatly. "An' y'all know thet's a fact." She glared back at him, challenging him. "I knows y'all been a-testin' thet, an' y'all knows I ain't lied. Not one word."

"And what if I decide t'stay here an' see if the gel turns up?" he challenged in his turn.

"Y'all c'n stay on thet side'a the stile till hell freezes over iffen thet's what y'all wanter do," her aunt countered with a shrug. "Y'all ain't a friend, so I ain't 'bout t' go outa my way fer y'all. *Mebbe* I'd call y'all a customer. I don' let jest any old person crost my threshold. An' I didn' make 'nuff supper fer a guest."

He guffawed at that. "I et good beefsteak an' taters fer dinner *an'* supper ev' damn day! Y'all thank I'm a-hankerin' fer beans an' hoecake?"

"When y'all's been a-standin' there till th' sun goes down, an' yore belly's plumb up agin' yore backbone, an' yore a-smellin my good cornbread, I reckon y'all'd beg on yore knees fer a chitlin'," she retorted. "An' I ain't a-feedin' y'all, an' I ain't lettin' y'all over the threshold. So y'all c'n stand there an' wait an' starve, an' then stand there in th' dark till dawn, an' *then* figger out how y'all is gonna excuse yerself t' the mine boss when y'all ain't there on time." She smirked. "It do git cold up here at night. An' y'all don' seem t' hev brought yoreself so much's a blanket."

McDaran's face turned almost purple with rage, and his free hand clenched and unclenched spasmodically. For a moment, Anna was afraid that he was somehow going to get past the shield and to hit her aunt anyway. Jinny just stared at him fearlessly, not moving an inch.

"Y'all ain't heerd th' last of this, Jinny Alscot!" he roared, shaking his fist in the air. "Don't think y'all hev!"

And with that, he wrenched the poor horse's head around, flung himself into the saddle, and spurred the beast so viciously that it leapt into a gallop from a standing start.

They watched as Jinny watched him disappear into the distance, then strode up the path between her garden plots up to the cabin.

The mirror misted over, and Anna thought that was all there was going to be. But neither Raven moved, and after a while it misted again, and her aunt's anxious face peered up at them. The anxious look cleared immediately.

"You got Anna," she said in Cherokee. "Good. Did you see McDaran?" she asked.

"Most of it, I think." Old Raven was the one to answer.

She shook her head. "I wish I hadn't made him angry, because he holds grudges, but maybe he'll concentrate on his anger and not on looking for Anna."

"I think we should keep her overnight, just to be sure he does not return," Young Raven suggested. "I would not be surprised that he should tie the horse up halfway down the lane, and come creeping back in the dusk to see if Anna returns to your home." Then Young Raven smiled. "But if he does that, he will either have to beg transport of Matt Holcroft, or walk, because the Little People would enjoy untying his horse and sending it back to its stables."

Jinny cackled. "I do reckon that the horse would be right pleased if that were to happen. You don't mind keeping Anna for the night, then?"

The old woman, who up until this moment had not spoken, leaned over Old Raven's shoulder. "And are you insulting my hospitality and manners, Virginia Alscot?"

Aunt Jinny finally laughed, if weakly. "No, Dawn Greeter. I most certainly am not. Thank you kindly."

"We will bring her back to you in the morning. And if he *does* stay, we will keep her with us for as long as it takes for him to tire of waiting fruitlessly," said Old Raven, and waved his hand over the mirror. It became a mirror again, and Anna became aware that every muscle in her body was taut with tension.

"Now you will discover if you like Cherokee food," the old woman said to her, conversationally.

"I will be grateful and thankful for Cherokee food, grandmother, and you are generous to share with me and make me your guest," Anna replied.

The old woman cocked her head at her husband. "She has good manners," she said, and went back to the stove.

A few moments later, she and the younger woman served the three of them a wooden platter, which had some round fried dough-balls and some fried rabbit on it, with some fried squash to fill out the meal. Under other circumstances, she'd have been eager to try it, but right now all she could think about was Billie McDaran, and that he was out there, trying to find her. And for no good purpose, she was sure.

17

In the end, she stayed three anxious days with the Cherokee, because the Little People came to warn them for three days in a row that McDaran was lurking around her aunt's home. Fortunately the piskies were still willing to carry notes between her and Josh, so she managed to tell him what was going on. The Raven family didn't have any paper, nor anything to write with, but Dawn Greeter suggested the ingenious solution of sewing a few words into a cornhusk with bits of colored thread unraveled from the edges of thriftily saved rags. Cornhusks there were in plenty, and Josh's equally short replies came back on paper she saved to use later if she needed to. Those replies made her worry, because things like *Stay safe, can't tawk now* were not exactly reassuring.

Dawn Greeter and Young Raven's wife Moon Daughter found plenty for her to do, and she was not backward in doing as many chores as they set her, but she was anxious the entire time. If she hadn't been so anxious she probably would have enjoyed the novelty of some of it—weeding in the garden was the same, and so was preparing harvested vegetables and drying them—but she learned how to grind corn in a stone bowl, learned how to make the corn-and-bean balls she'd been served the first night, and learned how to sew leather. Night-times were very different—everyone in the family, including her, was expected to pile together on skins and under blankets, on the floor, fully clothed. If anyone woke during the night, they often chatted to one another, or told stories, or sang to soothe the children. Old Raven told many stories in the evenings, anyway; some of them just seemed to be for the benefit of the children, but others were clearly tales with magic lessons, meant for her.

But her anxiety ramped up the longer she was kept away, and it was with great relief that the Little People finally reported that McDaran had abandoned his watch on the cabin and had returned to Ducktown. Young Raven volunteered to guide her home, and she could never have imagined she'd be so happy to see her aunt's weathered face as they came around the side of the cabin and climbed over the stone wall.

In fact, she practically flew the last few yards and threw her arms around Jinny in a spontaneous embrace, much to Jinny's consternation—and, if the look in her eyes was to be believed, pleasure.

"I missed y'all so much!" she cried.

"Huh. Reckon y'all missed my cookin'. Hello, Young Raven," Jinny replied, around Anna's hair.

"Greetings, grandmother," Young Raven said, gravely. "I bring Anna back. Now I must return. But if the evil one should come back, do not hesitate to send one of the Little People to warn us, and you, Anna, flee further into the Holler. It does not matter where you go, the Little People will be able to find you and bring us to you."

"I will," they said at the same time. "Thenkee kindly, nephew," Jinny concluded. Anna didn't hear him leave, but the next time she looked, he was gone.

"Y'all reckon McDaran's a-comin' back?" she asked, letting go of her aunt.

"Don't rightly know," Jinny said, clearly worried. "There's somethin' a-goin' on thet I cain't fathom. Dunno why he'd come all the way out here, then set down thar in the lane, waitin' fer three whole days. I ain't niver seed him stir his stumps fer nothin' afore, an' now, thar he is, jest waitin' fer a gel he ain't niver seed an' knows nothin' 'bout." She shook her head. "Wall, let's git yore bath an' some clean close on y'all, since I knowed y'all been a-sleepin' on th' floor."

"It weren't 'xactly on th' floor," Anna temporized, but she was glad enough of the offer. Not that she'd gone unbathed—

the women and children would go for a splash in a little pond that managed to get less-than-freezing by mid-afternoon. That was where they beat the dirt out of their clothing with rocks, then lounged in the water until their clothing dried. But it wasn't the same as a bath with soap, and she'd gotten used to Jinny's cleanliness regime.

As her hair dried in the sun, she was able to send a message to Josh via a piskie that she'd come see him the next day, and was relieved to get his almost immediate reply that he couldn't hardly wait. In the back of her mind there had been a fear that after having her there so much, he'd have found he missed his privacy, but it appeared that wasn't the case. But once that worry was out of the way ... her stomach started to knot up again. What did McDaran mean by coming here? *Did* he think he could just snatch her out from under her aunt's protection?

"Who d'y'all reckon tol' McDaran 'bout me?" she asked Jinny over supper. Jinny just shook her head.

"Dunno. Mebbe Abby at th' mercantile. Mebbe Cooper at th' Company store. But I wouldn't'a thunk Cooper, on account of I reckon he's still tore up 'bout losin' thet baby, an' likely ain't thinkin' of anythin' else." She shook her head. "Ain't no use worritin' 'bout it. Makes more sense t'figger out what we're a-gonna do 'bout it if he keeps comin' 'round. An' figger what in tarnation he wants. He's gotter know I ain't a-gonna let him meddle with y'all."

Jinny had made hoecakes with honey, and Anna sucked the honey off her spoon while she considered that. "Mebbe he figgers he's sech a handsome feller, it won't matter what y'all want, on account'a I'm likely t' take a shine to him?" she suggested.

Jinny hesitated. "I'm afeerd there's more to it then thet," she said finally. "He's a powerful strong magician. Prolly a Marster. An' when Marsters turn t'the bad, like as not they start lookin' fer people with the Glory thet they c'n use. Thet might could be th' answer. He might reckon y'all's here as my 'prentice."

"So you reckon he's done figgered out I got magic all on his own?" she asked.

Jinny shrugged. "Makes sense thet he'd show up now—it'd take his thick haid this long t'figger thet out fer his own self.

An'—wall, thet's where my figgerin' sorta falls apart. 'Cause there's a lotta mebbes. Mebbe he reckons t'offer t'take y'all as *his* 'prentice—'course thet'd end bad fer *y'all*, but he'd reckon y'all wouldn't know thet. An' he'd figger he could use thet power of his'n t' jest twist y'all round his liddle finger even if I'd tol' y'all 'bout him."

"Reckon mebbe he figgers I'd jest go, 'Oh, she's a old biddy, she's jest jealous he's a-payin' court t'me'?" she ventured.

"Thet do sound like his thankin'," Jinny agreed darkly. "He's a snake, an' he do thank there ain't a female critter can resist him. But thet's th' prollem. Like I done said, he's powerful strong. He might *could* get y'all a-dazzled and bewildered, an' I wouldn' be able to pertect y'all."

Anna hesitated, then said what she was thinking. "Jolene says I'm a-gonna be powerful strong too. Mebbe I c'n keep him off ..."

"All th' more reason why he'd come sniffin' 'round here now. He's figgerin' t' git his claws inter y'all afore y'all can defend yoreself," her aunt said bleakly. "We gotter figger us out some plans."

"Mebbe there's somethin' in Great-Granpappy's book I c'n use," she said after a moment.

Her aunt blinked, as if that had not occurred to her. "Mebbe. I ain't one fer readin' so I niver done more'n glance a bit at it," she admitted. "Y'all take it up on th' stove an' hev a read. I'll call out the Domovoy an' see iffen he c'n thank of anythin'."

She skipped over the part she would really rather have read—about how Pavel had met with Eagle Sight and the Cherokee up in the Holler for the very first time, how they had forged an alliance, and how the entire band had worked together to raise a cabin and make a garden for him in two days in return for his help in designing and building their new stone stoves. She even (mostly) skipped over the part where, no sooner had the mortar cured and the first fire lit in *his* stove, the Domovoy from his destroyed house back in Roosha crawled out from under it and made itself known to him.

No, what stopped her in her tracks was another part of the story altogether.

... we had gathered the last of our fall crops, protected those that would stay in the field with heaps of dead leaves, ferns, and

earth, and had killed and preserved our first wild pig and a deer. That, together with the fish and game I had smoked, lent us a feeling of confidence that we would survive our first winter here, and allowed me to consider making plans to celebrate with our Cherokee brothers.

And that very morning was the morning she appeared, standing outside my shield, at the rock wall we had built to shelter our gardens. In her green gown, with her blazing red hair and her special green lizard familiar spirits, she was unmistakable. And she was a creature I had never expected to see again.

Nor was I entirely easy about seeing her now.

Sometimes she was called The Malachite Maid, and was said to be the protector of miners against abusive foremen. But mostly she was called Hozjajka Mednoj Gory, and by that name she was a strange and enigmatic creature indeed, and that is how I knew her.

Just before our village had been destroyed, I had had several encounters with her. She had offered to be my patron, as it is said she does for craftsmen, for she collects them. Those she favors the most, she takes with her into her kingdom under the mountain. I had not quite accepted her patronage—for those who take her as their Mistress must never look at another woman, lest terrible things befall them—when the boyar burned our village to the ground. Had she come to me then—well, I probably would have accepted her, for where else was I to go and what was I to do? But she did not, and I followed the rest of my village, and then, went on my travels.

I never saw her again while I was within the borders of Rossiya, nor once I was out of them. I certainly did not expect to see her here, so far from both our native lands.

If she was powerful enough, and determined enough, to find me here ... I knew I had better go and greet her courteously and, if I was lucky, turn aside any anger she had with me.

I thought about telling Sally to remain at the cabin, but with a second thought, I knew that it was of little use to do so. She wouldn't obey me, and she had every right, as a Master in her own power, to know what we might have attracted—or be facing. Because if the Mistress was wroth with me, she would also be wroth with Sally.

So I cautioned her about what we were going to meet; on her own Sally went to get some of the balls of cornmeal and beans we had learned to cook from Blue Doe, a piece of honeycomb, and a wooden cup of our first brewing of vodka. These we carried down to her, as she waited, with the stillness of a malachite statue, for us to approach her.

I came first, and bowed low to her, as to a Tsarina, and addressed her respectfully. "Be welcome to my home, Hozjajka Mednoj Gory, and I beg you to accept hospitality of us." I spoke in the language of Rossiya, of course, but Sally knew enough of it to bring forward the wooden plate on which our poor offerings rested.

She stared at them, then at Sally, then at me. "And what of your promises, Pavel Lebedev, when last we met?" Storms threatened in her green eyes, but I knew she would punish falsehoods, not truths.

"Oh fairest of creatures, I made you no promises," I replied. "I said only that I must think upon your most generous offer. It was not by my will that my village was burned to the ground and my people sent away before I could make an answer to you. You are also the patroness of mines and miners, and I am neither of these. I thought you had forgotten me."

"This is true," she said grudgingly, her eyes flashing nevertheless. Or perhaps her eyes flashed in memory of what our boyar had done without her leave. Her next words proved my second guess true. "And the boyar has paid for his impertinence."

I did not ask her what she meant. In truth, I no longer cared, though once I would have been glad to hear all the details of his downfall—for downfall he most certainly would have suffered at her hands. "I did not dare the impertinence of calling upon you," I continued—which was true—"and I did not think you were still interested in my services"—which was also true. I had been greatly despondent, and saw little value in myself and my poor skills. "So I followed where the boyar sent my people. And then—I just kept going."

"And so you ended here." It was, obviously, a statement. Anger faded from her eyes.

"Even so. And on the way, I met one who to me is worth more than all the jewels under the mountain." I gestured to Sally, who once again offered the platter with a pretty gesture.

"*Even more than all the skills I could teach you?*" she asked.

This was a trick question. I must somehow answer it without offending her. "I am a different sort of craftsman now, Radiant One," *I said honestly.* "And I never was an artist. I know that now, and I am humble enough to admit it. Art without skill—well, that can be remedied. Skill without art is empty, and produces only pretty trinkets. I would not fit properly in your service, and would do you no honor by serving."

"*Hmmm.*" *She reached across the wall and took the cup of vodka, drinking it in a single swallow. Then she accepted one of the corn-balls, and the bit of honeycomb. I breathed a little easier. She was no longer wroth, and had accepted my hospitality.* "But would you enter my service to save your wife?"

"Instantly, Radiant One," *I replied.* "Even though my heart would pine for her every waking moment, and my dreams would be full only of her."

Then she turned to Sally, who had not followed more than a word or two of this questioning, and said in perfect English, "I am wroth with thy husband, woman. Yet you may save him. Would you enter my service, come under the mountain with me, and never see him again in order to so save him?"

Tears started up in my dear one's eyes, but she said, immediately and steadfastly, "I have crossed wide oceans and left my parents on the other side of the world to be with him. How could I do less than that to save him?"

Even knowing only that this was some powerful Earth Spirit, perhaps the equal or superior to any of the Great Spirits we had encountered here, she said that! Oh, my beloved brave one, what did I ever do to deserve you?

But of course, it was exactly the right answer, because at last, Hozjajka Mednoj Gory smiled, as if the sun had broken out from behind the clouds. "I see you are of no use to me, Pavel Lebedev. Prosper here in your new home, with your new allies. You may see me from time to time, for all Mountains are the same to me, and I can be here or back in Rossiya in less time than it takes to blink."

Well, that explained how she had made the journey. The Great Ones have powers that are astonishing, to be sure!

And with that, she began to walk off—only to turn back to me.

"There is a mine here, which interests me," she said. *"So I may be nearer than you think, more often than you guess, and you may see me in places you do not expect. If you do see me, in the future do not call me Hozjajka Mednoj Gory."*

"I hear you and obey, Radiant One," I said obediently, because obviously, there was no other answer to be made. "But what shall I call you?"

"Jolene."

At that, Anna nearly dropped the book. *What?*

She picked it back up again.

"Jolene," she said. *"I saw it on a tombstone. I like it."*

And with that, she turned and vanished.

"Aunt Jinny," she said, trying to catch her breath. "What does *Hozjajka Mednoj Gory* mean?" She stumbled over the unfamiliar syllables, and her aunt looked at her in puzzlement for a very long moment. "What Great-Granpappy called Jolene," she added, when Jinny continued to stare.

"Oh! So, y'all got t' thet part, hmm?" she replied. "I cain't wrap my mouth 'round thet palaver, but it means *The Queen of Copper Mountain.*" She shrugged. "Now y'all unnerstand why I said don't get twixt her an' what she wants?"

"Great-Granpappy didn' say, 'xactly …" But he certainly had implied more than enough. Anna sucked on her lower lip. "He reckoned she's purt powerful." And she remembered that forest spirit that Jolene had ordered about, the one bigger than a house, and shivered.

"Y'all know anythin' what c'n be in Ducktown one minnut, an' in Roosha th' next?" her aunt demanded. Anna shook her head, because obviously she couldn't. "Neither do I. Neither does any Marster I've arsked. *Purt powerful* don't begin t' describe her. Great-Granpappy was lucky to get shuck of her, an' he knowed it. It's might near as dangerous t' be somethin' she wants, as t' get atwixt her an somethin' she wants." Her aunt paused for a moment, searching for words. "She ain't human. An' she don't thank like one."

"Wonder what she wanted with me?" Anna said aloud.

Jinny's lips twisted in a sardonic smile. "T'plague *me*, most likely." But Anna wasn't at all sure of that. The only thing that she *was* sure of, was that Jolene wasn't all that different from Grandmother Spider, and that her aunt was right. She was far more dangerous than Anna had ever guessed.

Aunt Jinny turned her loose in the morning, right after tending the pigs and the chickens and eating breakfast. She couldn't get down the lane fast enough, and Jinny must have known she would be useless until she saw Josh again.

He must have heard her footsteps in the barn, because he met her halfway inside and caught her up in his arms and swung her around until she was breathless, and for a long, long time, wouldn't let her go.

She had a thousand things to say, and didn't need to say any of them. That embrace gave her all the answers she needed.

So instead she asked something else entirely. "The li'l angel?"

He heaved a huge sigh. "Done an' gone. An' it's been a rotten three days. On'y two thangs good outen 'em a-tall. C'mon in th' workshop an' I'll tell y'all."

He took her hand and led her to the shop, and picked her up by the waist to perch her on her usual stool, while he leaned back against his workbench. Now that she saw him, she saw he looked as if he hadn't slept for those three days. Shocked, she waited for him to tell her what was going on.

"So. Mistuh Cooper showed up with his cart an' hoss three days ago, an' McDaran with him, ridin' a livery hoss."

"What?" That hit her with another unwelcome jolt, although that corresponded to when McDaran had turned up at Aunt Jinny's. "Why? I mean, why did he hev McDaran with him, when y'all tol' me he couldn't hardly stand the man?"

Josh sighed. "Wall, he weren't too clear 'bout that. In fact, he weren't too clear 'bout *anythin'*, 'cept thet he wanted thet statchoo right quick, an' he weren't goin' back t'Ducktown wi'out it. Pa weren't a-tall happy about Cooper bein' thar, much less McDaran, an' then—wall, I dunno how the heck he done it, 'cause I know Pa thanks McDaran's a snake, but McDaran talked to him an' Ma fer 'bout an hour, an' next thang *I* know, they's invited t'stay, they's eatin' in the kitchen like guests, they's a-sleepin' in *my* room, an'

I'm beddin' down out here. Oh, an' Susie's so sweet on thet skunk McDaran thet I cain't even say 'boo' 'bout him without she crawls down m'throat. I ain't seen nothin' like it, an' iffen y'all hadn't tol' me 'bout magic, an' thet he had it, I reckon I'd'a thunk I was a-goin' crazy. As 'twas, took me most of the fust day t' figger out he'd done messed with their haids an' done it with magic."

"If he'd'a thunk y'all was a threat to him, he'd'a worked his weasel-magic on y'all, too," she said, darkly. "Then y'all woulda been givin' him good Lord only knows what."

"Or thet," he agreed. "But I reckon it's a good thang he reckoned me no-account, jest th' pair'a hands what made stuff, 'cause he left me alone. I jest wanted ter be shuck of both of 'em, so I did 'bout a week an' a half of polishin' in three days, barely slept a wink a-doin' it, an' they loaded the thang up in Cooper's wagon and took it an' thesselves back t'Ducktown yesterday. It'd been wuss if he'd been a-hangin' round m'shop like Cooper did, but he went off a-wanderin' somewhere fer most of the day, all three days."

"He reckoned y'all no-account, 'cause he don't know 'bout y'all courtin' me!" she blurted, and then told him, first to his astonishment, then to his anger, about McDaran's persistent lingering about Aunt Jinny's place and her going into hiding. She didn't tell him *where* she had gone. So far as she knew, he still didn't know about the Cherokee up in the Holler—and with McDaran around, working his wiles on folks, the fewer as knew, the better, she reckoned.

"Aunt Jinny made sure I was all right," she merely said. "I jest didn' hev no paper nor pencil, so I used them cornhusks an' threads instead."

"Thet was slick thinkin', Anna May," he said with admiration, and sighed. "I'd'a liked t'hev got away from Cooper an' at least sent y'all more than 'cain't talk,' with him hoverin' over me—but since I know thet was McDaran's doin', reckon I'll fergive him. Thet's why I didn' send y'all more messages—he was at m'elbow from th' dawn till bed. But thet's the fust good thang thet come of this. He paid me. Paid me right there on th' spot afore he loaded the statchoo inter his cart."

"An' the second thang?" she prompted.

"Th' second thang was *this*!" There was a big lumpy roll of canvas on his now-clean workbench, next to something bulky and covered with what looked like an old tablecloth, and he took the end and unrolled it with a flourish—and revealed that it wasn't a roll of canvas, it was a roll of *tools*, each in its own little pocket. Carving tools, exactly the sort of thing he had described himself as coveting, from tiny little things for carving pieces like knife-handles and cameos, to ones like those he'd already been using, plus a pair of mallets.

She stared at them in wonder—and concern. Because weren't these things supposed to be worth a fortune? She was about to ask where he'd gotten them, when he told her, and her blood froze.

"'Twas Miz Jolene!" he enthused. "Right arter Cooper an' McDaran rode off, she jest—turned up. Said she'd seed th' angel grave marker an' reckoned I deserved better tools than ole Cavenel was a-given me, an' jest handed these over! I arst her how I could repay her, an' she jest smiled."

She had offered to be my patron, as it is said she does for craftsmen, for she collects them. Those she favors the most, she takes with her into her kingdom under the mountain.

And as Josh gloated over his new tools, she was too paralyzed to think.

She managed, somehow, to feign happiness, because he was happy. But what had he done by accepting the "gift"? Had he actually bound himself to Jolene's service? Her gut clenched up, and she thought she might be sick.

"But wait!" he continued, still glowing with happiness despite his obvious weariness. "Lookit what else she give me!"

He whisked that old tablecloth off the lump, revealing—

Well, she wasn't sure *what* he had just revealed. It looked like a big piece of stone, but *what* a stone it was! Obviously cut from a much larger piece, the stone was a rough column as long as her forearm and as big around as a melon. And it was an eye-seducing, glorious swirl of vibrant blue-green and emerald green and pale green in layers and waves and chaotic swirls that had no regular pattern to them.

"What *is* thet?" she gasped, its *greenness* dominating the gray and brown and straw-colored workroom.

"It's malachite," Josh said, in a voice so full of the satisfaction of possession she almost didn't recognize it. "It's the biggest piece I iver did see, an' they ain't a flaw innit near's I c'n tell from lookin' at it. Jolene done give it to me, an' how a tiny liddle thang like her jest handled it like it weighed no more'n a egg, I niver will figger out. She said she give me th' tools, an' she give me th' material, an' now it was up ter me t' prove what I was made of."

Her dress, Anna suddenly realized. *That stone—it's like her dress*. Both the first, fantastical one she had seen Jolene wearing, and the second, more ordinary one, the one with the swirly pattern. The first dress had the colors and the silky sheen of this stuff; the second had the colors and the chaotic swirls.

"Where's it come from?" Her head was all a-maze, but her mouth kept asking sensible questions somehow.

"Same mines where y'all git copper," he said, hands gently touching the stone, eyes filled with the stone. "Reckon she must've got some deal a-goin' with the mine owners."

"Is it valuable?" she asked.

He shook his head, still gazing on the stone and not at her. "Not really. Not fer itself; it on'y gits valuable arter it's been carved an' polished. An' y'all gotter be careful; th' dust'll pisen y'all, so's y'all gotter sand an' polish it under water. Thet's what Jolene tol' me, anyways. She brung it, an' th' tools, jest afore y'all got here."

That, she was sure, was no accident.

"I cain't hardly wait t'set a chisel t' this," he continued, his voice still full of that acute satisfaction.

"What's stoppin' y'all?" She couldn't help it, she was afraid of the way he was gazing at that stone, she was heartsick thinking of how Jolene was getting her hooks into him, and the words came out harsh and sharp.

But he didn't seem to notice as he caressed the column of stone. "I gotter figger out what I'm a-gonna carve, thet's what. I ain't niver had a time when I was a-carvin' something jest I wanted to. The liddle thangs, they was allus what'd sell. The headstones, they was allus fer th' famblies. But this's fer me."

Instantly she felt ashamed of her tone. Just think of it, how it must have eaten at him, never having anything he had created just for himself. It would be something beautiful, because she already knew he that he loved and, more to the point, could make beautiful things. Just because he wanted to, and for no other reason than that.

She wondered what that would feel like, to set free that part inside of you that made beautiful things, and hopped off her stool to go stand at his side, one hand unobtrusively on his arm, staring at the stone. "I thank I'd be a-skeert t' cut inter thet stone, it's so purty," she said at last.

Now, once again, he finally looked at her. "Thet's part of it," he admitted. "I *cain't* go an' do somethin' thet'll mar it in any way. So I gotter thank this through. I gotter plan ev' liddle bit. It's all gotter be *right*."

"Let th' magic he'p," she suggested, surprising even herself. Where had those words come from? But she knew it was the right suggestion, even as he looked at her with pure astonishment.

"How?" he blurted, taking his hands off the stone.

"Le's jest give up on y'all larnin' t' scry," she replied, though it pained her greatly to say it. "At least fer now. Jest—put yore hands on thet stone. Let th' magic kinder sift inter it. Mebbe y'all cain't see ary flaws on th' outside, but let th' magic see if there's any hidden. Let th' magic tell y'all where th' stone's weak, an' where it's strong. Oncet y'all know thet, y'all will prolly hev some ideer of what kinda shape t'carve, an' the shape'll tell y'all *what* t'carve."

The look in his eyes gratified her so much she forgot her earlier hurt. And his next words made the sting of the fact that these things came from *Jolene* ease. "I swan, Anna May Jones, y'all's th' *smartest* gel I iver did see! How'd y'all thank of all thet? Not even Jolene tol' me the like!"

How had she thought of it? Maybe it was the things she'd learned this summer: how to use her magic with the earth and all the things that grew on it, instead of against the earth, forcing the earth to do things it didn't want to do. Maybe it had been learning to *do* instead of *be told what to do*. Maybe it had been learning to feel and think before she acted magically.

"It jest felt right," she replied. "Try it. Jest a liddle. See iffen thet works fer y'all."

He took a deep breath, placed his hands on either side of the stone again, and closed his eyes, the better to see the magic. For her part, she put one hand around his back and onto his right forearm and the other on his left forearm, pulled in magic from the stream of it running beneath the earth nearby, and let it slowly trickle into him to help his. And through him, she got a sense that this *was* working; he was seeing the piece of stone in a new way, right inside it, sensing everything she had promised he would.

But he was not used to working with magic for very long, and before too long it started to all slip away from him—not in a catastrophic sense, but as if his internal "eyes" blurred with fatigue, as if the tools were slipping from fingers too tired to hold them. She eased away from him and watched as his hands dropped from the stone, his shoulders slumping with exhaustion.

"Y'all need rest," she said firmly. "Rest inna bed."

"Oh," he replied, grinning wearily, "straw ain't so bad."

"Bed's better." She gave him a little shove toward the door into the barn. "Y'all go et somethin' an' git some sleep."

Hopefully McDaran's spell over his family had worn off, now that he was gone, so they'd *see* Josh was exhausted and fuss him into some good food and adequate rest. *An' I hope they's feelin' guilty too*, she thought. *They shouldn't oughta hev done thet to him, spell or no spell.*

But as she trudged up the lane to the cabin, her own steps were heavy, and her thoughts as gray as the clouds gathering overhead. Jolene had certainly taken notice of Josh ... which was the very last thing that Anna had wanted.

Now *she* knew what Jolene was—more or less—and this was not some simple town rivalry of two girls after the same boy. Now she knew why Aunt Jinny kept hammering on *Niver get atwixt Jolene and what she wants.*

And now Jolene knew everything Anna hadn't wanted her to find out. Now she knew what kind of a craftsman and artist Josh was. Now she knew he had magic! And Great-Granpappy had said in his book that Jolene had a habit of trying to claim artists and craftsmen for her own. Did that extend to artists and craftsmen who were magicians?

Likely. Prolly that makes her want 'em more.

Had she actually claimed him, with her gifts of tools and seductive stone?

No ... he'd'a tol' me if she'd got him ter make some sorta promise. She wanted to smack herself in the head now for not warning him before she had sent him off to bed—but there had been so much going on, and she *hadn't* yet told him what Jolene was, and would he even believe her if she did without some proof?

The proof's there in thet stone. Iffen thet there stone come outa the Burra Burra mine, I'll et it m'self.

She was so wrapped up in her own thoughts that it wasn't until she was over the stile and halfway to the porch that she looked up and saw Aunt Jinny waiting there for her, with a letter in her hand and a stricken look on her face.

She ran the rest of the way and seized Jinny's hands in her own. "*What happened?*" she all but shouted.

"Oh, honey-chile," Jinny blurted, her voice cracking. "Yore Pa's daid. An' yore Ma done kilt hersel' arter."

18

Aunt Jinny pulled her into the kitchen and pushed her down on a stool. Anna felt as if she must be in a nightmare. Any moment now, she'd wake up, and everything would be fine again. Jolene wouldn't be looming over Josh like a hawk mantling over prey. McDaran wouldn't be stalking her. Ma and Pa—

But she wasn't asleep. She sat there, feeling as if something had stolen all the breath from her lungs, her stomach a knot, and knowing there was no escape into waking from this.

The letter had consisted of two pieces of paper. The first was the official notice from some official in Soddy. It was a simple, harsh, two-line statement: Pa had died of Winter Fever—which was the official way of saying the mines had killed him with their smoke and dust—and Ma was dead as a suicide.

The other was from one of the neighbors, elaborating a little more. Pa stopped being able to work, then to get out of bed, and then just didn't wake up, all in the course of two weeks. The neighbors to whom Ma regularly sold potions knew nothing about his death until they noticed Ma hadn't come out of the house all day, went to see if she needed help, and found him stone cold in his bed and her dead next to him, hanging from the rafters. They went to get the authorities, who had been mighty displeased. A death in one of the Company houses was expected, but how *dare* Ma taint the place with her suicide!

But there was more. As if that was not enough.

Yur sis left owin a powerful lot to the Company, the letter went on. *They sold everthin in the house an it weren't nuff to cover hardly anythin. They's likely gonna try an find Anna May an git it from her one way or tother.*

Everything—everything gone. Ma, Pa, what little they had—all gone, as if it had all been swept away in the Great Flood. She didn't even have something to remember them by. She'd had no chance to say goodbye. If she'd been there, could she have saved Pa? Could she at least have saved Ma? And they were buried by now, in an unmarked pauper's grave, probably without even so much as a ten-minute graveside prayer. She felt as if she *ought* to be weeping, but all she could feel was emptiness.

Maybe that was because Ma and Pa hadn't ever really been to her what Josh's Ma and Pa were so clearly to him. Because Ma had been so wrapped up in Pa that she had nothing to spare for Anna—and Pa had been so wrapped up in himself he had nothing to spare for anyone. Maybe that was why she couldn't weep. Because the emptiness had been there all along, but it had been hidden by their physical presence, by the fact that she could *say* "My Ma is Maybelle Jones an' my Pa is Lew Jones."

And now she couldn't say that, the illusion of a family was gone, and the emptiness was just there, no longer hidden.

All that she *could* feel was a kind of flat, gray despair, that everything, *everything*, was so horribly falling apart. Ma and Pa, dead. Billie McDaran bound and determined to *get* her for some reason of his own. Jolene—with her sights set on Josh.

As she sat on a stool in the kitchen, feeling too numb and too overwhelmed to move, she finally picked one tiny incomprehensible bit out of both of those letters and looked up at her aunt, who was hovering over her anxiously, as if she expected Anna to swoon or have hysterics. "What'd thet letter mean, thet the Company was a-gonna try an' find me?"

Jinny straightened up, her mouth a hard, thin line. "Yer Ma an' Pa left a debt, an' their near kin—thet's y'all—is responsible fer thet debt."

"But—*how?*" she gasped. "I didn' go git thangs from th' Company store!"

"No, but y'all lived in th' Company house an' et what yore Ma got from th' Company store," Jinny pointed out, scowling at the injustice of it. "Thet's what they'll tell a judge. By *their* reckonin', y'all inherit debt jest like y'all inherit anythin' else. Iffen y'all cain't pay it, they c'n make y'all work it off, or go to jail."

She blinked, shocked. "Go to—but—thet cain't be legal, c'n it? There ain't no indenture no more, is there?"

Jinny shrugged helplessly, as Anna's stomach turned into icy knots, and her knees went weak. "Oh, they ain't a-gonna send y'all t'jail, not when they c'n sell yore debt t' some'un else. Folks'll do thet, buy a debt, t'git a free sarvant outen it. An' thet's what they'll do."

Anna whimpered a little in the back of her throat. "They'll—take me? Away?" Hauled away—where? Away from Aunt Jinny, away from Josh, to be someone's unpaid slavey—

"An' whoever gits yore debt'll jest keep a-pilin' more y'all owes fer yore room an' board," Jinny continued. "Lincoln was s'pposed t' hev got rid'a thet, but—" She shrugged. "It's th' Companies. They own th' judge, an' th' judge'll say y'all owe th' debt, work it off or go t'jail. They say it ain't 'indentured servitude' on account'a there ain't no contract, so it's all legal." She shook her head. "But thet ain't the wust thang I c'n think of. Iffen Billie McDaran finds out 'bout this, he'll go buy your debt, sure as sure, an' come a-lookin' fer y'all with sheriffs an' bailiffs. He'll take y'all, legal, an' with the sheriff t' he'p him."

By this point she was in so much of a panic that she could not move. She could only sit there, frozen, looking up at her aunt with horror.

Jinny stood beside Anna, looking into nothing for a long time. Finally, she seemed to make up her mind. "I'm a-gonna talk to Old Raven. I'll git him t'pass y'all along t' Oklahoma. He c'n do it 'long the secret ways he got, where no sheriff's gonna git wind of y'all. From there, y'all c'n git inter Kansas without no one knowin' there's collectors huntin' y'all. I got a brother in Kansas; y'all c'n stay with him till all this blows over."

Now the tears began, pouring down her face silently, as she gasped out sobs. "But *Josh*—" she wept.

Jinny took her shoulders in each hand and shook her, hard. "We got time. Time 'nuff fer y'all t'run down thar fust thang in th' mornin' an' 'splain ev'thang y'all need to t' Josh *an'* Matt an'

Maddie. We got mebbe three days at best, an' surely one at wust, afore th' Company gets a bailiff here arter y'all."

"But—" She stuttered through what Jolene had given to Josh, and what she had said to him. Aunt Jinny's mouth compressed, but her voice stayed steady.

"Now y'all lissen t'me, girl, an' lissen good. Y'all remember what Granpappy wrote 'bout him an' Granny? How set they was on each other?"

She nodded, vision blurring from the tears of despair.

"Wall, either Josh feels thet way 'bout y'all, an' it won't matter what Jolene tries oncet he knows what she is an' what she's gonna arst him, or he *don't*, Jolene'll take 'im, an' y'all are well shuck of him!"

Horror joined with panic and grief. "But I cain't niver—"

Aunt Jinny shook her shoulders again. "What'd I say? *Iffen it happens, y'all are well shuck of him!* Y'all wanter be treated like yore Pa treated yer Ma an' end up like her? Better git yore heart broke *now*, when it c'n mend. An' mebbe y'all ain't gonna *be in love* agin, but thet ain't th' end of the world. There's plenty more t'life than bein' in love."

Jinny's face had a peculiar look to it that Anna couldn't understand.

Jinny went and got one of the rags that served them as handkerchiefs, giving it to Anna. "Cry yoreself out, blow yore nose, an' lemme go talk to Elder Raven. We gotter git our plan an' git it a-goin' afore the bailiffs or sheriffs or, God forbid, McDaran shows up."

She gave herself up to tears, sobbing her heart out. In days at best, hours at worst, everything in her life would be gone. She'd be trekking into the west with nothing but what she could carry, heading for the dubious shelter of a total stranger, each step taking her further and further away from everything and everyone she loved. The bottom had dropped out of her universe, and there was nothing left for her.

She didn't sleep a wink, and in the morning she paced back and forth in front of the door until Aunt Jinny finally decreed it was probably late enough that the Holcrofts were also awake and about, and she could run down the lane to talk to them, and Josh.

"Josh'll prolly still be eatin' breakfus'," Jinny said, holding her by the elbow so she couldn't run off until Jinny had said her piece. "So mind y'all don't say nothin' bout magic nor Jolene 'round 'em. Jes' tell 'em 'bout yer Ma an' Pa, an' th' Company debt, an' how y'all's a-gonna go stay with—somebody—till th' Company gives it up. Thet'll be 'bout a year, I reckon. Mind, y'all ain't niver gonna be able t'set foot in Soddy agin, but I don' thank thet's gonna make y'all lose any sleep."

Numbly, Anna nodded.

"Don't tell 'em it's m'brother," she continued. "What they don' know, they cain't tell McDaran iffen he comes 'round usin' his Glory on 'em. Don't tell thet t'Josh, neither."

"But—"

"What he don't know, he cain't tell Jolene, an' cain't tell McDaran," she said sternly. "Would not surprise me a-tall iffen it was Jolene thet tol' McDaran 'bout y'all in th' fust place, oncet she found out y'all an' Josh was courtin'."

Anna felt as if yet another plank in an increasingly shaky support had been knocked out from under her. "But—*why?*" she wailed.

"T'git y'all outen th' way, a'course," Jinny said, as if she was an idiot. "*She ain't human.* Y'all might thank she was *yore* friend, but thet don't make y'all *her* friend. McDaran uses Earth Glory, same as she does, an' accordin' to Granpappy, she's got as much innerest in miners as she does crafters. Which means she don' give two hoots an' a holler 'bout what them mines does t' the land around 'em, I reckon. I figure she's as innerested in helpin' him as in helpin' y'all. An' she purely does not thank like a human woman. An' I warned y'all." Jinny sniffed. "Tarnation, by her lights, she might figger she's a-doin' y'all a favor, by puttin' y'all with someone with more magic power an' more money than Josh. Y'all cain't hold her t'what humans thank is good an' proper. *She ain't human.*"

"I'll 'member," Anna promised, her stomach turning and churning and tears rising up in her throat until they practically choked her. "Please, Aunt Jinny, lemme go!"

Jinny released her elbow. "Go," she said. "An' git right back here. They's a limit t'what I c'n do t' pertect y'all."

She flew out into the deep gray morning, in too much of a state to care about the chill ground on her bare feet. She cursed herself now for not having thought of using the scrying mirror to keep watch on Josh, so she could have had those last few hours to cherish when they were torn apart. There was scarcely any light under the trees in the lane, and she stumbled and nearly fell too many times to count, only momentum and the need to see Josh keeping her on her feet.

But when she emerged from the trees, she stopped dead for a moment.

She knew immediately that something was wrong, because the farmhouse had lights in every window, and Holcrofts running in and out of every door.

As she sped toward the house, Maddie somehow caught sight of her in the dim light, and waved frantically at her, face full of relief. "Anna!" she called, as soon as Anna was within hailing distance. "Y'all got Josh with y'all, right?" Her voice turned from relieved to a combination of relief and scolding. "What was y'all thankin' of, gallivantin' aroun' in the woods this time of—"

But her words brought Anna to a paralyzed halt, and Anna was close enough for Maddie to see what must have been her expression of horror. "N-n-n-no!" Anna stammered. "I ain't seed him since yesterday! I jest come a-runnin' down here t—*where's Josh?*"

Without waiting for an answer, she whirled and ran for the barn and the workshop. There was very little light, but what there was, was enough to tell her that her worst fears had been realized. The roll of tools and the block of malachite were gone.

There could be only one explanation.

Jolene had taken Josh.

The Holcrofts surrounded her, and babbled, but she was too sunk in shock and black despair to answer in more than monosyllables. No, Josh had not come up to the cabin last evening. Yes, the last time she saw him, it had been in his workshop, and she had sent him to the house to eat and rest. No, he hadn't said anything except a promise he would get some sleep. No, she didn't know where he was.

The last was a lie, of course. But what could she possibly say? *Yore son's been rieved away by a thang what calls herself The*

*Queen of Copper Mountain, he's been a-took Blessed Jesus on'y
knows where, an' we ain't niver gonna see him agin.* They'd think
she'd lost her senses. All she could do was stand there helplessly
while they gabbled at her; what she wanted to do was hold her
hands over her ears and think, or cry, or both—but instead, she
hugged herself tightly and listened to them, hoping against hope
that they'd say something that would give her an idea of what to do.

From the babbling she gleaned that Josh *had* gone in for dinner,
but that he'd eaten and then gone back to his workshop, saying
he'd had an idea for something. That wasn't unheard of; once he
got the shape of something in his head, he often wanted to get
the rough idea for it (sometimes literally) hammered out or he
wouldn't be able to sleep.

But in the morning he hadn't come down to breakfast, which
was unheard of, and when Susie went up to his room, his bed
was still made and had not been slept in since it had been used
by McDaran—Cooper having been bedded down on the floor
with blankets.

Eventually the Holcrofts stopped babbling at her and swirled
off again in their several directions, each one having an idea as to
where Josh might have gone—regardless of whether or not there
was any sense to their notions—leaving Anna standing alone in
the yard between the house and barn.

Her mind seemed filled with ice and blackness; her heart felt as
if it was being squeezed out of her body, and she could scarcely
breathe.

Jolene took Josh.

No use in going to Aunt Jinny—Jinny had made her feelings
clear. *Don't get atwixt Jolene an' what she wants and Iffen he goes
with her, y'all's well shuck of him.*

But she couldn't believe that of Josh. She *wouldn't* believe that.
Not until and unless she heard it from his own lips, something like
I pick Jolene an' what she c'n give me over you.

That was what it would take to make her believe.

And for that ... she'd have to go where he was.

With a Herculean effort she forced herself to go back up the
lane. Her feet were so cold they ached, but she forced them to
carry her through the frosty grass. Not to the cabin, but to the

spot about halfway to the cabin where she would find Jolene—
or Jolene would find her—the most often. She wasn't quite sure
what she was going to do when she got there, but—Jolene was a
creature of Earth, and the other Earth creatures recognized her.

I thank I know ... She could summon the little creatures of
Earth, as many as she could, and beg them to bring Jolene to her,
or lead her to Jolene.

Right now that was all she had.

Still walking, she pulled Earth power into herself, and prepared
to call for the piskies first, since those were the ones she knew best.
And it wasn't until the moment she sent out the first summons
that she realized the lane was blocked.

Someone, someone tall and broad, stood in the middle of the
lane, blocking her passage.

"Heh," said Bille McDaran. "Somehow I knowed y'all was still
here, Miz Anna May Jones, no matter what yore aunt said."

She froze in place, the magic to summon piskies still tingling at
the ends of her fingers.

"Oh, but y'all don't know me." He puffed out his chest. "I'm
Billie McDaran. I'm th' foreman of th' Burra Burra mine. I'm the
bestest, meanest magician betwixt Charlotte an' Memphis, I'm th'
best lookin' man in Ducktown, I'm wuth twenny puny pissants
like Josh Holcroft, an' ev'body'll tell y'all so."

"What d'y'all want with me?" she demanded. "I ain't no
concern o' yourn. We ain't livin' on Company land, we ain't got
no Company house, an' we got no debt at th' Company store."

He snickered. "Y'all's my concern iffen I makes y'all my
concern. Seems y'all's a witch, like yore aunt. An' thet makes y'all
my bizness. Ary a one in th' Ducktown Basin what makes magic
answers t'me."

"We ain't *in* th' Basin," she pointed out.

"Don't care." He cracked his knuckles. "Don't care nohow. I
makes m'own rules. I got a hankerin' t' hev a look at y'all arter
Jolene tol' me all 'bout y'all. Don't mind what I sees. Y'all ain't
bad lookin', an' y'all got power, an' thet's jest fine. I takes what I
wants, an' I reckon y'all are a-gonna be mine."

His words shocked her out of her despair—and into anger.
"*You!*" she spat. "*Y'all's* th' one what set Jolene fer Josh Holcroft!"

He laughed, still scarcely more than a dark gray shape with eyes gleaming in the thin gray light under the trees, and somehow all the more menacing for that. It was an ugly laugh. "Y'all's smarter than yore kin," he said. "'Course I did. I knowed Jolene since I come t'Ducktown, an' she knows me. We got a sorta arrangement, th' two of us. She lets me know 'bout thangs. Jolene tol' me 'bout y'all when I reckoned that ole cat Jinny was gettin' more powerful than she had any right t'be. An' she tol' me y'all was sweet on thet boy. So I done her a favor right back, an' tol' her thet Holcroft boy was jest the sorta tasty bite she likes best. Arter thet?" He shrugged shoulders. "Ain't no man nor woman c'n stop Jolene when she hankers fer somethin'." His eyes narrowed dangerously in the gray morning light. "Now, le's jest make this easy. Y'all come with me, now. I c'n make y'all fergit thet boy in no time a-tall, an' y'all is gonna thank me fer it. Play yore cards right, an' I'll even marry y'all."

"Y'all c'n go to *Hell*!" she spat, energized and surprising even herself.

"I prolly will, 'ventually," he agreed with a snicker. "But till then, I aims t' hev me some fun. Don' try an' fight me, girl. Y'all cain't win."

The power tingled in her fingertips, and all her senses, including the magic ones, were suddenly filled with an acute awareness of the forest around her. She gathered in even more power, cast a shield over herself, and before he could react to that, gathered even more, and summoned—

Not the useless piskies, but the herd of wild hogs she sensed rooting in the leaf-mold, eating acorns less than a hundred yards away.

He got little more than a moment's warning, as they turned as one, answering her call, and charged blindly through the underbrush straight for him.

What she *sensed* was the pigs' sudden rage, as they reacted to her call and identified McDaran as an enemy. What she heard was the same thing he heard: underbrush crackling and snapping, and squeals of anger.

He wasn't as stupid as she had thought he was; instead of standing there, puzzled, he reacted immediately. She sensed a darker version of the Glory surging from him, a power that actually nauseated her, as he held out his hands, turned them palm-up, and raised them.

And two monstrous critters rose out of the turf of the lane, one on either side of him.

Larger than McDaran, they looked like nothing so much as rough caricatures of humans made out of boulders. They weren't as tall as the thing that Jolene had summoned, but they were at least twice his height.

And they moved a lot more quickly than she would have thought, getting themselves between McDaran and the squealing herd of angry swine, swinging at the pigs with club-like arms.

She backed up involuntarily as the things reduced the herd of pigs to a pile of shattered carcasses in a matter of minutes. The few survivors fled into the underbrush, leaving her facing McDaran and his critters over the pile of battered bodies, with the rank smell of blood and entrails heavy in the air. She summoned more power from the line beneath her, filling herself with it until she was afraid she might start glowing.

McDaran just smirked.

"Tol' y'all. Yore no match fer me, girl. Y'all c'n pull whatever liddle tricks yore aunt taught y'all, an' I ain't even gonna break a sweat." He tucked his thumbs into his suspenders and chuckled. "Jolene didn' even teach y'all nothin' wuth havin', now, did she?"

"Why don' y'all arsk her yoreself?" she shot back.

He whirled as he sensed power and movement behind him—and there, floating in midair, was Jolene. Not the Jolene of Ducktown, nor the Jolene in her swirly dress, who was Anna's teacher—but the Jolene Anna had *first* seen, the one in the strange dress and apron of exotic materials, with trim of gold, and a halo-like headpiece of the same material. Her true form, Anna knew now. The Queen of Copper Mountain. Her eyes flashed with fury, and her beautiful lips were twisted into a frown of rage.

"*Illusions take less power to make and hold... What matters is not if it is real, but if you persuade someone or something else that it is real.*"

"McDaran!" the apparition shrieked. "How dare you try to steal my student from me?"

McDaran froze where he stood. But Anna was not going to wait around to see how long her illusion held him. Once the spell for the illusion had been set free, she ran.

She knew the game trails around here; he didn't. She grabbed up her skirts in both hands, freeing her bare legs, and ran, not for the cabin, because that was where he would expect her to go, but deeper into the wilderness. And while she ran, she sang.

He+! Hayuya'haniwa', hayuya'haniwa', hayuya'haniwa', hayuya'haniwa'.

Tsistuyi' nehandu'yanû, Tsistuyi' nehandu'yanû-Yoho'+!

He+! Hayuya'haniwa', hayuya'haniwa', hayuya'haniwa', hayuya'haniwa'.

Kuwâhi' nehandu'yanû, Kuwâhi' nehandu'yanû-Yoho'+!

He+! Hayuya'haniwa', hayuya'haniwa', hayuya'haniwa', hayuya'haniwa'.

Uyâ'ye' nehandu'yanû', Uya'ye' nehahdu'yanû'-Yoho'+!

He+! Hayuya'haniwa', hayuya'haniwa', hayuya'haniwa', hayuya'haniwa'.

Gâtekwâ' (hi) nehandu'yanû', Gâtekwâ'(hi) nehandu'yanû'-Yoho'+!

Ûle-'nû ' asehi' tadeya'statakûhi' gû'nnage astû'tsiki'.

It was the song to call bears, as Grandmother Spider had taught her, and into it she poured all the power that she could summon, spilling it into the magic and the song as quickly as she could gather it up.

She did not try to fight back her tears as she sang and ran, nor her terror. But she *did* fight back her despair. She refused to give up. Not yet. Not until there was nothing more to try, nothing more to be done.

"Bear is the spirit that you are most likely to need if you are in danger. Bear can run, and swim, and climb, and fight; Bear is fearless when that is called for, but does not lose himself in rage and will run when that is needed. And Bear is near to the Cherokee peoples."

The melody was simple and sad; she panted as she sang, tears trickling down her cheeks, and hardly able to get her breath between words, she ran so fast. But fear put strength in her legs, and anger in her lungs, and though she was lashed by branches and her hair came down and tumbled around her, still, she ran.

"He+! Little Sister!" she heard behind her as she crashed into a meadow and stumbled over a root. It was a rumbling growl

like thunder that carried words, Cherokee words she understood clearly. "*Stop running a moment!*"

She stopped and turned, almost falling, and gasped as a white bear as big as a horse lumbered to a halt before her. Thanks to Elder Raven and Grandmother Spider, she knew who this was! This wasn't just any bear. This was Medicine Bear, the Chief of all Bears, the Great Bear himself, the kin to Grandmother Spider!

"*Quickly!*" the Bear told her, before she could say anything. "*Climb on my back and grab hold of the folds of skin over my shoulders! We must run!*"

She scrambled onto his back, although she had never ridden another creature in her life, and did as she was told, splaying herself out face-down over his massive back, digging her frozen toes into the fur of his sides, and burying her hands in the folds of his skin just where the neck met the enormous shoulders. And as soon as she was secure, the Bear lurched forward and galloped off into the forest.

She would never have believed that something that looked as slow and clumsy as the Bear could run the way it did. But this was faster than she had ever traveled in her life, much, much faster than riding in a wagon, faster than traveling on a boat, fast enough to take her breath away. The great body heaved and surged under her, muscles rippling as he drove himself forward, tree branches lashing at her.

She hid her face in his fur to save herself from the branches, taking long, deep, slow breaths to try to get her own wind back. He smelled like dried grass or clover, sweet and fresh.

Somehow, he picked a path where branches weren't constantly whipping at her, and as the wind of their passing rushed over her, the warmth of his back and fur made her realize how cold she had been. Her feet, which had been like two blocks of ice, regained feeling.

Where were they going?

Don't care. Jest as long as it's away from McDaran.

What would she do when the Bear decided to stop running?

She didn't know that, either. She only knew one thing. For the time being, she had escaped McDaran, and now she *had* to find Josh, and find out, face to face, if he really had abandoned her for Jolene. After she knew that … she might be able to figure out what to do next.

Even if she did it with her heart shattered in a million pieces.

Suddenly, the Bear slowed for a few paces, and stopped.

"This is as far as I can take you, Little Sister," the voice rumbled, vibrating in her body. She raised her head and looked around.

There was nothing in this part of the forest to tell her where she was—except that it was not unlike the part of the Holler where Elder Raven's band lived. Huge, old trees, with moss-covered trunks; ferns as tall as her shoulders. They were not far from a steep mountain slope, rising up to the right, where trees somehow grew out of ground that was nearly vertical, and moss-covered rocks humped up between them. She pried her hands open and slid down Bear's back.

"This isn't where Elder Raven lives, is it?" she asked Bear. "I don't want McDaran following us and finding the band!"

"It is not. I would not do that," Bear reassured her. *"This is as far as I can take you to where you need to go. Over yonder is your guide."*

She peered toward where Bear was pointing to the right with his nose, and then, when it moved, she saw it. Green as the moss, but with a metallic sheen, it was one of Jolene's little lizards.

She moved toward the lizard, slowly, so as not to frighten it. But it didn't seem frightened. It raised its head, then bobbed the front half of its body at her, as if in greeting, and flicked its tongue at her. It wasn't a thin, forked tongue like a snake's; it was a glistening, fleshy tongue like a human's.

"C'n y'all take me to Jolene?" she asked.

It stared at her.

"C'n y'all take me to th' Queen of Copper Mountain?" she amended.

It bobbed its head once, whisked around in an instant, and faced the moss-covered rock wall.

She looked back over her shoulder to say "goodbye and thanks" to Bear—but Bear was already gone.

"Thank you, Elder Brother," she said aloud anyway, in Cherokee. "Thank you for saving me from McDaran. Thank you for bringing me here. Thank you for answering my song."

There was no direct answer, but a wind swept through the ferns, smelling of dried grass and clover.

"Where y'all takin' me?" she asked the lizard.

It bobbed at the wall, scuttled up to it—and vanished.

For a moment she thought it had abandoned her, but then she saw a space between the boulders that was just barely wide enough to squeeze through. If she'd been any larger, or her skirts bulkier, or, indeed, if she'd had one more petticoat on, she would never have fit.

She'd expected some sort of—building, perhaps. Queens lived in palaces, didn't they? Or at least some spectacular bit of scenery. But … this was a cave.

She shuddered. She didn't like underground places. Going underground meant danger, rockfalls, cave-ins, all the stories of terrible things that had come out of the mines and got spoken of in hushed whispers when men had drunk enough, or when women recounted the stories of those they had lost. And it would be dark in there, and not just like "night-dark," but a horrible empty dark that was so lightless it made your eyes ache.

But there was no help for it. According to Great-Granpappy, the Queen of Copper Mountain lived *inside* the mountain, so that was where Jolene would be. And so would Josh.

She took a deep breath and one last look around, and squeezed in through the crack.

19

She was afraid to move.

Behind her was the crack, spilling light—so very little light!— over the rocks in front of her. She stood with her hands against the rock wall behind her, and the little lizard posed in the spill of light before her, tail flicking impatiently.

Light's what I need. But for light, she would need power. Was there power around here that she could actually *use*? This was Jolene's territory; how would Jolene take to someone helping herself to whatever source of power there was?

But I cain't go futher without light. I gotter see where I'm a-goin'.

She'd have to chance it.

She stole a little—oh, so very little—power from the nearest source, which astounded her with its depth and breadth. This was not like one of the rivers of power she had encountered so far in her education. This was like—like a huge lake, an ocean, even, but one that was so still and calm and peaceful that it caught at her heart, and so deep she could not sense a bottom to it.

Taking power from this pool disturbed it a little, leaving ripples as she touched it, and she waited, heart in her throat, for retribution, or at least alarm. But nothing came. So, while the little lizard waited (patiently? Impatiently? She couldn't tell), she followed Aunt Jinny's instructions for molding the power into a ball between her hands, then sketched the glyph for "light" over it.

It didn't blaze up—she'd taken care not to have it do that,

because the last thing she wanted to do was to blind herself in here. Instead it increased in brightness slowly, hovering in the air just above the lizard, until she could see the area around the critter clearly. Clearly enough not to fall in a hole, or trip over something, anyway.

She waited again, but there was still no sign that anything or anyone cared that she had helped herself to power. With a sigh, she addressed the lizard.

"Can y'all take me t' the Queen? Or if she ain't here, t' Josh? But y'all gotter go slow. I ain't so spry in th' dark as y'all are."

The lizard skittered off, ball of light following along above its head.

She followed, picking her way carefully. It was warmer in here than it was outside, except for the cave floor. In no time at all, her feet, which had warmed up enough buried in Bear's fur to be comfortable, were aching with cold again.

The walls of this cave were close enough to touch, so she did, steadying herself as she picked her way carefully along the rocky floor. At first, it had been dirt, littered with small rocks, but the deeper they went, the more the floor changed. First came the dirt and rocks, then mud and rocks, then mud, and now she walked on smooth rock, as if it had been polished by water. And then there were little puddles. Everywhere, she heard the sound of dripping water.

Then the walls pulled away from each other. She kept her hand on the left one as long as she could, but the lizard wasn't obliging her; it kept taking a path that led away from the walls. And far too soon for her liking, she couldn't even see the walls, nor the ceiling. Not without increasing the brightness of her guide.

"Wait a minnut, please," she told the lizard, which obligingly paused. She raised the ball of light up above her head and increased the brightness. And gasped.

She found herself somewhere in a vast cavern, with a ceiling and walls and floor that looked as if the stone had liquefied and then become solid again, but not before it had formed pillars and gigantic wax-like drips. Or perhaps the structures were more like stone icicles. She couldn't make up her mind, and the sight momentarily drove all of her fear and sadness from her. Pa surely had never described anything like this. Perhaps neither he nor the other miners at the Soddy mine had ever seen anything like this.

There weren't just pillars and icicles either; here, the stone had formed into a kind of wavy, draped curtain. There it had been formed into a sort of gigantic mushroom. And *there*, icicle and pillar had fused into a ribbed column.

In the center was a lake, and they appeared to be walking along the "shore."

The color of all this stone was a sort of soft cream, with a hint of translucence. It almost seemed to be alive.

"All right, le's mosey," she said to the lizard, which was the only touch of color here.

She kept her light at its brightest as they traversed the length of this cave, heading for a narrow passage ahead. It was with some regret and a lot of trepidation that she dimmed her guide and brought it down to about waist-height again as they entered another narrow tunnel.

Anna had lost track of time, and the big caverns with their stone formations had ceased to amaze. Fear drained away, grief dulled, and all she was really aware of was the untiring little green lizard scuttling in front of her and her utter weariness. She hadn't slept at all last night, and hadn't eaten since—was it dinner, yesterday? She just put one foot in front of the other in a mental fog, until she nearly stepped on the lizard and it chirped angrily at her.

She jumped back and went to one knee. "I'm sorry, liddle feller! I didn' mean it!" she said pleadingly. "I were jest so a-weary—"

She held out her hand. The lizard regarded it suspiciously for a moment, then stuck out its tongue, licked its eyeball thoughtfully, and scuttled up onto her open palm. It raised itself up on its forelegs and jerked its head sideways. When she didn't react to that, it did so again, punctuating the movement with a chirp.

She looked. And realized that, for the first time, there was light in here that wasn't from her little floating ball.

She put her hand down and the lizard scuttled toward the light, taking her source with it. She followed.

She hadn't had time to raise the light and strengthen it before the lizard slithered off, so she had to pick her way carefully across flows of stone so cold and polished they felt slick.

The light source ahead was behind one of those stone curtains. Whatever the source was, it was bright enough to light up the entire curtain from the other side; other than that, there wasn't anything distinguishable. At another time she'd have stopped to admire the ripples, waves, and layers of subtly different colors—now she just wanted to get to whatever was behind that stone. Was it Jolene, at last? While majestic in its own way—this didn't seem grand enough to be the setting for a queen.

She edged around the sheet of stone, led by the lizard.

There was a formation of four of those stone icicles, close together. Tucked up among them was a light that she instinctively recognized as just like her own, only the size of her head, and too bright to look at directly.

Under that formation was a beautifully crafted workbench, at least ten feet long and three wide; part wood, part stone, and part metal. It was so beautifully constructed that her jaw just dropped when she saw it. Cream stone, pale wood, gray metal.

Sitting on the workbench was the only spot of color in the room—a huge chunk of malachite.

It looked familiar.

So did the canvas roll on the workbench beside it.

Something moved slightly at the back of the room, in the shadows. She ventured past the workbench on tiptoes. There was a platform back there ... a platform covered with what looked like a tumble of soft blankets and pillows in various creams and pale browns. And there was something—no, someone under those blankets.

"Josh!" She wasn't aware she had spoken until the sound echoed in the room. She wasn't aware she had run to him until she was sitting on the platform at his side.

He lay on his back, one arm thrown over his head. He still looked utterly exhausted, thin and drawn, and her breath caught as her heart ached. "Josh?" she repeated, leaning over him.

"Jolene ..." he murmured. And her heart went from aching to breaking.

With tears streaming down her face, she got up, backed away, then turned and ran. Somehow, the little lizard with her light had gotten in front of her again, and she followed it, half-blinded by the tears that scorched her cheeks, too wracked with heartbreak to think of anything else to do.

How long she wandered, she couldn't have said. She just followed the lizard, sobbing silently, eyes and heart burning together, throat closed, chest tight with grief. And when the lizard stopped, so did she, insensible to what was around her, until a polite cough made her raise her eyes. And her breath caught in her throat, despite her despair, because what lay before her was the most beautiful place she had ever seen in her life. Nothing even in her imagination came close to matching this.

Now she was in a "room" fit for a queen.

A sheet of that waterfall-like stone, three stories high and lit from behind, formed the backdrop for a platform of stone that had clearly been carved out of the native stone that had been there before. So had the throne that stood on it—or was the throne a part of it? In any event, the throne was marvelously carved, covered with sinuous, entwining representations of lizards, of the same sort that had brought her here. More of the lizards—live ones, this time—twined their metallic green bodies among the creamy stone of the carved ones. They were joined by a new set of lizards—and these were copper-colored. *Green fer th' malachite, red fer th' copper hereabouts?*

The throne was also illuminated, not from above, but from below and within. And sitting on that throne, glowing golden with her own power, was Jolene.

But this was not any of the three versions of Jolene that Anna had seen before.

Her hair looked like red, spun copper, and in it she wore another of those odd, half-moon-shaped crowns, but this one was in the form of a snake that twisted around and back and through its own coils, and it could only be what the old songs called "pure red-gold." The copper-colored lizards had entwined themselves in her hair, their shining hides hard to distinguish from her shining hair. Her green eyes glowed—actually glowed, in what Anna guessed was yet another manifestation of how powerful she was. But what she wore was more astonishing, in its way, than anything else about her! There could be no dress like this anywhere on the face of the earth.

In style, this gown was not unlike the first one that Anna had seen her wearing: a kind of whole-body apron with wide shoulder straps, over a chemise. But the chemise was of the thinnest, whitest, softest material that Anna had ever seen; the incredible gown was like no fabric she had ever laid eyes on. It looked like hammered copper, but it moved like silk. And the wide trim that formed the straps and the neckline and ran around the bottom hem of the gown was four inches wide, and sewn so thickly with genuine gems that nothing of the fabric beneath was visible. The gems winked and gleamed softly in the indirect light, sending off rainbows of color, daring her to disbelieve that they were genuine. So many gems, so many colors, and she couldn't have put a name to more than a handful of them. From reading her Bible, she knew rubies, emeralds, diamonds, and sapphires, but what were the tawny yellow ones? And the pink and pale blue? What were the purple and the ones that were half pale purple and half light green?

She found herself speechless in the face of this display of wealth and magical power. And yet all of it paled beside Jolene's beauty. All Anna could do was stare, rooted in place. And she might have stood there for an entire day, unable to make a start at addressing Jolene, except for the noise that interrupted them, the sound of a human voice, a man's voice, that came faintly from somewhere above and echoed down through the mountain.

"*Jolene*!" bellowed the distant voice. "*Jolene, Jolene, Jolene …*" cried the echoes.

"Tha's Billie McDaran!" Anna gasped, both hands spasming into fists, as fear gripped her once again.

"So it is," Jolene said casually, leaning on one arm of the throne and raising her hand to stroke a lizard on her shoulder. "I doubt that he has the wit to follow you—I doubt he has the wit to think you would come here. So he must be looking for my help in finding you." She raised an elegant eyebrow. "Why *are* you here? Shouldn't you be with McDaran? Really, Anna, I am greatly disappointed. I went to very great pains to arrange that the two of you should make a pair of it."

"*What*?" Anna gasped again. "No! Thet col'-hearted snake? I wouldn' go with him if he was th' last man on earth!"

The hand petting the lizard paused. For a moment, Anna was afraid she had made Jolene angry, but the green eyes did not flash, and the perfect lips only frowned a very little. "Really?" Jolene asked. "Whyever not?"

"'Cause I'm in love with Josh!" she responded with spirit. "An' he's in love with me!"

Jolene waved that off with one hand, as if it mattered nothing. "Mortals say that all the time, and it's seldom true. Think of all the advantages you'll have with McDaran! McDaran is *much* richer than Josh. He's quite handsome. He's in a position to make you queen of the Ducktown Basin, and if that isn't enough, between the two of you, you have the power, if you choose to exert it, to undo all the damage that the mine has done to the valley." She held out a hand and examined a ring on it critically. "I should think that last, at least, would interest you a great deal, since you seem to share your aunt's propensity to want to heal everything that is in need around you."

Anna paused at that last, thinking of all the good she could do, if that were true. No more choking air. No more dead babies. Green things would grow again and the rain would soak into the grateful, grassy earth instead of running off in poisoned rivulets ...

And then she shook her head violently. There was not a chance in hell any of that would come to pass. Billie McDaran never thought about anything but himself, would never move an inch to help anyone but himself, and would never, ever share his power with her. He was far more likely—if that was possible, as Aunt Jinny seemed to think—to steal *her* power to make himself stronger. "McDaran's *pizen*, Jolene! He's as pizened as th' Basin. He don't he'p people, ever. Not with his money, not with his power, not with nothin'. He thanks all them dead babies in Ducktown is funny. He *beats* th' men when they ain't workin' hard 'nuff for him! He laid one man out fer a week!"

Now she had Jolene's interest. "What?" she asked sharply. "Why do I not know of this?"

"On account'a he does it 'bove ground," Anna replied—guessing, but pretty sure the guess was correct. "Reckon at some time y'all must've tol' him what Great-Granpappy knowed, thet y'all pertect miners. So he niver does thangs where yore critters'll git wind of 'em."

Now the eyes flashed, and the mouth turned down into a decided frown. *Looks like I done got all her attention now.*

"Thet ain't all," she continued. "He's got two wimmin already, closed up in thet house'a his with him. He *says* they's is sarvants, but Josh's Pa reckons he's—" she blushed at her own indecency, but it had to be said, "—reckons he's a-lyin' with 'em both. An' folks in Ducktown reckon thet, an' thet he's a-beatin' them too."

"*What?*" demanded Jolene, half rising from her throne. "Why does—"

Then she settled back down, the frown turning into a snarl. "You need not answer that. Even in my land, women are of no account, and men may beat them if they will."

Anna decided to go further still. "Y'all reckoned t' set me up with him. But thet ain't th' way he sees it. He tol' me to m'face that he *might* marry me iffen I played my cards right. But once he finds out about Pappy's debt, he ain't a-gonna." Quickly she explained to Jolene what her aunt had explained to her, about the debt to the Company, and how she would be expected to pay it, as the green eyes darkened with anger. "... so you bet, oncet he finds out 'bout thet, he'll buy it up, an' he'll hev me all legal without ever havin' t' marry me. I jest bet thet's how he got them other two wimmin. He's got their debt, an' iffen they run off, he c'n set th' sheriff on 'em."

She had no idea how she had managed to put together such a convincing argument, much less where she had gotten the courage to say it all to Jolene's face. But it was clear that the arguments had all hit home.

Jolene was simmering with rage; Anna had never seen her like this before, and if that rage had been pointed in her direction, she'd very probably have fainted in terror. Power coruscated around the Queen of Copper Mountain, and the look in her eyes promised much, much worse than mere death. And just at that point, McDaran's voice rang through the caverns again. "*Jolene!*" he shouted ... and the inflection was not that of a man who was entreating someone. "*Jolene, Jolene, Jolene, Jolene ...*" the echoes came, only reinforcing that.

C'n I git her t' the boil?

"No matter what y'all wanted fer me," she said, steadily, "no matter what y'all thunk or planned, it'd niver be 'bout what y'all want. It'll on'y iver be 'bout what *he* wants. He don' reckon y'all's a Queen. But he sure do reckon *he's* a King, an' he reckons y'all's a-servin' him."

The eyes not only flashed ... so did her power, in a soundless, but contained, explosion of golden light. Anna shaded her eyes with her hand, and when her sight cleared and she looked back at the throne, Jolene was standing.

She looked terrifying. Something in her cold, anger-darkened eyes, something about her expressionless face, both these things were more frightening than the halo of pure power around her that radiated *actual* golden light. "Get behind my throne," she said in a flat tone of voice. "And may your God protect you if you have been lying to me."

Anna skittered behind Jolene's throne and crouched there, to find herself surrounded by a mound of copper and green lizards that were so quiet with fear that they could have been metal statues. Instinctively she gathered some of them into her arms to comfort them; when she did that, they all swarmed over her, tucking themselves as close to her body as they could.

"*Jo—*" the distant bellow rang out for the third time. But this time there was a flash of light that illuminated the entire cavern like a lightning flash, a sound like someone falling from a trivial height, and McDaran's voice finished, "—lene?"

"What is it?" Jolene's tone could have put ice on the pond in midsummer, but McDaran either didn't hear her tone or didn't heed it.

Likely don't care.

"Thet Anna May Jones y'all promised me!" he growled. "She done sassed me, disrespected me, turned me down flat, an' run off! Y'all git her fer me right now!"

"Are ... you ... *ordering* me, McDaran?" If Jolene's tone could have put ice on the pond before, it would have frozen it to the bottom now.

McDaran snorted with actual contempt. "Damn right I am, woman! Y'all promised me, now y'all make good on it!" Anna

286

could scarcely believe her ears. She had known McDaran was stupid, but she had no idea he was *that* stupid! Jolene was standing there in all her power *right in front of him*! Couldn't he see it? Couldn't he see the danger he was in?

Or did he think *he* was so powerful that he didn't care?

Jolene's tone turned ... silky. She all but purred her next words. Anna shuddered, without quite knowing why.

"Before I fetch the girl for you, I would like confirmation of some things," she murmured. "After all, it is going to take a strong man to handle the job of mine boss, don't you think? If I arrange for that, arrange for you to have a position where you will be completely in charge of the entire mine and smelting operation, answerable only to the owners, how do you plan to handle problems of discipline? The smelter workers don't know you; they might defy your orders."

"Then I'll lay 'em out on the ground, jest like I do th' miners thet sass me!" McDaran roared. "Woman, this is a-wastin' my time!"

"And another thing," Jolene continued. "The girl is a delicate creature, and she might not be able to take your attentions night after night; I'm concerned you might find yourself frustrated with her, and I would hate for you to be deprived of your very important needs because she might be indisposed—"

McDaran interrupted her with an angry guffaw. "Then I'll plow one'a my two hoors," he said crudely. "I ain't a-gonna break her. Not when I c'n siphon off her power t'add t'mine as long as I keep her breathin'. Y'all watch, Jolene. Purt' soon I'm a-gonna rule this here valley! There ain't nothin' an' no one thet's gonna git in my way. Now y'all fetch her! Give her to me like y'all promised! *Right now!*"

"I promised you *nothing*," Jolene spat. "You heard what you wanted to hear, you fool. And *you* are in no position to make demands of *me!*"

"Why, you furrin hoor—" McDaran snarled. And then, suddenly, he gave a yelp of surprise. "Wait—what? What y'all doin'? Jolene! *Jolene!*" He began to howl inarticulately, and Anna peeked around the side of the throne, arms full of lizards, who were trembling faintly.

Jolene stood where Anna had left her, arms crossed over her

chest, haloed with power. McDaran writhed where he stood, bellowing—

And he seemed oddly—shorter.

A moment after that he seemed shorter still.

And that was when Anna saw that Billie McDaran was knees-deep in the stone of the floor, and sinking.

Her hands flew to her lips, holding back a gasp of horror as she watched him flail and sink, his movements and inarticulate, animal-like shrieks growing louder and more frantic with every passing moment. Slowly, the stone engulfed him, giving him plenty of time to understand what was happening, and plenty of time to suffer as it did. Hip-deep. Chest-deep. Shoulder-deep, and his hands scrabbled uselessly at the rock.

Then his howls were cut off as his head was engulfed by stone.

His hands spasmed wildly on the surface of the stone.

Then they, too, were engulfed. The surface of the stone was as smooth as it had been before, with no sign of what had just happened. He was gone.

20

Anna remained where she was, crouching on the cold stone of the floor, hands crammed up to her mouth, staring at the place where Billie McDaran had been.

Jolene turned and looked down at her.

Anna stared back up at her, but the perfect lips no longer frowned, and the eyes had lightened again to a pure emerald green. The Queen of Copper Mountain gazed at her thoughtfully. Anna decided that discretion was in order, and went to her knees, bowing her head, cuddling lizards against her chest. A moment later, and the lizards slid away from her, returning to their mistress.

Jolene made a slight sound of amusement. "Oh, get to your feet," she said. "Now you need not concern yourself about McDaran. You can go home and go back to what you were doing before. I'm sure your aunt has plenty for you to do. You can tell her that everything will be fine."

She thought about telling the Great Elemental that no, she couldn't, because there was still that Company debt hanging over her, and that she was going to have to flee—

In fact, she had opened her mouth to say just that. But the words that came out were, "Not without Josh."

Jolene blinked at her and tilted her head to the side, inviting more.

"I'm a-beggin' y'all, don't take him from me, Jolene. There ain't nothin' under th' earth or 'bove it that's purtier than y'all," she continued, trying desperately to find the right words. "Y'all *know* thet, I seed it in yore face in Ducktown, when th' fellers there looked at y'all, an' y'all knew what y'all was makin' 'em feel. They ain't no way I c'n challenge y'all, not even iffen God His Own Self come down an' made me as purty as an angel." Now the tears started, not the horrible sobs that had wracked her before, but slow, painful tears that burned their way down her cheeks. "I found Josh, up where y'all left him. He was sleepin'. He called out y'all's name in his sleep, did y'all know thet?" she continued. "Y'all c'n take him, easy. 'Tween yore looks an' yore magic, I ain't got a chance. But y'all don' know what he means ter me."

"He's just the first boy that happened to take notice of you," Jolene said dismissively. "You'll—" But then she stopped and peered more closely at Anna's face, and her brows furrowed. "Go on," she said, and motioned to Anna to continue.

"Y'all's gonna live as long as th' mountains. By yore reckoning, I ain't gonna be aroun' but a couple'a seasons. Y'all c'n hev yore pick o' men, an' I reckon they don' mean too much t' a Queen like y'all. But I'm different from y'all. I c'n niver love agin …" She sobbed, once, and got control of herself. "I *know* it. I know it, like I know th' grass's green an' summer comes arter spring. I ain't niver gonna love agin, an' I ain't niver gonna be happy agin iffen y'all take him. But fer y'all—he's a-gonna jest be one more y'all collected. An' thet ain't no good reason t'part us. Please don' take him jest 'cause y'all can."

Jolene crossed her arms over her chest and tapped her right finger on her cheek. Anna held her breath. At least Jolene didn't look offended.

"Would you say he feels the same?" she asked finally. "After all, if I can take him so easily, wouldn't that mean he doesn't really 'love' you?"

She shook her head. "He tol' me he did. I b'lieve him. But …"

"*But iffen he don't feel thet way, then yore better shuck of him*," she heard in her memory. And was Aunt Jinny so wrong?

"Well. Let's just go find out, shall we?" Jolene asked, and before Anna could say anything in reply, she waved her hand.

There was a flash of light—and they were no longer in the cavern with the throne. They were in the cavern where Josh's workbench stood, and where that bed had been created for him.

He wasn't sleeping now, he was awake, one hand on the malachite pillar, the other on the workbench, frowning in concentration.

Anna didn't even get a chance to move; Jolene stopped her by gripping her shoulder. "He can't see or hear us," Jolene said calmly. "But just to be sure that you don't interfere—" For the first time in Anna's experience, Jolene sketched an actual glyph in the air, the lines of the sign glowing and pulsing with power before they faded. And when they had faded, Anna found herself completely unable to move.

"I can make him famous," Jolene said conversationally. "Or, if it's creation that he is interested in, and not fame, I can give him everything he could possibly need to execute the images in his mind. Never again will he have to work with inferior tools and material. I can even teach him how to shape the stone with his fingers alone, as easily as molding clay, and I can give him the power to make that possible. What can you possibly offer him?"

Her head dropped, as she understood that she really had nothing to compare to that to offer. Life sharing Jinny's cabin? Dividing his time between farming and his carving? Working with whatever he could get his hands on?

Oh, she *could* say that she could take care of him, but really, could she do that any better than the magical servants that Jolene surely already possessed could do? Down here in the depths of the caverns, life was very comfortable; it was neither blistering hot in the summer, nor freezing cold in the winter, and Jolene could surely give him a life of luxury surpassing Anna's wildest imaginings. She finally lifted her head again, tears trickling from her eyes.

Jolene nodded, as if reading her mind. "So, you agree that he would be better off with me than with you?"

She wanted to wail out her denial, but there was no arguing with facts. She could give him so little compared to what Jolene could.

If I was Ma and he was Pa ... Ma would'a scratched an' bit an' fought an' lied through her teeth. But I cain't do thet. It'd be a lie, Jolene'd know 'twas a lie, an' I know it's a lie.

Jolene turned her back on Anna and paced gracefully toward the circle of light cast by her magic above Josh's workbench. Her footsteps rang crisp and clear on the stone, and he looked up and smiled to see her. That smile felt like a dagger in Anna's heart.

"And what are you thinking, running your hands over that lovely piece of stone?" Jolene asked. There was nothing arch in her tone; it was just an honest question.

"Thet I reckon I know what I'd *like* ter carve," Josh said. "I'd *like* t'carve y'all, with your hair a-swirlin' round y'all." Those words were more daggers in her heart. He would never want to carve *her*. "But I dunno as I got th' skill. I ain't niver worked from life. An' I really oughter git back home, an' I dunno what my Pa'd hev t'say 'bout y'all hangin' about when I'm s'pposed t'be courtin' Anna." His smile made a joke out of that, but Jolene treated it as serious.

"And what if you didn't go back?" she asked.

"What now?" he replied, bewildered.

"What if you didn't go back home?" she repeated. "What if you stayed with me? I can teach you every skill in carving you need. I can give you skills you cannot imagine. I can supply you with tools you don't even know exist, and every material you could ever want. And if you want to become famous, I can arrange for that too." With every word Jolene spoke, Anna dropped deeper into despair, until it was no longer the spell keeping her from moving, it was the sheer weight of black despondence.

Because surely he would accept that offer. He'd be a fool not to. It was more than everything he had ever wanted, was everything he had ever dared dream of, and more.

He blinked at her, perplexed. "But I hev ter stay down here? Away from my fambly? Away from Anna May?"

"Yes to both," Jolene told him. "My craftsmen and artists are required to live here, with me, in my realm." She curved her lips in a sweet smile. "Think of what you could make! And you would never lack for tools or material, never need concern yourself for your daily needs, never be pulled away from creating in order to milk a cow again!"

He chuckled. "Y'all mus' be some kinda magical creature t' offer all thet," he said, skepticism tinging his tone.

She sketched a glyph in the air in front of his eyes. "Then look and see what is truly here, not what you think should be."

He gasped and looked around himself wildly. "Where am I?" he stammered.

"You are in my realm now, and I am the Queen of Copper

Mountain," she said proudly. "And I *can* give you all these things. I can give you your heart's desire."

He pulled himself together. "Beg pardon, Miz Jolene, but y'all cain't do thet. Not 'lessen y'all c'n give me Anna May, too."

Anna's heart spasmed, and she gasped.

Jolene shook her head imperiously. "That is not possible. My craftsmen and artists must devote themselves entirely to their work. There is no place here for distractions."

"But she ain't a distraction," he contradicted her. "She he'ps me thank. She rests me up. An'," he ended simply, "I love her, an' she loves me. Feller c'n make all the purdy thangs in the world, but iffen he ain't got love, they got no heart in 'em." He laughed. "Truth is, I druther make my own way an' do it all th' hard way *with* her, than git ever'thang y'all promised an' do it th' easy way *without* her."

With every word the weight of despair that had been crushing Anna to the ground was lifted. By the time he finished speaking she was light-headed with joy.

But Jolene wasn't done.

"What if I said—Anna May can come here, but to do so, she would have to give up her aunt, and her magic?" Jolene asked slyly. "After all, this would be a tremendous concession on my part just to allow her here at all. I have never offered this to another."

Josh paled, but he stood straighter. "Then I'd tell y'all I ain't niver gonna arst her t'give up nothin'. It ain't fair. It ain't fair t' make her do all the sacrificin', an' I won't do it."

"What if I said she would keep her magic, but it would all have to go to you, in the service of your art?" Jolene persisted.

"Then I'll say agin, I ain't gonna arst her t'give up somethin' thet important jest fer me. It ain't fair. Not only ain't it fair t' her, it ain't fair t' all the folks thet are gonna depend on her healin' ways and potions when Miz Jinny's gone." Josh crossed his arms over his chest, but his expression was apologetic. "I'm right sorry, Miz Jolene, but I reckon I'll hev t'do thangs th' hard way. I don't even blame y'all iffen y'all take back yore tools an' thet stone."

Jolene sketched a different glyph in the air, and Josh froze.

The Queen of Copper Mountain turned back to Anna. "Now *you* have that debt hanging over you. It is true that you do not have to worry about McDaran buying it, but the Coal Company in Soddy will still wish to collect it from you."

She felt the blood drain from her face, and felt faint. "It's true," she whispered. "I purely cain't saddle Josh with thet. It ain't fair! But if I was t'marry him, he'd be responsible fer it." Tears filled her eyes again. "I gotter do what me'n Aunt Jinny planned. I gotter high-tail it outa here, leastwise until th' Company decides they ain't gonna find me nohow."

Jolene regarded her thoughtfully. "Would you give over your magic to me if I allowed you and Josh to stay with me? I cannot have one of *your* kind living in my realm unless you are properly ... neutered," she added haughtily. Anna had no idea what she meant by that, but the prospect of escape from the Company *and* staying with Josh was worth any sacrifice.

"Please, Jolene!" she pleaded. "I'd even cook an' clean an' all fer y'all—" Then she realized that Jolene surely had any number of servant creatures to do that sort of thing for her, and stumbled to a halt.

And Jolene unexpectedly laughed, and snapped her fingers. Josh blinked his eyes and shook his head at the same time that Anna realized she could move again. And just as she shifted her feet experimentally, Josh cried out her name joyfully and rushed to her, picking her up in his arms and twirling her until she was dizzy.

"Now, Joshua," Jolene said mildly. "Do behave."

Josh stopped abruptly and put Anna down, blushing mightily. "Sorry, Miz Jolene," he said, shuffling his feet.

Jolene looked from one to the other. "Well," she said, a very real smile on her face. "You two have given me a very pleasant surprise. You are both faithful and true; you are both willing to sacrifice your own advantages to protect the other, and you are not merely *saying* this; when very real advantage presents itself, and when very real danger is present, you are still expressing the same determination. Such things need to be rewarded, as they so seldom are."

She turned to Anna. "Anna, you need to tell Josh what has happened to you, starting with the letter you received last evening."

When she had finished, Josh had been in turns alarmed, enraged, astonished, enraged all over again, and finally was left open-mouthed with amazement. "Wall, I swan, Anna May Jones," he said finally. "Iffen I weren't a-standin' here with magic lights an' lizards an' Miz Jolene a-lookin' like the Queen a' Sheba, I reckon I'd'a thought y'all was tellin' me tales."

Jolene gestured that Anna should hold out her hand. Obediently she did so as Jolene extended her own, and one of the little green lizards ran down from her shoulder to her hand and across to Anna's. "Follow my pet, and he will bring you out onto the lane," she said. "I leave it to the two of you to decide what you are going to tell your respective guardians. Josh, you may take the roll of tools. They will never break, and never need sharpening. Anna, this is for you." She suddenly was holding a box that looked as if it must have been carved from malachite. Anna would have *sworn* it had not been in her hand a moment before. "You need not flee to Kansas—wherever that is. Remain with your aunt. And any time you are in great need—but *only* when you are in great need—open that box, and use what you find in it."

Josh's eyes flitted momentarily—and with great longing—to the block of malachite on the worktable. Jolene saw the glance, and smiled again. "You will find that stone under your workbench when you return home. And from time to time you will find other materials worthy of your skill in the same place." Then she straightened and became every inch a queen. "Go now," she said imperiously. "I am saddened to lose such a fine artist—but we will see what you can become on your own. Perhaps you will be even greater without my teaching than you would have been with it."

The lizard scrambled down Anna's skirt and onto the ground, where it scuttled forward a few feet, then looked back at them. Obediently, they followed.

And when they looked back over their shoulders, there was nothing there but blackness.

The Queen of Copper Mountain was gone.

"I swan!" Aunt Jinny said, when she had finished telling her story for the second time. "Iffen it hadn't been y'all tellin' me this, I'd'a niver believed it. 'Specially not 'bout Jolene!"

Anna took a weary bite of the hoecakes Aunt Jinny had whipped up for her the moment she spotted Anna coming over the stile at the bottom of the garden. "Fer a liddle bit I was mighty tempted, when she said I c'd undo all thet bad what's been done t' th' valley," Anna admitted. "An' in a way, I kinder feel like I done let th' valley down."

"You an' me, we'll jest keep doin' what we c'n, an' ain't no one c'n arst more of us," Jinny told her. And in a rare display of affection, she got up and hugged her niece's shoulders. "Y'all *sure* y'all don't wanter go to Kansas?"

"Jolene reckoned we could figger somethin' out. Or more like, reckoned *y'all* c'n figger somethin' out, on account'a y'all's so smart," Anna replied, and yawned hugely.

"Git up on thet thar stove, an' take a nap, an' I'll git t'thankin'," Jinny ordered, with a glance at the malachite box that Anna had brought with her and left with Pavel's journal, her receipt book, and her Bible. "We'll see iffen Jolene's right."

Anna never knew exactly what it was that Josh told his parents when he got home, but whatever it was, the very next day he came walking up to the cabin right after dinner, before Anna had left to go down there herself. But instead of addressing Anna, he went straight to where Aunt Jinny was hanging clothing up on the line.

"Miz Jinny, I 'spect Anna done tol' y'all what happened ter us," he said, his face set in an expression of determination. "Now, I don' know much 'bout Miz Jolene. She been purdy good ter me, but that could'a been jest me bein' fatted up like one'a the pigs fer eatin' later."

"Wall, thet's sense," Jinny agreed. "She do seem ter have had what they call a 'change of heart,' though."

"But c'n we count on it holdin'?" Josh demanded.

"Reckon I don't rightly know," Jinny admitted. A gust of autumn breeze swirled leaves between them, and sent a chill down Anna's back. But it was a perfectly natural chill, and not a premonition, so she joined them.

"Yore Granpappy said her word was good," Anna pointed out, even though she had not been invited into this particular conversation. "Reckon he'd know."

Josh cast her a glance that said, *And that there is a tale I need to know, how you come to know this*. But he said nothing other than, "Wall, I aim t'make sure we don't have ter depend on thet. I don't reckon ter wait t'git married. My Ma and Pa are all right with thet. Pa's gonna go on down ter Ducktown termorrow, an' I'm a-goin' with him. We're a-gonna git the license an' talk t' all the preachers an' th' Justice a' th' Peace, an' the fust one thet c'n come on up here'll marry us. I tol' Pa 'bout yore Ma's debt," he continued, looking at Anna, "and he reckoned we better git married now, an' worry 'bout what happens iffen th' bailiffs git here."

Anna gaped at him. She never, ever would have expected Matt Holcroft to urge such a thing—she would have thought for certain that once he learned of the looming debt, he'd have urged Josh to break the engagement off.

"There's somethin' t' be said fer thet," Aunt Jinny agreed. She glanced at Anna. "It ain't a-gonna be no church weddin'. But thet purdy pink with th' white roses is purt near done, an' we c'n finish it iffen we both work on it ternight, an' thet'll do fer gettin' married in. They's still some roses out in Maddie's garden, an' I reckon we c'n fit ev'body inter her parlor."

She turned to Josh with a smirk. "I 'spect yore figgerin' on movin' in up here with me?"

Josh looked at his hands, awkwardly. "Wall … yes'm …"

"Good," Aunt Jinny said. "'Bout time I had a pair o' strong hands t'chop my wood!"

Josh blushed and mumbled his thanks.

"Now, jest one more thang. When y'all go inter Ducktown termorrow, I want y'all t' go by Billie McDaran's house, an' leave a note fer me." Aunt Jinny went into the cabin, leaving both Anna and Josh standing on the porch exchanging puzzled looks, and came back out again with a piece of torn-off brown wrapping paper that she handed to Josh. He looked at it.

"C'n I read it?" he asked.

"Go on ahead. An' don't show it to no one but McDaran's wimmin, not even yore Pa," Jinny ordered.

Josh read the note aloud. "*Yor no-account master com to a bad end. If I was u I would pak wut I cud carry an run.*"

"Oh!" Anna felt her eyes widen when she realized what Jinny intended. "Yore warnin' them t' take what they c'n an' run afore the Company figgers out Billie ain't a-comin' back!"

Jinny nodded. "I reckon at th' rate Billie was liven high, what with beefsteak an' drink an' all, he left a debt at the Company store hisself. Iffen they was held t'him by debt, Burra Burra will take 'em as part pay. An iffen them gels was jest held by his magic, it'll be broke now. So in either case, I reckon they oughter he'p thesselves to whatever he left lyin' around and git as fur away as they c'n go."

But Josh handed the note back to Aunt Jinny. "I'll jest tell 'em my own self. Might c'd be they cain't read. Might c'd be someone'd find th' note arter they bolt, an' start lookin' fer whoever wrote it." He smiled at her aunt. "Reckon I c'n use a liddle o' thet magic ter persuade 'em."

"Reckon I c'n show y'all how, in 'bout a hour," Jinny agreed.

"Reckon I c'n watch," said Anna.

It was about two weeks later that the bailiffs came.

Josh was around the back of the cabin cutting firewood, Anna and Aunt Jinny in kitchen putting up pickles with the last of the green tomatoes, when they were interrupted by a knock on the door, which was now closed most of the time against the autumn chill unless the day was unusually warm.

"*Trouble*," rumbled the Domovoy from under the stove.

Anna exchanged a look of resignation with her aunt. This could only be one thing.

"Wall, keepin' 'em on the stoop ain't a-gonna put this off," Jinny said with a sigh, and went to answer the door.

"Miz Jinny Alscot?" asked one of the three men standing there—the one with the shiny star on the front of his coat.

"So I be," Jinny replied, not inviting them in.

The sheriff was polite, the other two, not so much. They shoved their way inside, and one of them pointed at Anna. "Reckon thet'd be the girl, Sheriff," he said. "Reckon—"

"Whoa, now, slow up. We do this polite an' proper, or I'm a-gonna haul y'all both back t'Ducktown an' we do it in court," the sheriff said, clearly irritated at both of them. Anna didn't much like the look of those two, and it was clear that the sheriff didn't either. They were dirty, unshaven, and stank of strong tobacco and stronger drink. The sheriff turned to Anna. "Are y'all Miz Anna May Jones?"

"Anna May Holcroft," she said, hoping against hope that this would throw them off.

But the sheriff wasn't going to be fooled by such a simple ploy. "Till a week agone, y'all *was* Anna May Jones, am I right?" he asked sternly.

She bit her lip, and tried not to show her fear. "Yessir," she said faintly.

"Wall, these two fellers here is from Soddy Coal Mine Company, 'bout a debt yore Ma an' Pa owed the Company," the sheriff said sternly, but with a hint, at least, of some compassion. "Seems they died, which means y'all is responsible."

"How much is thet debt?" Aunt Jinny demanded.

"Forty dollars!" one of the two bailiffs said, loudly, as if by shouting he could frighten her into dropping dollar bills.

Anna felt herself growing faint. Forty dollars! That was more money than anything other than a bank could have! Josh had gotten five dollars for his little angel statue, and they'd hoped that would be enough—but *forty*? That was impossible.

The two bailiffs began shouting that she had to pay up or go to jail, and one of them actually took out a pair of hand-shackles and began rattling them at her. Then Aunt Jinny smacked the shackles out of his hand with the handle of her broom, shocking them into silence.

"Sheriff," she said into the stunned silence. "I'd admire if y'all would take these no-accounts out of my house. Y'all c'n stand on the porch, but my niece an' I need some time t'thank."

One of the bailiffs opened his mouth to bellow again, but the sheriff grabbed them both by the collars and shoved them out the door. "Take all th' time y'all need, Miz Jinny," he said, and shut the door behind them.

"I ain't got thet kinder money, chile—" Aunt Jinny began, her own face pale. "Mebbe if me an' Matt an' Josh—Mister Clay might could give us a loan, or Mister Cavenel on Josh's work—"

But Anna's eyes had lit on the malachite box that Jolene had given to her. "The box!" she gasped, and stumbled a little in her haste to get to the shelf where it lay.

It seemed a little heavier than it had been when she'd put it there. And when she opened it—

There were two worn-looking, slightly dirty, twenty-dollar gold pieces.

"Tell 'em t' come back in, Aunt Jinny," she said, holding out her hand to show her aunt what had been in there.

Aunt Jinny's eyes widened. "Gimme a minute to thank," she said. Jinny closed her eyes and stood there for about a minute, maybe a little longer. Then she went to the cupboard and brought out the oak-gall ink, a new quill pen, some of the pretty paper the lace collar from her wedding dress had been wrapped in, and a candle. "All right. Let 'em in."

The bailiffs came in pushing and hollering about how Anna was reckoning to cheat the Company, but this time it was the sheriff that had had enough.

"*Shut yore fool haids!*" he roared. When silence resumed, he turned politely to the two women and said, "Now. Did thet there time t'thank he'p y'all?"

Aunt Jinny nodded stiffly. "Reckon it did, Sheriff. Anna May, give th' sheriff th' Company's money."

Anna handed over the two coins, each a bit bigger than a quarter and much heavier. The sheriff looked them over carefully, bit them both, and nodded. "Reckon this's the correct amount, Miz Holcroft." He started to hand the coins to one of the bailiffs, when Aunt Jinny stopped him.

"Jest a minnut, Sheriff. I don' trust neither of them varmints not ter run off with th' money an' say we didn' pay it," she said sternly.

The bailiffs started shouting. This time the sheriff smacked one across the back of his head. "Reckon I don't neither, Miz Jinny. What d'y'all want ter do about thet?"

"Fust of all, I'm a-gonna write up a paper here thet says we paid it," she said. "An' Anna's gonna sign it, an' y'all as a witness, an' them. An' iffen all they c'n do is make their mark, I'm a-gonna write down their names. I'll make up two. One t'stay with us, an' one t'stay with y'all."

The sheriff nodded. "Seems like a good ideer," he said approvingly. "Anything else?"

"Then I'm a-gonna wrap up thet there money in a packet, an'

Anna is a-gonna sign a paper thet'll go in thet packet what says this's t'pay her Ma and Pa's debt, an' I'm a-gonna seal thet there packet up with wax. An' once it's sealed, y'all's gonna sign th' packet, Sheriff," Jinny said, her jaw jutting out with determination. "*Then* y'all c'n give it to 'em."

The two bailiffs looked extremely disgruntled by this point, which cheered Anna's heart no end, because she, too, had been afraid they were likely to run off with all or part of the money, leaving her with no way to prove that she had ever paid it.

"I do like how y'all thank, Miz Jinny," the sheriff said with admiration. "I reckon I'll do one thang more t'add t'thet. When I git back ter town, I'll send a letter m'self t' the Company, an' let 'em know their bailiffs took the full payment an' left th' same day as I sent th' letter. No need ter pay me fer a stamp," he continued, as Jinny made an abortive motion toward the cupboard. "I reckon this's official bizness. Since they come an' got me an' all, ter he'p 'em collect."

"Thenkee kindly, Sheriff," her aunt said, and in a remarkably short period of time, it had all been completed.

"Now," the sheriff said to the bailiffs, his face full of thunder. "It might c'd be y'all are thankin' hard 'bout two wimmin alone, an' iffen they got thet much money, they might hev more. I'm a-tellin' y'all now thet iffen so much as a punkin gits stole from here, I'm a-comin' ter look fer y'all. Am I clear?"

Just then Josh came through the front door. "I wouldn' say they's alone, Sheriff Tailor," he said with a nod to the sheriff, casually hefting the axe on his shoulder. "An' they's my whole fambly down the lane, an' the lane bein' th' on'y way t'git here."

"An' they's bears in them woods," Anna added. And right on cue out of the woods to the right came a bellowing roar.

The two bailiffs jumped, their eyes starting out of their heads in fear. Even the sheriff looked a bit intimidated.

"Reckon it might be time ter leave, afore night closes in on thet lane," Anna suggested.

The sheriff tipped his hat to them (the bailiffs did not), and all three trotted hastily down the path, collected their horses from where they had been tied up to the stile, and rode away at a canter.

Young Raven emerged from the woods to the right and hopped

over the fence, a grin on his face. When he reached them, he broke into a laugh. "Josh an' me was a-talking when them fools arrived," he said. "I slipped inter th' woods ter wait an' see iffen I was goin' ter be needed, or iffen I'd need ter bring y'all he'p. I heered y'all purty good where I was, an' when y'all talked 'bout bears, wall—" He chuckled. "Couldn' resist."

"Y'all couldn't hev done better if I'd'a arst y'all to," Anna said warmly. "Thenkee kindly, Raven. It's good t'hev friends."

And with a little gesture on a wisp of power, she added, *Thenkee, Jolene.*

For a moment, she thought she wouldn't get an answer. But then she looked down at her feet.

A little, jewel-green lizard looked up at her from the ground, bobbed at her once, and vanished.

But not before Anna had heard Jolene's reply in her mind.

"Yes, my dear Anna. It's good to have friends."

ABOUT THE AUTHOR

Mercedes Lackey is a full-time writer and has published numerous novels and works of short fiction, including the bestselling *Heralds of Valdemar* series. She is also a professional lyricist and licensed wild bird rehabilitator. She lives in Oklahoma with her husband and collaborator, artist Larry Dixon, and their flock of parrots.

www.mercedeslackey.com

For more fantastic fiction, author events,
exclusive excerpts, competitions, limited editions and more

VISIT OUR WEBSITE
titanbooks.com

LIKE US ON FACEBOOK
facebook.com/titanbooks

FOLLOW US ON TWITTER AND INSTAGRAM
@TitanBooks

EMAIL US
readerfeedback@titanemail.com